FRED HAMPTON'S BLUES

FRED HAMPTON'S BLUES

SEAN E BOYE

Copyright © 2024 Sean E Boye

The moral right of the author has been asserted.

Apart from any fair dealing for the purposes of research or private study, or criticism or review, as permitted under the Copyright, Designs and Patents Act 1988, this publication may only be reproduced, stored or transmitted, in any form or by any means, with the prior permission in writing of the publishers, or in the case of reprographic reproduction in accordance with the terms of licences issued by the Copyright Licensing Agency. Enquiries concerning reproduction outside those terms should be sent to the publishers.

This is a work of fiction. Names, characters, businesses, places, events and incidents are either the products of the author's imagination or used in a fictitious manner. Any resemblance to actual persons, living or dead, or actual events is purely coincidental.

Troubador Publishing Ltd
Unit E2 Airfield Business Park,
Harrison Road, Market Harborough,
Leicestershire. LE16 7UL
Tel: 0116 2792299
Email: books@troubador.co.uk
Web: www.troubador.co.uk

ISBN 978 1805142 799

British Library Cataloguing in Publication Data.
A catalogue record for this book is available from the British Library.

Printed and bound in Great Britain by 4edge Limited
Typeset in 11pt Minion Pro by Troubador Publishing Ltd, Leicester, UK

For my Mother and dedicated to the memory of Richard Bilkszto

FIRST THEY CAME

First, they came for the Brexiteers
And I did not speak out Because I was not a Brexiteer
Then they came for the Moderates And I did not speak out Because I was not a Moderate
Then they came for the TERFs And I did not speak out Because I was not a TERF
Then they came for the Working Class And I did not speak out Because I was not Working Class
Then they came for me. And there was no one left to speak out for me.

PROLOGUE

"Well, I just think we have more in common than what separates us, you know" said the young woman, taking a sip from her metal drinks bottle, before placing it on her lap and smiling at the man opposite.

Terry smiled back.

God, he hated that expression.

Try saying that to an asylum seeker floating about on a piece of driftwood in the middle of the Mediterranean or some pregnant mother mining Cobalt in the Congo, his thoughts scowled, while he slowly laced his fingers together on his lap, and pretended to listen some more

"And I know you hear that a lot these days, but I still think it's true, definitely. Although, saying that, it can seem as though it isn't, sometimes, if you know what I mean?"

Terry narrowed his eyes.

"Well, what I mean is, like when I went to the North recently. Have you ever been?"

Terry shook his head.

"Well neither had I actually, well not until the last election, just gone. Of course, my parents had taken us to the Lake District a few times when we were children, my brother and myself that is, and that's all lovely isn't it, but the places I went to with Momentum were totally different. In fact, to be completely honest, I was a little shocked. It was so run down and everyone looked so miserable. I mean the Tories have just allowed these people to just waste away, haven't they? And everyone was so angry, which I get, of course, but what really surprised me, was that they seemed more upset with Jeremy Corbyn, who was really trying to help them, you know make their lives better, than with the people who did this to them in the first place. I mean, don't get me wrong, I'm sooooo glad I did it. The atmosphere was amazing, all my friends from Uni were there, and it felt really special, especially travelling up on the train before we went to canvas. But then, even after all the work we did, it was so dispiriting when they just didn't get it. I mean some of them actually slammed the door in our faces, and we are the Labour party, for God's sake. The party that represents them. In fact, even now, I still can't believe, how people so disadvantaged, could vote for an upper class, racist bastard like Boris Johnson?"

"Maybe they're just stupid" said Terry, glancing, out of the window of the empty train carriage for a second, before returning all of his focus back to the young woman again.

"Well, of course, I'm not saying that. I mean, I think it was a bad decision, a really bad decision; but if only they knew the facts, you know, read around the subject a bit more, then I think they would have realized that Jeremy's plan was absolutely the right one for them"

"But they didn't, did they? So maybe they're just a bit stupid" repeated Terry with a sympathetic smile, before looking directly into the eyes of the young woman for the first time. Now, she was less certain, and straightening herself against the back of her train seat, she tried to impose some order on her thoughts again, until, without warning, it felt as if a huge wave was crashing over her face. Desperately, she tried to catch her breath, but still locked into the gentle eyes of the man opposite, she flailed around for that reasonable filter, which had always prevented any toxic thoughts pouring through or at least anything she could get canceled for. However, the wave was much too strong, and surged forward, seemingly without end, until out of the chaos a reassuring voice began to weave it's way through her startled mind.

"Are you sure? C'mon, Emma tell the truth. Say what you really think. You know you want to"

How did he know her name? was her next thought. They had only got chatting since she'd got on at Finsbury Park, but to her surprise, she didn't feel unsafe or in any kind of danger, if anything quite the opposite. Calm, relaxed, almost desired and yes, he was right, so right, she did want to tell the truth. Always holding back, always being good, always on the right side of history, she was sick of it; and what's more, he was so very handsome, brutally in fact, as if from another time, unlike those Northern Neanderthals, with their broken faces and harsh consonants.

"Yes, you're right! You're so right. They are stupid. Fucking stupid. Why can't they see that Socialism, Jeremy's kind of Socialism will save them? But they can't, can they? Because they are scum and just want a world where everyone sounds like them and looks like them. No wonder they voted Brexit. No wonder they voted for Johnson. No wonder they are poor. They don't even have the sense to make their lives better, do they? They don't deserve democracy, because they are just Peasants. Idiotic, prejudiced Peasants and worse still, they are probably transphobic. Yes, I'm glad I don't have to live among people like that and what's more I hope they all die from heart attacks from eating too many deep fried Pizzas or whatever in-breds like them like to live on, so the world can be rid of their disgusting ignorance once and for all".

Now she felt better, so much better. Like that time she'd thrown up, at her friend, Freya's party in Chiswick, after one too many Bellinis, and then laid down on the bathroom floor and felt the cold tiles against her face, and in that brief moment, she was completely at peace.

Terry smiled again.

"Its okay Emma, its okay. I understand, I totally understand" he said in a warm, consoling voice and then moving forward in his seat, he drew her face into his hands, before sinking his fangs deep into her slender neck.

CHAPTER ONE

The lights from the Burger Restaurant splashed over the delivery bikes, waiting patiently on the street outside, while Terry took a pull from his cigarette and stared down at his phone again.

Fast Food 4 U.

£8.56 per hour plus an extra £1 per delivery.

Being a Socialist Vampire did have its downsides, thought Terry giving his online payslip another derisory glance, before leaning back against his delivery box and closing his eyes. Bell-ends like his flatmate, Oscar, might virtue signal to the world that he really cared, whilst earning millions from a Green Venture Capital Fund, whatever the hell that was, but as far as he was concerned, if you said you were a Socialist, then you lived like a Socialist, even if that meant tearing around town on a scooter with 4 Big Macs and 3 KFC meal deals like a culinary version of Quadrophenia. Obviously, in the Blood-sucking universe, this was far from normal behaviour. *Quae semper cor tuum requirit* – whatever your heart requires, was the motto, and from fame or fortune to plain decadent desire, nothing was beyond the possibilities of the Brotherhood of Blood. Thousands of years of accumulated wealth and endless social connections made it virtually impossible to fail, but for some reason, this path had never really appealed to Terry; and so, despite the constant derision from his contemporaries, who regarded him as a bit of a crank and the odd reprimand from Lady Carswell, the Head of the Vampire Council, about "lowering the tone", he'd always managed to stick to his beliefs. Was a Docker in the 1950's, a Brickies Labourer in the Sixties, even a Binman in the Seventies.

Yes, the glorious Seventies.

Possibly, the greatest time in history to be Working Class, where grafting with your hands wasn't a crime and knowing your rights was a badge of honour. Okay, it was horrendously racist, sexist and homophobic but that being said, assets were low, wages were high, and nobody was struggling on a zero hours contract while paying a grand a month to sleep in a box room in Hackney. Even Barristers used to have the odd Findus French Bread Pizza now and again, but if you listened to the Mainstream Media, it was the worst of times, and a cautionary tale to be told to scare children on a dark winter night. *Don't give the rank and file any power, remember the Seventies, remember the Unions!* Such awful hypocrisy. The Middle-Class cock something up, like Iraq or the Banking crisis and it's just "one of those things", and "lessons to be learned", but poor people try and even up the playing field and it's "Never again", "A Social Apocalypse". Bloody Thatcher. Maybe he should have bitten her just after the Brighton Bombing in 1984, when he was down the road, working in a warehouse at the time, mused Terry, as he stamped his roll-up into the pavement, before speeding off in the direction of the Fulham Palace Road.

The slight chill of the Spring evening stung the back of his neck as he drove South and in no time at all, two Chicken Jalfrezis, four King-Size Burgers and a Chinese Banquet for six were delivered before his final drop at the Waverley Estate. "Can I really, be arsed" sighed the Vampire, staring up at the twenty storey building that now towered in front of him, and for a brief moment, contemplated running up the side of it, until he remembered that he'd nearly got caught pulling a similar stunt a few months earlier when a blurry photo from a local resident made page four of the Evening Standard with the headline "Cat burglar defies gravity". Naturally, Oscar had a field day over the incident. "My dear Terry, if you want a proper job, I can get you one tomorrow, you only have to ask, but for God's sake, don't get everyone caught for a bag of chips", he'd declared with his customary snide grin, as he planted the newspaper article on the kitchen table, while both himself and Errol proceeded to laugh their asses off for the rest of the evening. However, despite the irritation of being the butt of his housemate's joke, again, in this regard, the annoying prick was probably right. Thousands of years of craven confidentiality had to be maintained for everyone's safety, and was justifiably, the very first rule you learned, after being transformed into a Demon of the Night. *Reveal nothing or we all die,* was the decree and was deemed so important by the powers that be, they didn't even try and translate it into Latin, which, for a community as conceited as Vampires, was really something. Therefore, aside from some close shaves, which had been averted by wise Vampires like Polidori and Stoker, who employing Baudelaire's maxim, of the greatest trick the devil ever pulled was convincing the world that he didn't exist, gave the masses *The Vampyre* and *Dracula* to keep them off the scent, the darkest secret of human evolution had remained resolutely in place. "Best take the lift then", said the Vampire to himself with a lazy smile, slinging his large delivery pouch over his shoulder, before walking towards the entrance of the block.

"Oh hi, err, that was quick, thought you'd be ages yet" said a woman opening the door with a happy smile

"Oh well, you know, Fast Food 4 U. Good as our name, and all that" replied Terry, clapping his gloves together with a grin.

"Well, you're definitely quicker than the usual guys I get. Oh, I must get you a tip" added the woman raising her finger before running back inside her flat to get her purse. Terry shook his head. Why was it always the poorest who were the most generous? he thought, pulling a large Meat Feast Supreme Pizza and a bottle of Diet Coke from his satchel. When he'd been a builder, it was usually the old guy in the council house or the single mum with three kids in a Housing Association flat, who would hand you a cup of tea or try and make you a sandwich, while the best you could expect from the chattering classes was a dirty look and an instruction to wipe your feet. Naturally, this irritated Terry, and so, as a result, he'd made it a rule, never to accept any money from people in circumstances like this, who were usually broke or struggling to stand upright on the treadmill of Universal Credit and low income jobs.

"It's okay, really. You've paid by card already" said Terry, as the woman returned breathless with a pound coin in her hand.

"Oh, don't be silly, it's nothing. I know you guys don't get paid that much" she replied, almost giggling at the look of concern on her delivery man's face, as she reached forward to affectionately touch the elbow of his jacket, and the Vampire instinctively felt something malignant stir in his blood.

Her eyes were intelligent, warm, beautiful, and set against her black skin, he felt his pulse race, while the base voices in his head, demanded instant satisfaction. It would be so easy, and as the happy smile on the woman's face quickly turned into something more dependent and her body edged closer to his, he could feel the fangs in his mouth begin to push through his gums and ache for her blood. Like a syringe full of the most glorious narcotic, Terry stared intently at the woman's neck for what seemed like a lifetime, until a solitary voice inside his crippled soul finally screamed out it's dissent, and somehow the Vampire managed to drag his eyes away from his prey and force the demons of his nature back into their putrid catacombs to wait for another day.

"You okay?" asked Terry catching the falling coin, and pressing it back into the softness of her palm.

"Err, yeah, err, thanks. Sorry, been a long day" replied the woman blinking her eyes as she quickly looked around her doorstep to try and find her bearings again.

"There's really no need by the way" replied Terry,

touching her arm to slowly nurse her back to the present, before glancing at the box sitting under his arm.

"Oh, err, of course, the Pizza" declared the woman, still trying to find her way through the warm fog that had just rolled into her mind.

"Don't want it to get cold?" said the Vampire with another grin

"Err, no, you're right, my son will only moan" she laughed before adding "You know, you seem very familiar, all of a sudden"

"Really? Probably got one of those faces. I'm Terry, by the way"

"Oh, hi. I'm Lauryn", she replied and taking the Pizza and bottle of drink in her hands, she quickly turned around to place them on a side table in the hallway, before looking back towards the door again.

But it was an empty space.

He had already gone.

*

"It's an absolute disgrace! Complete disgrace. What do you think Terry?"

"About what?" said the Vampire, walking into the kitchen and placing his delivery satchel on the counter.

"About what?!" snapped Oscar

"Err, I've been at work, sorry. Has something happened?"

"Has something happened?! God's teeth, where have you been, man? Look!" said Oscar thrusting his phone into his house mate's face.

"Holy shit!" said Terry now watching a black man

being pinned to the ground and slowly choked by an American Cop.

"Oh, it gets worse. Keep watching"

"My God. Is he dead?"

"Err, yeah" replied Oscar, sarcastically.

"Jesus, that's disgusting. Who was he?"

"Does it matter?" spat back Errol, sitting with a drink, at a large oak table in the middle of the kitchen and joining the conversation for the first time.

"His name was George Floyd, and he was strangled for over 8 minutes before he died" confirmed Oscar, folding his arms in indignation

"God, that's awful"

"8 minutes 43 seconds, can you believe it?"

"American Cops, innit. Doing it all the time, aren't they?" said Terry, shaking his head, before turning around to take off his jacket

"And they're so much better over here," snapped Errol, not raising his eyes from his glass of rum.

"Well yeah, of course mate, they're pricks over here too, obviously" said Terry brightly.

"Not as bad though, eh?" scowled Errol.

"Well I didn't say that did I? Just that, it's different over there, isn't it? I mean, they've got guns and we don't, for a start," said Terry now a little taken aback, by the sudden hostility in his friend's voice

"Oh right, ever heard of Colin Roach?" said Errol, raising his head from his glass for the first time

"From the Sinead O'Connor song? Course I have. I was the one who told you about it, remember?" said Terry, instantly recalling the suspicious death from a gun shot wound of a black man inside Stoke Newington Police Station in 1983.

"Or Mark Duggan" said Errol, now sitting up and getting a little angrier, as he referenced the shooting of a young black man by the Police, which sparked the UK riots of 2011.

"Yeah, but that was from a few years ago, wasn't it?"

"Oh right, so that's alright then, is it?"

"No, of course not"

"You need to open your eyes, geezer. Still happening today. Still no problem killing a black man" said Errol grinding his fangs in fury and looking down into his drink again.

"Yeah I know, I get it mate" said Terry, now with a more conciliatory tone in his voice, while Oscar returned the faintest trace of an unconvinced smirk. "Well of course you do" he said before instantly returning all of his attention back to Errol again, to continue his rant about the murder, while Terry's eyes blinked furiously into the harsh fluorescence of the LED lights. Five minutes ago, he'd been happily thinking about the beauty of his Pizza Delivery Muse, and what kissing her might taste like, but now, felt as if he had just been hit by a flying brick. What the hell was this all about? the Vampire's thoughts demanded, and so quickly folding his arms, for the next thirty minutes, he tried desperately to demonstrate to his housemates, well Errol mostly, that he was, in fact, squarely on the side of the angels and had no truck whatsoever with Police violence against black people. However "I think they need to do away with the Cops completely now" and "I hope the bastard gets banged up for the rest of his life" seemed to come to nothing, and so after another neutral/ needy smile was rebuffed by his flatmates, Terry finally decided that he'd had enough of all the forced politeness, and instead sloped off for an early night. However, sleep was the last thing on his mind, and for the next few hours, as he stared up from his solid metal pallet, Vampires never used beds, as, because of their intricate exoskeleton mattresses generally caused them severe back pain, he tried to rationalize, what had just happened. It was nuts, thought Terry, especially over the subject of race, which had always been such a point of agreement between the two friends, ever since they had first met at a Steel Pulse gig in London in the late 1970's. Left in their politics and always favoring the underdog, their similar outlooks forged an immediate bond and although Terry was a little older, born in 1918 to Errol's 1951, in Bloodsucker years, they could nearly be considered as twins. In fact they were both part of Generation Delta, c 1810 – 1960, sandwiched between the Violent Generation 1640 – 1809 and the Pre-Millennials, 1961 – roughly 2110. Vampire Generations tended to last roughly 150 years or so by the way, and although Terry was white and Errol was black, what really seemed to matter to the young Vampires was the fact that they had both been "raised skint" and had the same dirt and resentment running through their veins. Rochdale meets Harlesden, Northern slum meets a West London ghetto, by the early 1980's, the two friends had joined the Anti – Nazi League and were regularly seen together after dark either battling Vampire Skinheads in Brick Lane, or joining protests against the SUS laws and the horror of the New Cross Fire. So, was all this for nothing? A fantasy of solidarity, just waiting to crumble, at the slightest touch? Terry thought as he continued to stare into the blackness of his cell for what seemed like hours, until eventually, failling into a deep sleep. The next evening, he rose late and still slightly unnerved by the events of the previous night, he padded into the kitchen craving a cup of coffee to raise his spirits, when, to his dismay, he discovered that Oscar's lackeys from EVC (Ethical Vampire Capital) were bloody everywhere. Around the kitchen table, lounging on sofas, leaning up against walls, the pandemic was fast becoming a serious pain in the derriere, thought the Vampire placing his cup under the Sage Barista Express, Bean to Cup Coffee Machine, while he waited for his evening triple espresso. If it wasn't fobbing off, Fast Food 4 U begging him to work days, which for obvious reasons had little appeal to a Demon of the Night, he was having to endure his flat-mates, especially the insufferable Oscar, on a virtually full-time basis. It was like being in an awful marriage, hissed Terry to himself, and for the next few minutes, he mooched around the kitchen, constantly sipping his coffee, trying to be as polite as possible to the well scrubbed insurgents, until his fragile mood took a further hit, when the door of the kitchen suddenly swung open and of all people, Lady Carswell, the Head of the Vampire Council, came into view.

"Ah, good evening everyone. No, no, please stay as you are, don't get up on my account. All looking very productive, excellent, excellent. Oh and Terence, still in your Jim Jams, I see? You've missed the best part of the day, my dear boy. I'm up well before the sun goes down. Remember we must grasp each day as if we were mortal, which of course, we once were "

"Err, yes your Ladyship" answered Terry, looking down at his tracksuit bottoms, and thinking it was the first time they'd ever been called Jim Jams, before returning his customary nervous smile, whenever he encountered Vampire aristocracy.

"No matter, no matter; Lassitude, the great advantage of youth. However, I was looking for a little word with Oscar. Is he here, by any chance?" said Lady Carswell glancing back towards Terry again.

"Err not sure. I saw him last night, but…" replied Terry, as he looked over to the other Vampires for some help, until the kitchen door swung open again and, on cue, his housemate appeared.

"Your Grace? What an incredible honour. If we had known, we could have prepared better " declared Oscar with his usual bombast before bowing his head and kissing the large ruby on a gloved finger of the Vampire Leader's hand.

"I was only passing, my dear boy, but I thought it might be nice to have a little chat"

"Of course, of course, let me take your coat and get you a chair and…"

"No need. I am not here for long, and I don't want to interrupt these glorious young men in their no doubt worthy endeavors. Perchance, is there anywhere, we can talk?" interrupted Lady Carswell, prompting Oscar to quickly bow his head again and after giving Terry and his work colleagues, a little conspiratorial wink, he ushered the Head of the Vampire Council out of the kitchen, and down the long hallway, towards a room at the end.

"Yes, I shall be going on the March later" replied Oscar, closing the door of the ante room and turning to

11

offer his guest a seat, before the Vampire Leader grabbed him by the back of the head and kissed his lips with a fierce passion.

"I thought you only marched against Brexit, my sweet" declared Lady Carswell, finally releasing herself from her lover's arms and stepping back to look around the room.

"Well, this is more or less Brexit again, don't you think? "White Cop kills Black Man", the horrors of the great unwashed once more."

"Brexit was just the Hors d'oeuvre, my darling. This is far more interesting. This is rebellion" said Lady Carswell with a knowing smile, and sitting down on the nearest chair.

"Rebellion? Are you sure? Mortals are far too stupid for that kind of thing. I can taste it in their blood" said Oscar pulling up another seat and sitting down opposite.

"Well, they never used to be, and that took effort"

"Of course. Three day week, unemptied bins, the Two Ronnies. I remember, bloody chaos"

"Exactly, but I fear we are going to need to do the same again" said Lady Carswell, placing her gloves on her lap.

"The same again?"

"My dear Oscar you need to open your eyes. The map is changing. We have all the money and very soon the restless hordes will pull their heads out of their bargain buckets or whatever they eat nowadays and finally realize, that they are being cheated and when they do, there will be hell to pay; and I don't want to go through all that unpleasantness again. Saw enough of that in Paris in 1789"

"But, surely it wont come to that?" laughed Oscar

"Oh, it might. History is always surprising us, my

love. Nothing stays the same forever. You've lived long enough to understand that much surely? However, I think this George Floyd affair has come along just at the right time. Keep the unwashed, as you call them, further apart, and then, we can deal with them separately, in our own time. What was it Madison said in the Federalist Papers? Proliferate Faction. Now Identity and Diversity, will be the new road-map for the coming century"

"Err, okay?" replied Oscar, folding his arms, a little confused.

"The individual not the collective? Push the real you? The personal is political and all that kind of thing, but this time we'll cede some ground to color. Usual drill, make sure 13% of billionaires, or whatever the proportion is these days, are black"

"Whilst making very sure, they're our blacks. I like it. But don't you think, it might be a bit risky, especially with Social Media, the way it is? Everyone and his cat wants to be a Lefty these days my sweet. Even Emily Vordermain is at it now and I remember when she used to flounce about in a sparkly dress doing quiz shows and giving hair-styling tips to Hello magazine. Point is, they might not all play ball" said Oscar, leaning forward for a kiss.

"Nonsense. It'll be just like Greed in the 1980's. A few worthies will throw their hands up in the air and say it's scandalous and how we're destroying the fabric of society, which of course we are, but then after a quick glance at their bank accounts and their children's school fees, they'll soon change their tune, and get on board the gravy train. Mortals are such fakes, it's what makes them so delicious. Therefore next week, I will announce at a special meeting of the Vampire Council, an embargo on biting black people for the foreseeable future and from that time forward, we will all take the knee at sunset and then every week after that to commemorate poor George Floyd. I shall also make sure all mortal Institutions do the same. That will annoy the Peasants and we'll keep pressing on the bruise until they lash out"

"Then we call them racists" said Oscar with a triumphant smile.

"Precisely. Make things seem ridiculous. In fact the more ridiculous, the better. Moral Relativism is now our new guide, my precious love. What was it Lenin said? Accelerate the contradictions. Such a clever man. I helped get him on that train to Finland back in 1917, you know. So yes, change the language, left is right, up is down, nothing is real, there is no objective truth. Keep them chasing their tails, while we distract their dull eyes away from what we really have"

"Power?"

"Control, you silly boy. Control. That's the real story of civilization" cooed Lady Carswell, leaning forward to kiss her lover again, before the sound of a yawn in the corridor outside brought their embrace to an abrupt end and the Head of the Vampire Council quickly rose from her seat and opened the door.

"So as I said Oscar, ensure everyone complies, which I'm sure they all will. Ah, Terence, there you are again" said the Vampire Leader with a big smile

"Oh err sorry, your Ladyship. I didn't realize you were in there, err..."

"You look a little fatigued my dear, if you don't mind me saying so"

"Terry's a Vegan your grace. Sadly not enough protein in badger blood. I've told him many times" interrupted Oscar with a look of mock concern.

"Yes, you mustn't believe all that nonsense by the Better Living Vampire Commission. Of course, they mean well, but Veganism is never good, we need the fat, you see. Yes, you must give yourself some proper food. In fact I insist that you come over to the Temple without delay, and I will treat you to some of my private stock. A young Scaffolder, AB positive, breathtakingly rich. It will definitely bring some color back to those pallid cheeks. Anyhoo, must dash, and remember what I said Oscar" said Lady Carswell, glancing at her lover one more time, before, in a blink of an eye, she had slipped through the front door and into the night.

"What the fuck she doing here?" asked Terry, still looking a little anxious after her departure.

"Came to see her favorite Vampire, didn't she?"

"Oh right" scowled Terry

"You should show a little more interest fella"

"No chance. She always scares the crap out of me. Anyway, not sure she likes me" replied Terry, sinking his hands into the pockets of his tracksuit bottoms.

"You're just being paranoid again. You really shouldn't worry so much, old chap. Life is for living, didn't you know. Oh bugger, is that the time? The Vigil" said Oscar, suddenly looking down at his watch

"Vigil?"

"Yes, Terry. The Vigil. Tonight, in Vauxhall. For George Floyd? God, of all people, I thought you'd know. You being the political conscience of the house and all that. Anyway, I'm supposed to be meeting Errol in half an hour, and I don't want to be late, must dash" declared Oscar, with a grin before racing out of the front door and leaving Terry alone in the corridor again. "Don't want to be late, must dash" said the Vampire, sarcastically to himself in the voice of his housemate, while he trudged back towards his cell and sat on his pallet. Oscar was never on time for anything, was famous for it, be late for his own funeral, he used to say, but that was before he could sense a new opportunity, of course. A few months previous, he wouldn't even lend Errol the money for petrol to get to work, he'd had to do it, but now, after the high profile murder of a black man, he was rushing around like a love-struck teenager. It made the Terry's blood boil and as he lay down on the metal base, contemplating the sight of Oscar standing among ordinary black people, gaily chatting about the injustices of a racist society, it felt like a cross between George W Bush calling Putin a war criminal or David Cameron telling us that he loved the Smiths. Yuk he mouthed to himself, and therefore placing some head-phones over his ears, he nodded his head to Small Talk at 125th and Lenox by Gil Scott Heron, and tried not to scream.

By 9pm it was getting late and deciding, despite the presence of Oscar, he should probably go to the Vigil, Terry finally rose from his pallet and got dressed before making his way towards South London. It was just after 10 pm, when he arrived in Vauxhall, and perched on a near-by roof, he smoked a cigarette, while he looked down, with a little amusement, at the large crowd assembled below. There had been some trouble earlier in the day on the Mall, with various statues being defaced, including, predictably, one of Winston Churchill, which made Terry smile. Back in 1990, in the evening, after the Poll Tax riots, he'd nearly done the same thing himself, but even then, as he stood in front of the fat bastard with a can of spray paint in his hand, intending to do his worst, he remembered the speeches in the darkest days of the War and in the end, couldn't bring himself to do it. Some history you just couldn't re-write, and therefore for the next few minutes, Terry was content to stay on the roof and take in the spectacle until a man with a megaphone asked the crowd to remember all the victims of racial violence over the years, before a deathly silence descended and everyone dropped to one knee. This was now the official riposte to racism, popularized a few years earlier by Colin Kaepernick, an African American Quarterback, who first introduced the practice before an NFL game to protest police brutality against black people, but despite the heavy symbolism involved in the gesture, Terry still found himself, wavering for a second.

It felt weak.

Hardly Tommie Smith or John Carlos at the 1968 Olympics, defiantly raising their fist in the air, was it? And try as he may, he couldn't really imagine Toussaint L'Ouverture, the black General of the only successful Slave revolt in history or Eldridge Cleaver, the Black Panther leader from the 1960's doing something so submissive. Therefore he remained stubbornly upright for a few more seconds, until, out of the crowd, Errol suddenly raised his head, to stare accusingly into his old friend's eyes.

Now, Terry felt an instant sense of shame, and embarrassed by his temporary belligerence, the Vampire looked away for a second, before quickly sinking to one knee, and staring blankly at the roof slates underneath his feet.

CHAPTER TWO

"You gotta get up Jordan"

"Yeah, yeah, just give me a few minutes"

"A few minutes? You've been in there all day. I wanna see you up in half an hour, okay? Or I'm coming back in"

"Y'okay" said her son, wearily turning his head back into the pillow, before Lauryn shut the bedroom door and walked back towards the kitchen.

"Don't know what I am gonna do with him"

"Kids innit? Love a kip, don't they"

"It's flipping nine o'clock in the evening Terry. He's been in bed all day"

"Oh well, you know what they're like. Has he got a job?"

"You're having a laugh aren't you ?" scowled Lauryn picking up a bottle of wine and pouring herself another glass, before adding dismissively "He wants to be a Rapper"

"Well, that's good, isn't it?" said the Vampire, brightly, now trying to make up for his treasonous comment towards his own sex, about mentioning, of all things, a job

"Not if you've heard him."

"It's hard though these days isn't it? Social media and all that. Half the planet judging you, every time you walk out the door."

"Oh, don't give him excuses Terry. Anyway I've had enough, he needs to sort himself out" said Lauryn emphatically shaking her head while the Vampire glanced down at the floor of her kitchen, and tried to suppress a grin.

"Don't!" said Lauryn seeing him out of the corner of her eye before walking over for a kiss.

"I won't" said Terry, leaning forwards to taste her soft lips and for a brief moment his blackened heart beat a little slower, while he tried to savor this silent joy. Following his last unscheduled exit, he had "accidentally" ran into her again a few evenings later outside her tower block. Naturally, the Ancient Texts strongly discouraged Vampires from engaging in romantic liaisons with mortals, as their emotions almost always weaken the resolve of creatures bound by extreme self-interest. "*Fuck em and bite em*" was the unofficial advice, but Terry wasn't so sure. Maybe it was his relative youth, a hundred years was a mere blink in the eye of a Vampire's life or maybe it was something more human that still dwelt in the deep recesses of his soul? However, whatever it was, he found that he couldn't resist. Of course, being a Blood sucker, with a pathological need to end human life, would challenge most relationships, but what was he to do? Turned at the height of the Spanish Civil War, he had traveled out from the misery of 1930's

Lancashire to fight the fascists and change the world, but, as usual, fate had something else in mind for him; and even when Hector, the Vampire who gave him extended life, whispered in his ear that "it's not for everyone my friend" and gave him the option to back away, he was still undeterred. Curiosity was his eternal curse. *"For what shall it profit a man, if he shall gain the whole world, and lose his own soul?",* his Sunday teacher had cautioned him once. Well the old bag would be laughing now, thought the Vampire with a sad smile, as he stared over the shoulder of his lover, and once more, dreamt of a possible path, out from all the blood and the guilt, before a tall figure dressed in ripped jeans and white T-Shirt, interrupted his perennial melancholy.

"Erm, sorry" said the young man.

"Oh so you finally got up then?" said Lauryn, pulling away from Terry and folding her arms, while her son groped for the handle of the fridge.

"Oh and don't drink all of that by the way. I want some for tomorrow, before I go to work" continued Lauryn watching him take out a carton of orange juice while Terry remained in the background, his eyes now eagerly seeking out the sanctuary of the kitchen floor once more.

He'd been here before.

Single mum scolding her son to show that she had some measure of control, while the boy wriggled around like a lizard in a jar, for a new and uninvited audience. Embarrassment was usually the bluntest implement in a parent's tool box, and so the Vampire continued to stare impassively at the floor, before the sound of a mobile phone ringing in another room, brought a welcome halt to the tirade.

"I'm Terry by the way" said the Vampire, puncturing the awkward silence after Lauryn had dashed out to answer the call.

"Oh, okay" said Jordan sullenly, his body tensing against reality of another man in his territory, especially a white man.

"I hear you're a Rapper"

"Err well, yeah."

"Who do you like?"

"You wouldn't know."

"Try me."

"Ghetts, Lowkey, Jme."

"Oh yeah, I know them."

"Really?"

"Nah! Ain't got a clue. I like ELO."

"Who are they?"

"Old drill band" replied Terry, as he allowed himself a little grin at the lameness of his joke, before adding.

"So who you support?"

"Arsenal, what about you?" replied Jordan, a little less defensively, as he placed the carton of juice back in the fridge.

"Man U" said Terry.

"Not doing so well."

"We need Lucius Noble."

"Yeah, he's good."

"The best."

"You sound different. You don't come from these Ends."

"Up North lad. More like Preston North Ends" replied Terry.

"What?" said Jordan, shaking his head.

"Nothing. Dad joke."

" You ain't that old."

"I use good moisturizer."

"You're a joker."

"Maybe" replied Terry with a warm smile and now turning his head, he looked deeper into Jordan's eyes, before whispering softly into his thoughts, that he was a friend and furthermore, would always treat his mother with love and respect. Now, after a moment of confusion from the brief psychic intervention, a big smile suddenly spread across the young man's face and quickly reaching into the pocket of his jeans, he pulled out a phone and marched over towards the Vampire.

"You wanna see my new video bruv? We filmed it yesterday."

"Definitely" replied Terry, as he looked at the screen held in front of him, whilst quietly admonishing himself for using his Bloodsucker powers to charm his way into the affections of his girlfriend's son.

"Is that a spliff?"

"Yeah bruv."

"Outrageous" replied Terry with mock indignation, as he continued to nod his head to the sound coming out from the phone.

"So you like it, then?" asked Jordan with a look of innocent concern.

"Well, it ain't Cole Porter or Billie Holiday, but yeah, it's great. You got talent" replied Terry, only half lying, as "Go With My Flow" wasn't the worst thing that the Vampire had ever heard.

"Cole who?" replied Jordan shaking his head again,

and the Vampire was just about to give the young man a quick resume of one of his favorite Composers of all time when Lauryn came storming back into the kitchen again, this time with a look of thunder on her face.

"That was your father again, complaining that you owe him money for some trainers, and now he wants to know when you're getting a job."

"Well, yeah, he'll get it."

"When?"

"Soon" snapped Jordan, now looking more than a little embarrassed in front of his new friend

"When?"

"When I get a job?"

"That'll be the day."

"You know, there's a bar, around the corner that's hiring. Lock down is finishing next week, I think, so maybe give them a call? Can't hurt. I can text your mum the number, if you want " interrupted Terry, before staring into the young man's eyes once more.

"Great! Cheers, Terry" replied Jordan, and after giving his mother, a cheeky wink, he placed his phone back in his pocket and then bounced out of the kitchen.

"How the hell did you do that? I've been trying to get him to go and get a job for months, so he can stop hanging around with those idiots from the Estate" declared Lauryn, placing her hands on her hips and shaking her head.

"It's a guy thing."

"Well keep doing it. Oh and while you're at it, maybe you can get him to clean his room now and again, as well" said Lauryn, reaching up to kiss Terry passionately on the lips again once more.

*

The Vampire Leader glided to the centre of the stage, and after lowering her head for a few seconds, as if in silent prayer, she raised her startling blue eyes to regard the two thousand or more Vampires who were now seated in front of her.

"Welcome to everyone, and thank you for interrupting your incredibly busy schedules to attend this emergency meeting of the Vampire Council, which although arranged in haste, I'm sure, due to recent events, you will appreciate our reasons for doing so. Therefore, with this in mind, would you join me in showing our utter abhorrence at the recent murder of George Floyd and our continued solidarity with our black brothers and sisters in Black Lives Matter, by first taking a knee" declared Lady Carswell, now looking pointedly over the heads of those assembled in the Great Hall of Blood, before instantly dropping to one knee and bowing her head.

"We gonna do this every fucking time we come here? It's like being in a bloody church?" whispered Terry into Errol's ear, as they both remained on the ground for a few seconds, before rising to look up towards the two large semi circles of tables set twenty feet above their heads signifying the First and Second Tiers of the Grand Council of the Ancient Order of Vampires. Only a few days earlier, Terry's customary flippancy towards Carswell and the Vampire Council, would have been met with the usual conspiratorial grin from his old friend, but since the murder of a defenseless black man on the streets of Minneapolis, any impish comment was now seen, as at best, misinformed, while, at worst, a little racist. This greatly annoyed Terry, especially as, over the years, he had taken enough beatings off real Nazis to feel he'd paid his dues. However, considering the circumstances and moreover, their little exchange of words in the kitchen a few nights previous, the Vampire decided now was probably not the best time to get over-sensitive about things, and so quickly drawing his eyes away, from the austerity of his friend's face, he looked up towards Oscar, who had suddenly appeared at an iron lectern, and was preparing to make the next proclamation.

"Greetings, my Brothers and Sisters in Blood, and a warm welcome to those who have traveled many miles from distant parts of our Realm to be with us tonight. From Glasgow, Belfast, Manchester, Liverpool, Exeter; your loyalty is always our greatest strength, it feeds our will to survive, so my thanks to you all again. And of course, our deepest gratitude to our esteemed and honored leader, Lady Carswell for setting the perfect tone of this emergency meeting of our Ancient Council. As always, your guidance is our greatest consolation" announced Oscar, directing his hand towards the Head of the Vampire Council, now seated in the middle of the first of the great semi-circle of tables, that towered above everyone, prompting some more applause from the audience, before he raised his hand for silence and started to speak again.

"And so, as we all try to process the truly appalling events of the last few days and are compelled to face the bitter realities head on, we find that our only option, is to finally speak the truth. George Floyd did not die because of one bad Cop, one bad apple, one rogue Actor in an otherwise fair and functioning Institution. He died because of a pernicious, racist, white supremacy. A Western, Colonial, Imperialistic vision of the world that no longer rings true in the second decade of the new century. For nearly nine minutes the knee of a white police officer squeezed the life out of a powerless black man and this time we could not look away. Nor should we. Yes it's uncomfortable, and as a middle class, Caucasian, and I was going to add middle aged, but at barely 550 years old, even my harshest critics, would not label me as that just yet, I hope, I, too,understand my privilege. Yes, because of course, that is the word, isn't it? Privilege. I can walk on the streets from dusk to dawn in any part of the world and be relatively sure that my color will afford me certain advantages and therefore insulate me from it's myriad of dangers. How many of our fellow brothers and sisters of color can say that? How many have been stopped by the Police for no reason? Denied career opportunities because of their surnames? Been subject to micro-aggressions on a daily basis? Yes I see the heads nodding. We've all seen it, haven't we? How many times has a person of color walked into a lift and the white person next to them, placed their bag over the other shoulder? Yes, yes, now we hear you, we are listening. Now we see you, our eyes are finally open. Those little cuts, and slights, too many to list here, must cease and with immediate effect. Therefore after an emergency conclave of the First and Second Tiers of our beloved Council, it has been decided, by a unanimous vote, may I add, that hence-forth, all black mortals will now be exempt from any Nocturnal Ex-sanguination. In short, no-body bites a black person for the foreseeable future.

Of course, this does not mean that the Council ignores the racism experienced by other minorities. We do not, and condemn it vehemently, whenever we encounter it. However, in the present circumstances, I think you will all agree that it is our black brothers and sisters who are suffering the most and, as a result, need our most urgent attention. Therefore, this new directive is immediate from Sunset tomorrow, and will be strictly enforced, so please abide by these rules, as, understandably, our sanctions against any non-compliance, will be, very harsh indeed. However, knowing many of you here, as I do, I am certain this course of action will not be necessary. We are essentially good people and have always known the meaning of the words, Honor and Duty, the twin pillars of a Vampire's life, for Millennia now. Indeed, it has been our principle purpose. To take the lead and push the base savagery of mortals onto greater things and we must do the same again today. It is our Destiny! We will thrive!" declared Oscar now stepping back from the lectern and raising his arms, as the whole chamber rose as one to chant back "We will thrive" the motto of the English coven for the last fifteen hundred years, before erupting into tumultuous applause once more. Terry, also rose to his feet and brought his hands together in a mechanical clap, as he forced out something resembling a smile. What a load of duplicitous tripe, he thought. Oscar couldn't give a toss about "people of color" and neither could, if the truth be told, most of the Vampires in the hall right now. How many times in the 1970's and 1980's, had Terry overheard racist jokes or comments in Vamp pubs and clubs all over the UK, and he knew of at least two

Brothers in Blood, applauding within eye-shot of him, who had been ex Chelsea Head Hunters, and back in 1982, had openly threatened to chase Paul Canoville, the first black footballer to play for the club, off the pitch. It was pure Vampire theatre, and although, Terry was naturally sympathetic towards the new directive, and had himself, since he'd been turned in 1938, studiously avoided biting mortals of colour as well as Jews, he'd been in a regiment that had liberated Auschwitz, the glaring hypocrisy of those now clapping like demented seals, left a very nasty taste in Terry's mouth, as he sat back down and stared up at the lectern once more.

"Thank you, thank you, I expected no less, and of course, as this is such a watershed moment, requiring fundamental change in all of us, particularly those of us who are not brothers and sisters of color, I think you will agree, a new purpose must be forged. Therefore, to aid us further on this voyage of self-discovery, I am very pleased to introduce to you, a woman who probably needs very little introduction. First Tier Vampire, with a Founder's Degree in the Occult and Philosophy, a visiting Professor at Oxford, Harvard and University of California, Berkeley. A noted Critical Race Theorist, author of the bestselling book, Fear and White People, and more recently appointed Co-Chair of the Committee for A Blueprint to a More Equal Planet, I have the immense pleasure to introduce to you, the very talented and may I say the very credentialed, Beverley Di Franco, everyone," announced Oscar, stepping away from the lectern to welcome, a petite white woman, with a blonde bob and penetrating blue eyes, that marked her out, to anyone aware of Vampire genealogy, as a high status WASP from the First Grade of the American Vampire Council. Again, the chamber burst into spontaneous applause, and everyone, including Terry rose again, to show their appreciation for the speaker, until the clapping died down and the audience returned to their seats.

"Thank you everyone, you are very kind, and thank you my dear Oscar, charming and to the point as usual. However I must correct you on one point. I am not a Critical Race Theorist. That is a separate niche, academic, legal discipline, which some of our enemies are now weaponizing against us, while ,as usual, not understanding a word of what the theory actually says. It's not actually what I do. However, in the febrile culture in which we live today, I can understand the confusion. So, my friends, to return to our subject, here we are …again!!!. I don't want to say I told you so, but as I have said repeatedly in my books, and podcasts, the systematic racism of our institutions will keep doing what it always does, because, not only, does it rely on the transience of our memories but also, more importantly, on our tacit compliance. The hand that killed Trayvon Martin, Michael Brown, Eric Garner, Tamir Rice, Walter Scott, Alton Sterling, Breonna Taylor has now choked the life out of George Floyd for nearly 9 minutes, and that hand is, I am sad to say, our hand. Yes that hand is a white hand, and we must now all face this undeniable fact. Just because we don't shout or even think the N word, does not mean that we are not part of the problem. Far from it. We are the problem! We support a system, like my dear, departed friend Edward Said said on many occasions, that is white, colonial, western and at it's heart, yes, racist. Prejudice plus power is now the accepted definition of racism and in the USA and the UK especially, as the events of the last week have shown, it is as alive as it ever was. In fact, whiteness doesn't even have a color does it?, but is rather the default position of modern society. The toys our children play with, the pictures on our currency, the very concept of beauty itself. Ask any beautiful black woman about colorism in her community and she will tell you about routine bleaching of skin and relaxing of hair to basically look more white. Of course, we can say things are getting better, but if we were to be truly honest, we would have to say, they are not. In fact I fear things are getting worse. Our racism is now so deep inside ourselves, that we cannot even see it, and has become as natural to us, as taking a breath. We live in a white Universe, and it's only getting whiter. If the Aliens ever arrived, it would probably be the very first thing they would notice. Take me to your White Leader they would exclaim and they wouldn't be wrong, would they? So what do we do? We can't keep finding refuge in the catch all excuse "I'm not racist, it's the other guy", and so we must find some real answers, and possibly a good place to start would be to check our privilege and…

"God's teeth, I have been hearing this nonsense for years! Privilege? What bloody privilege are we actually talking about here, may I ask, Miss Deee Franco?" interrupted a tall blond haired middle aged Vampire, now standing up in the middle of the hall with his hands on his hips.

"Err excuse me, who is that? Oh yes, I should have expected. Bane Vulpain ?" said the speaker, peering out into the audience.

"It's Vulpine actually, and I repeat, what bloody privilege?"

"Well, your obvious offense at the term, proves my point exactly. You are demonstrating your white privilege right now, aren't you?" rebutted the Speaker, to some sporadic applause from the audience, whilst instinctively taking a step back from the lectern.

"Really? So I'm white and therefore that means, there must be a problem does it?"

"You know, it never ceases to amaze me, why so many white people, well actually if we are to be completely honest here, white middle aged men, are so sensitive on this issue? Why do so many white middle aged men get so upset if we talk about race?" said the speaker again.

"Yeah sit down Bane."

"Shut up Vulpine, you dick."

"No I won't bloody sit down and listen like sheep to this absolute nonsense, and to answer your question Miss Dee Franco. No-one is upset about talking about race, we can talk about race as much as you want, but what people are upset about, is talking about race all the bloody time. Of course, it's awful, what's just happened in America, we all know that, but even if you put that to one side, I can't help thinking that everything seems to revolve around race today? Everything. And of course the irony is, we are less racist than we've ever been, any statistic will tell you that much. More mixed marriages, multiple surveys saying white people have no problem living next to non white neighbors, half the cabinet of the UK government is non white. What more proof do you need? In fact madam, if anything, you're the racist. Constantly pointing out the color of people's skin, highlighting their differences. I mean, aren't we all supposed to be color blind, or something. Didn't Martin Luther King say judge a man by the content of his character, not the color of his skin?"

"Well, actually that's part of the problem" replied the speaker, leaning back into the lectern.

"Oh really? So Martin Luther King is racist now. Brilliant. What about Nelson Mandela? Yes, I'd wager he had some type of internalized racism going on in there somewhere, and don't get me started on Gandhi, a white adjacent if ever I saw one" said Bane, to some laughter and applause from the audience on his side of the chamber.

"Now you are devaluing the argument for your own purposes, which of course is a typical response from a desperate white man, who doesn't want to face the truth. The reality is, that unfortunately, we live in a world that isn't color-blind and shows no intention of being so for the foreseeable future. Dr King was not incorrect, when he spoke of treating everyone with respect and understanding, as we all should, but the fact is, we are not the same, are we? Any casual look at the outcomes of people of color in our society will tell you as much. Education, Housing, the Justice system, the proof is overwhelming. Therefore, what we really want is not color-blindness, but rather clear sight, to see how everything really works and I think, you would have to be pretty myopic in 2020, not to realize that the world is exclusively run for the advantage of white people."

"As usual that made no sense to me whatsoever, but regardless, here's one for your ever so superior academic mind to mull over then. Like most healthy and fully functioning Vamps here today, my ability to survive relies mainly on the homeless or the totally destitute, all of which, by the way, are nearly ninety percent white. So, tell me, oh Enlightened One? These poor wretches living out of cardboard boxes, who are our unwilling food source. Privileged are they? Oh yes, my good man, I would feel infinitely more sorry for you, living on the streets, addicted to Spice and Black Tar Heroin, and being routinely picked off by Pimps and Vampires, if it wasn't for your awful white privilege!?"

"Now you are confusing race with class. It's intersectional."

"Oh of course, I forgot. It's intersectional! Another obscure term, made up by bogus academics to keep themselves in a job."

"And once more, Mr Vulpine, you show your ignorance to the world. Intersectionality, for those here, not acquainted with the term, is the idea that a person can face more than one kind of disadvantage in wider society. So, for example, if you are a black working class woman lets say, you would experience discrimination because of your race, your gender and your class. So, to your point, you do have a point. There are white people disadvantaged by their social conditions, and it's very clear that their lives are very hard, but they still have the advantage of being white, in a world, where, as I have said before, their skin color happens to be the default position."

"So what you're basically saying then, is maybe if they changed their accents or dressed in a certain way, they could improve their lives," said Bane, folding his arms.

"Well, conceivably, yes, and, of course, we have seen

white people do this all the time, haven't we? History is full of examples of white people from very poor environments, changing their accents, playing the game and then succeeding. Abraham Lincoln, immediately comes to mind, for example, and was a very dear friend of mine, by the way. He was the son of a dirt poor Kentucky Farmer and rose to be President of the United States in one generation. I very much doubt, at the time, if the same possibility would have been open to let's say Frederick Douglas. A black person, clearly, does not have the same option. Whatever they do, they are black and are therefore damned to be treated differently and as a consequence, condemned to far worse outcomes."

"Well, as usual, I think you people, might benefit from an up to date calendar. It's 2020 not 1860, if you hadn't noticed, but, of course, the idea of racial progress, doesn't serve your extremely divisive narrative too well, does it? However aside from this, let's suppose you are right. Let's suppose there is such a thing as white privilege. What if we don't want to change our accents? What then?"

"But you could, couldn't you?" replied Beverley Di Franco with a smug grin.

"That's complete rot," shouted back Bane, as a small contingent of Vampires around Bane now rose to start shouting and gesticulating at the speaker, while large parts of the audience in the front, turned around to abuse the dissenters.

"Fascists" and "Gammons" now rang out in the cavernous chamber, quickly followed by a chorus of "I can't breathe, I can't breathe," until the forty or so Vampires surrounding Bane decided that they'd had enough and promptly marched out of the meeting, to huge jeers from most of the audience.

"Fucking racist scum" shouted Errol, furiously, now standing on his chair and shaking his fist, while Terry looked at the joyous faces, all around him, and started to feel an uneasiness in the pit of his stomach.

CHAPTER THREE

"So is it just the white middle class you dislike, then?"

"Mainly" said Terry placing the heel of his boot on his knee, while glancing over at a print of Gustav Klimt's "The Kiss" on the wall opposite.

"And by middle class? Who are we talking about? For example, in America, the term could be applied to what we refer to here, as the working class."

"I mean the English version. Like the top 20% of society, you know the PMC, Professional Managerial Class."

"I see. And so using your metric then, how do we judge who is middle class or not?" said the man with a well trimmed beard, now using his fingers to make quotation marks for the words middle class.

"Well, it's not hard is it?" said the Vampire with a grimace, and as usual, annoyed by anyone indicating quotation marks with their fingers.

"How so?" said the man.

"Well, their manner for a start. You know, that slow way they talk. Considering every word like they're eating nouvelle bloody cuisine or something. Or that way they try and dress down, with a T-Shirt and ripped jeans, but have a two grand Apple Mac under their arm."

"But surely that could also be someone from a working class background, who liked to dress very casually, but made enough money to buy an expensive laptop" suggested the man, with an inclusive smile.

"What these days? Don't think so, Pal. Anyways, if you come from the streets, you always like to keep a bit of bling with you, don't you? You know, a bit of something, the wanker middle classes would never wear. Like an earring or big gold chain."

"Wanker middle classes? That's a bit excessive don't you think" said the man, raising his eyebrows in concern.

"Told you. I have a problem" replied the Vampire, looking away again with a yawn.

"Quite. Okay, so let's try and find some common ground, shall we? What do you require from the Therapy? Why exactly are you here?"

Terry had been thinking the same thing himself.

The very last place he wanted to be, on his only night off from delivering German Doner Kebabs, was in an office revealing his soul to a complete stranger. However, the plain truth was, he did need help. His frustration with the middle classes was now as bad as it had ever been, worse, even, than the 1930's when he had grown up during the Depression, and society was much more unfair and the gap between the haves and have nots was way more obvious. Not only had he knocked off a fresh faced young Momentum activist on a train recently, who also happened to be the daughter of the celebrated QC,

Sir Edgar Sheffield, but then, after watching a Channel 4 News interview with two Members of Parliament from the new intake of the 2019 election, where the Conservative MP was called Sandra, and spoke with a thick Mancunian accent, whilst the representative for Labour was called Petra and sounded like she'd just walked off the set of Downton Abbey, he'd spent the next two nights perched on top of the Left-wing Politician's roof in Richmond, debating whether to bite her or not.

And he was supposed to be a Vegan for God's sake!

Plus, he had something else to consider.

Lauryn.

They'd been dating quite seriously for over three months now, and he knew that if he didn't change, or at least cut back on all the fury, pretty soon his antics would come to the attention of the Vamps in suits, and life could suddenly become very difficult for the new love of his life. In fact Oscar was already beginning to make jokes about it and his new found fondness for "Bourgeois Beaujolais" as he put it and while the rules of the order meant that he was pretty much free to bite whoever he wished, if it looked like he was straying into Politics or affecting mortals of any power or influence, a nurse working for the NHS would pose few problems for their risk averse minds.

"I'm here because I want to stop hating the middle classes. It's making me ill" said Terry, suddenly cutting short his disaffected thoughts and turning his head back towards his Therapist again.

"Yes, I see. So do you think, it's an obsession?"

"Yeah. If you like?"

"Tinged with anxiety?"

"No, just hate."

"Okay, good, good. So not Bourgeouisphobia, which does exist, but simply an anger. A Misaristogny if you will."

"A what?"

"From the Greek, "Aristo" for ruling class, and "Mis" meaning hatred" explained the Therapist with a happy smile.

"Okay, whatever" snapped the Vampire, feeling none the wiser.

"And maybe some anger issues, as well" ventured the Therapist raising another eyebrow.

"Is that extra?"

"Err, no, probably all connected to the same thing, I would imagine. So good. Yes very interesting. So, may I ask, these ideas about class that you have? Have you ever considered that they might possibly be, a little outdated, now?"

"Well, that's a bit judgmental, if you don't mind me saying so. Thought you're supposed to be a Therapist?" replied the Vampire, folding his arms, and feeling, genuinely, a little put out.

"Err well, forgive me, but what I mean to say is: This whole notion of class conflict per se. It could be said to be a rather antiquated notion, don't you think? You know from another time" replied the Therapist, hurriedly, trying to clarify his position.

"You think?"

"Well, yes. Some might say things have moved on a great deal, from the last century for example" declared the Therapist, clasping his fingers together on his pad.

"I bet they would."

"And that it's divisive."

"Well, people are divided already aren't they, so we might as well be honest about it."

"How about the concept of envy? Do you think it might just be envy, rather than issues of class?"

"Not too sure you're that envious of the man burning your house down, know what I mean? Might be another emotion involved there. Like blind fury perhaps."

"Okay, yes, I get that, but, have you ever encountered the phrase, inverted snobbery, by any chance" said the Therapist, writing furiously on his pad, before looking up again.

"Means a skint bugger looking down on rich people."

"Just so. So would you describe yourself as that?"

"100 per cent."

"Oh excellent. Any particular reason?"

"Because of their hypocrisy."

"Hypocrisy. Could you expand on that?

"Well, you know double standards. Telling poor people to have single families, when they all get married themselves, and stay married, cos they know it's better for their kids that way or letting skint bastards live in lawless shitholes, while they ponce around nice neighborhoods or gated communities where none of that crap ever touches them or banging on about the environment and making everyone's energy bills higher, while pissing off on holiday three times a year and having two cars in the driveway or pretending to be Catholic to elbow their little brats into the only decent state school in the area that should really be for poorer kids or… "

"Yes, yes, I think I have enough there. Fine, we'll probably unpack that later, if you don't mind. So anything else? You know, that annoys you about the middle classes, then?"

"Other than saying "unpack", you mean?" replied Terry with a deadpan look.

"Well, yes, quite. But what I mean to say is. Are they any other aspects of middle class behavior that you find challenging? You mentioned, the accent, before" offered the Therapist, brightly, trying to placate his client's increasingly prickly demeanor.

"Well it doesn't help, does it?"

"You find it irritating?"

"You could say that."

"I have an RP accent, do you find that irritating?"

"A little."

"Why is that, do you think?" asked the Therapist.

"Because it stinks of privilege."

"But my father could have been anyone, a builder, a shop assistant."

"Was he?"

"Well no, he was in the Foreign Office."

"There you go then," replied Terry looking around the consulting room again, while the Therapist frowned a little, before putting down his notepad, to try a new approach.

"So, can I ask, have you ever had any positive views of middle class people?"

"Well, I suppose, they used to be alright, you know, Orwell, Tony Benn, Nell Dunn, the playwright, Joe Strummer, from the Clash. They came into poor areas to learn and find out how to make things better," replied Terry, remembering the time that he had met George

Orwell in Spain in 1937 and found him to be quite a nice guy, but a bit stingy with his cigarettes.

"But surely, they do the same thing today?" said the Therapist.

"Do they hell! They come to preach."

"Are you sure?"

"Too right, I am. They've lost respect for the working class, haven't they? Call 'em Chavs and Gammons and Neets and all that. I mean it's probably our fault in the first place for giving up on Unions and buying our own council houses, but it's still a joke, know what I mean?" snapped Terry.

"Do you resent them for this."

"Resent them? No, it just bugs me, what they do to normal people."

" But surely, middle class people are normal people."

"You're having a laugh, aren't ya? They might as well come from another fucking planet, son," spat back Terry, now beginning to lose his composure.

"Well again, I think that's a little extreme, and also, if it's at all possible, could you moderate your language. It doesn't help does it?" suggested the Therapist.

"Oh doesn't it? You see, this is what you people do isn't it? Please don't swear, please be polite, please do as we say. Don't you understand, fucking swearing is probably the only thing most poor people have left," barked Terry, suddenly sitting up in his seat, as his face began to redden with rage.

"Look, I don't think…"

"Oh, here we go. Don't like what I'm hearing, so lets shut you up shall we? Cancel and virtue signal, isn't that the strategy? Use politeness and shame like you used to use bullets and bayonets back in the day. Do as we say or we will crush you. Christ, you bastards never change, do you? You know Pol Pot might have been right all along. Stick the middle classes out in a big field and work them to death for a bowl of rice a day. Funnily enough, I met him once in a pub in Lancaster Gate, was quite good at darts."

"Erm, but wasn't he born over 100 years ago? How could someone so young have met Pol Pot?" replied the Therapist, crinkling his forehead in confusion.

"Because fuck face, I'm not quite what I seem, am I? Ooh, and apologies again for my foul mouth, but sometimes I just don't know when to stop" replied Terry, as he flew across the room, before sinking his fangs deep into the Therapist's neck.

*

By the first month of the summer, the lock down had started to ease, and so when Boris Johnson announced the end of the health purdah in the first week of July, most of the population had begun to tentatively poke their heads out from their front doors and try to remember how to live their lives again. Oscar, especially, seemed elated at the new turn of events, as he could now stop targeting care homes and finally get the taste of COVID out of his mouth, while Errol was still brooding over the events after George Floyd, silently swiping for hours through increasingly more militant images on his phone. Unfortunately, relations between Terry and his old friend still remained tense, where any inter-action between the two was either overly-polite or the subject quickly segued to white supremacy and the unfairness of being black in the 21st century. Of course he understood the reason for Errol's ire, the reality of being black in modern society was, up to about five minutes ago, problematic to say the least. However, in private, the Vampire still struggled to get to grips with this new racial narrative. For him, it had always been simple. If you were poor, you were right and if you were rich you were wrong, and anything including race was simply a side show. "*Culture may move through Class, but Class is still the water we all swim in*," Hector had once told him, and although he could see how this statement could be seen as Class Reductionist, willfully ignoring the very real effects that Race, Gender and Sexual Preference can have on an individual's life, for good or bad, he had always stuck by this maxim.

However, in 2020, this idea was seen as heresy, and while savvy journalists started talking about Anti-Racism, and decried the notion of Class Solidarity, and Human Resource Departments insisted on pronouns in "your bios", anyone finding themselves outside this progressive pincer movement, was quickly branded an, out of touch, bigot. "I haven't changed, they have" now screamed many on the old Left and although Terry was all for new ideas and radical change to benefit society at large, this new direction, also stank of something more ancient. When the rich or the large Corporations start to "Take the knee" or boast of "Stakeholder Capitalism", while still increasing their profits by 10 percent in one of the worst economic downturns in history, you know something is badly amiss. Therefore, sensing another clever ruse from the ruling classes, the Vampire was now finding himself increasingly dismayed on his side of the river, and, instead, began to reluctantly look across the water towards the other bank, where demagogues like Bane Vulpine, had planted their flag.

Naturally, when the infamous Right Wing Commentator and Pod Caster had flounced out of the last meeting of the Vampire Council, he had jeered along with everyone else and then eagerly joined in with all the insults and ridicule at the drink's reception afterwards. "What a twat," "Racist," "Worse than Trump". But, despite the worthy pile on, Terry also found, that deep in his soul, he wasn't as committed to the new narrative as he should be, especially with regards to the whole idea of "White Privilege". In fact, for the next two weeks, these two words were all that occupied his thoughts, and as a result to try and maintain his place within the ever shifting parameters of his own tribe, he started to read again. "Natives" by Akala, "Why I Am Not Talking To White People About Race" by Reni Eddo Lodge and of course "Fear And White People" by Beverley Di Franco, were all gobbled up by Terry, in a bid to restore his belief in this new updated version of "the Left".

Of course, he had heard of Critical Race Theory before, and even once, as the noted sociologist, Peggy McIntosh had requested, enthusiastically unwrapped his own "invisible knapsack", to realize how fortunate he was. Capitalism, Colonialism, Imperialism, and any other type of ism you could wave a stick at, had obviously made it much easier to be white than any other ethnic group on the planet, as even the so-called "Deaths of Despair" from the Opoid crisis of the last few years, affecting mainly white working class men in America had received way more sympathy than the Crack Epidemic of the Eighties which claimed so many young black lives. Obviously, a blind man could see the disparity, Terry thought, while instantly recalling his own memory of hitch-hiking around the world for three years in the last century, where he discovered that from Vienna to Bangkok, Melbourne to Lagos, he experienced only generosity and acceptance, as lift after lift from drivers of various colors and creeds brought him closer to the bosom of humanity. Of course, as a Demon of the Night with at least ten times the strength of any mortal, he was never in any kind of danger, but the people who regularly shook his hand and eagerly gave him directions to a good place to eat, or the sight of some historical interest didn't know this, and he was pretty sure that if he'd been black and mortal at the time, he probably wouldn't have got as far as Camden Town. Then again, that was nearly forty years ago now, and while things were still far from perfect, just the briefest look at the centre of any major city on a Friday night, with black, brown, white and any other hue, all drinking, laughing and loving together, would tell you that the world in 2020 was a very different place.

However, listen to anyone in the media these days and you would assume the total opposite, and instead of encouraging co-operation between people from different racial backgrounds to combat the many social problems of modern life, the new prophets of Race, like Ibram X Kendi and Ta-Nehisi Coates were, instead, preaching a Gospel of suspicion and separation, together with a new set of seemingly contradictory decrees. "Silence is violence" but "Never say anything to question the actions of a person of color" and "Past discrimination can only be defeated with present and future discrimination." Hardly the sentiments of W.E.B Du Bois, the famous black sociologist and socialist who wrote for all men to "Choose, their friends, enjoy the sunshine, and ride on the railroads, uncursed by color; thinking, dreaming, working as they will in a Kingdom of beauty and love."

Furthermore, advances in Biology and the recent mapping of the human, and even the Vampire genome, which was, admittedly, a little different, had completely blown Carl Linnaeus' idea of the hierarchy of the races, which had started all this racist nonsense of the past two hundred years in first place, completely out of the water. Human beings were, genetically, more closely connected than any other species on earth. *We're all the bloody same,* Terry's thought's now yelled with increasing despair, as screen after screen railing about white exceptionalism, white supremacy, and of course white privilege now appeared on his phone, until, in frustration, he typed in the 10 most deprived areas in the United Kingdom.

- Middlesborough
- Liverpool
- Knowsley
- Kingston upon Hull
- Manchester
- Blackpool
- Birmingham

- Burnley
- Blackburn with Darwen
- Hartlepool

Hardly all black ghettos, were they? And except for Liverpool, Manchester and Birmingham, most were towns in the North of England and pretty much full of poor white people. So much for your white privilege Terry's thoughts now howled, as Di Franco's words from before laid siege to his reason again.

But they could change their accent, couldn't they?

You think Beverley? Ever hear of accent snobbery? You think if Einstein had come from Cornwall or Appalachia, anyone would have believed him?

$E = MC^2$? Yeah right, whatever mate, now piss off back to Greggs for sausage roll, you Peasant, and leave the thinking to those who don't drop their H's.

Of course, what she really meant was, with all that advantage, all that immunity from white supremacy, all those lack of obstacles, and you still ended up poor, wretched and without hope? Well, there's only one rational conclusion to be made, isn't there?

It was your bloody fault.

This was just bigotry by another name, thought Terry, and nibbling on his bottom lip, in frustration at the political cul de sac he now seemed to find himself in, he continued to swipe through article after article demonizing the white working class, until thankfully, out of all the gloom, a new text appeared on his phone to lighten his mood.

"Bruv, I went to the job, can we meet?"

Immediately, Terry's face lit up and so forgetting all

about white privilege and everything else that had been driving him near to the point of insanity for the last few days, he soon found himself perched on the seat of his bike and staring at the eager face of his girlfriend's son.

"So what happened?" asked Terry, taking a pull from his cigarette.

"They gave me a try out and then they said they would get back to me" said Jordan excitedly.

"A try out?"

"Yeah, you know, they make you work an evening shift to see what you're like."

"What? How to pour a pint of beer? Joke innit? So how much did they pay you? Minimum wage I suppose."

"No, they didn't pay me bro."

"Pardon?!"

"No, they gave me a burger and a drink and told me that they would get back to me if they thought they wanted me," confirmed Jordan, with a triumphant grin.

"You what?! How many hours did you do?"

"Err, four" replied Jordan, now a little confused at Terry's sudden change in tone, thinking he would be happy that he had gone for the interview in the first place.

"Four hours and they didn't pay you?!"

"Nah, but that's fair enough innit, bruv? They have to know if I can do the job."

"Jesus wept. This is the reason your generation keeps getting shafted mate. No Jordan that is NOT fair enough. Its total bullshit. You should have got paid, the second, you started working for them. Bastards," said Terry, suddenly getting off the seat of his bike and pacing angrily around.

"I don't understand?" said Jordan, his head following Terry, in confusion.

"Jordan, you should be paid mate. Not given a burger and a coke and a "we might get back to you". This is not the flipping X factor son. You don't have to do a performance just to get a job."

"Yeah but they all do it, I asked someone there and they said it's like normal practice or something."

"It's only normal, if they say it's normal. Fucking hell, even back in my day, when the Pits were all closed, they paid you if you did any work."

"The Pits?"

"Err, another time, pal. Look, if you work for someone, they have to pay you, that's how it works. Not bloody surprised though. This is totally what happens when there are no Unions,

"What's a Union?" asked Jordan innocently and looking even more confused.

"Exactly. Years ago, you'd never even have to ask that question. You know the weekend people get off?"

"Yeah."

"Well it wasn't always like that. Back in the day, you only got Sunday off, but then the Unions stepped in and you got the whole weekend off yeah? And the 40 hour week? Used to 60, sometimes more. And you could get hurt or killed at work, by accidents, but then the Unions enforced safety standards, so it was safer and if you did get hurt, you got compensation and if you were sick, you got paid. It was all Unions mate. I mean you don't expect the bosses to do it by themselves do you? That's how you end up with a burger and coke for a night's work."

"Oh right."

"Dirty zero hour bullshit. It's Fortunes Bar, isn't it?"

"Yeah, but I thought you knew the guy" said Jordan, following Terry back to the seat of his bike.

"No, I just knew they were hiring," said the Vampire, just as from across the street, a well-built black man suddenly came into view.

"Oi bruv, ring me, yeah?" now shouted the man, making the shape of a phone receiver with his hand.

"Err, yeah sure Blake" replied Jordan, raising his hand and then lowering his head again.

"Who's he?"

"Just a guy I know."

"He looks friendly," said Terry, sarcastically, as the man walked on.

"Nah, he's alright, you know," replied Jordan hesitantly, and was just about to turn away, when Terry managed to catch his eye. Now images of knives being thrust in hands, young bodies pushed up against walls, packages of drugs, County Lines, threats, promises, smiles, warmth, belonging, loud voices, more promises, money placed in hands, obligation, all poured into the Vampire's mind.

"So he paid for the video, did he?" said Terry, touching Jordan's arm to bring him out of the Vamp mind meld.

"How did you know that?!"

"Calm down, Jordan."

"You 5 O?"

"No, I deliver Pizza."

"Then how the fuck do you know that then?"

"It's not hard mate."

"Well, I'm gonna pay him back."

"Oh I know you will. How much do you owe him?"

"£600."

"When's it due?"

"A few days."

"Look at me," replied Terry, reaching into Jordan's mind once more as he watched Blake handing over the money in twenty pound notes with a cruel smile, and for a second, was reminded of Oscar, before he stared back at the frightened boy standing in front of him.

"Don't worry, I'll get it for you. But you gotta do something for me. Keep away from him in the future, yeah?"

"Nah Terry, he's alright, when you get to know him."

"They all are, that's their trick. Why do you think he gave you the money, mm...?"

"To help me."

"Yeah right. He doesn't want the money back Jordan. It's a bribe. He wants you to work for him. Next he'll get you to stab some guy in another gang, probably in the same position as you, and then you're stuck, until you get stabbed yourself or banged up for 15 years. You know the craic?"

"There's no crack bro, they just sell powder."

"Very funny. Just keep away from him, alright? Send me your bank account details now and I'll put £700 in your bank account tonight, and when you pay him tomorrow, tell him you got it off your Dad and give him an extra £50 for helping you out, that will keep him off your back for a while?"

"But..."

"You can pay me back later, when you get a job. Better you owe me."

"Okay," replied Jordan brightly, before a shower of rain started to fall, and Terry said he should probably be getting back. Now, as the Vampire watched the young man disappear through the door of the tower block, he pulled out a pouch of tobacco from his pocket, to make himself a roll up, while his Vamp senses suddenly picked up someone watching from across the street. Blake. Neighborhood Bullies never changed, thought Terry licking the edge of the rizla paper with his tongue before casually returning the stare. Always making a bad situation worse. He had seen the same in his own home town during the depression of the 1930's. Big men preying on the weak, lending money and breaking bones for the interest. Anyone who has spent time on the streets, knows it only takes a few sociopaths to destroy a local area or an estate. They might as well be working for the Elites, keeping the poor fragmented and full of fear the Vampire's thoughts now scowled and for a second, he considered going over and taking the smile off the big man's malevolent face, until deciding he had a more pressing matter to attend to, he started his bike and roared off in the direction of Wandsworth High Street. Thankfully, the lights were still on when he got there and so moving around the side of the premises, Terry quickly prized open the lock of the back door, before standing in the main area of the restaurant, to observe a slightly overweight man in his late 20's stocking up the bar.

"Harry isn't it?" declared the Vampire, looking at the lanyard hanging from his neck before walking further into the room.

"Err, yeah, right fella, look you really shouldn't be…"

"Here? No I shouldn't, should I? But then again, you

shouldn't be ripping off poor little Gen Z'ers who don't know their rights, either," scowled Terry, as he flew behind the bar and shoved the man up against the back wall.

"My God, how did you just do that? Err, who are you? Ouch, that hurts," cried Harry, now getting his cheek pinched and in total shock at the speed of the attack.

"I'm a shop steward from the Union."

"Err, Union?"

"The CPBPFBEWEYAD."

"The what?"

"The Confederation of Poor Bastards who have to Put up with Fucking Bullshit from Exploitative Wanky Employers like You All Day. Now listen you dick. I hear you've been taking on people for a night, making them work for 4 hours and then paying them with a crap burger and a little smile that says we'll get back to you later."

"Err, what?"

"Try outs."

"Well, err, yeah, that's standard practice isn't it? You want to see how they shape up."

"Do that for every fucking job do they? Go for an interview as an Accountant or a Project Manager and they get you to work for a few days for an out of date donut from Tescos and a cup of milky tea?"

"Well that's different."

"Is it? You know what they used to do in the old days Harry? Have a quick chat, make sure you could complete a sentence and didn't piss on the floor, and then tell you to start the following night and pay you the going rate."

"Well our burgers are expensive," re-assured Harry with a nervous smile.

"That include service charge, as well?" said Terry, getting more angry, as he effortlessly raised Harry's 17 stone frame off the ground and stared deep into bar owner's terrified eyes, before images of a procession of young workers doing evening shifts came into view, while Harry laughed with his friends in a Gastro-pub in Islington. "I just give them a shift, and then let the fuckers go. I mean there are so many out there, the Pandemic has been a God-send and all it costs me is a burger and a diet coke. And I don't even give them one of our proper ones; frozen Birdseye fella."

Now Terry wanted to bite him.

He could see the glorious blood flood through the veins in Harry's pale neck. It would taste so good. Bite him. Bite the exploitative scumbag now, his thoughts urged, while his fangs pushed out from his gums, and the neck of his prey drew closer to his mouth.

"Please, please. Look, I'm sorry, I'm really sorry, but everyone does it, everyone," pleaded Harry, as the thirst tore through Terry's body, and he felt nearly powerless to resist, until the face of his recently deceased Therapist came into his mind again, and brought some balance to his fury. He had been deeply ashamed of what he had done, and vowed, if it was possible, to try and not bite anyone else in the future. Plus old Harry was right. Everyone was doing it. Britain had turned into a zero hours, reality show, where everything was up for grabs, and if he bit this prick, he would have to bite them all, thought Terry, as he slowly lowered the young man to the floor of the bar and then stared deep into his eyes again.

"Be at peace Harry. I am a friend. Now you mustn't exploit your workers ever again. It's unfair, and you know it

is and so in the future, always pay your workers for a shift, and make sure it's a living wage. Good. Now, you started a kid called Jordan a few days ago and you used him. That was bad Harry, so you must ring him immediately and offer him the job. And pay him £20 per hour, no let's make that £25 as I am seeing his Mother. And don't ask for a deposit for a uniform or any of that crap, just give him what he's due, okay? Oh and while you're at it, start giving out a few more chips with your burgers, yeah? Charging £19.50 a pop is taking the piss Harry and your know it," whispered Terry, as a warm hand now gently caressed the owner's thoughts and he felt completely at peace for a few seconds, before the Vampire, touched his elbow and brought him out of his trance.

"Err, sorry, can I help?"

"Yeah, the back door was open, so I walked in. Hope you don't mind, but I'm looking for a job," replied the Vampire, now safely on the other side of the bar and returning a re-assuring smile.

"Oh sorry fella, I have just hired someone," replied Harry, reaching forward to pick up a cloth to clean the bar

"Oh crumbs. So what's the pay like?"

"We pay £25 an hour."

"That's great. Do you have to do a try out?"

"God no. I mean I know other places do, but we just think it's a bit wrong. If you work, you should get paid, end of."

"Wow that's refreshing. Seems like a cool place to work."

"Well it's just a job at the end of the day, isn't it? Maybe check back in a few weeks, we get busy over the summer, especially now after the end of the Lockdown. Anyway, don't want to be rude fella, but I've got to ring someone about a job. Could you let yourself out?"

"No problem, have a good night," replied Terry with a grin, and thrusting his hands into the pocket of his jeans, he walked towards the exit of the bar.

CHAPTER FOUR

Terry cursed, as he looked down at another text on his phone from HR before quickly bringing his bike into the side of the kerb. "The Vampire Council has noted, with some dismay, that you did not attend your last two 'check your privilege' meetings. Please remember, these sessions have been specifically designed by industry professionals, in the wake of the murder of George Floyd, to educate and improve Brothers and Sisters in Blood, and therefore further non attendance may result in disciplinary action and appropriate sanctions."

"Industry Professionals my Northern derriere," hissed Terry. Probably a few overpaid Race Grifters hired from Oscar and EVC, who he had heard were now cornering the market in DEI, Diversity Equity and Inclusion and making millions as a result. It was obvious bullshit. However, being locked in his cell for a week subsisting on horses blood, the Vampire version of a jar of roll mops, or a £10,000 fine, which was the usual punishment for noncompliance was no fun either, and so texting back, a terse "I'll be there," Terry started up his bike again and headed towards the river.

The traffic on the Fulham Road was surprisingly clear for a week night, and crossing over Albert Bridge, he made his way south, until he found himself staring up at well presented Edwardian house on a tree lined street in the middle of Battersea. *Jesus, I remember when this place had a funfair and everyone lived on lard and smoked 20 a day* mused the Vampire recalling what the area used to look like when he had first come to London in the early 1960's, as he reluctantly slid off his bike and presented his eye to the scanner on the side of the house, before following the sound of raised voices and polite laughter to a room at the end of a long corridor.

"I think all the statues should be pulled down, all of them" declared a young black Vampire, while Terry crept in and sat at the back of a rows of chairs, arranged in semi circles.

"Surely not all of them, Jamaal? I mean Nelson's column is alright isn't it?" replied an older Vampire from a seat in the middle row.

"Nelson?! Are you mad bruv? Nelson was a pro-slaver, wrote letters in favor of it and everything."

"Err well pardon me if I'm wrong, but I think they have subsequently found out that Nelson's signature was forged on that particular letter," replied the older Vampire, with a knowing smile to the rest of the group.

"Oh, did they? Well, that's convenient, innit? You see this is exactly the kind of white supremacist claptrap, black people have to put up with, all the time. You think

Nelson liked black people bro'? You think he cared about what happened to African slaves? Don't think so. I mean I haven't read about any Petitions that he organized or Marches he went on, have you?" said Jamaal, shaking his head.

"Well actually I served with him as a first mate, in Egypt and Denmark, and he always seemed very reasonable to me" chipped in another older Vampire.

"Makes no difference. Put him in a museum if you want, I don't care. If it was down to me, I would dump him in the Atlantic Ocean with the bodies of all the other black people who were thrown overboard for being too sick or just talking back," snapped Jamaal, sucking on his teeth for greater effect, as some of the older Vampires now looked a little put out, while the younger Vampires nodded back enthusiastically in agreement. Typical, Jamaal Hedley, thought Terry, as he leaned back on his chair and grinned. Activist, Documentary Maker, Second Tier Vampire and rumored to have been turned by none other than Oscar, in Jamaica during the Morant Bay Rebellion in 1865, he was only seventy years older than Terry, himself, but despite his relative youth, this ambitious Vampire was fast making a name for himself and rising up the greasy pole of Bloodsucker politics. He was no fool and certainly knew an opportunity when he saw one, mused Terry, folding his arms, as he tried to zero out from the general hubbub of everyone trying to justify themselves in front of the social revolutionary, until Oscar tapped his marker pen against a white board and brought all the chatter to a close.

"Okay, okay, I think Jamaal has, as usual, made some

excellent points, but lets… Oh Terry, you've made it, at last?" said Oscar, suddenly noticing his house-mate at the back of the room.

"A few days on horses blood proved a bit too much for you? Don't blame you, ghastly stuff. Okay, this is Terry Anderson everyone, he shares my abode and is our all-round Socialist and voice of the North at breakfast time. Tried to re-distribute the Eggs Benedict the other day, nearly caused a riot. Anyhoo, it's lovely to finally have your presence and although you've missed the first few sessions, I'd wager a Blood B negative Tory, you are well aware of all the issues that we have covered, so you've probably missed nothing old chum," continued Oscar with a smirk, as Terry nodded to all the heads craning back to get a better look at him, while desperately trying to restrain himself, from telling his housemate to go fuck himself.

"Lovely, glad that's all sorted. Right, so before we get going, can we first begin, by all declaring our pronouns."

"Our what?" said Oscar, looking out into the meeting.

"Our pronouns, Terry. We are in 2020 now, if you hadn't noticed and we want to be inclusive, unless, of course, you don't want people to feel welcome?" said Oscar, accusingly, while a few of the younger Vamps, now turned around to stare at the potential heretic.

"Err, well, no, cool" said Terry, recoiling slightly from all the attention.

"Just as I thought" replied Oscar breezily, before quickly turning towards a middle aged attendee at the front.

"Err, well, I'm Barry, he/him" declared the Vampire, turning sideways to give everyone, a needy smile, while

Terry sat back in his chair and squeezed his arms tighter across his chest. Surely the only ones who should declare their pronouns, were those who were actually Trans or Non Binary, whatever the hell that was but not everyone else, where it was completely obvious what sex they were, thought Terry, watching with increasing unease, as Vampire after Vampire declared their pronouns, until, finally, the obligation came to him, and he blurted out Terry, he/him and tried not to throw up. The Spiral of Silence was indeed a powerful thing. You only had to look at the Witch Trials in Salem in the 1690's or Mao's Cultural Revolution in the last century to realize how that worked, and therefore Terry would have bet the full 2,000 years of his bloodsucking existence, that most of those in the room right now, didn't agree with this polite version of compelled speech, but did it anyway for a quiet life or the maintenance of their careers. In fact some high profile Vampires had already found themselves in hot water regarding the issue, including, most notably, Brutus Linehan, legendary warrior and hero of the Second Lycan War, who after announcing his pronouns as Fuck/Fuck off on a popular Pod-cast, was subsequently thrown off the First Tier of the Vampire Council by Lady Carswell and sent into permanent exile. If they could do it to war hero like Linehan, they could do it to anyone, had been the new whisper around the perennially paranoid Vampire Universe, and, as a result, very few had been inclined to rock the boat, including now, it seemed, himself, thought Terry as he tried not to call himself a spineless prick for the hundredth time, before bringing all of his attention back to the front of the room again.

"Perfect. Good to see we're all on the same page now. So I hope everyone got a chance to read the papers by Kimberle Crenshaw and Derrick Bell that I suggested and also the chapters in Delgado and Stefancics's seminal work, Critical Race Theory. Any comments, then?"

"Yes it was very good. Definitely made me think" said one Vampire brightly from the middle row.

"Yes, I agree, very enlightening" chipped in another.

"Excellent, so based on that, now when we look at White Culture, what springs to mind?" asked Oscar, turning to write on the white board behind him.

"Oppression?"

"Control?"

"Aggression?"

"Toxic ambition?"

"Hegemonic?"

"What about homicidal?"

"Yes, they could all be considered components of whiteness. Anything else?" said Oscar feverishly writing the words being shouted out on the board before looking back towards the meeting again.

"The scientific method?"

"Definitely."

"Punctuality?"

"God yes."

"Getting the right answer?"

"Spot on."

"Stoicism?

"Yes, nasty stuff. Excellent, well done, you've certainly grasped the Literature I gave you. I would also venture to include the whole Enlightenment period, in general, in the way that it promoted Western values as being the best, but was probably intellectually and morally bankrupt from the start. From what I recall, although I was in India for most of that time, Hume was closet racist and Voltaire, never shut the fuck up, more's the pity" said Oscar to general laughter from his audience, before a middle aged Vampire near the back raised his hand.

"Forgive me, Oscar, but surely being on time and the scientific method is a rather good thing, isn't it?"

"Is it Roland? Are we always right?"

"Well, I think we've done rather a good job so far. I remember when we all dropped dead from infections and then we discovered antibiotics and saved millions and of course there's air travel, modern conveniences, greatly improved food production, all, it could be argued, impossible without the scientific method. In fact I was a Professor at Oxford when Faraday…"

"But there are other ways of knowing. Isn't that right Jamaal?" said Oscar turning to the young activist again.

"Absolutely. Anything else, is just white supremacy bro," snapped the Vampire, as he glared at the insolence of the questioner, until the errant Vampire quickly nodded his head in agreement, before proceeding to scribble something random on his notepad.

"Precisely. You see when we really think about it, when we drill down into exactly what whiteness is, we discover that it's a world problem. Everywhere we look, we see the fingerprints of crimes committed by white people. Inequality, ecological disasters, and don't get me started on the Patriarchy. In fact, as we speak, there are over five hundred bits of discarded satellites floating about 10 miles above our heads, sent there mainly by white people, so even Space isn't safe from our rapacious natures. Yes, there's really no doubt about it. White people are the problem, and as Beverley Di Franco says time and again, "It's not, is there racism, but rather where is the racism?" It's always there, somewhere, lurking under the surface, we just have to look, you see. Therefore, as a practical way of moving forward, I thought it might be a good idea if all the white attendees here, which except for Jamaal, Haroon, David, Mohamed and Kemi, includes most of us I think, should spend the next part of our session, writing a letter of apology not only to people of color, but to black people in particular, for the hugely negative impact that we, as white people, have had on their lives over the last 400 years or so," said Oscar now walking through the rows of chairs, handing out paper and pens to all the white Vampires present. Again, Terry returned a perfunctory smile, as his time came to take a page of foolscap from his house-mate, before placing it on his knee and staring blankly at the empty page. This was way worse than anything he could have ever imagined, and instead of talking about the real reason why society was heading towards Armageddon, i.e. Neo Liberal economic policies, huge wealth inequality and the steady rise of feudal elites, they were going to spend the next half an hour or so writing virtue signaling crap, that most black people, couldn't give a toss about, anyway. In fact, he had heard of this type of thing before. Privilege walks in classrooms, shaming white students, rich American white women paying $5000 a time for "women of colour" to insult them over dinner, even some white people publicly washing the feet of black people in the street. It was nothing short of insanity, and the Vampire was giving serious consideration to tearing up his piece of paper and marching out of the session, but in the end, he didn't. Yes, horses blood was nasty and defying the Vampire council was never a good idea, as they could quite easily kidnap you and place you in Covens in less appealing parts of the world, if you caused them too much trouble, as happened apparently to Lord Lucan and that guy from the Manic Street Preachers, but what really stopped Terry in his tracks, was the sight of Sophie, Gary and Spence, who were old friends and good Socialists already fixed on their task and writing furiously over their page. The truth was, as with the declaration of pronouns before, he didn't want to stand out, to be the uncool one, to be the Bane Vulpine of the group, and so, dutifully lowering his eyes to the empty lines of the page, Terry nibbled on his bottom lip and began to write.

Dear Black People,

Just a quick line to say, that I have been thinking a lot about things recently, you know, the usual stuff: Who thought it was good idea to have orange Daim bars, will United ever sign a decent striker, and also that maybe we, as white people, might have been a little unfair and possibly a tad harsh to you over the last 400 years. Obviously, the Atlantic Slave Trade wasn't a good start, or, indeed, carving up Africa at the Berlin Conference in 1885, and letting, a lunatic like King Leopold of Belgium loose on the continent. Then, of course, after all the crimes of Empire, we, the British, had the bloody cheek to persuade you to come across and rebuild Britain after the Second World War, before treating you all like shit for 70 years and then not giving some of you, your full citizenship during the Windrush Scandal, because we destroyed your boarding passes, which, by the way, should've been in a museum, to recognize your important contribution to the UK, rather than at the bottom of a shredding machine somewhere. Furthermore, it was probably not a good idea to nick all of your music either, from Blues, Jazz, Reggae to Afrobeats and then call it our own, in the process elevating Elvis, the Beatles and Nirvana to superstardom and unknown riches, whilst giving fuck all back to the people who actually invented it. Cultural appropriation doesn't even cover it, oh and sorry for Cultural appropriation too, by the way. Sorry for bankrupting African countries with insane debt, while killing any Politician who might have put things right, like Patrick Lumumba democratically elected in the Congo in the 1960's and knocked off by the CIA for being a Socialist. Sorry for massacring the Mau Mau's in Kenya and generally supporting the Apartheid regimes of South Africa and Rhodesia, while endorsing absolute nutters like Charles Taylor and Jean -Bedel Bokassa to further our own disgusting Geo Political aims. Sorry for Edward Coulson, Cecil Rhodes, King Leopold again and of course Michael Bolton, and did I mention the Tulsa massacres of 1921, the thousands of lynchings, the Tuskegee experiments, Red-lining, or indeed the killing off of all the Tasmanian Aboriginals? We were pricks and no mistake, but rest assured, that despite all the carnage, I, as a person of a vanilla persuasion, am now committed to doing much better. In fact, more than much better, which I hope this letter clearly demonstrates, and if it doesn't then we can always arrange another diversity/get to know your privilege/ struggle session with Beverley Di Franco to ensure that we are ticking all the right boxes, instead of getting to the root of the real problem as to why we are at each other's throats, ie Class and Crony Capitalism.

Then again, that might actually solve something, so we'll probably give that a miss.

Anyway hope that puts everything right,
All the best for the future,
Yours
Terence Anderson

Five minutes later the Vampire handed his completed work to one of Oscar's smiling acolytes, before sitting back in his chair to listen to even more reasons why western society was a general blight upon the planet, until feeling bored and a little mischievous, he raised his hand to ask "Other than the UK, which other white majority country was better at race relations", prompting an immediate shaking of heads and shoulders edging away from him, before he added with a warm smile, that this was not something that he, himself, believed, being completely on board with the whole anti-racist agenda, but simply a point that a fellow Vamp had raised in a bar recently and he just wondered what might be the right response to that kind of question.

"Yes that does come up quite a bit from those who haven't read around the subject. However, we counter such ignorance by clearly stating that this is not a race to the bottom, and just because black people don't have to sit on the floor to eat their food, it doesn't mean that the restaurant is giving good service, does it?" replied Oscar to knowing laughs from everyone, while the shoulders gradually leaned back in Terry's direction again and he was safely amongst the enlightened ones once more. Further pointless chat then followed for another fifteen minutes or so, after which Oscar made a few announcements about suggested reading for the next meeting and also a "Marvel Universe themed Orgy fundraiser for BLM," before the evening was brought to a close with a solemn taking of the knee. Maybe the horses blood wasn't such a bad idea thought Terry as he quickly exited the meeting and marched down the hallway to find himself a roof top across the road, to smoke a cigarette.

He had been to Communist meetings in the Thirties, Anarcho-Syndicalist happenings in the Seventies, Socialist Worker get togethers in the Eighties, and in all that time he had never, ever, EVER felt as indoctrinated as he did just now; and that's saying something, because it was the old Left who more or less invented the practice, thought the Vampire, sucking on his cigarette, and mumbling manically to himself for another few minutes until the sight of Oscar and Jamaal coming out of the house, made him duck down on the roof for a moment. From his position, his superior Vampire hearing could just about make out a joke regarding an older member of the Vampire

Council, plus a plan to meet up for a drink prior to the Marvel themed Orgy, before Jamaal walked away towards his car, while Oscar took a quick step left and suddenly disappeared down a side street.

He was very fast, so Terry found it incredibly difficult to keep up with him as they both tore off towards the darkest depths of South London, traveling over roofs and high buildings, in one or two bounds, as their enhanced physiology, rather like that of a giant spider, meant they could cover great distances with very little effort. In no time at all, Oscar had reached Catford, while still Terry kept a discreet distance and after running along some railway tracks, his house-mate finally came to a halt outside the locked gates of a small park somewhere near the borders of Surrey. *Where the hell was he going, he usually fed locally?* thought Terry as a dog barked in the distance, whilst he spotted Oscar vault some railings, to perch inside the foliage of the closest tree. This was a standard Vampire tactic, as most victims were taken near parks, and then bled in comparative peace, before the body was taken somewhere else to disguise the manner of death. So who was the unfortunate sod tonight?, mused Terry, crawling forward across some roof slates to get a better look, as a middle-aged white man walking his dog came into view. A warm breeze rustled the leaves of the over-hanging trees, as the man stopped to allow his pooch to relieve itself by the iron railings and looking up at the night sky, he was just about to start to whistle when a hand reached out from the darkness.

Now the little dog let out an anguished howl, and ran about on the pavement in confusion, while Terry bounded down from the roof of a near-by house and then over the iron spikes at the other end of the park to circle back and get a better look at Oscar and his latest victim. However, as he lay flat on his stomach and gazed along the damp earth of the park, for a moment he lost him, until, by some bushes, he finally located his house-mate sucking on the man's neck. Now, in glorious agony, he bit down on his bottom lip and drew in a deep breath from his diaphragm, as his Vamp Mindfulness App had taught him, to find some temporary release from the terrible blood urge. It was a poor substitute and Terry lowered his head to calm the yearning in his soul for a moment, until he looked up again, only to see Oscar taking selfies of himself and his victim. That was weird. Vampires rarely took pictures of "a feed" as it was kind of an unwritten law not to glorify a kill. In fact, even before camera phones, Vampire Art showing the bloody practice was severely frowned upon by the authorities and rarely shown in public, and so deciding to get a closer look, Terry snaked forward in the grass, only to find that when he glanced up again, Oscar had completely disappeared from view.

"Looking for me dear heart" declared Oscar, suddenly standing behind Terry.

"Oh, err, hi Oscar."

"Mother of God. Did you just jump? How very mortal of you. Been following me, have you?"

"Well, err…"

"Don't worry Terence, I saw your moped parked across from the house when I came out with Jamaal; assumed you'd be somewhere close."

"Well, yeah, well, err…"

"You wanted to see what I was getting up to."

"Well, you usually feed locally don't you? Just weird you coming out all this way," said Terry, following his intuition that his house-mate was up to no good again.

"Not a crime is it?" asked Oscar.

"Of course not. But why were you taking a picture? That's not allowed, you know?"

"Well that's more of a convention, I think you'll find. Was just doing a little thing for my Vampbook page. Actually, I was taking a leaf out of your book. Getting one in for my own side, so to speak. Poor old Danny over there was in the paper the other day, whining about Black Lives Matter. Says it was hateful and divisive. I love blood, infused with a strong opinion, don't you? Still a few pints in him, if you fancy it?"

"Err no, it's okay."

"Of course, Vegan Vampire. Very ethical. Good for you. Oh and next time you feel like joining me on a hunt, you only have to ask Terry. It's always good to have the company. Well, best get back to Danny, think he is going to have a little accident with a night train out of Paddington. Says on his Twitter-feed, he's been experiencing a bit of depression recently, especially during Lockdown. Poor man, his children will be distraught" continued Oscar, slapping his housemate hard on the back, before turning around and disappearing back into the darkness of the night.

*

Terry sat back on the park swing, and quickly tapped his fingers on the screen of the phone.

"White van man, tasted a bit gammon, but well worth the trip" was the predictable tagline on Oscar's Vampbook page, as bloody image after bloody image appeared on his screen, until the Vampire could take no more of the Gorefest, and angrily rammed the device into the side pocket of his black jean's.

Dick.

Then again, could he hardly complain.

He'd been played at his own game.

How many middle class white liberals had he taken out over the years.

Bourgeois Beaujolais.

Now he was getting a bit of his own medicine.

Poor Danny from Wallington.

Electrician, 48, 2 daughters, had a Spurs tattoo.

Wasn't one of life's winners, an ordinary bloke who happened to be white, and just wanted to have his say. A year previous, he would have been seen as harmless, funny, even, but now, in the noxious world of your tribe against mine, it was: words are violence, he's a bigot, he must be silenced. The battle lines in society were being re-drawn by a madman, thought Terry, anxiously looking at his phone again, as Oscar and his ilk, all predictably piled in with big smiley emojis and thumbs up, while even fabled Left-wing comedian Tudor Dee chipped in with a favorable comment. This was particularly sad for the Vampire, as he had always loved the comic for his edgy, anti-establishment take on modern life, previously tearing apart anything that took itself too seriously, but now he was ridiculing the death of a working man, because he didn't have the correct thoughts.

"Prick," spat out Terry, and for a second, he considered going around to his nice little house in Stroud Green and gorging himself on his treasonous blood, until he reminded himself that, not only, did he not do that kind of thing anymore, but also, as a First Order Familiar, Tudor was under the protection of Carswell herself, and so exempt from any Vampire attacks. "Now that's privilege," laughed Terry, swinging back and forth on the swing for a few minutes, until a quick glance at the night sky up told him it was probably getting late, and he should head for home. However, the trip back took longer than expected, as, not being very knowledgeable about South London, he lost his way and somehow ended up in Greenwich, and thought he might be in danger of a "singeing", as Vampires referred to the effects of exposure to sunlight, which although embarrassing, was quite a regular occurrence for Demons of the Night, especially the older ones who drank too much, but despite this, he managed to find his way back to the river, where after recovering his bike, was safely inside his house in Fulham before the sun rose.

"Oh you're still up?" said Terry, walking into the kitchen and slightly startled by the presence of Errol, sitting in the dark.

"Yeah, had a late one. BLM meeting uptown," replied his friend raising a glass of Wray and Nephew rum to his lips.

"Oh right. how did it go?" asked Terry, brightly.

"Yeah, it was great, where you been?"

"Just out" replied Terry, pulling a bottle of Stolichnaya Vodka from the freezer and pouring himself a drink.

"Yeah, the meeting talked about a lot of good things. I would have invited you, but you would have probably just laughed," scowled Errol, taking another sip from his glass

"What?" said Terry, turning around quickly.

"I saw the letter that you wrote, apologizing to black people."

"How the hell, did you see that?"

"Oscar left them lying on the side, when he got back."

"Oh, I bet he did. That's totally out of order! It's supposed to be private."

"Ashamed of it?" grinned Errol, at Terry's outraged reaction.

"Not at all, but its…"

"Thought it was a bit snidey myself."

"What?! Fucking hell, Errol, it was just taking the piss. Or aren't we allowed to do that anymore?"

"Not about this, you're too naive geezer."

"Oh for God's sake."

"Bit too much, bruv?"

"I'm not disagreeing with you, am I? I've always been on your side."

"Oh that's damned decent of you, old chap" replied Errol, affecting a posh accent.

"Oh, whatever" replied Terry wearily, as he quickly put the bottle of Vodka back into the freezer and prepared to leave the kitchen to avoid another argument.

"You know we chatted about geezers like you tonight" said Errol, sitting back in his chair, as he watched Terry move towards the kitchen door.

"Like me?" said Terry, quickly turning around again.

"Yeah, you know old school, Labour. Black and White,

Unite and Fight, and all that fucking foolishness, but deep down you like things just the way they've always been. Working class white wallahs still in love with Oasis and Ken Loach movies who think owning a few dub reggae albums and knowing who Angela Davis is, qualifies you as some kind of Saint. You make me laugh geezer."

"What you on about now? What's Oasis got to do with anything" said Terry, shaking his head and nudging back into the kitchen.

"Nothing, but didn't see too many black faces in Brit-Pop, know what I mean."

"And I didn't see too many white faces in Grime. What the fuck does it matter?"

"Nah, it's all good spar. Just saying, that's all" replied Errol with a sour grin before returning to sip his drink.

"Fuck's sake! You know I ain't like that" cried Terry, with his hands on his hips.

"Nah, it's all good" repeated Errol, running his tongue over his teeth.

"Jesus, I can't believe this. How many racist Vamps have I fought with you, hey? How many times have I stood up for you against the patronizing bullshit from those wankers on the Vampire Council?"

"Oh thank you, my White Savior" replied Errol, throwing his hands up to mock worship his house mate.

"Oh just, fuck off, Errol," snapped Terry, shaking his head and preparing to leave again.

"No I mean it. How will I ever be able to repay you, bruv? But just for the record, do you know how many times, in his life, my brother, David, got stopped by the old bill? Every fucking week for 30 years! I ain't joking geezer, and always for the same shit. "The back lights of your car aren't bright enough," "You look like someone we're interested in," "Your music's too loud." Every week without fail. In fact if they ever missed a week, he'd give 'em a bell, to see if anything was wrong, you know, was anyone sick or gone on holiday? Oh and then surprise, surprise, he ups and dies at 48. Forty fucking eight! From high blood pressure and a heart condition apparently. You kidding me?! The guy was a top athlete, represented South of England in 100m hurdles, had trials for QPR, but now he's dead before he's 50? It's called weathering Terry. The day in, day out abuse, of micro-aggression's, not getting a break, constantly feeling like you're being watched, where you know one false move and the system jumps down on your head and keeps jumping. No let off like with your white mates. Nah, none of that spar. No, "I was your age once laddy, now off you go and don't do it again." Nah, just the hard word every time. It's joke man and by the way, do you know how many black men have died in this pandemic? 5 times more than white men. Why? Because we are working in the shittiest jobs, that's why. Oh and don't give me, all that Vitamin D deficiency bollocks, you see online, now. Yeah, maybe it's because we don't swim as well, hey ?" declared Errol now rising to his feet with fury in his eyes.

"Yeah, okay, I get it" said Terry, becoming less agitated and nodding his head at the power of his old friend's words.

"You keep saying I get it, but I don't think you do?"

"Okay, so maybe I don't, Errol. Maybe I'll never know what it's like to be black, fair enough. But do you really think siding with Oscar and Carswell is going make it any better?" said Terry, moving slightly towards his housemate.

"At least they fucking understand what's going on."

"Now who's being naive? What, you think you're the first ones they've fucked with? Mate, the white working class have had bastards like Oscar and Carswell all over them like a rash for years. *Cathy Come Home, Kes, Scum*, they couldn't get enough of us. Oh, the deprivation! Oh, the working class mystique! Oh the noble Pleb!. You wanna talk about Brit-Pop? Half those jokers, were mockneys anyway or middle class tossers from Wilmslow getting a taste of the ghetto in their new Adidas Sambas and pretending they were the fucking Happy Mondays or something. Then, of course, when it all gets a bit too samey for their sophisticated palates, they do the usual middle class thing and stick their finger in the air again and wait for the next new trend to wander by and suddenly, low and behold, they all decide, they want a bit more color in their diet and anything white and skint is sooooo last year dahlink."

"Well good, fucking good is what I say. I'm sick to death of hearing about poor white people. Oh no, poor white boys aren't doing too good in school, oh no, poor white people are getting panic attacks, oh no, poor white people can't say what they want now. Don't make me fucking laugh, Terry."

"So that's it, is it? Fuck poor white people."

"Yeah, that's it Terry. Fuck poor white people."

"You total wanker. Oscar's really got his claws deep into you now hasn't he? Been up all night explaining his

Critical Race Theory to you has he? That must have been cosy. Let you in the big house and treated you like an equal did he?"

"So I'm an Uncle Tom now, cos I want to change the shit wankers like you have been shoveling us for years, yeah? Oh, read this Errol, it's E.P Thompson, it's about us poor people or watch this Errol, it's by Eisenstein, he really gets it. Just white people keeping the black man down, but, at least this time, I'm reading about my own reality for a change."

"What reality? You're getting used mate."

"Mate? We ain't mates Terry. Don't you fucking understand? You know the way you look at Oscar, yeah? You hate him for his privilege and all that. Well, guess what? That's the way we look at you. You don't live our lives, you don't walk in our shoes, you don't go into a bank and know you're not gonna get a loan. Fucking joke, man. Always stepping on egg shells, always agreeing with white people all the time, so they don't take offense. Oh yeah mate, I totally agree. Society isn't institutionally racist. Yeah, yeah probably some geezer playing the race card again, ain't it? You get me Terry? So how the fuck can we ever be friends, then?" said Errol, now finally losing his temper and punching his friend hard in the side of his mouth, sprawling him on the kitchen floor. However, almost immediately, Terry had sprung back to his feet and aiming two punishing blows to his abdomen, Errol was quickly forced back against the red Smeg Fridge Freezer, before tables and chairs flew in every direction and the two Vampires traded furious blows for a minute or more, neither gaining any real advantage, until from the doorway, Oscar made a sudden appearance.

"What the hell is going on here?!" demanded the older Vampire, stepping in between his two house-mates.

"Oh, err, it's nothing, we just had a disagreement, that's all" replied Errol, a little embarrassed, as the two combatants stopped brawling immediately and took a step back.

"About what?"

"Err nothing" mumbled Terry.

"Nothing? This is my kitchen you have just wrecked. I've a good mind to report the pair of you to Carswell. You know fighting between our kind is strictly forbidden, now what's going on?"

"Well, you should fucking know Oscar. You caused all this" said Terry, wiping some blood from his mouth.

"Excuse me?"

"You heard. The obsession with all this Woke bollocks, taking the knee every ten minutes, checking your privilege, it's driving normal black and white people apart."

"As usual Terry, I haven't the faintest idea, what you are going on about. No-one I know of, is talking about driving white and black people apart. In fact, last time I checked, I think we were trying to do the complete opposite."

"Oh, that's typical Woke bullshit."

"Woke? That's the second time you've mentioned that word. Woke what, exactly? If I'm not too much mistaken, the word "Woke" actually comes from the Black Community, itself, and was used to encourage people of color to wake up and change their reality. In fact, Jamaal was kind enough to explain it all to us at one of our diversity meetings; which, if you could ever be bothered to turn up, you would have heard as well. As far as I can see, "Woke" just means trying to build a kinder society."

"Does it fuck. It means agree with me or get canceled. It means do exactly what I say, when I say or I will call you a racist. The very last thing Woke is, is kind."

"You know that's exactly the sort of thing the Daily Mail or a Tory Back-bencher would say. I thought you were a Socialist, Terry?"

"I am, but I'm also on to bastards like you. Playing games with the poor, as usual."

"Playing games with the poor? Excuse me? Again! No idea what you are going on about. Seriously fella, think you should consider seeing a doctor or something. Actually, not surprised. All that badger blood can't be healthy."

"Jesus. Gas lighting me now, are you? Mad, am I? said Terry shaking his head and placing his hands on his hips.

"Well definitely, a tad confused. Following me around tonight, as well, very peculiar. Of course, you're entitled to your opinion, but quite frankly, Terry, if that's the way you feel, then maybe you should look for somewhere else to stay?"

"What? said Terry with a look of complete shock on his face.

"Yes, thinking about it now, maybe it's for the best."

"But I've been here from the start. I found this place remember?"

"Well things change, don't they and last time I looked, my name was on the mortgage. I won't charge you for the damage, which I think, in the circumstances, is more than fair, but make sure you have found an alternative place to stay by the end of the week."

"Hey Oscar, c'mon, there's no need for that. It was just an argument."

"I can see that Errol, but it's pretty obvious that Terry is on an entirely different path to us now, which will only make living here, virtually impossible. End of the week Terry, and please don't make me involve Carswell, you know how that will end" declared Oscar coldly, before quickly spinning around on his heel and disappearing back down the hallway again.

*

Terry untangled himself from the crowd, and quickly moved to the back of the Hammersmith Odeon, while still keeping his eyes fixed on the singer who was now standing motionless in the middle of the stage.

"Of all the shows on this tour, this particular show will remain with us the longest, because not only is it the last show of the tour, but it's the last show that we'll ever do."

There was now a slight pause, as the audience processed David Bowie's words before they looked around at each other in mild confusion at the unexpected announcement, wondering if he was joking or it was another stunt from the mind of the Genius of Glam. However, the Vampire allowed himself a little smile. He had known for the last hour, as after barging to the front and staring into one of the lead singer's different colored eyes, he had gleaned that the controversial rock star was just about to make another dramatic turn in his already remarkable career. He also knew what he was going to play for an encore, and so not really caring for the songs, Terry was just about to turn around and leave the gig, when "What a total bastard," suddenly stopped him in his tracks and a tall man emerged from the folds of the back curtain, smoking a cigarette.

"Didn't even tell the bassist or the drummer, he was going to do it. Fucking talented though. Of course I knew two weeks ago" continued the tall man, as he started to make his way towards Terry.

"Oh right. You his management or summit?" replied Terry, placing his hands in his pockets and staring dismissively at the over-confident mortal.

"No darling I was at a party at the Sombrero and I looked into his eyes, just as you did, I'd wager."

"Pardon?"

"Don't look so surprised, Terry."

"How the hell, do you know my name, Pal?" said the Vampire stepping forward with his fists clenched.

"Because I am the same as you, dear heart" came the reply, as Terry now stared back into the eyes of his new acquaintance, before a thousand images flooded into his mind.

"Oh right. Well, I've just arrived from New York, actually," said Terry, flicking back his long hair, and referencing his recent four year residence in the American city, in an attempt to counter the confidence and poise of his fellow bloodsucker.

"Sounds more like Near York," said Oscar, casually, and taking another pull from his cigarette.

"You what, Pal," snapped Terry, stepping forward again.

"Only joking Terence, fancy some Spag Bol?"

"Spag Bol?"

"Spaghetti Bolognese. Do catch up," said Oscar and quickly grabbing Terry's arm, as David Bowie sang the chorus of "Rock and Roll Suicide" hustled towards the exit, before the two vampires walked out into the bright lights of

Hammersmith Broadway and in the direction of the nearest tube. Soon, the District Line deposited them in Sloane Square, and after a decent march down the Kings Road, they arrived at a spacious house at the end of a narrow tree lined street.

"This yours?"

"Fraid so," replied Oscar.

"Very nice."

"It'll do, I suppose. So Spag Bol, I'm fucking starving," said Oscar, opening the front door and leading them both into the kitchen.

"So where's the tin?" said Terry opening up one of the cupboards and looking around the shelves.

"Tin?"

"Yeah, tin. You know Spaghetti Bolognese? Heinz?"

"God's teeth, Terry, it's 1973, in case you haven't noticed?" said Oscar, shaking his head, before reaching into the fridge to grab, some garlic, onion, and minced beef, while, at the same time, picking up a packet of spaghetti lying on the counter, to finally announce to his guest "Spaghetti Bolognese!"

"You'll never get all that on a slice of toast," said Terry with a grin.

"Peasant" said Oscar, howling with laughter, and then placing all of the items back on the kitchen counter, he rolled up the sleeves of his dress-shirt and started to cook.

"This is fucking lovely," said Terry, fifteen minutes later, whilst shoveling mouthfuls of pasta into his mouth.

"So you've only ever had Spag Bol from a tin?" said Oscar sitting back in his chair and folding his arms.

"Didn't even know it was called Spag Bol."

"Incredible."

"Well you know what you know don't ya? Ever had Dandelion and Burdock?"

"Not unless they were at that orgy I attended last week."

"It's pop, like a soft drink."

"Northern pop? Bet it tastes ghastly."

"It's lovely."

"I'll have to take your word for it."

"Ah but that's my point, you see. Didn't know it did ya? Anyways, what's with the fucking green beans?" said Terry, pointing at a bowl sitting by Oscar's plate.

"Oh, I always have vegetables with my pasta. Have some."

"Jesus, they're not even cooked" cried Terry, taking a bite out of a green bean, before spitting it back out onto his plate.

"Al dente."

"Al who?"

"Al dente."

"Well, I don't care about the name of the bastard who cooked 'em. They're fucking raw, pal!"

"Priceless" replied Oscar now laughing hysterically.

"What? Is this you taking the piss again? Serving me up raw vegetables," said Terry, sitting back in his chair and looking a little offended for the first time since they arrived in the house.

"Not at all. Mea Culpa. Look, Terry, they ARE cooked but just not the way we do them over here. Vegetables shouldn't be boiled to death, but brought to the boil, for maybe, five minutes, no more. Like the Italians do. Al dente, isn't a person, it's an expression, it means "to the tooth"."

"To the floor more like."

"They're very good. Taste them again, go on," urged

Oscar with a warm smile.

"Actually, that's not too bad," said Terry biting into another green bean again.

"You can taste the vegetable, yes?"

"Yeah, I can. Flipping hell, my mother used to have them in a pot for an hour."

"They must have tasted like mush".

"We quite liked mush."

"You've a lot to learn Terry."

"Don't worry, I know enough."

"Tut, tut, that Northern pride will get you nowhere, you know?"

"I do alright."

"Well you can better, trust me. Look you've just arrived back in town, let me be your guide."

"Guide to what?"

"To life and love. Vampires, of all creatures, should have a bit of class, don't you think. I mean look at your shoes."

"What's wrong with my shoes?"

"They're cheap."

"Oi. They cost me a fiver from Freeman Hardy Willis, I'll have you know."

"And in 6 months you'll need another pair. However go to Churches and buy a nice pair of Brogues for Fifty quid, last you a lifetime. Plus they look better. Female Vamps love a nice pair of shoes, Terry. First thing they look for," said Oscar raising a well polished brown brogue towards his guest.

"Dunno if I could pay Fifty quid for a pair of shoes though," said Terry dolefully, but visibly impressed by the sight of Oscar's footwear.

"You will in time. So shall we have some Tiramisu then?"

"What the hell is that?"

"Like trifle."

"Can't we just have trifle?"

"No we can't, now get the plates," said Oscar, with a big grin, before rising from his seat and walking back towards the fridge again.

CHAPTER FIVE

Terry didn't wait for the end of the week, and so by the following afternoon, he had risen early to pack what possessions he had into a holdall before slipping out a side door to a waiting Uber, just as the sun started to set. The cab, turned into Woodlawn Road and trying not to stare too closely, at the hair sprouting from the neck of his driver, the Vampire's thoughts dwelt on his present predicament, and how depressing it was that after nearly a hundred years on this toxic rock, all he had to show for his sorry existence, was 3 shirts, 4 pairs of black jeans, some underwear and a treasured copy of the Communist Manifesto given to him by Hector back in 1937. At least he had a decent pair of shoes, he thought admiring his hand made Chelsea boots for a moment, until the events of the previous night came back into his mind and his mood darkened again. Didn't count that he had fought on the right side in the Spanish Civil War, the Second World War, had marched for Disarmament, the Civil Right's

Movement, the Miners' Strike, Clause 28, the Iraq War, or gone door to door for Attlee, Wilson and Corbyn, because, now, in 2020, he was officially, a Nazi.

Of course, Errol had mumbled something about not having to go, and he would "definitely talk to Oscar later", but Terry knew, in his heart of hearts, that this was purely window dressing, and, in reality, his old friend was probably happy he was leaving too.

Maybe he was right?

Maybe black and white people could never be friends?

Maybe the Past posed too many obstacles?

In truth, over the years, he'd even asked himself the same shitty question.

Can the oppressed ever forgive the oppressor?

Can 400 years of brutal, unforgiving, relentless dehumanization, be forgotten in a few decades?

Terry shook his head and bit down on his bottom lip.

In truth, he doubted if he would have been able to forgive, so why the hell should he expect his friend to do the same, just because they both happened to grow up poor and shared the odd spliff now and again over the sounds of Burning Spear or Augustus Pablo.

In the end, everything had to be paid for, even if the currency in question, was friendship Terry's thoughts now lamented, and so dragging himself from the back of the cab, he walked through some automatic doors into the reception area of the Vamp Inn, the Bloodsucker version of a Travel-Lodge, with his heart feeling like a bag of cement. He couldn't even text Lauryn, as she was upset with him now as well, following, of all things, a pointless argument about "Statues" and whether the one of Gandhi in Manchester should be taken down , just because he had made some disparaging remarks about black people when he was a lawyer in South Africa. She'd said "Yes", he'd replied, "Are you mad, it's bloody Gandhi for God's sake," resulting in a huge bust up, this time with him, jumping out of the bed and running down the side of the tower block, not caring if he ended up on page 4 of the Evening Standard again or not. It was all a giant mess and therefore, feeling about as miserable as he had in a long time, he lay on his hotel pallet and sucked wearily on a sachet of Grey Squirrel blood and morphine, he had just purchased from a machine in the hotel lobby and tried not to weep. However, the opiated animal blood, brought little relief to his despair, and he was just about to trudge over and get himself another sachet from the bedroom table to double the dose, when the buzzing of his phone made him turn his head.

"Heard you've fallen out with Oscar? Whats going on? – Sophie."

Now, his dopamine quest was put on hold, and quickly clicking on a thread attached to the text, Terry rubbed his face with his hand, before reading an article from the Blood Post.

"Why I Asked My House Mate To Leave by Oscar Fitzgerald – It had been brewing for some time, but sadly, the relationship with our long time housemate Terry Anderson has finally broken down and regrettably, we, ie myself and Errol McKenzie, have been forced to ask him to leave the property. Ever since the murder of George Floyd, Terry, who had lived with us for over 30 years, had been in mixed spirits, displaying, on recent occasions, behavior

that was both concerning and problematic. Instead of showing solidarity for one of the most important issues of the 21st century, he continually mocked the taking of the knee, and even the idea of "Lived Experience", whilst, at the same time, creating a very unsettling atmosphere for everyone in the house, especially Errol who happens to be a Brother in Blood of Caribbean heritage, and needless to say, needed support and re-assurance after what had happened in America recently. However, this was not forthcoming from Terry, and finally, in an alt right rage, he launched an unprovoked attack on Errol, if that isn't white privilege, I don't know what is, before proceeding to cause thousands of pounds worth of damage to my kitchen. These actions are particularly puzzling, because, as a long time Socialist, Terry had previously espoused many good causes over the years, including fighting in the Spanish Civil War and joining the Civil Rights Movement, and therefore it is unclear to me, how he has now found himself in this reactionary place. I suppose a progressive future is not for everyone, but whatever the reasons, it is now very clear that his present views do not align with the values of the house and as a result, we have, somewhat reluctantly, been forced to move on. However, despite all the unpleasantness of the last few months and the damage to my kitchen, which although extensive, I have decided not to charge him for, I would like to confirm, that we feel no acrimony towards our old housemate, but rather a sense of lingering disappointment at how things have worked out. It is indeed a sad day for everyone"

"Problematic" Unsettling", "Do not align with the values of…" Of course, the buzz words of the new weasel faith, thought Terry, as he stared at the article again and tried not ram his fist through the flimsy walls of the hotel room. What values are those exactly then Oscar? Maybe the values of being one of the biggest Care Landlords in the country, exploiting the most vulnerable in society, whilst trousering the profits from over inflated rents, and services you never provide, or maybe it's siphoning off all your profits to the Cayman Islands and paying no tax, or perhaps it's making big deals with China, where the Uighur Muslims are getting brutalized every day in concentration camps or indeed it could be securing investment for EVC, from Saudi Arabia, where homosexuality is against the law, and if you try and live a normal gay lifestyle, some prick will try and throw you off the nearest ten storey building. "Complete bullshit didn't really cover it," scowled Terry, shaking his head, before reaching over for another sachet of Squirrel blood to sedate his increasing fury. Ironically, it wasn't even the crony capitalism, the double standards or the pointless decadence that really got to Terry. Oscar was a Vampire, after all, and programmed for self interest from the start, so what did he expect? But what really galled him, was how his former house-mate and people like him, continually got away with it. How could people not see through the charade? How could everyone be so shallow? Well, of course, there was a very easy answer to that one. Charm. It goes a very long way and like most of his class, Oscar was a master at it. It was their superpower, as even Sophie, who knew full well what a duplicitous dick Oscar was, now seemed completely seduced by his bullshit. "What's going on?" That was just a new Lefty speak for "Apologize quick, before it gets any worse," and reminded Terry of the recent rehabilitation of George W Bush and all the other architects of the Iraq War by the Mainstream Media during the presidency of Donald Trump. It was vile and hypocrisy of the highest order and even though, he had little in common with someone as divisive as Trump, he could also see it for what it was. The expediency of the Elites and the criminal indifference of everyone else, and so tossing his phone on his pallet in disgust, Terry lay down and turned his face to the wall of his hotel bedroom while he tried to shut out all of the farce, until another ping from his phone made him look around again.

"Haven't always agreed with you Terry, but that article was low. You were in the war, FFS, fighting real Fascists! Give me a text if you need anything. I know how it feels to be canceled by your own side. It's pretty awful – Bane Vulpine."

Jesus Christ! That's all he needed.

Support from Bane bloody Vulpine, supporter of Brexit and general loud mouth right wing pain in the arse, thought Terry, suddenly sitting up again and glaring at the offending message on the screen of his phone. "How the hell did he get my number?" was the Vampire's next thought, and he continued to look at the text, as if he had been accused of liking the music of some particularly naff pop group, until his eyes began to soften and a guilty smile, crept onto his face. In the whole of the Bloodsucking Universe, it turned out that Bane Vulpine was now his only friend! It was like getting succor from a Wolf or a Hyena. Or was it? Wasn't Bane just saying exactly the same thing as himself? That, in the end, the identity game, only turns into a circular firing squad? The same dance, the Left had been performing for years. In fact how many times, in the last century, had he stood and watched, while the eternal purity spiral wiped out many a good comrade from Trotsky onwards. They would never learn and maybe, when all was said and done, there was more freedom with his "so called" enemies" than with his "so called" friends, thought Terry, now hesitantly tapping his fingers on the screen of his phone.

"Don't worry Oscar's a joke, no-one listens to him, anyway."

"Sadly they do Terry. Wokeness is now a new Faith."

"Well I know it's been getting out of hand, but it's still pretty niche, don't you think?"

"Not sure about that. They have no platformed Germaine Greer, John Cleese and even Elaine Bounty."

"What?! Elaine Bounty of Elaine Bounty and the Lethal Injection?"

"The very one, for saying Tranny on Facebook" texted back Bane, while Terry now, placed the phone on his lap and shook his head in utter disbelief. He was okay about Germaine Greer and John Cleese, they were public figures who played the establishment game, so who cared about them anyway, but Elaine Bounty? That was a different matter entirely. How many times, in the late 1970's, had he seen the Transgender Punk Rocker perform her outrageous act, in glorious dives like the Nashville in West Kensington or the Windsor Castle in Maida Vale. Such courage, such verve, in a time when the average man in the street would, not only, have sympathized with her meeting a violent death, but greatly encouraged it, for dressing like a woman and flaunting it like she just didn't care. These cancelers and trolls had no bloody idea, what Gay and Trans people had to put up with back then, and in fact, he fondly remembered stepping in to save her one rainy November night on the Earls Court Road from some particularly vicious Gay Bashers, to be then duly rewarded for his timely intervention with a kiss on the cheek and two lines of biker speed. God he loved that woman and now bastards like Oscar had punished her for saying, the word Tranny. Fair enough, these days, the phrase might be a bit outdated, but surely an icon like Elaine Bounty, who had blazed a trail for years, owned the word, didn't she? It was ridiculous thought Terry and as a result bit hard on his back teeth in fury at the pointless outlawing of a cultural legend, before another ping brought his attention back to his phone again.

"Come to Manchester Terry. You can't stay in the Vamp hotel for the rest of your life, you'll get roped into a nasty 3some."

Terry smiled and then didn't.

What the hell should he do?

Bane could be just as bad as Oscar, if not worse, reasoned the Vampire, while his mind mulled over the numerous examples of old Lefties being jettisoned by their own side only to find less amenable surroundings on the right side of the argument. It was never a good look and so he chewed on his bottom lip again as he pondered what to do next until Errol's words suddenly elbowed their way back into his thoughts again.

"We ain't mates Terry."

"Yeah, well maybe we ain't," scowled Terry, quickly grabbing his phone and texting again.

"Good idea, I'll come up tomorrow, where shall we meet?"

"I'll have someone pick you up from the station."

"Fine" replied Terry, and after sliding off his pallet to pick up another sachet from the side table, the Vampire began to suck on the opiated blood, while outside his hotel window, the rain began to pour down from the night sky.

*

"So thank you so much for joining us tonight, and before I start, could I just say what an incredible privilege and honor it is to have you here and giving us some of your precious time."

"My pleasure" said the Guest.

"Oh excellent" said the female host, nearly blushing at the sight of the handsome young man sitting opposite her, before adding "And I must disclose, before we begin, that I'm a huge football fan, so please forgive me if I gush somewhat."

"Gush away," said the Guest with an easy smile.

"Thank you. I will try and control myself. So after your powerful speech at the Black Lives Matter protest in Hyde Park recently where you called for zero tolerance to race hate and that real opportunities must now be provided to black people in society, is it true, that you are now setting up a Charity to deliver food parcels to deprived families all over the country during the pandemic?"

"Yes, that's right."

"And furthermore, that you are actually using your own money to do this?"

"I am."

"Well, this is incredible. And forgive me, if I've got this wrong, but is it also true that you only pay yourself £23,000 a year?"

"£23,579.34 actually. That's the average wage for people in the area where I live."

"Oh I see."

"And actually, it's a lot better than what most have to put up with."

"How so?"

"Well my income is guaranteed isn't it? But someone from where I come from, is usually on a zero hours contract, so they can be thrown out of their job anytime, can't they?"

"Oh yes, of course, I didn't consider that. But, forgive me for asking again, but isn't the contract with your club for £250,000 per week," said the interviewer, narrowing her eyes.

"Actually, it's £300,000 per week now. I just negotiated a pay rise."

"Oh wow? Well, this is very different, if you don't mind me saying so. You've just been made England Captain, you've won three Premiership titles, two Champion's League, a Ballon d'Or, and you have the best goal to game ratio in Premiership history and you're still only 26. On top of that you're also a person of color from very humble beginnings, a one parent family I believe, and yet you don't feel, some would say, the very natural desire to acquire the trappings of a better life? Moving to a better area, a bigger house, etc."

"A gold plated Jet-ski or a guitar shaped Swimming Pool? Those things don't really interest me."

"That's amazing. So how do you spend the rest of your money, if you don't mind me asking?"

"I do a lot of drugs" replied the Guest with a deadpan look.

"Oh?" replied the Interviewer, raising an eyebrow, and now a little unsure, if he was joking or not.

"I wish, I get tested every week, don't I? No the rest goes into a Trust, where a board decides how to spend it. Our main mission is to establish a Construction Company to purchase land and then build new houses at cost. It'll be non profit, so any profits go back into the business."

"That's incredible. So when does it start?"

"Well, that's the problem. We have to secure the land first, and that's difficult, cos most of the big Building Companies obviously want to hoard it, to keep property values high, and increase their profits, like the model citizens they are. So, until we can get that going, we're just giving out food, and raising awareness about other important issues, we feel strongly about."

"Oh excellent. Like what for example?"

"Well, for instance, how someone like you, got their job."

"Err, pardon" said the host, narrowing her eyes again.

"You know the first question I usually ask, when I meet someone new that is?" said the footballer, sitting back in his chair.

"Erm…"

"What school they went to?"

"Oh, okay," said the Interviewer, now looking visibly confused, at where the conversation was going.

"You went to Benenden didn't you?"

"Well, err…"

"And that's a Private School, isn't it?"

"Well, yes but…"

"So this is one of the questions we look at. Why someone gets the jobs they do. I mean, I know some incredibly intelligent women from where I was brought up, who could easily do the job that you're doing right now."

"Well, with all due respect, Mr Noble."

"Call me Lucius."

"Err yes, well, as I say, Lucius, with total respect to your point of view, but I did work on the Financial Times for five years, then spent six years as a political correspondent for Sky and…"

"All supported by an unpaid internship when you started out, no doubt, which, of course, ordinary people have no chance of being able to afford. Working for nothing to develop your career, while staying in London to be close to where everything happens. You used to live in Chiswick, am I right?"

"Erm, well, yes, but…"

"Bet that wasn't cheap, even 15 years ago, and I'd imagine your parents helped you with your rent, you know, while you built your career?"

"Well, yes, at the start…"

"And the connections you made in public school and Oxford University. You went to Oxford?"

"Well Cambridge actually, but it's not always the case that…"

"And of course there's the little unwritten rules, aren't there? All about the way you dress, the accent, with that just about the right amount of emotional detachment?"

"Yes I accept that, but I think we are getting off the point here a little…"

"You think? But your researcher said you were keen to talk about White Privilege? Think her name was Verity? You know her?"

"Well, of course, she works here…"

"Very well spoken. Told me she went to a Russell University. All that education to hand me a cup of coffee and tell me when the Green Room was."

"Well that's her job, but if we can get back to…"

"So I take it, you believe in White Privilege, then?" persisted Lucius.

"Well, yes, of course."

"And Equity?"

"Err yes, well I think it's a very valid idea and…"

"Why, may I ask?"

"Well because it helps people who have been held back in the past."

"What like that poster with the small black child not being able to look over the fence, until you give her a box to stand on?"

"Yes, exactly."

"But surely isn't that just saying black people are small? That they can never grow, that they'll always need to be given a leg up? You know, not make them pass tests like everyone else, treat them like children until the end of time?"

"Well no, I think what it's saying is…"

"Actually I prefer Equality myself. Equity makes no sense at all, does it? I mean people have all sorts of privilege, don't they? Height, two parents staying together, how good looking they are? Did you know ugly prisoners get much longer sentences than more handsome ones? Pretty Privilege, I think they call it. Now, that's the biggest advantage. In fact, makes you wonder how half the Politicians these days, ever made it in the first place, doesn't it?"

"Err, yes" laughed the host, nervously.

"But okay, let's suppose you do believe in Equity. Why not make a start yourself now, then? Give up your job up to a working class woman of color?"

"Well, err, like I said, she may not have the necessary experience or…"

"So I couldn't take a black working class woman off the street and teach her how to do your job in 4 weeks then?"

"Well I'm sure she would be just as capable, but I would respectively say that it probably would take longer than 4 weeks."

"Really? why? I have watched your interviews before. Your questions are hardly career ending, are they? You never really get that much out of your guests, do you? I mean, look at what you did, with me just now. You were incredibly patronizing, maybe even a little sexist. Imagine if a male interviewer had talked about "gushing" to a female guest."

"Well I didn't mean…"

"And, of course, you got turned over a few years ago by that academic Niles Bateman didn't you? Spending the entire interview trying to ridicule him, rather than do what you should have been doing, ie find out the truth behind what he was trying to say. That would have been interesting, he's a really clever guy. No wonder he took you to the cleaners. No working-class woman of color would have ever fallen for that. She would have just done her job."

"Now look, I don't think…" said the interviewer now moving uncomfortably in her seat and desperately trying to get the conversation back on track.

"But this is the problem isn't it? 53% of the Media went to Private School, most of the Judges, CEOs, top positions in the Civil Service and don't get me started on the fucking Labour party."

"Look, please, can you…"

"Not say fuck?! Of course, keep it clean, before the watershed, might be kiddies watching. You know I didn't want to do this interview in the first place, because I knew how it would turn out. Same nonsense, same crap. I don't even know why I do them. In fact, you know what? Bollocks to it. This is going to be the very last time, I get interviewed by someone who went to a Private School or a Grammar school for that matter. Yes, that sound's good. Be my new rule. In future, anyone from the Press or the Media who wants a word with me, must have gone to a Comprehensive first, and not one of those nice ones over-run by Tiger Mums, but proper ones with too many Supply Teachers and Knife Detectors at the gates. Ha! that'll fucking narrow it down, won't it? Probably be about four journalists left in the country who I can talk to now. Brilliant! Anyway, glad that's sorted. This interview wasn't such a hideous waste of my time after all. Oh and by the way my sincerest apologies for shattering your illusion and the illusion of the thousands of your progressive viewers out there right now. I know, I should really be spouting all that truth to power malarkey that gets you people so turned on. You know, loud angry voice, shaking my fist, in righteous fury, being a good marginalized celebrity and all that. I get it, I really do and I know, I should be more fucking grateful, but then again what else do you expect from a black man with his own mind," replied Lucius, removing the microphone from his shirt before casually strolling off the T.V set, while the presenter's words of apology for "the offensive language" trailed in his wake.

CHAPTER SIX

"Alright Pal, names Kevin, Bane sent me to pick you up," said a stocky, red haired young Vampire, suddenly appearing from behind a metal pillar.

"Oh cheers" said Terry a little taken aback, before shaking his hand.

"No bother at all. Night-trains can a bit tricky, so best to show you where to go, and anyways, always a pleasure to welcome a Northern lad back home. Rochdale, isn't it?"

"Aye, originally."

"Can always tell. Still got some of your twang. Never lose that do you?, unless you want to, of course," said Kevin, as the Vampire smiled at the familiar bluntness of a fellow Northerner, before following his guide towards the exit of Manchester Piccadilly station.

"He's great isn't he?" said Terry, walking onto a main road and noticing a billboard opposite, with a huge poster of the footballer, Lucius Noble.

"The best," answered Kevin, opening the door of a

black Audi Quarto, while Terry allowed himself a little smile of relief.

Only a few weeks earlier someone had hired a light aircraft and flown an All Lives Matter banner over Turf Moor, the home of Burnley Football Club, which, although not in itself a controversial statement, was considered by many observers, as an insensitive response to the Black Lives Matter movement and the recent murder of George Floyd. In fact, it was the main reason, why he'd hesitated about coming back in the first place and had nearly canceled the trip at the last moment, fearing that he might be jumping from a Lefty frying pan into an Alt Right fire. However as they drove away from the station, and Terry looked out on a city he knew so well, he was satisfied that, for the moment at least, he wasn't joining Lancashire's version of the Proud Boys.

"There's the site of the Peterloo Massacre back in 1819. Bane was there, would you believe? Probably pissed up and trying to chat up the local birds, and over there, is the school the Bee Gees went to, before they emigrated to Australia. You gotta love, Gotta Get A Message To You, don't you? total classic, and of course, on your right, the old Hacienda. Fuck me, did some pills in there. Still mates with Shaun and Bez, you know," said Kevin, randomly pointing out local landmarks to Terry, who dutifully nodded his head at the impromptu tour until forty-five minutes later his driver pulled up outside a plush apartment block at the end of a side street. "Right Terry, lovely chatting to you. Probably see you later, you're dossing with me I think. Anyways, he knows you're coming, just take the lift to the top floor, can't miss it," said Kevin gesturing to the entrance, and so following his guide's instructions, the Vampire soon found himself in a sumptuous top storey apartment and shaking the hand of Bane Vulpine, scourge of all things woke and the most controversial Pod-caster in the Vampire world.

"Sorry I couldn't meet you straight away, had to grab a bite, so to speak, another bloody care home, I'm afraid. Unfortunately mortal blood is not like wine, and the older the vintage, the worst the heartburn, so I am on the water at the moment. Would you like a drink, by the way? I have a very good malt if you fancy a taste," said Bane walking towards a drinks trolley.

"That would be great."

"Splendid. Kevin look after you adequately?"

"Err yeah, had a good look around the city."

"Yes Kevin is very proud of Manchester, as he should be. I've been here over thirty years myself, and although lacking a good tailor and a decent Art Gallery, I find it doesn't have the awful conceit of London, if you don't mind me saying so. I know you have been down there for some time now."

"No, you're right, London can be full of shit," said Terry as he was handed a whiskey, and his host motioned for them to sit down on some leather sofas situated in the middle of the apartment.

"Couldn't have put it better myself. So Oscar kicked you out for daring to challenge his Wokeocracy did he?" said Bane resting his elbow on the arm of a Chesterfield and getting straight to the point.

"You could say that."

"Priceless. What a piece of work is a man! You know,

I've known him for years, ever since his Chartist days back in the 1840's."

"Chartist? Oscar?"

"Why, of course. He was a charlatan, even back then. Always playing the revolutionary card, reading out the Masque of Anarchy by Shelley in the very best drawing rooms, whilst, at the same time, pouring oodles of cash into the new Cotton Mills of the North, and breaking the backs of 9 year old girls and boys in the process. Always likes a nice profit, does Oscar. Very free market. Oh and did you know, he was in John Edward Taylor's "Little Circle", you know the founder of the Guardian newspaper? Yes, they used to meet up regularly in wood paneled dining rooms to make "wise decisions" for the masses. How dreary and they were dead against giving the common man, the vote, don't you know? Didn't think he had the intelligence. In fact, just like today, if you can be bothered to read anything that awful rag pushes out. They still hate the Oi Polloi with a passion, don't they? Especially after Brexit, and to make the irony even more delicious, Oscar and his Guardian owning chums were vehemently for the Confederacy in the American Civil War. Hated Lincoln and the North with a venom, and on more than one occasion, I witnessed Oscar in the Garrick, pounding the table with his fist, as he furiously declared that it was a scandal and "an attack on the very concept of Freedom itself" that the South couldn't decide it's own destiny, when in reality he was just hacked off about losing his investments in Slave Plantations in Tennessee. And these are the same frauds, who, today, demand any statues with the slightest whiff of slavery, be pulled down. Maybe they should pull themselves down instead?"

"Really, I didn't know that?" said Terry with genuine surprise.

"Of course, look it up. I think he was against Home Rule as well, the General Strike of 1926 even on Chamberlain's side in '39, but of course you'd never suspect it now, by the way he floats about as "The Champion of the Oppressed," but that's his genius, you see. Never dwells on the last mistake. Take a knee and move on, very clever."

"But they could say the same about you," said Terry, taking a sip of his whiskey.

"Oh and they do. Public school, successful acting family, lives in indefensible comfort, friend of Disraeli, dined with Lloyd George, threw fundraisers for Thatcher, never worked a day in his life, which is absolute tosh, of course. I work very hard, I just don't let you see the sweat. But, you see Terry, my greatest crime has always been, my refusal to prostate myself in front of the court of the Cognescenti, the intellectual Elites, and this is, naturally, why they come after me. That's the last refuge of a scoundrel, I'm afraid. I don't apologize for who I am. Anyway by today's puritanical standards every white person before 2015 is a racist, sexist, homophobic transhater and should be canceled on sight. But that's the problem isn't it? No context when looking at the past, and therefore no redemption unless you are willing to completely submit yourself to the prevailing religion and beg forgiveness for all your sins?"

"You think Woke is a religion?"

"Well don't you? It has original sin, racism. Holy Texts, lived experience. Irrational belief systems, a woman can have a penis. It's all there. The only surprise is that it has come from the United States of all places. I mean, I used to love all the American exports. Poe, Twain, T.S. Eliot, Maya Angelou, Buddy Holly, The Stooges, House Music, it was all so fabulous. They would give us the culture and then we would sell it back to them for twice the price. The Beatles, The Stones, Punk, Rave, it all originally came from them, but, as usual, they were too brainless to know what they had, in the first place. It was a beautiful symbiotic relationship, which enriched everyone, but now the most powerful cultural powerhouse, the world has ever known, has suddenly gone rogue. It's terrible. Fucking Hollywood preaching to us, instead of telling us a story, the Universities turning into woke Madrassas, big Corporations flying the rainbow flag. It's truly frightening, Terry. You see, the trick is to keeping pounding you until you completely crumble under their dictates and if you don't, they will spend every waking hour trying to destroy you. Actually, it's nothing new. They've been at it for years. Robber Barons at the end of the 19th century, our way or the highway, I mean look at what they did in Vietnam."

"Or Central America."

"Exactly. Or Chile, in fact. I mean, look at what the CIA did to poor old Allende? I'm no Socialist, as you well know Terry, but I really think, we are all Allende now. Forget climate change, Woke ideology is without doubt, the biggest challenge to humanity today. Mark my words, it will be the main source of the next global conflict, have no doubt about it. I used to think it would be over resources. Water, Oil, Micro-chips, but now I am utterly convinced, it will be over Pronouns."

"Are you sure? Surely it's not that bad?" said Terry, laughing and shaking his head.

"Remember, I am considerably older than you, I have seen the history repeat itself again and again and I think what we are experiencing today is exactly the same as I witnessed as a young man in the 14th Century. I was the second son of an innkeeper in Lincoln would you believe, and at the time, Feudalism was all the rage. Power brokers like John of Gaunt had all the land and the power, very much like Jeff Bezos and Bill Gates have today. Huge figures with enormous wealth, and while that religious lunatic, King Richard the Second was flapping about in the wind, men like Gaunt controlled everything and made very sure, they kept the common people down with their knights, like John Hawkwood, Henry Percy or Sir John Chandos. Exactly like the celebrities do today. Jay Z, Taylor Swift, Benedict Cumberbatch they're all just doing the same thing. All singing from the same hymn sheet and keeping their Feudal masters in power. Of course, back then, if you didn't play ball, they cut off your head, while today they cancel you. It's just the same. Hilarious."

"You could say that about any century, the poor have always been shafted."

"And so they have, but I think when you dig a little deeper, you'll find the circumstances of the 14th century are uncannily similar to today's. Elite over production, too many smart-arses going for too few jobs, and what happens when the smart arses don't get their dream job? They fuck with society, that's what, hence all the bloody rebellions they were at the time. Also back in the 1300's culture was on the wane. God, don't I remember, bleak doesn't even describe it. Awful Mystery Plays and except for Dante and Chaucer, everything else was simply a regurgitation of the 12th century Renaissance, just as artists today, struggle to compete with the glories of the 20th Century. I mean where are the artistic movements now? I don't see any Cubists or Pop Artists or even Abstract Expressionists running about, do you? Well you can keep the last lot, Pollock was such a bore, but you see what I mean. Philosophy the same. Back then everything was dictated to by the Church and Scholasticism ruled, so as a consequence, free thought was crushed, as everybody argued about how many angels you could fit on the end of a pin, as today we argue over the meaning of ideas and words that have been settled for generations. I mean what the hell is Non-binary, when it's at home? It's not even a medical term is it? They just made it up, didn't they? And to top it all, there was the daddy of all pandemics, the Black Death, just as we have COVID today. Thankfully I had been turned a few years earlier, so I survived, but I was old enough to witness half of Europe being wiped out. Perfect for Vampires of course, but what was left afterwards was anarchy. And then what came next? The Peasant's Revolt of course and we can see the seeds of that today can't we? Poor getting poorer, given less choices. It's definitely on the cards my dear boy."

"Yeah, but the Peasant's Revolt was no bad thing, was it?"

"God, you Lefties love a nice re-set don't you? Two hundred thousand unwashed oafs outside Smithfield's Market? And they would have succeeded, as well, if Carswell hadn't persuaded her husband at the time, William Walworth, the Lord Mayor to stick his sword in the neck of their leader, Wat Tyler. I was ten yards away when she hypnotized him. Incredible, took a millisecond."

"Carswell?"

"Of course. Our great leader is always on hand to give history a little nudge. Intervened in the Putney Debates by whispering in Cromwell's ear that the soldiers who had just won him the Civil War were traitors to God, and then managed to get poor Robert Lockyer executed and Honest John Lillburne imprisoned on the Isle of Wight, before wiping out all the Levellers and the Diggers. Hypnotized Melbourne to deport the Tolpuddle Martyrs, buggered up the Chartists, with the help of Oscar I might add, even got poor William Cuffay transported."

"William Cuffay?"

"Yes no-one knows about him, do they? Amazing man. Black guy, Tailor, Chartist, Trade Unionist…"

"What he was black? In the Nineteenth Century?" said Terry, sitting forward in his seat with amazement

"Oh yes. This is what people like Di Franco miss, you see. There have been black people, standing up for their rights here for centuries. He was only 4ft 11', would you believe. Incredible speaker. I heard him once at Aldgate, but he shot his mouth off one too many times for Carswell's liking, so she got him sent to Tasmania; and now she talks about BLM. The irony is quite exquisite, don't you think? What else has she been up to? Let me think. Oh, yes, infiltrated the General Strike of 1926, so it failed completely, even corrupted the Miners in the Eighties."

"No, that's bullshit Bane. I was there, there was no corruption."

"You sure, my dear boy? Call a strike in the Summer

when the coal stocks were high, not take a ballot, and somehow find a way to unite the country against it's membership? Carswell got to them alright, maybe not the top brass, like Scargill, much too principled of course, but definitely some of the ones below. In fact, one of her personal guard told me, a few years later, at a New Years Eve orgy when he was out of his mind on Chinese heroin. It never changes, Terry. Any time the lower orders try to organize, there she is, disrupting, corrupting. She is the master. Actually, I have it on good authority, she is at present advising Meghan and Harry. Personally I give that marriage 10 years at the most. Americans and English rarely make good couples do they? But you see, that's how she works? Use whatever weapon is popular at the time. Once it was a sword in the neck, now its victimhood. The ultimate Elite Couple, complaining they are put upon. It's genius really, and if I didn't find the whole thing so completely nauseating, I would be tempted to join forces with Carswell and her ilk, but sadly I can't bring myself. This Di Franco woman and her Critical Race detritus is forcing us to choose sides, so even an old Red like you, has been left without a home."

"Well, err..."

"Oscar kicked you out for being in "a reactionary place" didn't he? What does that even mean? Christ the fucking Wokies constantly accuse our side of dog whistle politics, when they virtually invented it. "A reactionary place?" Means you are a racist Terry."

"Yeah but we don't want to live in different camps, do we? I mean there's no future in that, is there?"

"Well the future is here already, I'm afraid," replied

Bane, as Terry took a sip of his whiskey and stared out of the huge windows of the apartment into the blackness of a Manchester night. This thought had been bothering him for some time. Was this the future? Separate camps? A new Segregation? My truth against your truth? Be an ally? He'd rather be a friend. Used to be a time when black kids and white kids crashed into each other for fun in clubs like Shroom, the Fridge, Cream and the Ministry of Sound whilst finding common ground in Pirate Radio stations like Solar or LWR, but not anymore.

"So what do we do?" said the Vampire, turning his head back towards his host.

"We stick together Terry," replied Bane with a warm smile, before rising from his sofa, to get his guest another drink.

CHAPTER SEVEN

It flopped like a greasy fried egg in the middle of the road, its sides pushing unevenly, onto the cars and buses, that sped past, desperately trying not to touch its verges for fear of sticky contamination. The Green or the Common, as it was officially called, was a municipal park, elliptical in shape, and measuring about 8 acres in area, and in a former time, the local alcoholics, would patrol its threadbare pastures like alcoholic Stalinists, taking a very dim view of anybody doing the slightest thing that could be considered as beneficial to their minds or their bodies. They ran a tight ship, and on more than one occasion, Errol had witnessed a hapless jogger innocently starting to do a few push-ups in a corner of their domain, only to be approached 30 seconds later, by a shuffling group of drunken bench dwellers, and told "to fuck off and do that kind of thing somewhere else", while in the same breath, being cordially invited to join them for an afternoon of drinking extra strong lager and shouting at passers by.

For a moment, the Vampire's face broke into a smile at the old memory, while he sat motionless on the roof of a tower block opposite staring down at the playground of his youth, until his eyes hardened again and he suddenly rose to his feet.

Gentrification.

Yesterday, Ireland, the Caribbean, and India, today, Hackney, Walthamstow and Bethnal Green. The destinations might be different, but the intention was still the same, as ambitious young men and women, rowed up to the shore with their false smiles and duplicitous hearts to stake out virgin territory. Of course, it was a reliable playbook, except this time, they didn't bring beads or Lee Enfield rifles, but rather a deposit from the bank of mum and dad and a recipe for really good hummus. Okay there had been a little resistance back in the 1980's from some of the natives, who instantly recognizing the ancient chicanery, refused to show the new settlers which plants to eat or not to eat, or provide food when the winter nights closed in, but in this new Jamestown, the odd mugging or dirty look in a newsagents, was nothing more than a minor inconvenience. In fact, it would only increase their resolve, and at some future date, be told as war stories by a blazing Chiminea, over a reasonably priced bottle of Montrachet in some leafy garden in Dalston. By the mid 1990's, the infection had firmly gripped it's host, while the former bastions of working-class culture, the Local Café, the Pub, and even the rubbish Second Division Football Club crumbled before their ever so helpful suggestions.

"Don't you think it might be healthier, if you cooked your "fry up" in olive oil?"

"Have you ever considered serving food in the bar?"

"Do you think, it's appropriate for football fans to swear when there are children about?"

It was relentless and very soon property prices soared, as the rapacious and the curious swarmed in, marveling at all the potential, before rolling up their sleeves to lick everything into shape. Inevitably the alcoholics from the Green would be respectfully gathered up and moved on to more "appropriate retreats", whilst his old manor would soon receive it's inevitable slave name from its new masters, alongside those of other conquered territories. Clarm (Clapham), Brighton (Brixton) and Chez Boo (Shepherds Bush). Probably wasn't Clarm or Chez Boo, when his mum and dad had rocked up from Grenada with a battered suitcase and a bag of chips back in 1950, Errol's thought's now scowled as he stared down again, and crinkled his nose. Now, kids didn't play out on the streets anymore, there was nowhere to play pool, and probably two pound on the pint. Shame progress, was so fucking boring, thought the Vampire, as a deep sigh from the pit of his soul, mixed with the chill of a winter's night, until a quick look at his watch, forced him to scuttle down the side of the tower block and walk off in the direction of the nearest tube.

The journey on the Central Line took no time at all, so by 7pm, he was safely inside the office and as usual was the first one in. In fact, strictly speaking, it was impossible be late anyway, as according to his contract, he could, in theory, stroll in at any time. However, after years of working as an electrician for London Underground, Errol had always preferred an early start. Not that it was any kind of sacrifice, as his new environment now more closely resembled a holiday camp than any work place he had experienced before. Free breakfast, insane coffee machines that made perfect cappuccinos, X-boxes, even a Pinball Machine in the corner. *How the hell did anyone get any work done*, thought the Vampire, taking a warm croissant from a plate on the kitchen counter, before ambling over to his lap-top to start his night's work. For most of his adult life, he had run cables through dark tunnels or fixed the points, so the 7.38 to Cockfosters didn't end up in a tunnel with everyone having a panic attack. It was hard graft, but he had never minded. He liked working with his hands, plus he enjoyed the company of the men on his shift.

Football, Women, a few drug stories, *and* a distinct lack of bullshit.

"Not much chance of that around here," mumbled Errol to himself, as he took a bite from his croissant and recalled the reaction of his new colleagues, since he had started working there, a few months earlier.

So white and so full of fright.

George Floyd had really done a number on them, and in the sum total of his 70 years, he had never received so many approving smiles from so many Caucasians. It had to be exhausting thought the Vampire and on a few occasions, he had been tempted to climb on a desk and tell everyone to "calm the fuck down, before they pulled something". Then again what did he expect from *"EVC, Ethical Vampire Capital, raising finance for a better world"*. Wind farms, Green Apps, even a scheme, using a children's roundabout to drill for water in Mali, which ultimately ended in failure when the kids eventually got bored of going round and round all day and only really used it if the, mainly, white investors ever turned up, to be shown "what a difference it all made". It all sounded too much like bullshit to Errol and one of the main reasons why he had turned the job down, when Oscar had initially offered it to him. However, after an invitation to one of Lady Carswell's "Shepherds Pie and Champagne Soirees", he'd had a re-think, and the very next day, found himself signing a six figure contract to be, of all things, personal assistant to Beverley Di Franco. He half suspected that the Vampire Leader had hypnotized him to change his mind, but what was he to do?

Then again, over-thinking things wasn't really his style, and so finishing the last of his breakfast, the Vampire opened up his lap-top, and set to work. For an hour or so he tapped away happily, until stopping to stretch his arms a familiar voice made him turn his head.

"Oh, could you be a dear and pass me that book, there's quote in there I need" asked Beverley Di Franco, with a big smile, while Errol reached over to a pile of books on his desk and handed over a copy of Gender Trouble by Judith Butler to his boss.

"I know I could get the information online, but I am terribly old school. I just love to get my hands on the pages, and as much, as I love Judith, her writing style is so appalling, one has to concentrate. She's not exactly Durkheim or Horkheimer, is she?"

"*Err, no, probably not,*" thought Errol burying his head in his lap-top again, as he wondered who the hell Durkheim or Horkheimer were, and did either of them play for Chelsea or Real Madrid? It was like another language to him, and although, he wasn't a complete philistine, and in common with most people from the British Caribbean diaspora, had heard of Marcus Garvey, and even rumors of the great Jamaican historian, C L R James, for Errol, his new work environment was still, way too wordy for him. He'd always preferred books like Trick Baby by Iceberg Slim or Dopefiend by Donald Goines, which spoke of people he could recognize, trying to fight an unfair system designed to batter down the brothers, instead of this new diet of Critical Theory, which just seemed to over-complicate everything. Of course he got it. Systematic racism had it's structure and you had to understand it, before you could dismantle it, but, that being said, the discussion felt a little false, especially as most of those making all the noise, seemed to be cut from a very different cloth altogether. In fact, his co-workers, Patrice, Shola, and Femi, were a case in point, who, although, black, like himself, because of their upbringing, education and general attitude, sounded as if they had arrived from a completely different universe. Their parents were doctors and engineers, who had come to the UK in the Eighties from places like Nigeria and Ghana, where no-one had been a slave, unlike those from his own background, who still had the fury of Sam Sharpe and Peter Tosh running through their veins. Back in the day, these differences had always been a bone of contention between these two distinct sides of Black Britain, where tensions between "Nerdy Africans" and "Street wise Caribbeans" were particularly marked; and although things had greatly improved since, there was always a nagging suspicion from his side of the argument, at least, that these relatively new arrivals, somehow looked down on their lower achieving cousins. Even their jokes, weren't the same, but were, rather, more forensic and controlled, as they smiled derisively at people who didn't quite get cultural appropriation, or the concept of privilege. It seemed a bit like snobbery to Errol and mildly irritated him, as even Jamaal, who came from a similar background to himself and had, in fact, turned him in the mid Seventies, was getting in on the act; and where, once, the two of them could sit down and just laugh freely at anyone in their neighborhood who thought a bit too much of themselves, now that kind of talk was suddenly considered out of bounds.

"It's self-hate bro."

You sure? Maybe it's just taking the piss, thought Errol with a sigh, as he continued to tap away on his lap-top until Beverley said it was time to go and he rose to follow her into their weekly "catch-up session" with Oscar and Jamaal.

"So we have been looking at your work for the last quarter" declared Oscar, brightly, before looking down the long mahogany table towards his housemate, as the meeting started to come to a close.

"Err, well, I've only really been here for the last quarter" replied Errol, with a laugh, as he was about to pick up his laptop to leave.

"Exactly, which only shows how well you've done. And let me just say, while I'm here, that it has been a pure joy to work with you, Errol. You bring a much needed humility to our collaboration" broke in Beverley now turning towards her assistant with another happy smile.

"Err okay" said Errol putting his laptop down again.

"No seriously fella, your effort and industry has been noted by everyone" chimed in Oscar again.

"Well you know I just arrange the meetings and keep the press off Beverley's back."

"Well if I am not mistaken, that's called PR, and normally we would pay thousands of pounds an hour for what you do by instinct," replied the best selling author.

"Well, I just answer the phone and tell the idiots to get lost" said Errol with a self effacing smile.

"Well you do "get lost" very well, if I may say so, and in the process, you have taught me such an incredible amount, not only about my own privilege, but also about the on-going whiteness of an organization, even as progressive as ours. I mean, it's one thing to write books or take seminars on the subject, but quite something else to see it in action, and I really have to say that the way you have conducted yourself, has really confirmed to me how people of color have been held back for so long," continued Beverley Di Franco.

"Stamped on more like," interrupted Jamaal.

"Quite and much worse, of course. Therefore, with this in mind, we thought we'd like to do something about that," said Oscar pouring himself a Mortal Mary from a large jug on the table, made from Vodka, Frozen human blood and Tabasco Sauce.

"So we have recommended you to the Second Tier of the Vampire Council," announced Beverley Di Franco, clapping her hands together with barely suppressed joy.

"Err, what? But, I'm not even on the Third Tier yet," said Errol now, with a very confused look on his face.

"Well, that's only tradition and as you've probably noticed, it's horribly white and so we need to change all that, pretty asap. What do you think?" said Oscar, with a warm smile before taking a sip of his drink.

"Err, well, I'd probably have to think about it."

"It's where we need to be bro'. It's a great opportunity," said Jamaal now staring directly at Errol, with almost a look of reprimand in his eyes.

"Err well, I suppose and I could work with you," said Errol, hopefully, looking back at his mentor.

"Err well, not exactly. Jamaal has now been promoted to the First Tier," interrupted Oscar.

"But that takes years doesn't it?" said Errol, without thinking.

"Precisely, and it still ends up looking the same," announced Beverley, clasping her fingers together in front of her.

"Oh right."

"So, bro?'" asked Jamaal.

"Well, erm..."

"Oh, for God's sake just say yes Errol, so we can avoid another Shepherds Pie and Champagne doo at Lady C's again. Being trapped by one of those old Czech aristocrats talking for hours about some fucking peace treaty or other in the 17th century will be the death of me," said Oscar rubbing the side of his nose, while everyone around the table started to laugh, before Errol nodded his head in agreement.

"Err, well if you're sure? I would be honored."

"Excellent, that's the ticket. I'll get the paperwork done today and arrange the ceremony with Carswell and the Council, whenever's convenient. Congratulations. You must be very proud Jamaal."

"Errol was never in doubt. Easiest decision I ever

made" said Jamaal nodding his head towards his younger charge.

"And of course two housemates on the Vampire Council, that hasn't been done since, well you and Bane," added Beverley mischievously.

"Well lets not talk of the dead, shall we? I think this time it will work out a little better than that last debacle," replied Oscar slightly grimacing at the memory of sharing a flat with Bane Vulpine and Aleister Crowley in Bloomsbury in the 1890's, which became somewhat of a scandal at the time, before quickly changing the subject again to discuss moving EVC into the lucrative world of Transgender Surgery. Meanwhile Errol sat motionless at the table as he tried to process what had just occurred. Second Tier of the Vampire Council and he was barely 70 years of age? There were only ever twelve Vampires elevated to the Second Tier of the Council at any one time, and qualification usually involved gaining some great victory over the Lycan hordes or bringing great wealth to the Brotherhood of Blood, and was never offered to one so young. It was like a 19-year-old being appointed Chancellor of Exchequer, or made the head of a large Corporation, and was completely unheard of, and therefore the more cautious voices inside Errol's mind wondered that if Derek Chauvin hadn't leant so hard on George Floyd's neck, a few months earlier, whether he would still be running lines of cable under Holborn Tube, whilst looking around for the odd homeless guy to feed on. In fact, after the meeting, he said as much to Jamaal privately, but received a typical admonishment from his "Spirit Father", which was the name Vampires gave to the ones who had turned them, who then quickly advised him in hushed tones to "Fake it, 'til you make it, cos that's what the white boys do" Easier said than done, thought Errol, who had always instinctively been against any form of affirmative action or positive discrimination, preferring to get by on merit rather than any favors. However, resolving not to over-think things again, the Vampire decided to take Jamaal's advice and after asking Beverley, if he could finish early for the night, he texted an old girlfriend if she fancied meeting for a drink, before taking the lift down to the underground car park. Soon, he was in his Range Rover Discovery with the sound of Jill Scott ringing in his ears, and as he took a left off the ramp onto the Grays Inn Road, he started to sing the chorus of "Getting In The Way" at the top of his voice, while tapping his fingers against the steering wheel. Now, he could barely contain his excitement, and felt the blood fizz around his body, while he thought of how proud his Father might have been, if he was still alive and understood anything about Vampire Politics, of course. Yeah, the old man would definitely have got a kick of this one, thought the Vampire with a grin, and he was just about to reach over and change the track on his car stereo, when out of nowhere, a police car suddenly appeared and flashed it's siren for him to stop.

"Hello Officer, yes Officer, any reason why you stopped me Officer."

"Err yes, sorry sir, but we've just had a spate of car robberies in the area and a man fitting your description, yadda yadda yadda."

Now all the hope and energy of the past few hours,

suddenly vanished into the cold night-air.

Despite all the promotions, all the slaps on the back, all the positive feedback, he was still a black man, thought the Vampire now looking deep into the eyes of the white Police Officer standing by the door of his car.

"How the fuck does someone like this, get this kind of motor? I could never afford it on my 30 grand a year. Probably drugs or a Pimp. It really pisses me off."

All his life, Errol had heard this kind of rubbish, so, in the end, what really was the point? It was a game, black people could never win and now getting out of the car, he was reminded of an interview with a famous black British actor, he'd recently watched on YouTube, where the film star described spending two months in the Dominican Republic and loving every minute of being surrounded solely by people of his own color until on the flight back to his home in London, he, inexplicably, burst into tears. Tears that told him he was coming back to a pantomime of harmony, where his heart-rate would increase and his body would be in a permanent state of tension waiting for the next assault on his self-respect, thought the Vampire, as the cold metal dug into his wrists, and he could feel the fangs, push through his gums, and for the briefest of moments, he considered snapping off the cuffs and feasting on their bigoted blood. However, he didn't. Even after George Floyd, biting a cop was still considered very off limits by the powers that be, and would definitely end his new career before it even got off the ground, and so deciding discretion was the better part of valour, the Vampire took a very deep breath, before looking deep into the policeman eyes again.

"Be at peace my friend. Yes, I was too quick to talk

back, you deserve respect. I am with you, I understand your pain. Of course, society is unfair today and why shouldn't ordinary white guys, make it too? You've been here longer, I get it. This was your country long before we all got here, wasn't it? However be careful Officer Lawrence. You don't want to be a racist, do you? Of course, I know, you're not like that. Good, now uncuff me and tell your colleague that you've made a mistake and I'm that celebrity, who does the DIY programme on BBC2. Yes the one, who laughs a lot and everyone loves. Your type of black guy. Hitch's up his pants, never plays the race card and keeps his hands off your daughter. Yes, I'm on your side, so you can let me go, just let me go."

"Err really sorry sir, I think we've made a bit of a mistake here. It was dark. Err not that being black in the dark should, err well you know. Err, if you'd like to make a complaint, I have a form in the car that you can complete. My colleague and I would be more than happy to…"

"Take a knee?"

"Err would you like us to? If that's what you'd prefer?"

"No, it won't be necessary."

"Err well, if you're sure and again I'm very sorry to have bothered you."

"Not a problem, Officer," replied Errol with a polite nod, and after turning around to get back into his car, he then placed both of his hands on the soft foam of the steering wheel, and slowly started to squeeze.

CHAPTER EIGHT

Terry opened his eyes and for a few seconds, stared out, in confusion, at the unfamiliar surroundings of his new cell, until his thoughts re-focused and he realized, he was back in the North again.

Home.

Or was it?

D. H Lawrence, Hockney, or Lennon had never made it back and for some reason, he'd thought, it would be the same for him. A romantic exile, fighting the good fight in warmer climes, but here he was, back, like an old library book that goes missing for years and is finally returned, so as a result, Terry could now feel the very air he breathed, passing judgment on his unexpected homecoming.

What's he like these days? Why did he stay away so long? Bet he thinks he's better than us?

Last time he had been in a bed in the North, he'd had cockroaches running all over his face, with his brother's knee stuck in his back. Hardly an incentive to stay was it?

thought Terry now mounting a stout defense against the denunciations going on in his head and for the next half an hour, he railed against his imagined accusers until a shout of "Breakfast" finally released him from the dusty web of toxic nostalgia.

"So what time is it?" asked Terry wandering into the kitchen with a yawn.

"4."

"Jesus, you get up early."

"Best time of the day Terry, me old son, anyway get that down ya."

"Oh right, err a fry up? Okay, err, what's that?"

"Black pudding."

"Human?"

"Is there any other kind?"

"Think I might give it a miss mate."

"Don't know what you're missing Tel. You've spent too much time "dan sarf", that's your problem. Oh and don't worry, I didn't put any sugar in your tea, I know you London boys, don't like it. I have two myself" added Kevin forking the two human black puddings off Terry's plate and placing them in his mouth with a grin. Two sugars in your tea. That's proper working class, mused Terry, bringing a mug to his lips, while he stared at the floppy fringe and Inspiral Carpet's T-Shirt sitting across the table from him. It was like being back in an episode of "The Word", from the early Nineties, but then again, he shouldn't have been that surprised. The previous evening, Bane had told him that he had turned Kevin at the famous Stones Roses gig in Spike Island in 1990, and as it usually takes about 30 or 40 years to shake off your former influences, he himself, had been wearing a trilby hat and whistling George Formby tunes well into the 1960's, Terry would probably have to put up with this form of extreme Laddism for the foreseeable future.

"You chat to Bane then?" said Kevin, wiping his mouth with his hand.

"Yeah."

"Mental in' he? Totally brilliant but fucking intense, know what I mean, I get lost most of the time, when he starts going on, but he's still amazing."

"Yeah, he's original, alright."

"And the rest, clever as fuck, and he likes his Charlie. Nutter. Talking of which, fancy a gig tonight? I know this Pulp tribute band playing later"

"Thought there was another lockdown?"

"There is, but we don't take any notice of Carswell up here do we? Up for it?" said Kevin with another grin, while Terry stared blankly at a poster of Shirley Manson from the band Garbage on the wall opposite and took another sip of his tea. He wasn't completely sure that he fancied a night out of getting hammered on "E's" and shouting "Mad for it" at pissed up Vamps in bucket hats. He had done enough of that, first time around, in clubs like Smashing and PopScene in London in the nineties, plus his mind was elsewhere now. He was still thinking about Lauryn. Thankfully, within days of their last falling out, they had patched up their "Gandhi argument", as she liked to call it, laughing that they'd probably both gone a little too far and what the hell, he was much better in the film anyway. The first argument between lovers was always the best, and so the sensual bond between them, was now stronger than ever, as they texted each other constantly, and retreated into that private world of complete intimacy, where only the two of them really existed. Of course, there was the little matter of his sudden absence from London, which the Vampire explained away as having to help his brother, who had a construction business in the North and recently had an accident. This was partly true, as Jimmy, his older sibling and a bricklayer, had indeed fallen off a ladder and broken his back, but that was over 60 years ago, and he'd long gone, but in the circumstances it was the best he could think of at the time.

"So you coming then? Forget the bird," said Kevin with a sneaky smile, after he glanced into Terry's eyes and momentarily read his thoughts.

"Oi, don't do that, you nob," snapped Terry, a little angry that he had forgotten to put up a mind shield, as Vamps, especially, the younger ones, were always trying to find out what you were thinking. Then again, maybe his new host was right. A night out could be better than staying in and mooning about Lauryn, especially after all the drama of the last few weeks, and so deciding to accept Kevin's offer, Terry quickly grabbed a shower, before Suede, The New Fast Automatic Daffodils, My Life Story and Rialto filled the air, and the two Vampires proceeded to knock back a bottle of Stolly Vodka and 3 grams of more than acceptable cocaine laced with fentanyl. Thankfully, due to their enhanced physiology, Demons of the Night could never over-dose, but nevertheless, the narcotic still had a similar effect, as it did with mortals, so by midnight, they were nicely out of it and after taking a short cut across the roofs of South Manchester, where somehow Kevin managed to fall off twice, they then made their way to "The Hole In The Floor", so named as the entrance was through a manhole cover in the middle of a back street.

"No cunt will ever find us in here," shouted Kevin over his shoulder as they quickly disappeared down a narrow ladder to then snake their way through a succession of corridors towards a bar area, where a passable version of "Do You Remember The First Time" was being blasted out from a tribute band playing at the end of a cavernous room. Soon drinks were bought and the evening settled into a routine of filthy jokes and football talk, before Kevin declared, that he wanted to do some MDMA with his mates and promptly disappeared to jump around a darkened dance floor. Terry decided to pass, and so ordering himself a Jack Daniels and Coke, he settled his back against the bar and for the next few minutes, watched as his new flat mate waved his hands around to a very ropey version of Disco 2000 until a voice from the side, made him turn his head.

"So you know Kevin, then?"

"Doesn't everyone," replied Terry, addressing a tall, auburn haired woman in a tight fitting black dress with the filthiest red lipstick that he had ever seen in his extended life.

"You're not wrong there. Lovely boy, shame he's still stuck in 1995."

"Thought it was 1991?"

"Probably. A floppy fringe is a floppy fringe, I suppose. I'm Maxwell by the way."

"Terry."

"I know. Saw your picture in the Blood Post."

"Err, okay."

"Oscar is such a fraud, don't you think?"

"He's a dick," scowled Terry, taking a sip of his drink.

"Precisely. You're best without. Actually, I used to have dealings with him myself."

"In finance?"

"Nothing so boring. Art."

"You're an artist?"

"Not exactly, I help artists. I have a company called Art Qaeda, which promotes the curious and the truly bizarre, and like most greedy boys with an eye for a bargain, Oscar wanted a piece of it. Fancied himself as the next Saatchi, but I told him I wasn't interested. Like most dealers today, he doesn't care about the Art, just loves the money. Personally I think it's disgusting, on a par with child trafficking, so I told him to piss off," said Maxwell, turning to glance around the bar.

"Bet he didn't like that" laughed Terry.

"No he did not. Tried to hypnotize me. The cheek! I'm nearly the same age. Anyway, I don't need his money, I do okay."

"Oh yeah, so what do you do, then?"

"Property, a bit of Tech, a few Clubs."

"Clubs?"

"Yes darling, you're in one. This is mine. "The Underground for the truly Underground", except these days the truly Underground is depressingly, very much above the ground. The internet has totally destroyed the mystery, don't you think? Years ago it took 18 months for a scene to truly evolve, you know under the radar of all the straights. I was there at the start for Mod, Disco, Punk, Rave, Grunge, and they were all made that way. No more than 60 people at the most involved at the start, but now, as soon as any green shoots start to appear some clown with a camera is revealing it all to the world and so the dream is gone. Like stealing off a Ganja plant before it has budded. Never a good smoke. Do you know we have an Aphex Twin tribute band coming in next week and people are actually looking forward to it? it's very sad really" replied Maxwell with a mischievous grin, as Terry laughed out loud, before bringing his drink to his lips again and gazing into the beautiful brown eyes of his host. Naturally, his thoughts were still very much occupied by Lauryn, but, as the conversation continued by the bar, he found himself drawn further into the orbit of this amazing creature of the night.

"Bringing up kids is easy darling. Don't have sex with them, teach them how to wire a plug and don't be around them all the time."

"All celebrities should be forced to die young, so normal people don't have to feel so bad about their own mediocrity."

"Having Luxury beliefs is like a Vegan with chicken eating tendencies."

She was like Oscar Wilde on Meth, and as the aphorisms continued to trip off her tongue, gradually his problems with Oscar, the new Progressive Left, and even Lauryn, started to drift away and for the first time in months, Terry started to have some real fun. Soon, more drinks were ordered and after an hour of chatting and laughing, they decamped to a back area to smoke a cigarette.

"That was nice," said Terry with a grin, as Maxwell leaned forward to kiss him on his lips.

"Yes it was, but shall we give it another try? and maybe this time, try not to give me an impersonation of your grandmother at Christmas."

"My granny was a wonderful kisser."

"Mine tasted of mead and stale bread" replied Maxwell, as she leaned forward and tasted his lips once more, before Terry suddenly pulled away and lowered his head.

"You have someone else?"

"Well you know I have."

"Sorry, force of habit."

"No problem. I tried to stop you, but you are stronger."

"A little older, perhaps."

"She's a mortal" said Terry, dolefully, shaking his head.

"I saw. They're the worst and a Pisces to boot."

"I know. High maintenance," said Terry with a grin.

"Not as bad as Geminis. Like being in a threesome all day with that lot, very exhausting. So is it love?"

"Could be."

"Lucky you. In fact I nearly envy you, all that conviction. You must have been a very chaste mortal is all I can say."

"Probably."

"I was a slut. Still am for the most part."

"Well, maybe it's the best way."

"Or maybe, it's not. Anyway who cares, leave psychology to the boring bastards is what I say, for would you believe, I have just come into possession of some amazing cocaine, just off the vine from Bogota," said Maxwell with a grin leading Terry out of the smoking area, before wandering off to find her handbag behind the bar.

"Alright Tel, having it are you?" said Kevin, suddenly appearing out of the darkness of the club.

"No-one says "having it" anymore Kevin."

" Ha! I fucking do. Maxwell is amazing isn't she?"

"Definitely."

"Saw you two having a little snog," said Kevin, giving Terry, a playful punch on his arm.

"Hardly a snog."

"Looked like it from where I was standing. You do know, she's a he don't you?"

"What?"

"You know Tranny."

"You mean Trans?"

"That's the one. Surprised she didn't tell you. Fucking hot though, I'd have her," replied Kevin, with a wink, and then just as the band started to play "Common People", the young Vampire raised his arms in the air and shouted "Yes my son", before tearing off direction of the dance floor again, while Terry placed his hands in his pockets and began to nibble on his bottom lip.

*

"So here I am. Tudor Dee in Hartlepool. Yes, the glorious North East. Fuck me it's gorgeous, isn't it? Oh to be Hartlepool when Spring has sprung. Van Gogh definitely missed a trick here, didn't he? I mean fuck Provence, the light here is soooooo amazing. In fact, one might say inspiring; he may even have kept his ear, who knows. Jesus what a dump! Can you believe people wanna live here? So yes, here I am, the day after the by-election result, where Boris buttock faced Johnson, persuaded the local constituency that a racist, sexist, homophobic future was just over the horizon and surprise, surprise the idiots went for it. No wonder they hung a monkey up here. I mean, seriously, what else do we need to know that the Apocalypse is already on it's way? Brexit, Trump, Johnson and now Hartlepool. There must be a quatrain in Nostradamus about this somewhere? Something like "when the fat yellow haired scum bucket lies down with the lamb" together with a prediction about premium bonds. Even Schopenhauer couldn't feel this gloomy. What a crap country we truly are? So called Culture Wars being waged left and right as the "proper working class" fool themselves that they are standing up for "What's right guvnor". Really? Of course anyone with half a brain knows that the Culture War is just a ruse designed by Nazis to keep our attentions away from systemic racism, outrageous sexism and general transphobia. My God! Don't you just want to leave now?! In fact can't we have our own Brexit, pleeeeease?! Don't we deserve that, at least, especially after the last four fucking years!? I mean I live in North London and we have loads of green space around me. We could grow our own vegetables, graze the odd chicken or free range goat in Clissold Park. Gotta be better than this. Yeah let's break away now. Join up with the rest of London, Brighton and Bristol maybe. Form an alliance of common fucking sense, for a change. What do you think?"

"Bit strong?" said Cressida leaning over Oscar's shoulder to pause the video, before looking sideways for her boss' reaction.

"Not at all, he's an edgy Comedian, it's what he does."

"But what about the backlash?"

"Cupcake, didn't you know? We own the backlash. No,

keep it, it's just right," replied Oscar, now moving his hand slowly up the inside of his assistant's leg, while she smiled and stroked the back of his neck.

"But won't the tabloids go mad darling?"

"With any luck," laughed Oscar, now turning around to attempt a kiss, before a sharp rap at the door, forced his assistant to step back and quickly fold her arms.

"Brett!" declared the Vampire standing up and walking around the desk to eagerly shake the hand of the man entering the room.

"Good to see you Oscar."

"No, the pleasure's all mine. Err that will be fine Cressida, and make sure it's uploaded onto all platforms for maximum effect, will you," said Oscar smiling at his assistant, before motioning his guest towards the two armchairs, that sat in the corner of the office.

"They been looking after you? Hotel okay?"

"Incredible, very luxurious," replied Brett, in his lazy West Coast tones.

"And the extras? The Orgy Rooms are powered by Green Energy, you'll be glad to hear."

"Err, well I am not as enthusiastic as you Brits for all that kind of thing, but, yes, it's been fabulous just as I would expect. So, as I said on the zoom call, we are looking to our expand operations into Northern California," said Brett, crossing his legs and getting straight to the point.

"Well that seems a good idea. World is going full veggie now and your brand of vegan sausages and hamburgers, seem to be hitting the right spot from what I hear."

"Have you tried them?"

"Not really my bag, still very much a carnivore, but my

assistant says they are exactly like the really thing and of course, from our point of view, it's ethical."

"Oh incredibly. Everything is sourced from Eco-friendly products."

"Good to hear?"

"Yes, we even bring in our ingredients from abroad by Sail Ship. Greta, was on the last one," said Brett, proudly.

"Greta?"

"Greta Thunberg."

"Oh, of course."

"Yes, we definitely pride ourselves on our ethical standards, it's not just about the money, is it?"

"Heaven forbid. Well we're all on board here. Top marks in ESG, you'll find."

"Oh Environmental Social Governance? Of course, that's de rigueur now, but it's all moved on again, Oscar. Effective Altruism is the newest thing."

"Yes I heard something about that on a TED talk recently."

"It's fantastic, really. Doing good, whatever the cost."

"How wonderfully extreme. California, never sleeps does it? Well, we're all for that here of course but to the matter in hand. I had a quick glance at your books, and everything seems tickety boo, however my contacts in San Diego tell me, that you've been having some staffing issues recently," said Oscar, breezily, not wanting to get sidelined by another insane idea from America, he couldn't really be bothered with.

"Err, well I wouldn't call them issues Oscar. Just a few employees who want to start a Union," said Brett, moving a little uncomfortably in his seat.

"I hear it's a bit more than that, old chap."

"Well, err, you know, ever since the whole Bernie Sanders thing blew up, everyone, on our side of the pond, is very keen to promote worker's rights, and…"

"But surely, our friends in the Democratic Party, managed to nip all that nonsense in the bud, didn't they?" interrupted Oscar.

"Not entirely. But we have spoken to our staff and totally assured them that we only have their very best interests at heart, because obviously with our values at Embrace Vegan, we would never do anything to exploit them."

"Of course; and did you tell them that joining a Union would take money away from their wages and be wasted by corrupt officials."

"Yes, we did that and even had a special showing of "The Irishman", you know the new Scorsese film about Jimmy Hoffa, the corrupt Union leader from the Seventies."

"Yes shame about Jimmy. I was good friends with the man that "clocked him", as they say. So did it work?" said Oscar, raising an eyebrow.

"Well, err, kind of. They could see what we were trying to say, but they were still very insistent that they wanted a Union. A man called Pagan Magner is agitating them."

"Does he work for you?"

"Well, not anymore. We fired him, for taking too many toilet breaks, but he has refused to go away and is still very popular with most of the work-force. In fact, he has started his own Union from the outside. Embrace Vegan Workers for Fairness and Justice. This is the last email he sent me," said Brett showing Oscar the screen of his phone.

"Mmm… no pronouns?" said Oscar with a frown.

"First thing I noticed too."

"Not one of us then. Okay, let's see what the little fascist has to say. Dum de dum, we need more guarantees and control over our working lives, better pay, improved safety, sick leave, usual nonsense. Yes, I think we'll have no problem extending you a loan here, Brett, but first, we must sort out this Union issue. They can be very messy things and in my experience, have a tendency to stand in the way of real progress."

"But, we still give them their rights, yes?" said Brett with a face of concern.

"Of course, but not too many rights, my dear boy. Ethical Capitalism, also has to make a buck, n'est-ce pas?"

"Err, well, of course."

"Lovely. So you'd better leave this one with me then. More our area of expertise. That's what EVC Management Consultancy is all about, isn't it? That's why you pay us the big bucks. So, why don't you go back to the hotel and freshen up and I'll meet up with you later and we can talk some more" said Oscar with a big smile, quickly rising from the armchair, to show his client out of the office, before taking a phone from his trouser pocket.

"Angelina. *Como estas?*"

"I'm from Boston, Oscar, you dick. My grandparents were from Puerto Rico. I don't know a word of Spanish."

"Sorry darling. Only teasing. Got a bit of problem in California."

"Doesn't surprise me. Place is a basket case."

"Democrats, don't you just love 'em."

"Not our fault, place was fucked up well before we got our hands on it."

"Of course, of course, and all that lovely Fentanyl, you must send me some by the way, ours tastes like half baked sludge. Anyway, remember those shares I advised you to buy in Embrace Vegan?"

"Oh yeah, I forgot to thank you for that Oscar, made me a fortune. They're the biggest vegan food producer in the US right now."

"Well they may not be for much longer, darling. Unions are turning up, to spoil the party, as usual. In fact, I thought, we'd shut most of them up with a few promises and a couple of sweeteners."

"We did and most of the main Unions are onside, but some of the workers have cottoned on to what we were doing and started their own ones now."

"Blast. That explains it. Well some idiot called Pagan Magner is making a nuisance of himself."

"Oh yeah, I've heard of him. Keeps sending me messages in my DM's asking for me to show my support. I usually fob him off with a few memes. So whats this to do with me?"

"Well, I thought, as you're the darling of the Left right now, might be a good idea, if you go and meet this Magner fella, you know, tell him he's fighting the most important battle of his life and how he's on the right side of history and all that tosh, and then drip feed to our friends at CNN and MSNBC, that the best thing to do all round, is deal with this at a Federal level and now's not best time to start anything in a Pandemic etc, etc. You know the drill darling. Kill them with kindness. Use the old "not this time but definitely next time" routine, never fucking fails."

"Oh really Oscar?! Christ, I'm going to Florida this weekend and I have the Met Ball in 2 weeks."

"Please, please, just for me buttercup. They have 10,000 workers. If they win this, who's next? Amazon? Starbucks? We'll all lose a fortune."

"Okay, but you owe me Oscar."

"Of course. You know you're my favorite Familiar."

"Yeah, yeah, not even sure if I want to be a fucking Vampire now, after all this hassle."

"Rest assured, it will be worth it. Thanks again. Ciao Bella " said Oscar, ending the call and placing the phone back inside his trouser pocket. If anyone could fuck up a strike it would be AFM. Angelina Felicia-Mendes. She'd even managed to derail Bernie Sander's little socialist moment in 2016, calling him "an old time racist", and handing the Democratic nomination to Hilary Clinton. Didn't matter that poor old Bernie had marched with Martin Luther King in the Sixties, and never uttered a prejudiced thing in his life, he wasn't "Our man". *That's why we always win,* grinned Oscar, and licking his lips at deliciousness of the irony, he walked towards the large windows of his office and stared out into the blackness of the night.

CHAPTER NINE

"You're beautiful," cooed Terry, resting his elbows on the kitchen table and staring deep into her soft brown eyes, before bending his head to do another line.

"So are you."

"I know."

"Why do guys always do that?"

"Do what?"

"Err I know," said Maxwell, affecting a deep male voice

"Because we're great, that's why. Anyway, why do girls always do that?"

"Do what, pray?"

"Try to knock down a man with a bit of swagger."

"It gives our life purpose. So I'm a girl then?"

"If that's what you want me to say," said Terry, wiping some powder from his nose.

"I do. But you won't fuck me."

"I have a girlfriend."

"Suppose you didn't?"

"Probably not."

"But I'm a girl, you said so."

"With a cock."

"It's only small."

"Still a cock."

"But I'm a woman."

"Well, strictly speaking Maxwell, you're a Trans woman."

"Cheek. But you thought I was a woman."

"I did."

"So I'm a woman then?"

"And you are Trans."

"Suppose I had surgery, and got a plastic pussy."

"I dunno."

"You want a real one?"

"Is that so wrong?"

"It's a tad transphobic."

"Is it fuck, Maxwell. I can't believe you're guilt-tripping me for not wanting to shag you?! Look, like most Vampires, I'm sex attracted."

"So Sex is biological then?"

"Of course. XX Chromosomes for women and XY for men."

"Not always."

"What? Intersex? That's less than one percent or something," said Terry with a grin, who after recently listening to a Pod-cast about Vampire De-Transitioners had subsequently done extensive research on the subject.

"It's more than that."

"No, it's not. It's a tiny, tiny percentage and anyway the exception doesn't make the rule, does it? Some people are born with six fingers, but we generally say humans have five, yeah? Same here. We are a Dimorphic Species, simple as."

"That's a little disputed, I think darling. The science is not settled."

"Yes, it is. If you're male you've got small Gametes, ie sperm, and if you're female, you've got larger Gametes, eggs. There's sooooo much evidence Maxwell. It's like in every cell of your body, for fuck's sake, even Vamps," said Terry, laughing and shaking his head.

"Yes, okay, smarty-pants but other cultures, like India and the Samoans had Trans for centuries, didn't they?"

"The Hijra and the Fa'afafine?" said Terry with a grin.

"That's them."

"But they were, never, ever considered to be actual women. Their cultures just recognized that they were men, who wanted to live as women. There's a big difference, Maxwell."

"Well, okay what about the Native Indians of America? They had a Two Spirit sex, which is the same as Trans."

"C'mon, everyone knows that was only invented in the Nineties in Canada, by some fucking idiot who'd done too many mushrooms."

"Okay maybe you're right about all that. But all I m saying is, I feel like a woman" said Maxwell, plainly.

"Good for you."

"So I'm a woman then?"

"I feel therefore I am?"

"Ooh little twist on Descartes? Very clever," said Maxwell, laughing and clapping her hands together.

"Not really, stole it off a Nathaniel Noyce Podcast.

Point is, just because you believe something, doesn't mean it's true."

"Yes it does."

"No it doesn't. That's such Post Modern bullshit. You can't turn Tuesday into Wednesday, just because you fancy it. There's such a thing as objective truth, you know," said Terry, lighting a cigarette.

"Well my truth is I am a woman."

"And my truth is, I think you're Trans."

"Trans rights are human rights."

"Of course."

"And Trans women are women."

"No. Trans women are Trans women."

"Can't I just be a woman?"

"You can be whatever the fuck you want, Maxwell, just as long as you don't force me to say what I don't want to say. You know, it's funny, but years ago, no-one gave a toss about all this, did they? I remember talking to loads of Trans people down at Madam JoJo's in the Eighties and Nineties."

"I loved Jo Jo's," said Maxwell, starting to chop out another line.

"Yeah it was a great club wasn't it?, and back then no-one gave a fuck, did they? Trans was just Trans, and no-one said a dicky bird about all this crap. They just got on with it. But now it's gone completely nuts. In fact, do you know, who I was talking to the other day? Sammy Stagg."

"Ooh I remember him, the old Indie guy."

"That's him. I used to be his roadie, nice bloke, still is, as far as I can see, but now he's gone completely mental. Not sure, if it's for his career or if he wants to keep in with the kids or something, but when I knew him in the late Eighties, he was all about Class and Unions yeah? The very last thing he was into, was anything to do with Identity. Even had a song on his first album called Identity Politics Is No Politics At All, it was great. But then I ran into him in a pub in Soho the other night, and all he kept banging on about was how Julie Moore and Hilary Bundle are…"

"TERFs."

"Yeah, Trans Exclusionary Radical Feminists. I had to look it up. And the way he was going on, it was like they were witches or something. I mean, I know those women, really well. Used to be around them all the time at gigs and marches and all that. They were proper Lefties, spent years in Greenham Common."

"Walking around all day in dungarees and yellow wellies from what I recall. Never a good look. But Terry, my sweet, you don't understand. It's all different now, believe me. It's just like Clause 28 back in the day," said Maxwell, leaning forward to touch his arm.

"That's what Sammy Stagg said! But it's not, I looked into it. In fact, it's nothing like Clause 28. I mean Gays weren't forcing people to use pronouns back then, were they? Or issuing death and rape threats if you disagreed with them or canceling people and getting them fired, if you had an opinion they disagreed with? All they wanted was to be accepted like everyone else, and from what I can see, these TERFs or whatever you call them, aren't saying Trans people can't lead normal lives. If anything they're pro Trans."

"But Trans people do live in fear, Terry."

"Where? Not in the UK, they're not. You know, I hear this all the time about a "Trans Genocide", but the figures just don't back it up. You know how many Trans people were killed here between 2008 and 2017? Nine. And most of them were domestic disputes and had nothing to do with, if they were Trans or not. Most of the figures they use for the "Genocide argument" are from Brazil, where there's a lot of Trans prostitutes, and that's a dangerous profession anyway. Look Maxwell, I just don't buy it, love. Course it's hard being Trans, everyone knows that, but, as far as I can see, no-one is targeting you, certainly nothing like what gay people got back in the Seventies, and if anything, right now, you're probably the most protected group on the planet, cos if anyone says anything about you, they get canceled, don't they? And you know what makes all this bullshit even funnier? Guess who started the campaign back in the late Eighties against the Tories and Clause 28, in the first place? Julie and Hilary that's who. Actually I mentioned this to Sammy and he just shook his head and still said they were Fascists. I couldn't stop laughing. I mean this is the bloke who had a top ten hit with "A Man Cries Out For His Mother."

"Oh, I remember that one."

"Yeah, the anti war song. What would it be titled now? "A Man Cries Out For His Birthing Person?" It's a joke."

"Actually, thinking about it now, you do have a point. All this anti-TERF behaviour is getting a bit too much, isn't it? I supose they're not really saying anything about hating anyone Trans are they? I mean, to be honest I don't feel that threatened," said Maxwell, taking a pull of her cigarette.

"Thank you! At last some bloody sense!"

"I like to please a man," said the Trans Vampire leaning forward with a cheeky grin.

"I'm not shagging you, Maxwell," said Terry, firmly.

"Don't be so hasty. So you fucked the one who turned you, yes?"

"Jesus this is harassment."

"Answer the question."

"No. Hector, only bit me; that was always friendship."

"All the boys say that. And what about Oscar, then?"

"Jesus, can you stop reading my mind!"

"Sorry cupcake. Force of habit."

"Unbelievable! No Maxwell, I didn't shag Oscar either. We were close, very close, but nothing physical."

"You sure? Oscar is notoriously bi-sexual."

"Well, not me. Not that I have any problem with gay sex, before you start all that crap, but like I said, I'm sex attracted."

"So the only cock you want to touch is your own."

"Precisely."

"Poor you."

"Anyway, if you really wanted me to fuck you, all you would have to do was make me."

"Yes I could. Second Tier Vamps like me, can hypnotize little boys like you in a heart-beat."

"Maybe you have, and I didn't know. Was I any good?" said Terry with a grin.

"Incredible. But it's not my thing, I'm afraid. I have a hard on for Free Will. So one more try, Lover. I look like a woman, I smell like a woman, I almost always act like a woman and you fancy me, yes?"

"Of course."

"So why don't you want to fuck me?"

"Because you've got a cock."

"Any circumstances where you might re-consider?"

"Maybe if I was in prison, doing a ten stretch."

"Okay, let's rob a bank then."

"No," replied Terry in mock defiance, and then turning away from Maxwell, he lowered his head to snort another huge line of cocaine mixed with fentanyl, before leaning back on his chair and falling into an opiated bliss.

*

It was just past 3 pm, when the Vampire came around again, to find Maxwell had gone, together with all the cigarettes. Typical, thought Terry, smiling to himself, and so after a general clear up of the debris from the previous evening, he made himself a cup of tea, before shuffling off to his cell to try and sleep off his hangover. However, the drugs in his system insisted that he stay awake, and so sitting up in his pallet with the heart-rate of a small hamster, he proceeded to watch various vacuous You Tube videos about "How Clever Crows Are" or "Why Tears for Fears Split Up" until completely bored, he finally decided to get up and seek out an early breakfast.

"Any chance of getting some brown bread now and again, Kev?" said Terry taking a reluctant bite out of his slice of white processed toast before looking across the table at his flat-mate.

"Don't like it."

"It's healthier."

"Precisely," said Kevin now opening his mouth, to show Terry, the coco pops inside, before returning to read a back issue of Loaded magazine from 1996.

"Classy."

"That's me," grinned the younger Vampire, and Terry continued to chew in outraged silence until a ping from his phone interrupted his fibre free breakfast.

"I haven't seen you in weeks, you're making me cry xxx."

Now his blackened heart skipped a beat.

It was Lauryn again.

Only a few days earlier, Sophie, who was the only Vamp from London, he still kept in touch with, had texted him to say that she'd heard through a friend, who was a Temple Guard, that Oscar knew he was with Bane now and that he was also monitoring his old girlfriend, "Just in case she proved a security risk". Of course, Terry knew what that meant. Oscar was keeping the pressure on. Join Vulpine and his gang and this is what you get. Maybe your girlfriend might fall off a tower block or be crushed under the wheels of a high-speed train, who knows, so easy to arrange, old chum? Vampire Politics was a very dirty business, especially with regards to mortals, who were seen as collateral damage at the best of times, and therefore, despite his feelings of almost constant and desperate longing, for the moment at least, Terry had decided to keep his distance. So, deciding not to answer her text again, he finished his breakfast, and dolefully plodded back to his cell to sleep some more, until the sound of Kevin and his mates playing the Verve's Urban Hymns at full volume in the front room, rudely brought him out of his slumber. He rubbed his eyes as Richard Ashcroft wailed The Drugs Don't Work through the walls, before instinctively reaching across to the table at the side of his pallet to check his phone.

A missed call from Lauryn.

Now his heart beat a little faster, as it always did at the sight of her name and quickly pressing 5 on the keypad, he placed a bud in his ear.

"Err hi Terry, it's only me. I suppose you're helping your brother again, so didn't want to disturb you, but thing is, I haven't seen Jordan for a few days and I'm getting really worried now. He hasn't been home for the last two nights or been at work. I rang Harry at Fortune's Bar and he's been really helpful actually, and says he's missed a shift and will ring me if he hears anything, but I just don't know what to do now? I know, he hasn't been himself recently, something's definitely on his mind, I can feel it. I think he might be in some kind of trouble. A few boys on the estate have been asking for him, and someone told me, he was with a guy called Blake, who's a bad lot, apparently. Look it's probably nothing, but is there any chance you could call me back? I am really worried and he seems to listen to you, err, sorry about this. I love you, please ring me back."

Now, the muscles in the Vampire's neck tightened, as he remembered the well built man staring at him from across the street with pure malice in his eyes, while he glanced over at the Vamp clock on the wall of his cell.

12.07, with a second clock showing that sunrise was at 7.06.

He could make it.

Vampire technology was almost in a golden age and so after quickly getting dressed, and grabbing some keys from a drunken Kevin, within minutes of hearing the phone message, he was astride an 8500 *cc Ducati Vamp* and heading for London. In fifty minutes, he had already reached Brent Cross, and after roaring down the North Circular, and successfully avoiding any speed cameras, with a specialized cloaking mechanism that made his bike virtually invisible, he soon found himself a few street's away from Lauryn's tower block on the Waverley Estate. No doubt, Oscar would have his spies out, thought the Vampire and so he made his way carefully along the side of the Estate, checking for any signs of his own kind. However his senses picked up nothing, and so taking a chance that, as it was the weekend, and therefore everyone was probably having a night off, Terry quickly sprang up the side of the block, before finding himself on the gangway outside his girlfriend's flat.

"Oh thank God you're here Terry, I've been out of my mind with worry. He's gone, he's gone, I've looked everywhere," cried Lauryn, opening the door and throwing herself against the Vampire's chest, before he quickly closed the door behind him and carried her through the darkness of the flat. Now, as they sat on the sofa and the Vampire gently stroked her hair, he listened intently, as she explained that she hadn't set eyes on Jordan in two days, how she had asked around the Estate and that the last time anyone had seen him was a few days ago by a newsagents on the main road, talking to a man called Blake. Instinctively, he leaned down to kiss her, while the pain of his unwilling absence from her soft lips, departed his mind for a few happy moments, until realizing that he had more pressing matters than his own desire to think about, he looked deep into his girlfriend's eyes, to quell the terror of her frantic thoughts. Now, in the silence of the flat, she slept, while the Vampire rubbed his face and decided what to do next. There was no doubt, Jordan was in real danger and he'd always known that paying off the debt to Blake, would be, at best, a temporary solution. Living in a place like the Waverley Estate, wasn't easy, especially for a young black man, and so, it was only a matter of time before the natural forces of the streets, would extend its gnarled fingers around his fragile shoulders and start to pull his head under the surface. It was an all too familiar tale, and one played out in every major town and city in the UK, however, for the moment, Terry couldn't concern himself with these abstractions His only mission now was to find Jordan; and so marching out of the door of the flat, he was down the walls of the tower block in no time and heading South on his bike. A few months earlier, he had made it his business to scope out "Blake's centre of operations", just in case anything silly happened, and so now perched in a tree on a quiet street in Kennington, he stared into a top floor window, and saw Blake and his Gang, together with Jordan, smoking a spliff, and looking completely unconcerned.

"Little prick", but at least he was safe, thought the Vampire, shuffling further along a branch, before giving his watch a quick glance. 1.45 am. Plenty of time, and eventually the boss man would need a piss he reasoned, and so springing from the tree to a better position, he sat crouched on a ledge by the bathroom window, while he

watched a succession of teenage boys spend a ridiculous amount of time checking themselves out in the mirror, until twenty minutes later, sure enough, his quarry entered the scene.

"Fuck, bro', what the…" gasped Blake, as Terry was now inside the toilet and an inch off the Gang Leader's nose.

"Hey Pal, remember me?" said Terry placing his hand over the man's mouth and staring into his terrified eyes.

"Yes you do, don't you? I was the guy who got Jordan the job, paid off your dirty debt, and generally fucked up your plans to destroy his life. I wonder why you wanted to do that? What was the motivation? Lets see, shall we?" continued the Vampire looking deep into Blake's mind and reading all his thoughts.

"Usual stuff. Jealously, bitterness, ego. Didn't want Jordan getting out of the swamp, sets a bad example to the other young 'uns, doesn't it? Plus it pisses you off, as well, yeah? Why should he be different? Why should he have talent as a Rapper, when all you can manage is slapping faces and selling drugs. It's not fair Blake or is it Andrew, Andrew Stone. Ooh your dad was a bastard wasn't he? Beat your mother terrible, left when you were young, must have been hard. The abused, abuse, I get it. My sympathies, but still, it's no excuse, is it? So what's your plan for Jordan, then? Get him to stab someone tonight. Someone at a party later. Someone you don't like. Someone who took your girl. Lame excuse Blake, my son. Not nearly good enough. Your soul is rotten, pal. Everywhere I look in this cesspit of a mind, all I see is rage, envy, violence, no coming back. Oh dear Blake, I thought I might be able to talk you out of this, but you will never change, will you? The system has destroyed your soul, and you'll keeping hurting until someone stops you. So it'll have to be me, then" whispered Terry, before he brought out a knife from inside his black leather jacket and plunged it 3 times into the gangster's chest, instantly stopping his heart. Slowly the big man's head fell back, and as the light disappeared from his eyes, a patch of red, began to appear on the white T-shirt, he was wearing. It looked glorious and turning his head for a second, the Vampire tried to resist, but the urge was now too great; and so placing his mouth over the puncture, he began to gorge on the fresh blood. It tasted like paradise. Like the best food he had ever tasted, the most exquisite drug, the sweetest sin and Terry was just about to lower his head again for another taste of the forbidden ambrosia, when the door swung open and, of all people, Jordan was standing in front of him.

"Shit, I thought, I locked it," cried Terry, immediately pulling the young man inside and slamming the door shut.

"Terry! what are you doing here…"

"Don't say a word. Don't even make a sound. You saw nothing here. Run out and tell everyone Blake has been stabbed and then call the ambulance. Don't think, just do it now, do it now" whispered Terry, as he quickly moved around the young man's mind, to erase the memory of his mother's boyfriend being a homicidal Bloodsucker, before quickly opening the bathroom door and pushing him back into the party again. For a few seconds, Terry remained perched on the window ledge to make sure his silhouette was seen by at least one other person, so Jordan wouldn't get the blame, and then quickly crawling down the side of the house, he disappeared into the night, as the screams and shouts of the party followed in his wake.

He had broken his own "No People of Colour and No Jews" rule, which had lasted for over eighty years now, but, surprisingly, he didn't feel guilt or shame, but rather satisfaction for a job well done; Of course, he knew, like every other Vamp, that there was no such thing as evil, that it had to be cultivated in the petri-dish of an unfair society, but he also knew that once it had been nurtured in an innocent host, it never lost it's grip. A virus like Blake could be particularly harsh, preying on it's immediate surroundings to ensure it's own survival. Only the poor can truly oppress the poor, as they don't have the confidence to punch up. That's why, when there's a riot, the downtrodden burn down their own areas, loot their own shops, kill their own people. The system programmes them for self harm, so instead of marching on Mayfair and Knightsbridge, where their real enemies lay, they prefer to watch as their own lives go up in smoke. Of course there would be another Blake to fill the vacuum, the ghetto had a production line of willing sociopaths waiting in the wings, but for the present, Jordan and boys like him would be safe, thought Terry, climbing to the top of a near-by Tower Block to get a better view of proceedings before reaching into his jacket pocket for a cigarette. For a few minutes, he stood and drew the nicotine into his lungs, as he watched people run out into the street and the flashing lights of the police cars arrive until satisfied that he had avoided any chance of being spotted or recognized, he was just about to make his exit down the wall of the block, when "You couldn't help yourself, could you?" suddenly made him turn his head.

"Err Errol, what you doing here?"

"Following you."

"How? I checked," said Terry, stepping towards his old house-mate.

"New Tech geezer. Blocks out our scent. Oscar reckoned you'd be back."

"Look, you don't understand, the kid was in trouble."

"So you thought you would do your White Savior thing," said Errol, putting his hands on his hips.

"What the fuck has color, got to do with it? He would have been forced to kill someone tonight. I read the guy's mind. It was lucky that I got there when I did," snapped Terry, shaking his head.

"Wasn't your call. We don't get involved with mortals."

"Oh really? Like you don't spend all day helping black kids from joining gangs?"

"I'm black" said Errol, firmly.

"So if I see a black kid drowning, I should wait around for the next black life guard to turn up, should I?"

"Bullshit response."

"Bloody hell Errol! Your mind's been infected mate. You were never like this."

"Wasn't I?"

"No, you weren't!"

"Maybe I've woken up, then."

"So not friends, just allies then, huh?"

"That's right."

"Really? You fucking twat," replied Terry, now finally losing his temper, before delivering a punch to the side of

Errol's head. However his old house-mate managed to duck the jab and driving his shoulder into Terry's chest he drove him back across the roof top, where for the next thirty seconds or so, the two Vampires fought bitterly, giving no quarter, as they landed blow after blow on each other's bodies until Oscar suddenly appeared out of the darkness to stop the fight.

"Okay, step away Errol. Terry, this is the second occasion you have struck a fellow Brother in Blood, and this time, it cannot be ignored. Bind him and take him into custody, we will convene a meeting of the Disciplinary Council immediately, and they can decide what to do with him then" instructed Oscar, waving his hand towards the three Vampire Guards, who now appeared out from the shadows to grab Terry by the arms.

"Oh cheers mate, you fucking traitor," barked Terry, spitting some of his own blood in the direction of Errol, before he was swiftly dragged from the roof, to a van waiting in the street below.

"What the hell you doing here?!" snapped Errol, storming up to Oscar with his fists clenched.

"Now don't be silly old chum," replied Oscar, folding his arms.

"You said just follow him, that's all," cried Errol, taking a step back, as he realized, the older Vampire could snap him in two, if he fancied.

"He broke a rule."

"We break rules all the time."

"He assaulted you and he killed a black mortal, which is against the new directive."

"What? How did you know that?"

"We had back up. We've videoed everything. Standard procedure," said Oscar, looking up towards the night sky.

"Standard what? Look I don't get it Oscar. We're interfering with mortals all the time. I mean I hypnotize kids on a regular basis to try and stop them stabbing each other, you know use their fists instead, have a bit of honor, for a change. It's what we do, isn't it?"

"But you never killed one."

"Haven't I? How do you know? Sometimes they have to die. Like the one Terry done tonight. I've heard of Blake. He's all bad and I might be black but I ain't gonna be crying any tears, when a scumbag like that gets what he deserves."

"Terry's methods are wrong and his thinking is wrong, you know that. He's out of control Errol and for security reasons we can't have him running all over town, killing who he wants, just because he's got the hots for some mortal. We need to be progressive fella. That's the most important thing right now. Remember, the future is ours. We will thrive," said the older Vampire with a knowing wink, before walking away across the roof.

Fucking white people. They hated each other, way more than anyone who was black or brown, thought Errol, now watching Oscar, saunter cockily towards the edge of the building. It was like, he enjoyed it. Got a big kick out of sticking it to his poorer white relation. No-where was the class system as toxic as it was in the UK, as even his old man used to say immigrants like him, had stepped into a war that had been going on for a thousand years.

"Yeah, well, it ain't my fucking war," muttered the Vampire to himself and then marching purposely across the roof, he quickly raced off into the darkness of the night.

*

"Come on, there's this place I know," said Errol as they staggered out of the Churchill Arms and Terry felt his eyes water from the chill of the night air.

"Ahh, mate! It's not another Jazz Funk night, down that karzhi in Ken High Street, is it? You know I hate all that shit" replied Terry, now taking a petulant step back from his friend, while Errol started to laugh and shake his head. Ever since they had known each other, music and their differing tastes had always been a bone of contention, between the two Vampires. Terry, since he'd shaken off the ghosts of his youth, now generally favored songs with loud guitars and angry lyrics, as in the sound of the new British Punk bands like the Ruts and the Clash, while his fellow Vampire favored something more mellow, preferring soul bands like Frankie Beverley and Maze and Shalamar. It was a classic impasse of young working class black and white men at the time, and other than One Nation Under a Groove by Funkadelic and 20th Century Boy by T Rex, which they could both agree were classics, everything else was a bit of an issue. Well, everything that is, except for Reggae, of course, and in particular, Dub Reggae. Here the two young Vampires found complete synergy, and as a consequence nodded their heads in blissful harmony for hours on end to the heavy bass-lines of King Tubby and Scientist, whilst usually under the influence of some very good weed.

Therefore when Errol suddenly declared "Nah, it's down the Grove, innit?" and started to walk away from the pub, towards Notting Hill Gate, Terry had a sudden change of heart. He loved the Grove, or Ladbroke Grove, as it was *officially called, not only, because it was the home of the Portobello Road, his favorite street in the whole wide world, where even now, in the mid 1980's, this cultural artery still maintained that beautiful collision between the possessed and the dispossessed, but also, as it was the spiritual home of Dub Reggae in London. "Perfect" slurred Terry, as the two friends soon got into a good stride, and in no time at all passed the Lonsdale Arms and Finches, until a sharp right, brought them onto Lancaster Road.*

"Where the fook, we going?" said Terry, now sounding much more Northern, after 10 pints and 4 double whiskeys.

"You'll see lad" replied Errol, with a wink and then walking to the end of the street, they took another sharp left, before they finally found themselves in front of a large Victorian house. Drunken knocks were then visited on the paint splattered door, until about five minutes later, a thin black man with a sour look on his face, came into view, who after reading their minds to ensure they were not mortals, and then enquiring, "Why the fuck hadn't they used the bell?" gave them a dirty look before letting them in.

"Is this a party?" said Terry, enthusiastically as he walked behind his friend down a narrow corridor, to enter a large room with a short bar at the end and packed with people either seated at tables or dancing.

"It's a Shebeen" declared Errol over his shoulder, while Terry's initial eagerness now gradually started to evaporate as he started to take in his new surroundings.

Everyone was black.

Everyone.

In fact he had never felt so white in his extended life and as he exchanged glances with some of the patrons and produced the first of one of many needy smiles, he was instantly reminded of scenes in films like Animal House *and* Live and Let Die, *where the white boy wanders into an openly hostile black bar and gets a good hiding.*

"So what do you want?" asked Errol, interrupting his anxious thoughts.

"Err, what?" said Terry, still distracted by his mild panic.

"Drink? What drink, do you want?"

"Err, just beer, thanks" replied Terry nervously.

"What beer?"

"I dunno, err, whatever you're having."

"Two Red Stripes" Errol said to the barman, before looking sideways at his friend again.

"You okay?"

"Yeah, course. Erm, are all the Vamps in here, older than us?" asked Terry looking furtively around the bar once more.

"Yeah, ancient. Some of them been here since Norman times."

"Wow, that's old? They must be really strong?"

"Very... and they're black," laughed Errol, as if he was reading his friend's mind, before handing him a can of red stripe. Terry returned a nervous smile, and sipping on his beer, he tried to nod his head in time with the bass line of the song playing in the background, as he had done, quite expertly, many times before, but, due to his present state of self imposed anxiety, he now found that he was losing his place in the rhythm, and, at one point, looked as if he was on the verge of having a fit. Therefore, to avoid any further embarrassment, he resolved to keep his head very still for the moment, and continued to grin like a village

idiot at anyone who caught his eye, until, inadvertently, his attention found it's way over to a skinny Vamp seated at the end of bar.

"I don't think that bloke likes me," whispered Terry to Errol, after being stared at for thirty seconds straight before his friend turned his head to take a casual look over at the Bloodsucker in question.

"Yeah, he's a bit mad that one. Think he's a crackhead or something."

"Oh well that's a comfort, then. I mean, if I get stabbed or glassed, at least there'll be a reason," said Terry, a little alarmed.

"What you going on about?"

"He looks dangerous mate. He's making me feel on edge."

"Well now you know how I feel then," replied Errol with a grin before looking away, which only increased Terry's sense of unease, as he took another nervous sip of his beer and looked around the room once more.

Is this payback?

Has my so called friend been storing up all the slings and arrows of outrageous racism, he has suffered over the years, and now I'm gonna get battered to settle the account? Maybe they're all in on it and it's a secret society of discontented Caribbeans? Terry's irrational thoughts now yelled back to him, as he sipped on his beer again and tried to control his increasing feelings of dread.

"Okay fair enough, Errol. You've made your point. White Vamp boozers are rubbish and racist, I get it, but can we now fuck off before someone stabs me through the heart with a chair-leg," hissed Terry, breaking the silence between the two friends again and nearly hyperventilating from all the tension.

"Relax, you idiot. They're not allowed to kill a fellow Vamp, are they? Even a cracker."

"Yes but they could fuck me up."

"Very true. They could fuck you up."

"Jesus" whimpered Terry.

"Oh give it a rest and stop being a pussy, will ya? I like it here, so we're staying. Anyway, I'm off for a piss" said Errol shaking his head and walking away.

"Well I'm coming too then" shot back Terry, almost childishly, and after placing his beer on the counter of the bar, he quickly followed after his friend into the rest-room.

"You're pathetic, you know that?" snapped Errol as he unbuttoned his 501's and started to relieve himself.

"Actually I wanted a piss," replied Terry, defiantly, as he looked down at the bottom of the urinals and tried to think of running taps and waterfalls.

"Yeah looks like you were bursting. You know what Terry, I have to put up with every white prick in the universe calling me Chalky, or saying play the white man or bumping into me in the pub and then checking his pockets, and I just keep cool, smile and move on. But, as soon as you're the only white face in a gaff full of black guys, you shit yourself."

"Well, that ain't my fault."

"I'm not saying its your fault. All I'm saying is, that's what I have to put up with."

" Okay, I get it," said Terry, straining to urinate.

"And another thing. Notice how you got in here no problem, yeah? Not like all those fucking clubs in the West End, with their quotas for black men. "Not tonight geezer, we're full", just as twenty pissed up, badly dressed white blokes walk in. Didn't hear that tonight did ya?"

"No, you're right, I get it."

"I get it. I get it. You're always fucking saying that, ain't ya?"

"I know."

"Pathetic," said Errol again, and now buttoning up his jeans, he headed towards the exit of the toilets, while Terry quickly did the same and hurried after his friend.

"Anyway mate, you can hardly talk. How many white birds, you shagged? You're always shagging white girls, ain't ya? I reckon you wanna be white," shouted Terry at the top of his voice, a few paces behind Errol, as he desperately tried to claw back some credibility before there was a sudden break in the music.

Now everyone in the Shebeen turned around to stare at them, before a symphony of 40 Vampires sucking their teeth filled the air, and the music quickly started again.

"You're a fucking idiot, you know that!" hissed Errol, in his friend's ear. now looking extremely embarrassed, while Terry mumbled "Sorry mate" and another needy smile returned to his face once more.

CHAPTER TEN

"So you definitely didn't go to Private School or Grammar School?"

"God no, it was a comprehensive in Sheffield," replied the reporter, now accentuating his northern accent even more, to increase his chances of getting an interview, with the famously belligerent Footballer while his subject looked down again at the piece of paper in his hand. It was best to make sure thought Lucius, as only a few weeks earlier he had been rather embarrassingly duped by a journalist who produced proof that he had attended a sink school in Birmingham, when in fact he'd gone to Eton and as a result, the prank was splashed all over the tabloid press for days. Even he had to laugh, but, in saying that, he didn't really want to make a habit out of making himself look like a dick too many times, and so studied the documentation a little more forensically, before handing it back to the journalist.

"Looks genuine enough to me. What's your first

question then, and don't start it with "So". That really annoys me."

"Err, s…, I mean, well Lucius, great game as usual, a wonder goal and 2 assists, but before we talk about the game, can you explain to our audience why you didn't take the knee again before the kick off?"

"Because it means nothing. Virtue signaling by celebrities who are too thick to realize that they are achieving jack, except maybe a few more clicks to improve their brand."

"Err, well they might say that's an unfair summary of their actions and that they are making a valid stand against racism."

"Yeah they might say that."

"But, isn't it a just stand against unfairness?"

"It's a pointless gesture, that means nothing because it's costs nothing."

"But isn't this just playing into the hands of those fans who routinely boo the taking of the knee?"

"What do you mean? I'd boo as well, if I was them. They know they're been preached at by a bunch of self interested no marks. Assuming they're all racist and have to be re-educated, to start thinking the right way. It's insulting and these fans, you go on about all the time, the ones who spend all the money by the way, they know enough to realize, it's an empty gesture. As far as I'm concerned, they are no more racist than me."

"So black lives don't matter, then?"

"12 years ago they made a black man President, yeah? Did that change anything in America or the world, for that matter? Eddie or Sam or whatever your name is?"

"It's Simon actually."

"You sure you didn't go to Public School?"

"Err, yes."

"Well Simon, did things change with Obama being president?"

"Err well."

"You do know he dropped more bombs than George W Bush don't you? And he kicked hundreds of thousands of black people out of their homes, after the 2008 crash? Didn't see anyone taking a knee about that, back then, did you?"

"Err, okay, fair enough. Well, I think we should probably return to the game now…"

"No, you started this Simon. So here's another question for you then? What do the ones with all the money and all the power really fear, other than a shortage of quinoa down their local Waitrose, of course? I'll tell you shall I? Ordinary people, whatever their color, realizing they have loads in common with each other, and getting together to do something about it. You see, that's what really keeps them up at night."

"Yes but…"

"Cos we all know how the world works don't we, Simon? You got a million pounds, you can make two, two gets you four, four will bring you ten, but earn 30 grand a year, and you'd have to be a fucking genius to make that last without having to bankrupt yourself on loans. Oh and God help you if you've got any kids."

"Excuse me Luciuis but could you…"

"Stop swearing? Not really Simon, I'm on a roll. So here's another thing. You know the Stock Market is going up, at the moment, but we're actually in the middle of a Pandemic. How's that work? You'd think as everything's being shut down, Corporations might be going to the wall, or at least losing money, but they're not, are they? It's because of Quantitative Easing. Free money from their mates in Government and the Central banks, but when they get it, instead of investing it in their businesses, with new technology or heaven forbid, giving their workers a pay-rise, they buy back shares in their own Companies, to keep the Stock Price artificially high, so they can give themselves huge bonuses. You know in 1970, the average CEO was getting 30 times, the wage of his average employee, now it's 300 times. This is how they work. The Bosses and the Professional Managerial Class. They want cheap labour and no back-chat from anyone without a degree, and heaven help you if you want to build any Social Housing in their area, cos then it's all "I agree in principle" until they block it in the courts. It's a stitch up, mate. The 80% are getting crushed. It can't go on. We can't keep walking down the old roads anymore, because they just go around and around, going absolutely nowhere. The fact is, we have to build newer ones, straighter ones, so we can all get out of this hateful misery, and so that's why I'm arranging a March in four weeks time in Trafalgar Square. There you go Simon, big exclusive for you, there. It's gonna be called *Time for a Real Change*. I want millions there bruv. Let's forget taking a knee and all that fucking virtue signaling bollocks and do something useful for a change. March with me in four weeks and let's show these jokers once for all who's really in control," said the Footballer, pushing past the Journalist to speak directly into the camera, while Lady Carswell, pressed her finger on the remote control, as a frozen picture of Lucius Noble in mid rant, now filled the huge television screen on the wall opposite.

"He's dangerous."

"Oh darling, he's just another gobby Sports Star. Only difference is, he's actually quite good. Saw him play Chelsea last year. Absolutely destroyed us. Such a sweet left foot. Very similar to Messi but puts it about like Roy Keane. Probably get the Balon d'Or again this year. I mean…"

"Oscar. He is dangerous," interrupted Carswell, with a cold stare.

"But not as dangerous as you my petal. Come back to bed, you're gorgeous, when you are irritated. Your lip curls up on one side" said Oscar, patting the metal base of the huge double pallet.

"Stop flirting Oscar, this is serious. He is talking about revolution."

"Oh, he's hardly Che Guevara is he? He's a footballer, sweet-pea. It's all performance with that lot. I mean I should bloody know, we represent enough of them at EVC. They're complete idiots. Half the time, they just spout whatever their fucking agents tells them, while the rest they prattle on about "Their brand" and "Having a Legacy"," said Oscar, affecting a generic working class accent.

"Well this one is different. The modern world is perfect for malcontents like Lucius Noble right now, especially with Social Media. Do you think if the Diggers had Twitter, we could have ground them into the dirt, as we easily as we did?"

"Oh, that was years ago, come back to bed petal, my body yearns for you," said Oscar leaning over for another kiss.

"He's planning a March," snapped Carswell, moving her head away and folding her arms.

"So what. They did the same for Iraq and we still did what we wanted."

"Well not any more. People are wiser this time, and never forget the power a Poet or Revolutionary has over the masses."

"I thought that was just women" said Oscar, with a slippery grin, as he moved across the bed again.

"Some women. Can't you see Oscar, the more he talks, the harder, it will be to shut him up? He is unorthodox. Lives on the same wage as everyone else, very clever. Yes, this is new. Very, very new. Before we could always get the Celebrities on our side, especially the poor ones, because they loved the money so much and would do anything to protect it. Look at Richard Burton or Tupac Shakur? Both supposed Socialists but despite their bluster, they loved the lifestyle more. But this Lucius doesn't care about how many shoes he can buy or houses he can live in."

"He has his detractors too cup-cake. Don't worry, I will get Jamaal and Tudor Dee to write a few columns about how he is letting black people down and playing a white man's game. You know turn him into a race traitor, like we did with Calvin Sewell."

"Calvin Sewell is religious and a conservative, so he's easy to ignore, but it won't be so easy with this Lucius. The dispossessed rarely see the sky, because most of the time, their eyes are fixed on the ground and it has always been our job to keep them there. That's why I don't care about loud mouthed Populists like Bane Vulpine, they do our job for us, keeping the Culture War going, keeping everyone distracted. But this Footballer is something else entirely. He represents true jeopardy, like Fred Hampton before."

"Fred Hampton? who's he, pray?"

"Precisely. No-one really knows about him. We erased his memory, but, in reality, he was the most dangerous man in the Sixties. More dangerous than Malcolm X, Martin Luther King, and Bobby Kennedy all put together. He was the head of the Black Panthers in 1969, and his idea was to bring poor Whites, Blacks, and Latinos together. And he was getting somewhere, as well. Had a meeting with White Miners in Virginia, and Latino gangs in New York, it was just the seeds you understand, but it was incendiary and could have gone anywhere. That's why our American allies had to extinguish him. Brother Hoover and his half-crazed FBI were a blunt instrument at the best of times, but they got the job done. We need to do the same with Lucius Noble. He could easily become our Fred Hampton and much worse, if don't do something."

"So what do you suggest? Take him out like the FBI?"

"Nothing so crude, my dearest. Deal with him, yes, but in a more English way perhaps."

"Without fuss?"

"Precisely. Find him, hypnotize him in the manner I showed you, so it lasts for a day and then make him download child pornography or say something extremely vile about women, you know rape is acceptable for a husband, that kind of thing, but he needs to be silenced."

"Perfect," said Oscar leaning over for a kiss.

"And tonight," added the Vampire Leader, pulling away from her lover and walking into the middle of the bedroom.

"But can't we at least have a little…".

"No! I have chosen you for greater things my darling boy, because I see your talents, but if you fail…"

"I wont fail" replied Oscar, wiping the smile from his face, before sliding off the pallet and putting on his clothes.

*

Oscar quickly exited the bedroom, and deciding to ignore the comfort of the internal lift, raced down the stairs of Vampire Palace to the car park below. This was serious, he thought, sliding into the front seat of his Tesla and putting on his seat belt. The one thing he didn't want was a disappointed Carswell and although she had as much affection for him as any Vampire her age could be expected to have, in reality, she was absolutely ruthless, and so if he didn't come up to scratch, he could quite easily find himself back in the shallows paddling about with all the other losers. That's why she had ruled for so long, and that last look she'd given him just before he left, confirmed he was probably hovering close to something quite unpleasant.

Of course, he didn't need the Vampire Leader to tell him, Lucius was a danger, any fool could see that. However he'd decided a few years ago, when the footballer had first started to make his pronouncements on social issues, that it would be more judicious, to play the long game. Death by a thousand compromises was usually the best solution, where he either conformed and started to behave like a proper celebrity, a la John Lennon preaching "Imagine there's no possessions", whilst swanning around multi-million-pound mansions and being best buddies with Ronald Reagan, or found himself on the margins, ridiculed. Anything else was completely off the menu and as it seemed, early on, that the young Lucius wanted to be some kind of working class martyr, he had decided that "the silly little boy" would have to learn the hard way. A well-placed article here, some innuendo there, maybe the odd prominent black voice decrying Lucius for letting down his race. Uncle Tom, was always a reliable assassin, and he was pretty sure, given time, he would have eventually gotten his man. But now, Carswell, wanted results yesterday, he would be forced to shelve his original plan and drastically change tack. "Blast" mumbled the Vampire to himself and grimaced again, while he tapped an address into his Sat Nav before making his way out of the underground car park.

Not that finding Lucius Noble would be difficult.

The whole world and his cis-gendered wife knew that he lived in a council flat on the 12th floor of a tower block which he had inherited since he was eighteen from his single mother, who'd died from cancer. It was all part of the mystique, and when he burst onto the scene a year later, scoring a hat-trick in his very first game against the League Champions , no -one believed for a second that a Premiership footballer would be staying for long in an Estate notorious for drugs and gang violence. In fact, even after a year, of remaining in the council flat, everyone still thought it was some kind of a hoax, until Lucius showed the Local Authority, who had been busily trying to evict him at the time, and everyone else incontrovertible proof that he was, in fact, living on the average wage of his local area, whilst also donating the rest of his multi million contract and boot deal to a Trust, dedicated to promoting true equality in British society. Of course, the Mainstream Media, certain he was as fraudulent as themselves, had ferreted around his financial details like demented auditors, looking for a crack in the ice, while older rock stars, from similar working class backgrounds, like Conor Fitzgerald, sneered from their North London mansions that he was just a "Do-gooder and a stupid twat". However, nothing stuck, and after a few more years when the footballer, continued to take the bus to work and even made his own sandwiches, "Cos no-one who works for Primark gets free travel and lunch, do they?" a modern-day legend was born. The Pandemic, further elevated him to God-like status, and after rapidly establishing Social Clubs in working class communities all over the country, and distributing free food to nearly five million of his countrymen, badges with "Lucius speaks for me" started to be worn by everyone from Supermarket workers to those on the front line of the NHS. Predictably his fellow professionals, scrambled around to get in on the act, quickly declaring their support for his initiatives, whilst making financial contributions to various Local Charities, only to find themselves, condemned by the man, himself, on his regular podcast, *Noble Endeavour*. "These are the same so called Role Models, who kiss their badge when they score a goal to make the fans think they love the club. But, if they were to be really honest, they should have their bank account numbers stitched on their shirt instead, because that's what they're really kissing. Don't trust them, they're fucking frauds and will always let you down." Destroying this paragon of Prole virtue would be an absolute pleasure, thought Oscar as he pulled up outside the tower block, before nimbly crawling up its walls and letting himself in by an open window to find his way towards his prey.

However, "I'm having some oven chips, if fancy any," soon halted Oscar in his tracks, as a light in the front room, suddenly came on and Lucius stared back with a big grin.

"McCains?" replied Oscar, coolly, placing his hands in his pockets, whilst desperately trying to disguise the shock of being caught in the act.

"Supermarket brand, I'm afraid. Bit broke this week, but they're very good."

"Think I'll pass," replied Oscar before flying across the room to stand in front of Lucius and stare into his eyes.

Nothing.

"I picked up your stench, as soon as you hit the roof, Vampire. That cloying mustiness of Orchids mixed with dried blood. Never forget it," said Lucius edging past Oscar's astonished face to remove a tray from the oven and empty some chips onto a plate.

"Lycan."

"Wolves of the Night if you please, and we do like a beard. I often think, it must be awful for you Vampires these days. All that skin like a baby's arse, while everyone else is sprouting whiskers and getting mental health counseling from their Barbers. You must feel very excluded?"

"Never really went for that look myself. Bit too Bronze Age, for me. By the way, you wouldn't happen to have a drink, anywhere around here, would you?" said Oscar, regaining his poise, while he looked around the council flat with increasing distaste.

"Bottle's over there."

"Thanks," replied the Vampire walking over to a coffee table and picking up a cheap bottle of Scotch to pour himself a drink.

"I was half expecting a call sometime from you lot. What was it? Not taking a knee? Annoying Channel Four, Pissing off the Guardian?" said Lucius, placing a chip in his mouth.

"Amongst other things. You'll have to stop, you know. It's unsettling the order of things."

"The order of things? Of course. Yes, best keep the order of things, or all hell will break loose, won't it? Hardly fair Bloodsucker."

"Neither is competing with mortals. All that latent strength."

"Thought you'd approve. Trans men competing in Women's Sport and all that" said the Lycan with a grin.

"They are women."

"You don't believe that for a second, charlatan. But for your information, I am the same as mortals, except when I change, which I'm hardly likely to do in the middle of a game am I? Think of all the hate, I'd get from the Mascots. No, the talent is my own, you can check my Testosterone levels if you wish."

"Still unfair, I'll have to talk to Keevan about this. It's against the Pact."

"Keevan doesn't rule me."

"Well, you need to stop."

"Why don't you stop?"

"We're not doing anything."

"Priceless. Tell me Nosferatu? Do you get chosen for your bullshit, or is it something that naturally occurs, when you are turned? You have a perfect plan, don't you? Keep the attention on identity, keep people at each other's throats, while no-one sees the sleight of hand?"

"You have us wrong dear boy."

"I think not, but, don't worry, a change is coming. But this time, the pitchforks will have black, white and brown hands on the shafts. The 80% are rising up and when they do, it will be so beautiful. I am Aufidius, motherfucker and I will haunt bastards like you for as long as it takes."

"Shakespeare, by God? Aufidius? Didn't he betray Coriolanus?"

"You can't betray your oppressor, Demon."

"Really? Anyway, didn't you know? Shakespeare was a fraud, old chap. A failed actor, who could barely read or write. Everybody knows it was Edward De Vere," grinned Oscar, taking a sip of his whiskey.

"The Earl of Oxford? Another Vampire lie. He was a Lycan, as well you know. That's why pricks like you have been trying to discredit him, for years. Still can't believe something that incredible didn't come from your own stinking class. Does it annoy you Bloodsucker? Answer me you privileged dog!" replied Lucius, now suddenly transforming into a Lycan, before bounding across from the kitchen to pin Oscar's neck against the living room wall."

"Aagh, I can't breathe."

"How very George Floyd of you. Nice to see one of the Elites struggling for air for a change. How does it feel? Frightened? Embarrassed? Humiliated?"

"Aaghh, yes, aagh."

"Welcome to our world, Deceiver. I could squeeze the

life out of you now, but a Black Lycan killing a Tier One Vampire and white to boot, would be too much trouble, even for me. Don't come here again, because the next time I may not be so hospitable," spat Lucius, letting go of Oscar's throat, as the Vampire staggered back with terror in his eyes, before quickly hurling his body towards the ceiling and then scuttling to safety through the window he had entered by.

Oscar had encountered Lycans before and although incredibly strong, it usually didn't take that much for a mature Vampire, like himself to defeat one. His kind were an older form, so their ancient DNA made their muscles much denser than the average Werewolf, but, there was no doubt, that Lucius could have killed him just now if he'd wanted to. This thought slightly unnerved the Vampire as he clambered down the side of the tower block, and feeling a rare moment of vulnerability, which he only really experienced when talking to Carswell, he suddenly lost his grip, and tumbled from 40 feet to the ground below. A few yards away, a local fox looked on in quiet bemusement, until a hand shot out, and Oscar brought the animal's neck to his mouth. The blood brought a little optimism to his mood and he continued to feast on the unfortunate animal's neck, until he sat up and stared blankly at the pale moon floating above his head. He couldn't tell Carswell about this, she could reject him, and after centuries, of being her lover and confidante, all his plans of becoming Chief Imperator of the European Alliance could crumble into ashes before his eyes. No, he would have to sort this out himself, thought the Vampire and although Lucius might be immensely powerful, even he, would be no match for more than one Vampire and so dropping the limp body of the fox on the frozen tarmac, he pulled his phone from a side pocket and started to text.

CHAPTER ELEVEN

Terry winced as he brought the cup of the horse blood to his lips and hoped he wouldn't retch again, before steadying himself to attempt another sip. It reminded him of rotting herring and fruit cordial, if that combination was even possible, and for a few seconds, he lay back on his pallet, trying to recall long cool glasses of sparkling water to mitigate the awful taste, until his mind returned to the unfairness of his present condition again.

Hypocrites!

How many random mortals had Vampires killed for no good reason, over the years?

Probably in their millions, and even though it was supposed to be the Third Law of the Ancients, *Never take a mortal life unless to feed*, a bit like a Catholic wearing a condom or a Muslim having a sneaky Gin and Tonic, this was largely ignored by the majority of Bloodsuckers. In fact, only recently, he'd heard of a fellow Sister in Blood, who after being told in an overly aggressive manner during the

Lockdown to walk around the block to access the last train for the Victoria Line, had spitefully bled a ticket collector around the back of Tottenham Hale tube station, and received nothing more than a slap on the wrist and a £500 fine. While, because he had joined Bane on the other side of the argument, they were throwing, not only, the book, but whole bloody bookshelf at him. Typical Woke bullshit. Get caught wearing a Nazi uniform in your youth or sporting black face in the 1990's but prostrate yourself before the altar of Critical Race Theory and Gender Ideology and bingo, you are absolved from your sins, but refuse to bend a knee and stick to your principles and you are canceled and sipping horse blood for the rest of your life. "It's a complete joke," mumbled Terry bitterly to himself ,and this was even without taking into consideration the blatant treachery of Errol, "his so-called" friend. Now, any road back for the two of them, was, as far as the vampire was concerned, permanently closed. How could he sell him out like that? It was one thing to stand by when he had been ejected from his house in Fulham, although Terry still expected a little more loyalty from an old comrade, but quite another to actively conspire to actually get him nicked. "Fuckhead", spat out Terry into the fetid air of his Prison Cell while he continued to think unwholesome thoughts about his old house-mate, until finally tiring of his internal rant, his eyes drifted towards the stone floor again. Couldn't they just text?, he thought as he lit a match and brought an old vellum parchment to his face for another look. Three months, subsisting solely on "Equine Blood" in "Bloodwells", or the Well of Blood Penitentiary, to give it, it's formal name, and a year's banishment from London, his rudimentary grasp of Latin now told him, plus more importantly, an order to stop seeing *"The mortal, Lauryn"* or face the consequences. Consequences? Of course that meant death for his former lover and probably her son, to make sure there were no loose ends. The Vampire Establishment was nothing if efficient, and so faced, with very few options, Terry had agreed to the terms, as he scratched his signature in his own blood, on the parchment to vow to never see either of them again. At least they would be safe, thought the Vampire, placing the document on the stone floor again, as part of the agreement, negotiated by his Solicitor from Vamp Aid, was that she and Jordan would automatically be added to an official list of mortals considered exempt from the attentions of his own kind. However, it was scant consolation, and, in truth, Terry would have welcomed five lifetimes on horse's blood rather than endure the hell of permanent separation. Lauryn was still his only link to that little part of himself, slowly being consumed by the passage of time and the expediency of experience. In the end, he would end up like Oscar or Carswell, calculating and detached, as only those who lived within the limits of a mortal life, knew the true nature of compassion. Longer life makes you cynical, savagely intellectual and pointlessly cruel. Yes, of course, she was better off without him, he was a Vampire for God's sake, but this did little to offset the terrible ache he now felt in his heart and so curling himself up in a ball on his pallet, Terry tried not to weep, as he resolved to set his face against the vagaries of destiny and grimly accept his fate. Therefore, the next few months of his incarceration were predictably miserable but thankfully passed quickly and without incident, until one night, he found himself, sitting on Kevin's old motorbike, and told to "piss off and not come back for a year". Terry duly nodded his head and after roaring off down the M1, by 12.45am, he was sitting in Maxwell's Manchester, bougie canal-side apartment, on a chez longue shaped as a pair of lips and sipping a very good malt.

"You're staying with me, I insist," announced the Trans Vampire, chopping out a big line of cocaine on a mirror with her American Express platinum card and handing it to her guest.

"You sure," said Terry lowering his head towards the narcotic.

"Absolutely! Oh my God Terry, you can't go back to living with that autistic savant, Kevin, can you? I mean, I love the boy to bits, but two more seconds of watching him shovel sandwich spread into his Salford gob every evening, would be absolute torture for any man, Trans or not. You do know that he thinks Neo Liberal, is that guy from the Matrix and I have it on very good authority that he's freezing his Big Macs now, so he can microwave them later, when he gets back from the club. Barbarian doesn't even cover it. No Terry, you are far too sophisticated for all that unnecessary squalor. Oh and don't worry, I might fancy the arse off you, but I won't make it too obvious," she said with a cheeky grin.

Terry smiled back.

Of course, she was right.

Living with Kevin was not really an option, and a few days with the younger Vampire would have had him running back to Bloodwells and demanding to be let back in for another three months. In fact he had come to this conclusion long before his release, and had even considered renting a little studio flat through the Vampire Accommodation Service, but their properties were always so basic, with very few comforts, only dual clocks on the wall and tiny freezers to store your blood, plus by the time he had forked out for all the deposits and agency fees that you had to pay, in advance, these days, he would be broke before he could even start. Gone were the days of just turning up and handing the Landlord a few quid and sticking your suitcase on the top of a dusty wardrobe, as renting privately in the 21st Century, even for a Vamp, was nothing short of a complete scam. Furthermore, even though he was loathed to admit it to himself, thirty years of living somewhere like Fulham had turned Terry into something of a snob, and therefore, as he scanned the luxurious interior of Maxwell's apartment, with it's huge chandeliers hanging down from vaulted ceilings, illuminated by hundreds of pieces of art on every wall, he found that he didn't need too much persuading to stay.

"And, of course, what happened to you, was absolutely awful" continued Maxwell, as she walked past one of Goya's black paintings and shook her head. "Mortals die all the time, don't they? and you get 3 months and a year's ban. Well screw them. Anyway, you've lost nothing. London's been dead for years. Scummy little middle class mono-culture. What's on at the National these days? What's showing at the Tate Modern? Sanitized nonsense, that no-one will remember in five minutes time, never mind in a hundred years. No, as far as I'm concerned, all the good Art is being done in Margate, now. Like Paris in the 1920's, but with a few more tattoos."

Terry smiled again.

As usual, his host was unstoppable, and only recently from his prison cell, he had watched the Trans Vampire, debate with Sharon Denim, the celebrated YBA from the nineties, on BBC's Newsnight about the importance of working-class art. The Artist, who's previous work had famously included a quilt made up of her own used tampons, stated that it didn't matter where the Art came from or who made it, whereupon Maxwell called her "a thick bourgeois bitch" and threw a glass of water over her and then the tinned excrement really hit the fan. Calls for an immediate apology and even her arrest quickly followed, but undeterred, three days later at a night launch in a Morrisons supermarket in Stockport, Maxwell announced to the waiting Media and a small crowd of confused pensioners, that she had officially given up on the Art world, and would now focus all of her attention on the written word, by establishing *Stay In Your Lane Publishers*. The choice of the name of her new company was particularly ironic, taken as it was from the world of diversity training, where this phrase was regularly employed to encourage people to stay within the limits of their own ethnicity and experience. Of course, Maxwell's intention was to be the polar opposite of this sentiment, and stated as much, a week later, in a famously controversial interview with the popular Podcast TriggerFinger. "In 2021, 80% of the publishing industry is not only female, but also comes from the same privileged parts of society. So, the question is, with all these stuck-up cows calling the shots, where will the next D.H. Lawrence, Shelagh Delaney or Irvine Welsh come from now? The answer is nowhere. So, fuck the publishing industry, is what I say. Telling stories is like cave art, and they don't own the caves."

Unsurprisingly, the Mainstream Media went into an immediate meltdown. "Racist", "White Supremacist" "Bigot", were now all thrown in the direction of the Trans Vampire, as Journalists and Columnists, mainly from the Left, it must be said, immediately declared that *Stay In Your Lane Publishers* only seemed to be interested in the lost opportunities of white working-class men and women and not the working class in general. However, Maxwell quickly dismissed these comments, as "boring and cliched" before declaring that, not only, would all working-class writers be welcome, whatever their color, creed or sexuality but that the "real racists, in this case", were in fact the white middle class liberals themselves or WML's as she liked to refer to them now, "who wanted poor people to remain eternally ignorant and disabled, so they could be more easily mocked at their wanky little soirees in Highgate". Again, the internet blew up and calls for the new publisher to be banned covered the front pages of the more Liberal newspapers for days, but instead of causing any real harm, this barrage of fresh abuse only played straight into the hands of the Art Entrepreneur. "Lots of lovely free publicity, the saps" she shouted waving her hands in the air, during an interview with Sky News, so by the end of the month, every working-class kid who could string more than four words together had sent manuscripts to the new Publishing House and the money began to pour in from eager investors.

"So why don't you work for me," now declared

Maxwell, hoovering up some more lines of the excellent cocaine before looking over at her amused guest again.

"Doing what?"

"Whatever you want."

"I don't know anything about publishing, Maxwell."

"Neither do I, but you read don't you?"

"Well, yeah, of course, but…"

"Who's your favorite author?"

"Steinbeck, probably."

"Mine's Jilly Copper. See, you're an expert already."

Terry laughed out loud again while he told Maxwell to "Stop taking the drugs and talking shit" but after further pestering from his host, plus a few more lines of cocaine, he finally agreed to be an "Editing Consultant" for *Stay In Your Lane Publishing,* whatever the hell that meant. However, to Terry's surprise, the offer was real, and as good as her word, the very next evening, Maxwell made an office for him, in one of her many ante rooms, and so for the next few weeks, under an original Warhol print of Marlon Brando, Terry set to work reading the thousands of manuscripts that had been sent to his lap-top. In fact, after all the lunacy of the past year, it was just the diversion, the Vampire needed, and to his absolute astonishment, found that, he did indeed, have a talent for spotting good writers, and ninety years of reading Joyce, Fitzgerald, Baldwin, and Thompson, had not been in vain. Now Bentley Armitage, Kai Thomas, Mohamed Sarkar, and Hayley Higgins spoke of dead-end jobs, pointless violence and a stolen future and as a result, were all quickly signed up by Terry, to shake the literary establishment to it's very core for the first time since the late 1950's and early 1960's. Back then, the Obscene Publications Act held sway, and the Vampire could clearly remember the moral outrage when book's like Colin MacInnes's Absolute Beginners and Alan Sillitoe's Saturday Night Sunday Morning, were published and so was greatly amused at the irony of history repeating itself again, but this time with the "so called Progressives" replacing the post war Establishment. Now high street booksellers, steadfastly, refused to stock any books by *Stay In Your Lane Publishers,* considering them to be "Triggering and Unsafe" while the critics could hardly contain their excitement, as they all, eagerly, queued up to stick their collective boot into the new genre, complaining "Too Simplistic" "Full of hate" and "Not knowing what a semi-colon was".

It was the standard response from an out of touch Media, and as before, only served to advantage the new enterprise, as the public quickly lapped it up. And why shouldn't they? For years now, British Art and Culture had been devastated by fear and self censorship, where so-called Artists anxiously marked their door with Rainbow Flags and Be Kind Hashtags, so the Woke Angel of Death would fly over and leave them alone in relative peace. Ordinary people sensed this lack of courage, and instinctively craving something with a little more bite, gradually abandoned their previous indifference to the written word, and began to buy the new literature by the truckload from the Publisher's own website. Even, Maxwell, was amazed by the rapid rise of her new venture, commenting to a reporter that "It's just like the Hull Truck Theatre Company back in the 1980's. If you tell stories relating to their daily lives, the great unwashed will have no problem consuming the Art", and as the months passed, and the successes continued to pile up, it seemed as if *Stay In Your Lane Publishing* was definitely here to stay.

Predictably, the North and Manchester, in particular, began to experience a Mini Renaissance, similar to that of the early 1990's, as new Clubs and Art Galleries quickly sprouted up around the city. Meanwhile Maxwell had opened another club called "The Tony Bar" named in honor of the deceased Northern Entrepreneur and Visionary Tony Wilson, as she attempted an art chaos version of the Algonquin Round Table from the 1920's and Studio 54 from the 1970's. The Club was an instant success, as everyone from the new Counter Culture turned up. Bane Vulpine, of course, the film – maker, Piers Montage, the cult graphic novelist P.B Maguire, and legendary 90's Rapper, Point Break. Obviously, the establishment kept it's distance and seethed from afar, but there was very little they could do as a new generation of working class Artists, and Taste-makers, drove their Standard into the ground and gleefully staked out a new claim.

Terry also, had no problem joining in with the new Zeitgeist, consuming copious amounts of drink and drugs, while flitting from grand opening to new book signing like everyone else in his circle. However, despite all the fun, in his more reflective moments, the Vampire sensed that there was still something lacking from the new movement. Yes, he had signed and promoted writers from working class backgrounds, but, despite his best efforts, most of his roster remained stubbornly one color, and so the general perception that "the Working Class" being code for white and poor, continued to be a hard stain to scrub away. If the new divisive ideology of Social Justice Authoritarianism, was ever going to be defeated, it could only be achieved in solidarity with all working-class people, of all colors and if this wasn't achieved, then surely *Stay In Your Lane Publishing,* could well be committing the same crimes as their enemies, mused the Vampire, and this dissident thought nagged away at him for months, until late one evening after work, he eventually mentioned his fears to his boss.

"Working class, should mean all working class, don't you think?"

"Of course Terry. That's what we do, isn't it?" said Maxwell absentmindedly, while she looked around for her cigarettes.

"Yeah, but most of our writers are still white aren't they?"

"No! What about Mohamed Sarkar?"

"Okay, one."

"And whatshisname? You know, Kai."

"Kai Thomas? His mother's Italian. And there's something else Maxwell. All our readers are white."

"Really? You sure?"

"I checked. Over 95% and only the other weekend, Gary Juvenile wrote a big article about us in the Observer. Why Class has still got a color? He made some good points."

"Oh forget Gary Juvenile, Terry. Last month he was complaining about a Mexican character in a book written by a white woman. Ridiculous. What? You can only make Art, if you're from the same ethnic or sexual group? I mean, no-one complains, when they write A Shark Tale or the Tiger Who Came To Tea, do they? I mean did anyone bother to ask the Sharks, if they minded, were the Tigers ever consulted?" said Maxwell, triumphantly, as she finally found her cigarettes.

"Yeah that's bullshit, but I think the other stuff he said about us, might be right. In fact, to be quite truthful mate, I've been thinking about it for ages myself."

"Ooh, such a worrier. Stop fretting, cupcake. We're on the right path. Have faith" declared the Trans Vampire, now dismissing his objections with a kiss on the cheek, before quickly inviting him along to "another doo" in the City, this time to celebrate Bentley Armitage's, "The Spice of Life" a story about drugs and homelessness, which had recently sold 500,000 copies in the first six months of it's publication. As usual, Terry found himself returning a weak smile to his old friend and although still unconvinced, he reluctantly put on his black leather jacket, and followed her out of the door.

The party was on the other side of town, and predictably, a manic Manchester affair, as the sounds of New Order, Audioweb and Nineties Rave filled the air, while faces from all over the North-West crowded into the small club to celebrate the return of the working-class voice after 30 years in the middle-class wilderness. It was definitely a wild party, but Terry's mind was still mulling over his previous conversation, and as a result quietly sipped on a Vodka Sour, while Maxwell disappeared into the bathroom to bite a Sensitivity Reader that she'd just recognized from a previous visit to London. Fortunately the other mortals fared a little better, as all the Vampires present, remained on their best behavior although a female Vamp on way too much Crystal Meth was seen hovering dangerously close to Bentley Armitage's neck, and had to be swiftly ushered away, before she ended the career of the young novelist, before it even had a chance to start.

"Fucking great though innit, Tel" said Kevin, slapping his old house-mate on the back and suddenly wrenching the Vampire out of his unanswered thoughts.

"Yeah, definitely" replied Terry, with a forced grin.

"This is what we want, hey? Our boys back on top again."

"Yeah, but its not about that is it, Kev?" said Terry, irritably.

"Course it is. Look what's fucking happened since the working class stopped making music, mate. You know 60% of all guitar music is now made by cunts with a Private Education. Can you believe that? Pistols, Specials, Prodigy, even the Spice Girls, all normal people from normal backgrounds, and now all we have is Ed bastard Sheeran"

"What about Stormzy and Dave?"

"Not the same though is it, mate? Don't think they'll all be around the Joanna in forty years' time banging out old songs from Stormzy, know what I mean? C'mon Terry, you're a Northern lad, you know the craic. Grime is shite. Fucking bollocks if you ask me. I haven't heard one good song. In fact, all urban music is crap, innit?"

"Urban music? So you mean black?"

"Oh don't start on all that Tel, you know what I mean?"

"Kev, Black people invented Indie Music. Without Black music, there is no Rock n Roll, there is no Beatles, there is no Pistols."

"Mate the only things Black people gave us was fucking Jerk Chicken and Motown."

"What?!"

"Nah, I'm only taking the piss, in' I? I've got Black mates. But, yeah, I see what you mean. Want another drink?" replied Kevin, as Terry shook his head, while the younger Vampire grinned back at him before stumbling his way back into a crowd of people again.

Now, amidst all the rattle and hum of the party, Terry continued to sip on his Vodka Sour as he tried to dismiss Kevin's words and the rest of the toxic thoughts from his mind and just have a good time. However, this nagging feeling persisted and looking across at the back of his old flatmate's head, bouncing up and down to "Fool's Gold" by the Stone Roses, he was suddenly reminded of Errol's comment from the previous year.

"Didn't see too many black people in Brit-Pop."

"No there weren't, were there?" mumbled the Vampire to himself, and quickly finishing his drink, he took one last look at the party before making his way towards the exit.

*

"My dearest Keevan, you do choose the most frightful places to meet" replied Oscar leaning against the railings of Highgate cemetery, with a look of bored amusement on his face.

"Don't talk to me like one of your filthy breed, Bloodsucker. Anyway I thought you would like it here – close to Karl Marx, you're new hero," said the Werewolf Overlord, flanked by two very large attendants.

"Oh Please. Ghastly man, met him in Soho once, had the breath of a stout. Wanted to be a familiar I recall. Should have sent him to you."

"We have no use for such fools. But enough of this prattle. I am busy Vampire, what is it, this time?"

"We have a problem."

"Yes, and all you have to do is walk out into the sun. I can get one of my men to give a ride to the nearest beach if you'd like."

"Hilarious. I mean Lucius. He needs to be stopped."

"He is no concern of ours," snapped Keevan, walking away from the Vampire.

"He should be. I tried to talk to him last week."

"Give you a slap did he?" said Keevan, turning back with a grin.

"Let's just say he wasn't receptive."

"Benin pack, very dangerous," said Keevan.

"What, really? I thought we'd wiped them all out," said Oscar, narrowing his eyes, and now more than a little disturbed by the new revelation, until the vexed faces of Keevan and his two large attendants, forced a quick change of approach.

"Of course, no disrespect, intended. But, I'm pretty sure, I saw Carswell kill Tamur in a backstreet in Prague with my own eyes," continued Oscar.

"Tamur had a son."

"Lucius," said Oscar, raising his eyes to make the connection.

"I supported his mother, loved him like a son, but then, when he became a man, he was as his father. The same stubborn streak that nearly brought down our kind in the last War."

"Well mark my words, Keevan, it will happen again, if we are not careful. He is causing chaos with the mortals, if you haven't noticed. Rising them up, agitating the rank and file, breaking asunder every convention we've spent years carefully putting in place."

"He cannot be spoken to, I have tried. It is pointless."

"Then you must try harder, Great Wolf Overlord."

"There is nothing else to be done. A wall of bricks. So I have set him adrift," spat back the Lycan Leader, lowering his face to hide his rage.

"Well he must be dealt with and if you can't rein him in, others must. Remember Lycan, you have as much to lose as the rest of us. Your stock is in the same companies, you have the same interests, just look at the Pandemic? A windfall to everyone. How much money have you made in the last few months? Maybe more than us, I'd wager. This is dangerous my old friend. You saw the March the other week? Time for real Change? Three million on the streets of London and joined by others in Barcelona, San Francisco, Melbourne."

"It will pass Vampire. Like Occupy Wall Street."

"My dear Keevan, don't you remember? We arranged that. Got a few Familiars to cause a ruckus and persuade that ignoramus Barry Funk from Dark Stone, to push all that ESG malarkey, to keep the Proles away from asking too many questions after that little hiccup in 2008. It worked a treat. But this is serious, my friend. This is real people," said Oscar, moving closer, to Keevan, who still looked unconvinced.

"And what will your friends in Davos say, when they find out that it was you who raised Lucius, mm…?"

"They will say nothing Night Demon," barked the Werewolf Overlord suddenly stepping forward into the Vampire's face.

"He must go Keevan," declared Oscar holding his ground.

"We do not kill our own."

"You won't have to. I mean that's what friends are for, isn't it?" said Oscar, waiting a few seconds for any further objections, before producing a coy smile and then walking back into the darkness of park.

CHAPTER TWELVE

Still another another 3 hours left until sundown, thought Terry, as he looked down at the illuminated dial of his old carriage clock, before squirming about in his hastily dug hole, and hoping that something small and furry wouldn't piss on his face again.

Sweet Jesus, there had to be another way?

But after the loss of Lauryn, the treachery of Errol and the attitude of Kevin and some of those at *Stay In Your Lane Publishing* , it seemed to Terry, that the only option now, was to flee to the woods and just escape from everything. As a result, he had decided to join the Ascetic Vampires, older Bloodsuckers, so disgusted by their own natures and the outside world in general, that they had withdrawn from everything, and like the monks of antiquity, spent their lives in quiet contemplation whilst feeding off the local wildlife.

"You can bite anything except mortals and Red Squirrels, because we rather like them" declared a mud caked Vampire in a solemn voice, after his arrival in the community, a few week's earlier, before immediately demanding his mobile phone and then handing him a shovel to dig a pit in the forest for his daytime slumber. It was hardly Maxwell's luxury apartment or even the Vamp Inn, thought Terry, but despite the isolation and privation, his new circumstances seemed the perfect solution to all his woes, and for the first few days he had reveled in the peace and silence of Mother Nature. However his addiction to the 21st Century was strong and very soon his mind started to howl in pain, at its absence from the online world. His phone had been quite literally his life, and now, without its constant stream of input into his brain, he wiggled about in his earthen tomb, as if withdrawing from a drug. Once upon a time, he could sit for hours and just be, but not anymore and recalling a recent experiment at an American University, where after being deprived of their phones for only twenty minutes, students had pressed electrodes against their bare skin, preferring the pain of an electric shock to the tyranny of an un-stimulated mind, he now found himself digging his nails into his own flesh for some perverse relief.

Could it get any worse?

Not only was he a Vampire cursed to stalk the earth, living off the blood of his fellow mammals for the next two thousand years, but now at 103 years of age he was actually self-harming. How bloody humiliating was that? He'd be masturbating next? his thoughts whined, and for the next two hours he continued to excoriate himself for his unhappy existence until out of the darkness, a hand reached into his shallow grave and without warning, suddenly wrenched him to the surface.

"What? err…"

"Don't worry Terry, the Sun has dipped behind the trees. You are safe."

"My God! Hector!?"

"At your service my beautiful friend."

"Hector!"

"Yes, yes, it is me."

"What? Where the fuck!"

"Yes, yes, it has been a long time."

"But! HECTOR!" screamed Terry, throwing his arms around his old friend, and hugging him with shouts of intense joy until two Vampire heads quickly popped out of the earth to interrupt their happy re-union.

"Do you mind, this is an Ascetic Community," said one.

"I knew we shouldn't have let him stay brother Julian, far too young for this kind of life," said the other.

"Come Terry, let us leave these good men to their thoughts, and go for a walk, we have much to talk about," replied Hector nodding apologetically to the outraged Ascetics before leading Terry towards a winding path in the woods.

"How the hell did you find me?"

"I talked to Maxwell and she told me that she had caught you looking at a brochure for the Ascetics once or twice before, and after that I just followed my nose."

"My scent," confirmed Terry with a knowing smile.

"I am bound by it and you mine. It is our bond since I turned you."

"Oh yeah and thanks for that, by the way. You were my Commanding Officer," said Terry, with a playful smile.

"And you, a raw recruit from England, come to fight the Fascists. A face carved in poverty, but I set you free. What? You regret your decision?" said Hector, coming to a halt with a sudden look of concern on his face.

"Well, no, but you never know how these things will turn out do you?" said Terry, shaking his head.

"But, you were perfect for this life, no? Curious, principled, singular even."

"Principled?"

"Of course, I am extremely careful. I only turn the best of men."

"Not sure about that Hector."

"Well you should be. You know in a thousand years I have only turned six mortals. Three men and three women and except for two mistakes, I have always chosen well."

"Mistakes? You?"

"Yes Terry. One man, I should have given the gift of extended life to, and one man I most definitely should not. But enough of that. What are you doing here Terry?"

" Well…"

"Life is hard my friend."

"Not like this Hector. It's fucking awful, at the moment, seriously."

"You always swear so much my gentle boy."

"Well, so would you, if you'd seen what I'd seen. I don't know where it all went fuc., err sorry, well you know, wrong. I'm Socialist, but now I am without a home and the work of the last 80 odd years has come to absolutely nothing. It's all twisted. The Tories have now become the party of the poor, while the bloody Elites and the top twenty percent have completely taken over the Left and hate the people they're supposed to represent. How the hell has that happened? I mean, it was bad enough in the Seventies, with every Tom, Dick and Harry out of Public School hi-jacking our causes, but, at least, back then you knew when they hit 30, they'd be off to become the Tory gits you always knew they were. But now the fuckers are staying. Scuse the French. Seriously Hector. The last Labour party meeting I went to, I didn't hear one working class voice, not one and then all they did for most of the evening was make snidey remarks about knuckle dragging bigots who voted Brexit.

"Brexit? I have heard this word many times, since my return."

"Well it's driven everyone mad, and the chattering classes, got their noses put out of joint, big time, because the poor ruined their little racket, so now the word is basically code for white working class racist who shouldn't be allowed to vote."

"Ah the chattering classes. Yes. Maxwell tells me that you started biting them."

"I did."

"It solves nothing. How many my boy."

"A few. A posh girl on a train, a political Speech Writer, a privately educated Radio One DJ. Even my Therapist."

"You bit your Therapist?"

"He was called Jasper."

"Is that a bad name?"

"Not really. But his attitude did my head in, so I bit him. It's really fucked up. In fact, you're completely wrong about me, Hector. I'm not good or principled or anything like that. I'm a psychopath, seriously. You should have bled me on that beach in Barcelona."

"I know your heart, Terry, you are good. However, these homicidal tendencies, are not right. You will have to stop."

"I'm trying, but it's really hard. Fucking WML's."

"WML?"

"It's what Maxwell calls 'em. Stands for White Middle Class Liberal."

"Well then, my friend, I'm a WML too."

"No you're not, you're Jewish."

"My dear Terry, the Jews are the original White Middle Class Liberals."

"Yeah well you're different aren't you, and anyway its not just the Boutique Left, is it? I started hanging around with the other side as well, didn't I? You know right wingers like Bane Vulpine and his mob and they're the bastard same, well except for Maxwell of course, she's great."

"Yes, Bane? Such an idle boy, always has been. You mustn't listen to him."

"Well people do and his followers basically just want to keep everything the way it's always been and then there's Errol, who's a mate of mine, but sold me out and has been entranced by Oscar."

"Oscar? Oscar Fitzgerald, you mean?" interrupted the older Vampire with a frown.

"Err yeah, sorry, do you know him?"

"Oh yes, I know Oscar. So, still up to his old tricks then?"

"And the rest and then there's this mortal called

Lauryn, who I love but I can't see, cos the Vampire Council will kill her and her son if I do."

"You love a mortal?"

"Crazy, isn't it?"

"It's your youth, you still have human instincts. You must never love a mortal my dear boy. I told you that. Dear me, such trouble and so you come to the woods to stay with the most dead of the undead."

"It's better than going back."

"This is no way to live my friend, you must fight."

"I have no fight left, Hector. Its total rubbish, all of it, and I would rather stay in a shallow grave and let foxes piss on my face all day, than go back and endure all the hypocrisy and double talk. At least here, there's some peace" spat back Terry sitting down on a tree stump and placing his face into his hands in resignation, while a woodpecker rapped his beak against the bark of a nearby Elm to break the silence of the forest.

"People are tribal Terry. It is the great curse of our existence and the hardest challenge for those who think as we do. It never changes and has broken my heart for a thousand years. All those people with so much in common, killing each other, hating each other. Fred Hampton knew this."

"What, the Black Panther?"

"The Socialist, I prefer to call him. You know I knew him, well you met him, didn't you when you came over to see me in New York in 1969? He was the brightest of all the stars in that time. He had such a fierce intelligence, the kind that you cannot teach, together with charisma, and an incredible heart. He understood that working class unity was the only important thing and that's why they killed him. In fact, I was with him the night before and I even offered him the gift of extended life."

"He was one of your regrets?"

"My greatest. I thrust my hand into his mind and asked him as I asked you, but he was unsure. I should have tried harder to persuade him, but then he went to a meeting and the next day he was dead. The FBI assassinated him with 200 bullets in his bedroom wall. I found out Dierdra Carswell was behind it."

"That doesn't surprise me, she's a bitch."

"She wasn't always so. But I lodged a complaint with the International Vampire Council, that her actions were totally unnecessary and in direct contravention of our ancient remit not to interfere with mortal progress, but it was turned down, and so in my grief, I removed myself from the world."

"Yeah, I remember that. I went to look for you, at your address in Brooklyn, but you'd gone."

"I am sorry my friend, I should have said something, but I was not myself. A world that could kill Fred Hampton with such impunity was not a place I could live in so easily, and therefore I retreated to my books and shut everything out. But now I have returned, because I realized Fred Hampton was right. He was right in 1969 and he is right today. The direction of the new Left, may have been betrayed by Marcuse and the rest of those intellectual frauds who abandoned the workers and instead exploited minorities, so they could spread their ideas of Repressive Tolerance, shutting down any kind of debate, but, in reality, we do not have the choice to despair. Especially those, of us, blessed with extended life. So, we must fight on. This is what I learned in my exile. It is never over."

"Not sure about that Hector, it's proper bleak at the moment."

"What about Lucius Noble?"

"You know him?"

"Not yet, but he intrigues me. He could be a new Hampton, a new James Connelly, a new Rosa Luxemburg. His eyes burn with the same passion."

"True. He's about the only decent one left," said Terry, raising his head with a little more optimism.

"So, it's agreed. You are coming back with me. After 50 years, I have returned to the world and you will join me. Come, let us tell the Ascetics that you are ready to leave. I'll wager everything, it will make their day."

"Oh definitely," replied Terry with a grin, as the two Vampires began to stroll back, while a full moon in the night sky illuminated their way through the trees.

"By the way who was that other Vampire you mentioned? You know the one you shouldn't have turned." asked Terry, lowering his head under the branch of a tree,

"Oh him? Oscar," replied Hector softly, before the two Vampires re-joined the path and wandered back towards the Ascetics.

*

"And Noah began to be an husbandman, and he planted a vineyard:

And he drank of the wine, and was drunken; and he was uncovered within his tent. And Ham, the father of Canaan, saw the nakedness of his father, and told his two brethren without. And Shem and Japheth took a garment, and laid it upon both their shoulders, and went backward, and covered the nakedness of their father; and their faces were backward, and they saw not their father's nakedness.

And Noah awoke from his wine, and knew what his younger son had done unto him. And he said, cursed be Canaan; a servant of servants shall he be unto his brethren. And he said, Blessed be the Lord God of Shem; and Canaan shall be his servant. God shall enlarge Japheth, and he shall dwell in the tents of Shem; and Canaan shall be his servant."

"There's no mention of Ham being black, here?! Where the fuck does it say that the guy was black?" Errol's thoughts now demanded as he lay the copy of his mother's King James Bible on the kitchen table and shook his head.

The curse of Ham.

The Book of Genesis, Chapter 9, verses 20–27.

Ham was supposed to be black and was banished by his father, Noah, for apparently seeing him naked, although later biblical scholars said that this was merely a euphemism for something more serious and the old man might have actually been sodomised by Ham.

Who the hell would shag their own dad?

Well maybe only a black man.

Oh and let's not forget "A servant of servants shall he be unto his brethren."

Wasn't wrong there was he?

The excuse for Slavery.

Noah, the original white supremacist.

You couldn't make it up, could you? thought the Vampire, as everywhere, he seemed to turn, there was some more bullshit about the color of his skin. Africa was the dark continent, when in fact, if you could be bothered to read a book, about the Empires of Axum, Mali, and Greater Zimbabwe, you would realise most of it had been just as civilised as anywhere else. People had black hearts. Societies came out of a Dark Age. The Asians had issues, the Arabs routinely called black people "Abeed", which means slaves; even the Aliens were racist, as Errol had never heard of a black man ever being abducted by little green men.

No wonder one billion people felt more than a little left out.

In fact, forget white people, even other black people were at. Dragging each other down, like crabs in a bucket, where centuries of no confidence and constantly having to justify your human status, exacted a terrible price on the collective psyche. Now Errol's fangs forced their way through his gums at the multi generational impotence of his own race and he seethed in silence for the next hour until the buzzing of his phone suddenly interrupted his increasing rage.

"Hi, really loved your profile, you sound perfect. Shall we meet in a Hotel. Naturally, everything will be paid for, plus your fee of course. Do you prefer cash? Might be easier. Anyhoo, meet you there Saturday at 8 pm, if that suits? By the way, I will have a hand-held camera, instead of a phone, hope that's ok? The resolution is so much better. Text me if any issues, cheers Ben."

Never trust anyone who puts "Naturally" in a text thought Errol staring at the message on his phone for a moment, before replying "Cool, I'll be there" and then walking across the kitchen to pour himself a Scotch. Three days later, as arranged, the Vampire made his way to the reception bar of an exclusive hotel in the centre of London, and after looking around at the well coiffured heads of the wealthy clientele for a few seconds, he quickly recognised the couple from the picture on his phone, standing over at the corner of the bar.

"Hi?"

"Oh hi. I'm Ben and this is Sarah, pleased to meet you"

"Nice to meet you too."

"Oh great, err didn't know if you would recognise us or not," said Ben.

"Yes, we are still a bit, err…" said Sarah

"Uncomfortable?" offered Errol

"Precisely. This is the first time, for both of us, and we're, err, a little nervous," confirmed Sarah with an anxious smile.

"Err have you come far, so to speak?" chipped in Ben, with a cheeky grin.

"West London," replied Errol, smiling benignly at the little double entendre.

"Oh not far. We're North. Err where in West London?" asked Sarah.

"Fulham."

"Oh, lovely. We could only afford Canonbury."

"Oh that's nice too," said the Vampire.

"Yes, we like it. So what do you do?" said Ben.

"I'm in PR."

"Oh, really? That's unusual. I mean, err, I wouldn't have expected…"

"Oh God, shut up Ben, that's so racist," snapped Sarah

"Well err, no, no, all I meant was..."

"You didn't expect, me to have such a professional job?" interrupted Errol, trying to diffuse any embarrassment.

"Well..."

"Or come from Fulham?"

"Err, well..."

"That's fine, don't worry. Appearances are designed to deceive, aren't they? Especially in London. It's totally understandable," said the Vampire with a re-assuring smile.

"Oh thanks. Well obviously, I didn't mean."

"Oh God, shut up Ben. Would you like a drink?" interrupted Sarah, now turning towards Errol.

"Yes a whiskey, would be great," said the Vampire, placing his elbow on the bar, while the woman in her mid thirties turned to order some drinks before they all proceeded to chat away for the next hour or so, mainly about the horrors of Brexit and how awful Boris Johnson was.

"Oh I feel much more relaxed now. Amazing what a few Martinis can do for you, isn't it? Err, so shall we go up?" said Sarah, placing her glass on the bar and smiling at Errol.

"After you," replied the Vampire finishing his drink before following the couple out of the bar towards the lift. A few minutes later, they all entered a large, luxurious bedroom, at which point Sarah nipped off to the bathroom to freshen up, while Ben immediately pulled out a small wrap of cocaine from his pocket and started emptying the contents onto a desk by the window.

"Oh, would you like some?"

"No I'm fine."

"Oh really? It's very good. Got it from a guy in Tottenham, I know"

"No you're alright," confirmed Errol, seating himself on the corner of the bed, just as Sarah returned from the bathroom, and then watched in silence as the couple busied themselves with snorting the cocaine and kissing each other, before Ben suddenly reached down for a hand held camera that had been lying on the floor.

"So, if you two would like get to know each other and I'll find the best place to stand," announced Ben, now circling the bedroom, as if he was filming a nature documentary.

"Cool, but before we start, please feel free to say anything you want. This is for you, after all. So just let yourself go, tell the truth. If you want to say I love your big black cock, then by all means say it. Have no filters, just say what you feel," said Errol with a smile, as he rose from the bed and started to remove his jacket.

"Oh that's fantastic," said Ben.

"Yes, that makes it so much easier. Err okay, well erm, shall I take off your shirt, then?" asked Sarah, shyly moving towards Errol.

"If you like."

"Oh I would so like. In fact, I couldn't help looking at you in the bar. You have an amazing body."

"Thank you."

"And I saw that picture of your erm, you know on your profile. I hope it's the same in real life?"

"Well, have a look for yourself," said Errol, lowering his eyes towards his groin.

"I will. Oh my god it's gorgeous," said Sarah, after unzipping his fly.

"I will just put the camera here, and... Oh wow, didn't see that," exclaimed Ben, now resting his leg on the end of the bed to get a better angle.

"It's heaven darling," said Sarah, giving her husband a filthy smile, before she started to suck the Vampires cock.

"Do you like it" asked Ben, moving in closer.

"I do."

"How much?"

"So fucking much."

"Do you like to suck his big black cock?"

"I fucking love it, its so big and black."

"Is it better than mine?" asked Ben

"So much better, this is a huge gorgeous black dick and yours is nothing in comparison."

"Oh, can you say that again darling? But this time, can you say cock instead of dick, it sounds so much better."

"Oh, of course darling. Yes, he has such big black cock, and it's so much better than yours and I can't wait to feel it inside my wet pussy," gasped Sarah as she continued to concentrate on Errol's mid-riff until the Vampire put his hand under her back and expertly eased her body onto the bed.

"Oh my god that's fucking amazing," cried Sarah, as Errol now began to rub the end of his cock against the lips of her pussy for a minute or two, before finally sliding himself inside her.

"That's just Incredible. Let me film his big black cock going in and out of your pussy, yes that's just perfect" said Ben sinking to his knees to shoot upwards, while his own penis started to harden inside of his chinos.

"Oh Jesus, oh God, that's it, that's it, oh my God, oh my God, that's divine, keep it there, keep fucking me with your big black cock."

"Yes, keep fucking her, incredible. In fact, you can turn her over, if you'd like," offered Ben, helpfully.

"Oh that's so deep, so fucking deep, I think I'm going to come again, Jesus you're ramming me so hard, that's right, that's right, that's right, fuck me, fuck me, black cock is so good, so fucking good," cried Sarah, arching her back.

"Err, also, could you possibly spank her and call her a white bitch," suggested Ben moving to the centre of the room to get a better shot.

"Sure. Something like, take my big black cock, you white whore," said Errol looking back towards the camera.

"Perfect," said Ben approvingly.

"Yes I'm a white whore," joined in Sarah.

"Well you're a white fraud actually," said Errol with deadpan eyes, as he continued to fuck her harder.

"Err what? Err, yeah okay, that could work," said Ben with a slight frown.

"Yes, a white hypocrite. Sign up for Black History Month, have BLM posters in your windows, but call the Police if you see more than two black kids, hanging around a lamp-post," continued Errol, as he continued ram Sarah from behind.

"Look fella, err loving the new turn, but it's a bit strong, don't you think?" replied Ben, now looking a little concerned as he lowered the camera from his eye.

"You think?" said Errol turning his head towards the lens.

"Well yeah. Lets just keep it civil, shall we? We just want to have some fun," said Ben, now letting the camera fall by his side as he placed a hand on his hip.

"Well, I'm having fun and Sarah's having fun."

"Yes I am, oh God that's unbelievable, I'm coming again," exclaimed Sarah, continuing to push back on Errol's cock.

"Look we have paid you, and all we want is…"

"Is to get what you paid for? Course you do Ben. Big Black Cock wanted for curious couple. I get it. Want a new kick, bored with the same old same old. But you know, these days, I see so much of this crap online, that every time I see BBC now, I'm not thinking of Match of the Day or Have I Got News For You any more. I'm thinking of sex. Fucking racist sex."

"Actually, I work for the BBC, in marketing," offered Sarah, breathlessly, and coming again on the Errol's cock, while Ben now stared back at Errol with a look of betrayal in his eyes.

"But you said that it was alright…"

"And I did, but you didn't have to do it though, did you? And it didn't take too much persuading to see the people you really are. So black men are good for Rapping and Fucking yeah? And maybe knifing each other to death in Tottenham so you can bang some Charlie up your nose?" said Errol, suddenly pulling his cock out from inside the woman and placing his hands on hips.

"Look, I don't know what's going on here, but like Ben said, we just want to have a good time" said Sarah, now more than a little upset that the sex had stopped so abruptly, before sitting up on her knees and deciding it was time get to grips with the situation. However, the Vampire completely ignored her protests, and instead, lunged forward, to grab her husband by the shirt. In seconds he had plunged his fangs deep into the man's neck, and as the blood spurted everywhere, the Vampire drank deeply for a few seconds, before he quickly turned all of his attention towards the terrified face of the woman.

In less than five minutes it was all over, and as Errol stepped away from the bed and grinned at the reflection of his crimson mouth and blood spattered body in the full length of the bedroom mirror, he felt no remorse and their blood tasted good.

CHAPTER THIRTEEN

Oscar continued to run his hand up the inside of his assistant's leg, while he looked out from behind his desk and talked into his phone.

"Don't be silly Brett, everyone is upset at the so called Woke at the moment, whatever that means, but relax. It's just the birth pangs of a new idea. Trust me. they said exactly the same thing about the Printing Press, the Steam Engine, even the Internet. It will be fine, don't worry. Now tell me about your Union problems; did they go away in the end?"

"Yes, eventually. Pagan Magner met with AFM and she made a big thing about the strike on CNN. In fact at one stage I thought she might have gone too far and we would really have to Unionize, but then she said she was going set up a Special Committee in Congress to look into it and assured the members, that although worker's rights were top of her list, right now wasn't the best time for any disputes."

"Perfect and you still have your ethical reputation in tact."

"Kind of. Well, in fact there's been a bit of a backlash from some of our customers, you know saying that we have sold out. That's why I don't think we should be going any further down this progressive path right now, Oscar. I mean what does it prove?" said Brett, very unconvinced.

"It's all about signals my dear boy. Lets us know who's on our side plus there's your Corporate Equality Index score to be considered."

"But what about business Oscar? We're here to make money aren't we? You said so yourself?"

"And you will, but without a good Corporate Equality Index score my dear chap, no investor will touch you with a barge pole. That's where the money is now. Customers are so last century Brett."

"But how do we make a living, then?" said Brett, a little amazed.

"By playing to our base. Make them feel part of something, special. A tribe is the most powerful thing in the world, especially a new one. Make it specific and show the world that we are the victims, under attack from an out of touch majority. Remember, Christianity started with a few followers, didn't it, and so it takes time. Use that energy, especially with the young. My God, Tik Tok is packed full of consumers just waiting for a new meaning to their pointless lives. Fuck me half of them think they are autistic or LGBTQ or some such shit, so let's give them what they really want. A purpose, a flag to stand behind."

"Well, err..."

"And Diversity, Equity and Inclusion? You met with our consultants, I trust."

"Err, yes, but I didn't expect it to cost so much."

"Well, quality doesn't come cheap."

"Of course, I see that, but, to be completely honest with you Oscar, it's actually causing more division in our work place, not less. Now everyone is complaining about micro-aggressions, and making grievances about each other every other day and even lunch times are much more segregated now. We never had that problem before, everyone just sat with whoever, but now the atmosphere is actually quite unpleasant" said Brett, desperately.

"It's just teething problems. Look trust me on this Brett. It is the new road-map to success, so just continue denouncing anyone who disagrees with the progressive agenda, sack anyone who won't use their pronouns, keep the pressure on. Show your side that you are not only listening to them but you are it's new leaders."

"But I just want to sell sausages Oscar."

"And you will. But you must remember, everything is ethical right now and investors get very nervous about loans if they think you might be on the wrong side of the argument."

"Oh, there's no problem with the loan is there?" said Brett, nervously.

"Well, you never know with these things, but if you do as I say, the Fund Managers will love you and green light whatever money you want. In the end, it's just good business."

"Well if you're sure?"

"I'm more than sure. Look, to put your mind at rest, I'll send one of our best DEI consultants over to you next week, Kike Crenberg. She was on Dr Phil recently, and wiped the floor with a right wing Podcaster, she's completely brilliant and this time, I'll only charge you the normal rate."

"What's that again, I forget."

"$30,000 for the day. Oh damn, someone has just walked in Brett, so I'll have to dash. Talk later, ciao," said Oscar promptly ending his call before looking up at the three large Vampires who had just walked into his office.

"Fucking twitchy yanks, how we ever got turned over by them, I'll never know. Ah, Rory, Chester, Samuel, here at last. Took your time, I texted you six hours ago."

"Carswell wanted us to drain a couple of homeless guys for a party tonight, sir."

"It's Lady Carswell to you."

"Err, sorry Sir" said Chester.

"Homeless? that's a bit low rent for her isn't it?" said Oscar.

"COVID sir."

"Okay, but as I said, I don't want her to know about any of this, so make sure, when she talks to you, you block your minds just the way I showed you."

"Sir" said all three in unison.

"Good. So, our target will be Lucius Noble," said Oscar, as he began to open a folder on his desk.

"The footballer, sir?" said Chester, a little surprised.

"Yes."

"Oh, that's a shame I quite like him," said Samuel.

"Yeah he's a Lege. Did you see that goal he scored last week against Liverpool?" said Rory.

"It was sick bruv and the celebration afterwards? Epic!" said Samuel clapping his hands together.

"Are we finished?" snapped Oscar, looking up from his desk.

"Err, sorry sir," said all three again, this time, lowering their heads towards the floor of the office.

"Lucius Noble is an enemy of everything the Brotherhood of Blood stands for. He is like the first rays of dawn on our flesh, a sword in our heart. Do you understand?" said Oscar, leaning forward menacingly in his chair.

"Sir. Got a bit carried away, sir," said Chester, placing his hands behind his back.

"Because it would be an awful shame to take away all those lovely privileges of being the Private Bodyguard of the Chief Imperator wouldn't it? And suddenly, you find yourselves back in the same Essex sewer, I found you in. Good. So have we scoped the location?" said Oscar, satisfied he had made his point, before looking down at his folder again.

"Err yes we did. It's all been spec'd out. But question sir."

"Yes, Chester."

"Why will it take four of us?"

"Because he is a Lycan."

"A Lycan?" said all three in amazement.

"Yes, that a problem?" asked Oscar, not raising his eyes from his desk and still studying the contents of his folder.

"No sir. But surely, a Lycan wouldn't take all of us, would it?" said Chester, probing further and now a little confused.

"He is enhanced, from the Benin Pack," replied Oscar, casually.

"The Benin Pack?! But I thought they'd all been wiped out in the last Lycan war, sir."

"So did I Chester, but one remains."

"Err, okay. It's just I've heard a few stories about the Benin Pack, sir," said Chester, now a lot less certain, while Rory and Samuel gave each other an anxious glance.

"Afraid?" said Oscar, looking up with a grin.

"Err, well, no sir," said all three.

"Well you should be. The Benin Pack, were the cream of the Lycan breed. Fast, immensely strong and very clever. Only Lady Carswell and Hector before he left, could lay a glove on them, so we don't want any mistakes," continued Oscar.

"No sir," said Chester, firmly.

"Yeah, suppose it can't be that hard, can it? End of the day. Still only a Lycan, ain't he?" said Rory, slowly warming to the task.

"Yeah, and we can give the hairy scumbag a proper dig, for all the crap they give us half the time."

"I'm afraid, it will be more than that Samuel. He has to die," said Oscar, lacing his fingers together, in front of him.

"Die?! But won't that start a new war sir? Keevan won't stand for it, surely," said Chester, stepping forward from his two colleagues and looking increasing alarmed.

"Don't worry about Keevan, he has as much to lose as the rest of us. Lucius is dangerous and he has to go. There's no other way" said Oscar, easing back in his chair to indicate that the meeting was over, before the three Vampires nodded their heads and quickly departed the room

*

"Oh, its so wonderful to have you back among us again," declared Lady Carswell, as she strode down the steps of the Great Hall to kiss both of Hector's cheeks before directing him to a seat at the highest table of the Vampire Council.

"It's always been here, always empty, waiting for your return."

"Full of mischief as usual Dierdra, You never change," said Hector, with a wry smile.

"It's true! The chair has always been there. Tell him Oscar. Oh what a brute," protested Lady Carswell turning in mock outrage towards her Lover for confirmation.

"It's true Count of La Mejorada, ever since you sadly left us 50 years ago."

"Well I am touched and it's Hector, you don't always have to massage my posterior, Oscar."

"I would never dream of it," said Oscar, with a slippery grin, before they all took a seat and the Vampire Leader began to speak again.

"So you're back my darling Hector, what fun. And what brings you out of isolation, may I ask? Much has changed, you know."

"Yes I heard the Beatles are no longer together. I was in Cordoba, Dierdra, not Mars," said Hector leaning back in his chair.

"But I know how you go to ground when things are not to your liking. I can never forget how upset you were after I intervened with the Paris Commune in 1871."

"Well maybe it was just my little aversion to 30,000

people being slaughtered in the streets for wanting a fairer society."

"Ah, always so sensitive, it's what I love about you, Hector. But enough of the past, spill the beans. What has really brought you back?" said the Vampire Leader with an impish grin.

"Oh, nothing in particular. Just seemed like a good time. The wind is changing, and I felt I needed to be back amongst my own again."

"And we are overjoyed to have you. Ah, the Council will be abuzz with such gossip once again. The Great Thinker has returned. And yes, you are right, things are changing and your advice will be needed now more than ever."

"Well, you always have things under such good control Dierdra, but of course, if I can assist in any way, I will be more than happy to help. However, for the present, I am a little weary from my travels. Is my apartment still here?" said Hector, suddenly rising from his seat.

"Just as you left it. Kaspar, take the Count to his quarters, and attend to his every need. Make the Legend welcome in our midst once more" said Carswell, turning to stare in the direction of a heavily set guard, before Hector bowed his head to the Chief Imperator, and left the table.

"What the hell is he back for? This is the last thing we need right now," hissed Oscar, as the doors of the Great Hall closed and the two Vampires were alone again.

"He is re-rejuvenated, I sense new life in him. We must keep a close eye, Oscar, but use discretion. Hector is one of the 7 Elite, so be very careful."

"He looks older to me."

"He no longer lives in your heart, my love?"

"Don't remind me, I was very young and he had more hair."

"Such ingratitude. But do not dismiss him so quickly, my sweet. He is powerful, beyond even your ken and he has come back for something; I can see it in his eyes."

"Don't worry, I will make sure he doesn't get up to anything."

"Excellent, and our little friend, Lucius the Lycan?"

"Oh you know?" said Oscar, taking a step back, and unable to mask his surprise that his little subterfuge had been uncovered.

"Of course. I read the thought's of your little Gang. You didn't think your mind block would work, did you? Like all men, you under-estimate me, my dearest love. So, he is Tamur's son. Well, it took all I had to kill the father, the son will be just as difficult. Is Keevan on board?"

"He knows," said Oscar, lowering his head.

"Excellent. The world has very little time for romantics, and Keevan was always a pragmatist. Oh and in future, Oscar, please don't lie to me, you know how much it disappointments," said Carswell, coldly, before stepping forward to grab her lover's shirt and press her mouth against his lips.

For the next few nights, as instructed, an army of Oscar's informants, both Vampire and Familiar, dogged his every move, and as a consequence, Hector led them on a merry dance around London, as he caught up with old friends or leafed through rare manuscripts in the British Library in the early hours of the morning. Gradually, all of his trackers revealed themselves to him and so one by one he hypnotized them to tell their master that all was well and "The old man" was just catching up with the new century, after his long absence. In reality, this was not too far from the truth, as Hector's eyes now sparkled with wonder, at the sudden transformation of the Ancient City, and like the great actor it had always been, London was now relishing its new role at the centre of a globalized world. So many languages, so many different faces. Gone was the grey homogeneity of the past and it would indeed, now be a pleasure to spend some time in the home of John Dee and William Blake.

However, for the moment, this delight would have to wait, and so making very sure that he wasn't being followed again, Hector made his way to a suburb in North London, to perch on the roof of a terraced house and stare in at a bedroom opposite.

"So here I am Colin. Tell me to my face that I'm a second-rate chimpanzee. We're all alone now. Don't be shy."

"I'm sorry," blurted out Colin.

"Too predictable asshole. You're a racist, troll, aren't you? A fucking useless bully, who's shitty life means that you want to infect everyone else with your disgusting misery. Fortunately, your abuse, means nothing to me, but you have been persecuting my brethren Colin. Black footballers, black singers, black MPs, probably even the next door's dog because he isn't white enough. I have traced your accounts, very clever to register abroad, but not clever enough my dear little bigot, but now you are going to die" replied Lucius producing a chloroform-soaked handkerchief from behind his back and pressing it over the face of his victim. In seconds Colin's body went limp, and quickly walking across the room to pull a belt from a pair of jeans lying on the floor the Werewolf was just about to wrap it around the skinny neck of the young man, when a familiar scent, made him quickly turn his head and scowl.

"Vampire!"

"Do you think, it will hold?" asked Hector, looking towards the hook on the back of the bedroom door.

"They usually do," said Lucius, casually before returning to his gruesome task.

"So this is not your first?"

"It's my fourth. What do you want Bloodsucker? I told your friend, Oscar to keep out of my business."

"Oscar? Oh he's no friend of mine. By the way, my compliments on your transformation, Lycan. In fact, it reminded me of... but they are sadly all gone now."

"Not all."

"You are of the Benin Pack? How? I saw you Father perish in..." said Hector, his eyes now widening in genuine shock.

"I am his son."

"My God. Tamur had a son? Of course, this makes sense, now. Your father was a great leader, I remember him well. You have his strength and fury."

"What do you want old man," said the Werewolf, wincing at the sound of his father's name, while he continued to drag the body towards the door.

"Nothing in particular. Just here to observe. Pray, what is the reason for this random homicide? Lycans are rarely so psychopathic."

"He's a troll, sending filth to Singers and Actors, so I decided to show him where his words can lead."

"Protecting celebrities? Surely, that's not your style, Lucius?"

"Life has consequences. But fear not, Vampire, it's not just about race, the other three I killed organised pile ons, got people fired for no reason, ruined lives."

"Everything has to be paid for?"

"Exactly."

"I have a dear friend, who is doing the same. Killing white middle class liberals, would you believe? You should meet. You'd make quite a team."

"Is he a Demon?"

"Yes."

"Then I'll pass."

"Well, at least, let me help. I will hold the head, while you pull on his legs" said Hector as Colin hung on the back of the door and started thrash about wildly for a minute or so, until the life finally departed his fluorescent pink body.

"Do you feel better now?"

"Very. What do you want Vampire?" asked Lucius again, placing his hands on his hips.

"Hector, please."

"Hector? The Spanish Scourge?"

"At your service."

"You killed many of my kind," said the Werewolf, backing away slightly, now with a little less assurance in his voice.

"Only in defence, I was an unwilling soldier in a pointless war."

"Of course, you parasites are never the victims are you? Anyway, I thought you'd disappeared, gone to ground," said Lucius, regaining his poise.

"I had. But I always make an appearance when things get interesting and you are very interesting."

"Glad, I entertain", said the Lycan, with a wry smile.

"I want to help. What you are doing is radical."

"Frankly, I couldn't care less what you think, Bloodsucker. You stink of the Elite. I have nothing to say to someone like you," said Lucius suddenly, unconvinced by Hector's words and preparing to leave the bedroom.

"But I was born a poor Jew."

"Well suck it up muthafucka. I was born black," said Lucius, turning around again.

"So you get more points?"

"Much more."

"A competition then?"

"It's the only one, we can win."

"Are you sure? Try Hadrian wiping out half a million of my people in the First Century" said Hector with a grin.

"Try the Atlantic slave trade."

"The Expulsion of Jews from Spain."

"Jim Crowe."

"The Russian Progroms."

"Lynching."

"Auschwitz."

"What about Israel?" said Lucius folding his arms.

"Ah, a terrible nightmare. The Palestinians deserve a home, but then so do the Jews. I sometimes, think it was a pity that the Promised Land wasn't located somewhere in Antarctica or Idaho, then we may have peace. However, let us not argue over impossible problems, last of the Benin Pack. So, like your father, you make waves. What does Keevan say about this?" said Hector, with a warm smile.

"He says nothing."

"The Lycan Overlord does not approve?"

"He says I'm a heretic."

"The good ones often are. That's why I am here to help."

"Help? Don't make me laugh. Vampires only help themselves."

"But you know of my reputation?"

"They say you are just. They say, my father thought well of you," said the Lycan lowering his head, less sure now, as he was reminded of his dead father once more.

"And I of him. Look, you may not believe this, but we are on the same side Lucius. You must let me help," repeated Hector.

"Oh, like you helped my father, when Carswell, tore his throat out. I know the stories," said Lucius, baring his teeth in fury.

"We were at war, my boy. These things are beyond our control. Your father would have done the same, if it was me. You see this is why we must join together to stop the Carswell's and the Keevans causing more conflict, more misery and bring real change to this world. You have made great strides, Lucius, and you will make many more. I sense your power. But there are great dangers out there for you, right now. More than you know. Therefore, I implore you with every beat of my corrupted heart; let me help you?" said Hector, now with his arms almost outstretched, as the young Lycan stared back with uncertain eyes.

However, the fury in his blood, overtook him again and scowling "Then get out of my way," he barged past Hector and through the bedroom window, leaving the Vampire with a sudden sense of dread in his heart.

CHAPTER FOURTEEN

Even after all this time, Terry still couldn't shake it, and like a hopeless addict stumbling through the streets looking for one more score, he found himself, inexorably, drawn back towards her door again. In fact it had been the worst aspect of his return to London, and despite Hector's intercession on his behalf, having his year-long ban reduced to 3 months, staring across now from a roof at midnight, for probably the sixth or seventh time in ten days, it actually made him wish that he'd stayed in the woods with the Ascetics, rather than endure any more of this awful pain. Why was lost love such a hellish force? Shredding your mind, destroying your reason, imprisoning your soul? No sane creator could have devised such despair, thought the Vampire, as he scrolled through her unanswered texts for probably the thousandth time and prayed for some kind of release.

"Why aren't you answering me?!"

"What have I done wrong? Are you ghosting me?!"

"I love you and now you have broken my heart. You won't answer me. So everything you said was a lie. Goodbye you *fucking prick.*"

She never cursed, well at least not on text. Something to do with her strict Jamaican upbringing she'd always said, so when she called him a "fucking prick" he knew it was over. He had ceased all contact to save her life and as a reward, he would now be hated and forgotten forever. Erased from the record. Yesterday's man or Vampire if he was to be completely accurate. Of course, women were masters at this, as only men mingled with the ghosts of their past looking for redemption and some trace of hope, while to compound his misery even more, Terry now also discovered that she had found a replacement. Handsome, tall, he looked like fun, plus he was black. Maybe she'd had enough of whiteness. A plague on the world, thought the Vampire, smiling sourly to himself, as he watched the couple kiss under a lamp-post and felt like a miserable stalker again, as the jealousy poured through his veins like a polluted stream. The agony was exquisite, and as he slunk down the side of the house and heard the door of his ex-lover's house slam shut with all of it's erotic promise, he vowed to himself once more, that this would be the very last time. However, deep in his splintered heart, he knew he'd be back, and so accepting his fate for the moment, at least, he climbed reluctantly onto his bike and headed north. Thankfully, there was little traffic on the roads and so Terry made good time, driving towards his new home, a studio flat in Warren Street that a friend of Hector had lent him, and he was just about to take a left off the river towards the Strand, when out of his peripheral vision, he noticed a figure standing alone on the ledge of Blackfriars Bridge.

"Err, you okay mate?" asked Terry, now pulling his bike beside the kerb of the pavement, and looking up at a young man in his mid twenties with a well trimmed beard.

"Oh yeah, err hi."

"Think the stop for the night bus might be across the road" said the Vampire with a grin, as the young man gripped tighter onto the lamp-post standing by the side of the bridge and returned a polite smile.

"Erm, yeah, I'm okay actually."

"You look it. Smoke?"

"Err no."

"Bad for your health innit?"

"Err, yeah," said the young man, returning a nervous laugh.

"Mind if I do?"

"Err, no."

"Cool."

"Look, seriously, I'm okay, you don't need to worry about me. You probably need to be somewhere, yeah?" said the young man, with nervous concern.

"S'okay, I've got some time" said Terry now looking anxiously at the night sky, and sensing the onset of the dreaded dawn in his nostrils, also added "So what you doing up there then?"

"Well…"

"Things not going too well?" persisted Terry.

"Erm…"

"It's okay," said Terry, turning to glance over the side of

the bridge at the river sliding past in the darkness below, before the young man punctured the brief silence and started to talk again.

"Well, it's all just shit isn't it?"

"Fucking too right. Makes me wanna top myself sometimes. Err, sorry. Stupid joke," said Terry raising his hand in contrition.

"It's okay. Even brushed my teeth before I came out."

"Did you? That's funny. So what's your name, then?"

"Joshua."

"Cool, I'm Terry. So what's occurring then Joshua? Why the high wire nocturnal stroll by the river? You a poet or something, plumbing the depths of your soul?"

"Ha, no."

"So what's going on then?"

"Err I dunno, it's just, err, well it's mental isn't it? Like they tell us all the time, to be kind and open and all that, but then when we are, they… Oh, fuck, I can't really explain it. Look please, please leave me alone, please go."

"I will in minute, but just let me finish my fag. So who's "they" then?" asked Terry, looking up at the young man again.

"Oh you know. Parents, friends, Social Media, my girlfriend. Its really difficult, you know."

"Always wanting more?" interrupted the Vampire.

"Well, yeah."

"Lot of pressure?"

"Definitely."

"Like a big fucking tick list."

"Completely. Like I know I'm privileged and all that, and I should be grateful. Had good parents, nice home, great school and I didn't have the start that some people have, you know like you see online, with abuse, drugs, and being in care."

"But you're still human, yeah?"

"Exactly. I mean I even did what I was told. Got the GCSE's, A Levels, went to a Russell Uni, you know got the 2:1. But then when I graduated, there was nothing. Applying for job after job, and then I ended up working in a clothes shop, which don't get me wrong is great, and obviously I don't look down on anyone doing that kind of work, I mean, it's really important, look at the supermarket staff during the Pandemic."

"But you don't wanna just work in a clothes shop, for the rest of your life, do you?" interrupted the Vampire.

"That's right!"

"And that's not even the half of it Pal."

"What do you mean?" said Joshua, letting go of the lamp-post for a minute.

"Your generation is basically fucked. Can't buy a house, gonna earn way less than your parents, can't get in a fight without getting stabbed, dating is terrible, and nothing is gratis anymore. You know in my day Tapas was free, now it costs a tenner a pop. Even your drugs are kiboshed, because some dick puts Fentanyl in your Charlie without you knowing, making you OD', when you just want a good night out. Plus to top it all, the Boomers and Gen Xers, who spent all day giving you Participation Trophies and not letting you play out on the streets now turn around and call you useless bastards, cos you can't deal with the shit world that they fucking invented and didn't prepare you for in the first place."

"Yes! Yes! That's it. You're so right. We are fucked. The

Pandemic, the climate, no decent jobs, everything costs a bomb. It's awful. God, I wish I was born in the Nineties. It was so much better then. Tarantino, P J Harvey, Massive Attack? I mean what do we have now? Marvel movies and Billie Eilish? My generation is so shit."

"Oi, not so fast, Josh. Okay your generation might be a bit off when it comes to Culture, but you don't get the Renaissance every day, do you? That was a really creative time, mate. Probably only happens once every 200 years, if that. Remember. Comparison is the thief of Joy."

"Oh, that's really good. Who said that?"

"Theodore Roosevelt."

"Who's he?"

"The bassist in Nirvana. Anyway mate, I'm not buying this bullshit. You're not gonna jump into the river over the Nineties are ya? What's really up?" asked Terry with a knowing smile.

"Err, well, yeah, you're right. It's not really that" said the young man lowering his head.

"Thought so. Go on," encouraged the Vampire folding his arms,

"Well, thinking about it now, it's kind of silly. But, well, I really like JK Rowling yeah? You know the Harry Potter author. I mean I read all of her books when I was young, seen all the films, but then a lot of my friends I do stuff with, you know people who are into Social Justice and all that, think she is really Transphobic, and, of course, I can see what they are saying and all that but I also think that she's entitled to her opinion, yeah? And as far as I can see, all she is really saying is that sex is a biological and women are not "People who bleed", or "Cervix havers", which I think is a bit insulting, if I'm being honest. I mean I seriously looked through all of her tweets and I couldn't find anything that was hateful and even when I asked some of my Trans friends, they just said she was and if I wanted to be an ally, I should accept their lived experience and leave it at that; which didn't make much sense to me. I mean ideas should be based on facts, yeah? and we should be able to listen to opposing views, right? So anyway one night, I got drunk and shared a tweet that JK Rowling posted about biological men in women's sport and how it can be unfair, as they've gone through puberty and all that, which I thought was fair comment, but then I got piled on by everyone else, who called me Transphobic and evil and started to super-impose pictures of Boris Johnson and Donald Trump on my head and even Hitler, and then when I started to argue back, it just got worse and they sent my posts to the company I worked for who a few days later sacked me, which I didn't really mind because I hated the job anyway, but now my girlfriend has left me too, and it's a joke. I mean, you read about things like this online don't you? Ganging up on someone and ruining their life and, if I'm being truthful, I even did it, once or twice myself, but then when it happens to you, it's really bad."

"Bit of payback?" said Terry, smiling as he remembered that Maxwell had very recently, after the case of Professor Kathleen Stock being forced to leave Sussex University because of her Gender Critical views, completely changed her mind about the whole Trans debate and as a result, on a very popular You Tube channel, whilst wearing a T-Shirt emblazoned with "Adult Human Female" on the front, which is the dictionary definition of a woman, offered a

Rothko painting, valued at £70 million, to anyone who could prove that JK Rowling was transphobic, and as yet there had been no takers.

"Yeah I suppose," replied the young man lowering his head again.

"Actually, I think you should jump," said the Vampire with a deadpan face, as the young man now looked back a little betrayed, before Terry assured him that he was only joking and then reached out his hand to guide him down to the pavement.

"You ever notice, the biggest bullies, have their pronouns under their names," said Terry leaning his back against the side of the bridge before gazing up at the night sky.

"And taglines like be kind," said Joshua.

"Classic. You just need to forget them son."

"But you don't understand Terry. These days you can't. It's like it's everywhere you go, like a mark on your face that says you're unclean, a bad person."

"What? Because some wankers canceled you from their whats app group?"

"It's way more than that. You don't understand. My life is literally over."

"It is fuck. How old are you?"

"25."

"Jesus that's nothing. I'm a lot older than you."

"You don't look it."

"Well, trust me I am and when I grew up, me and my brothers and sisters couldn't care less, because we weren't the most important thing in the house, know what I mean. Food was, paying the rent was, making sure the range didn't go out"

"The range? What's that?"

"Like a cooker. Look, the point is Joshua, from what I can see, guys your age were always the most important thing in the house and it turned you into little Princes and Princesses. Problem is, life is hard, mate."

"Oh God, not that again. We're all snowflakes?! Yeah right. We don't spend all of our days eating avocado on toast you know?" said the young man, suddenly losing his temper and stepping away from the bridge.

"You sure about that sunshine? You were just about to top yourself, because some scumbags said something that made you feel bad. Mate, you can't go through life without being insulted, or feeling uncomfortable or unsafe, whatever the hell that means. Point is, there's always been bullies. It's what humans do, they fucking love it. You just gotta fight back. I mean these are the same pricks who say babies are racist"

"Yeah, I saw that in the Metro the other day. It's a bit fucked up, isn't it?" said Joshua, walking back to the side of the bridge again.

"And the rest. They call themselves Progressives, but they're the opposite. They're Regressives. You know the easiest dogs to train are the clever ones, yeah? It's group think. On a major scale your generation is dying from bullshit Joshua. Bullshit, risk averse parenting and politeness is literally killing you mate."

"So what do I do?"

"Leave home for a kick off. You still live with your parents, yeah?"

"With my mum," said the young man, nodding his head.

"Then leave."

"But I cant afford to. It's not that easy, you know. I don't have any money and you need loads to get a deposit, and there's nowhere to rent and…" continued Joshua, as he tried to explain his circumstances to Terry, but the Vampire had already zoned out from the predictable excuses and suddenly realizing it was getting very late and not wanting to end up as a pile of ashes, he quickly threw his cigarette into the river and turned his head to stare directly into the young man's eyes.

"Be at peace Joshua, you are a good man, and so believe this. Life is shit most of the time and what's more it couldn't care less if you fucking lived or died. So deal with it. Welcome the obstacles. In fact run towards them and hug them like your best friend. We need adversity. It gets us out of bed in the morning. Think of what people did years ago. Like the Irish when they first got to New York in the 1850's, 10 to a tiny room, or those from the Caribbean, when they arrived in London in the 1950's, called all the names under the sun. They made it through. Everything is possible. You'll find a way, humans always do. In the end, all you really need is courage Joshua, it's our greatest quality and it brings you the most happiness. Oh and while we're at it, can you tell your generation to stop saying, "It's amazing" and "I'm honored" or being fucking humble all the time. It gets really annoying. Forget all that crap. Remember you're not a Yank, you're British, so (a) Stop taking things so literally all the time, (b) Have a bit of swagger now and again and (c) Just take the piss. Life's a lot more fun, that way"

"Yeah, okay, cool. I totally get it now. Fucking hell I feel brilliant now, err, no forget that, it's too much isn't it? Yeah I'm good, just good, that's all I need to say, isn't it? My God, my God, that's it. Just believe in yourself and forget all the haters. I don't know how to thank you Terry, you've really helped me. Definitely. Wow, you saved me, you don't realize how much, you saved me," declared Joshua, joyously jumping around for a few seconds before stepping forward to give the Vampire, an enormous hug.

"Well, okay, that's good, glad to help, happy you're sorted now. Oh and while we're at it, don't be going online looking for me, with all that "I was saved by a stranger" bollocks, that you see in the papers now and again. That's only looking for approval from the same bastards who nearly killed you tonight. Remember Josh, every piece of generosity doesn't have to be shown to the world, okay? Charity should always be anonymous, not for self advancement, know what I mean? So just be thankful, that I've helped you and then quietly pass it on to someone else, you know, if you ever get the chance. Okay?"

"Err yeah, okay?" said the young man, a little confused.

"Not okay. I mean it, Josh. Don't tell the world about tonight. This is just for you alright? Trust me, it's so much better that way. I'm serious mate?"

"Okay, I get it. I will definitely just keep it to myself." confirmed the young man, a little taken aback by the sudden firmness in his savior's voice

"Well see that you do. Right then, I'm off. Be lucky lad. Oh and do me a favor, will ya? In future, keep the fuck away from bridges at 4 in the morning. Some of us have to get home before sun comes up, know what I mean," said Terry climbing onto his bike and then with a big smile and a wave of his hand, quickly sped off in the direction of Warren Street.

*

"You know I still remember my first block party. Yes I was in my mid-twenties and like, most of my peers, I was simply blown away by Outkast and Dr Dre and the whole Hip Hop scene. Yes scene, we did say that back then, and, of course, because I was a nice white girl from the "Burbs", I had no knowledge at all of black people. I had only grown up amongst my own kind, i.e. white people, with maybe some Latinx, here and there, but these were usually gardeners or house cleaners, so as a result when I encountered black people for the first time at this gathering in Ohio, I was actually quite terrified and literally told every story about my racist parents that I could think of, to try and assimilate myself into my new environment. How pathetic. Trying to show I wasn't racist and, in the process, showing just how racist I really was. Now this story may be familiar to a lot of people here, and if it is, it should tell you that whatever we do, however we act, white people are irredeemably racist. It is baked into our very DNA. It is present from the moment we wake up to the moment we fall asleep and…"

"But Beverley, that cannot be true for everyone, can it? I mean, of course, racism is awful, but not every white person is racist, surely?" interrupted a black woman from the front row.

"And here we see white fragility in it's most reasonable form. I'm sorry and I'm sure you are a perfectly nice person, but the fact that you challenge something as obvious as systemic white supremacy shows just how bigoted you really are."

"But, excuse me, I am actually a person of color?!" protested the woman, before looking around the audience, increasingly confused.

"Are you? Are you really? I think a true person of color would understand how the system has disabled them for centuries. A true person of color would see that white supremacy has many allies within people of color themselves, who have internalized their own racism and instead, become apologists for the very tyranny itself. A true person of color would know that the idea of the melting pot or Dr King's idea of judging people by their personality and not the color of their skin is actually a way to control people of color. You know I used to be very conciliatory to any push back against my ideas, especially from members of minority groups or poor people, but now that time is past, I'm afraid. In fact, I'm tired of pandering to liberal arguments, tired of trying to explain my position to well- intentioned, misguided fools, who just want us all to go along to get along. My friends, like the black community searching for justice for 400 years and coming up short, every time, frankly, I'm just tired. So, for those, who are still unsure, here's the deal. Look inside yourself and ask this question. Are you helping the oppressor or are you helping the oppressed? It's really just as simple as that" declared Beverley Di Franco raising her hands in the air and smiling as everyone in audience, except her previous questioner, who remained in her seat shaking her head, then immediately got to their feet and started to clap wildly.

"How the fuck did she go to a house party in Ohio in her mid-twenties? That would have meant it was about 1650. Don't think Dr Dre was making records then, bro."

"She got that story off a white woman in a struggle session, before she bled her dry in the car-park. She's a genius," said Jamaal, standing in the wings and casually bringing his hands together, while Errol looked on a little unimpressed.

"You don't think it's a bit much, then?"

"Ain't nearly enough, bruv. The system is creaking and like brother Gramsci said, once you take over the Institutions, get the Culture on your side, boom, you have all the power. De long walk to paradise, Rastaman. We got the Universities, the Media and since the end of Trump, we got the Government too. Look at Biden, in America, recently? You think, it's a co-incidence, the first thing he did was overturn the ban on Critical Race Theory? Everything is captured geezer. It's gonna be our time."

"Yeah but it's all about victimhood Jamaal. Can't see how that helps a black man? Telling him he's never gonna get ahead," said Errol, shaking his head.

"Preach that to George Floyd."

"Yeah I get it, but you know, I think it's getting a bit silly now. The other day, I saw a demonstration in London on the news, and they were shouting "Hands up don't shoot!", you know like they do in America, but our Old Bill, have only got truncheons. What's that about?"

"It's just frustration, bro'. People are frustrated by all

the bullshit," said Jamaal, placing his hands behind his back.

"I know, but even what happened to George Floyd, it happens to white guys too, you know. In fact, I've been reading this thing online about a bloke called Tony Timpa, you ever heard of him?"

"Nah."

"Me neither, but he was white and a couple of years ago, he died in exactly the same way as George Floyd did, but you know nothing was said."

"So, who cares about one cracker. Black men are getting killed all the time, Errol."

"I know that, but most of the time, it's usually by other Black men innit?"

"Because the system, fucks them up, yeah? You know how it works?"

"Of course, I do, but sometimes, maybe we should sit back and have another think about it all, you know?"

"What is there to think about?" said Jamaal, cocking his head to one side.

"Well, for a start. Why don't we get BLM, marching all day, when thirty black blokes get shot in Chicago over a weekend, hey? There only seem to do it, if someone white is involved. Just seems a bit wrong, that's all and in this same article, I was reading, they talked about the deaths of black men by the Police. Do you know how many unarmed black people are killed by the Police every year in the America?" said Errol, brightly, now warming to his subject.

"Probably thousands."

"That's what I thought. But it's less than 30. I couldn't

believe it. Apparently, this Black Professor called Roland Fryer wrote a paper about it and…"

"Fuck Roland Fryer, who the hell is he anyway? Probably some Oriel, who doesn't know he's black bro'. Look, there's only one side in this war, yeah?" said Jamaal, finally losing his patience, to stare menacingly into the eyes of his Spirit Son.

"Well, yeah of course. I was just telling you about what I'd read, that's all," said Errol, shrinking back from the violence in Jamaal's voice.

"It's all white supremacist propaganda put about by Fox News and Tucker Carlson to weaken the Black man. You need to watch what you're reading, Errol. You get me?" said Jamaal, holding the stare for another few seconds.

"Yeah sure," said Errol, nodding his head before lowering his gaze in submission.

"Good. Anyway stop looking like you're gonna burst into tears and help me get Beverley through this crowd before they try and kiss her to death," said Jamaal with a grin, now turning to walk away, while Errol's eyes remained stuck to the floor, unconvinced, until the sound of more applause from the auditorium, brought him around again and then rubbing the side of his face with his hand, he moved towards the stage again.

CHAPTER FIFTEEN

Terry sucked harder on his cigarette, as he began to read the top two headlines from the news website

The first told of the sudden disappearance of Lucius Noble, who had not been seen since scoring a hat-trick in the semi final of the Champions League while the second dealt with Joshua Norton, a 25-year-old graduate, who had recently tried to end his life on Blackfriars Bridge, only to be saved by a "Good Samaritan on a Delivery scooter", and now wanted to track him down and thank him personally.

"Of course, he did," scowled the Vampire, disappointed but not altogether surprised at the actions of the young man he had helped the previous week. However, the lack of integrity from another Gen Z'er, was the last thing on Terry's mind as he rose from the table to pour himself a drink. Lucius Noble had been missing for five days now, without a word to anyone, and more troubling still, there had been no posts on his Social Media accounts, which considering the amount of time the Footballer spent on Twitter and Tik Tok, waging a daily war against the hypocrisies of the status quo, was concerning to say the least. Needless to say, his club issued numerous pleas for their star player to get in touch, as did a small number of his team-mates who were still on speaking terms with him, while the Mainstream Media, could hardly contain their glee at the temporary departure of their long time nemesis. Headlines like "Let's pray for his swift return" and "Please come back to us, Lucius" complete with photographs of little boys and girls holding up pictures of the sporting superstar boomed out from all the front pages for the next few days, whilst inside these publications, rumours of "struggling with depression", and "possible drug issues", began to spread. Of course, this was a standard tactic from the scribes of the Oligarchs, using whispers and innuendo from "a credible source" to question the reputation of a popular figure who was not completely onside with the beliefs of the Establishment, before setting them up for the final plunge of the knife. It stunk of Carswell and Oscar, who's tentacles, Terry knew, stretched deep into the corridors of power and therefore, as far as he was concerned, the situation was starting to look very bad indeed. Unsurprisingly, Hector came to a similar conclusion and had been texting Terry on an almost hourly basis since the vanishing, until finally, he requested that they meet by the river, just after sunset.

"Apologies for asking you here, my dear friend. How are you, by the way?" asked the older Vampire walking to the side of the Embankment with a look of deep anxiety on his face.

"Good."

"Excellent. Yes, this Lucius business is extremely concerning, and so I have arranged a dialogue with Keevan tonight. Will you come?" said Hector, with an expectant smile.

"The Lycan Overlord? Why him? Surely he can't help?"

"Lucius is a Lycan."

"What?!"

"Yes, from the Benin Pack."

"My God! I thought they'd all been wiped out," said Terry, slightly shocked.

"One remained, the son of Tamur."

"Jesus, I never knew he was a Lycan."

"I sensed it straight away, when I saw him talk on Spanish television. The anger behind the eyes is impossible to completely mask, and then when I met him, he confirmed my suspicions."

"You met him?"

"Yes, and he was all I anticipated. A new Hampton, but now this. It is troubling indeed, so, I have contacted, Keevan."

"Thought, the Overlord never dealt with Vampires, only Carswell."

"We've known each other for centuries. In fact, he was nearly the end of me, one time in the Black Forest. A stubborn man, but generally honorable and he has agreed to meet. Will you come?" asked Hector, more impatiently this time, and after a quick nod of the head from Terry, the two Vampires quickly marched across Waterloo Bridge towards the huge wheel that stood on the south side of the river.

"This is new," said Hector climbing into one of the pods

and then respectfully bowing to the Werewolf Overlord.

"I thought you would enjoy the drama, Vampire. So I heard you were back. Spanish blood not to your liking then," said Keevan with a grim smile.

"I prefer it to the English. Less chilled."

"Thankfully Lycans are simply warriors, not parasites."

"I think you know Vampires can fight Keevan."

"Ha! Demon, you got lucky that day. If my brother had held his nerve, you'd be ashes by now."

"How is Fionn by the way? Still has the limp?"

"What do you want Spaniard?" snarled Keevan.

"I am here for Lucius."

"Everyone is looking for brother Lucius, isn't that right Bran?" laughed the Lycan Overlord, looking over at the tall figure of his son, standing at the back of the pod.

"You are not concerned?" asked Hector, folding his arms.

"Why should I be? It's a stunt, nothing more. I'll wager you a cohort of my best men that he is in a bar somewhere, enjoying the attentions of a female, foolish enough to listen to all his nonsense. He is more hyena than wolf. Don't worry, he'll re-appear, full of ignorance and rebellion, as usual."

"But he has been missing for a week now," replied Hector with a genuine look of concern on his face.

"And what of it? He is fully grown. I am not his keeper."

"Are you not his Overlord?"

"Lucius goes his own way now. Anyway, what business is it of yours Bloodsucker?"

"I met him once, I liked his ideas."

"His ideas are heresy. He seeks only anarchy and division."

"I think, that is what he is trying to prevent."

"He is foolish and brings shame upon himself and his breed. He says he is fighting for what is right, yet he allies himself with those who would bring us ruin. We asked him to use his celebrity for good, yet all he does is attack the Institutions that make us strong. We begged him to stop, but he would not listen, so we have cut him loose. He is no longer any concern of ours. Lucius only ever thinks of Lucius, he does not want progress."

"Upon my word Keevan, if I didn't know you, I would swear that was Carswell talking, just now," said Hector, throwing his arms out in mock outrage, before Bran suddenly sprang forward to launch an attack. However the older Vampire, easily deflected the ponderous swing of the younger Werewolf, while Terry stepped forward to bare his fangs, and stare down the other Lycan guard.

"My apologies Spaniard. My son has yet to learn how to control himself."

"It's nothing, we were both young once, old friend," said Hector, wiping down his coat.

"But with more sense, I think. But no matter, there is nothing more to say, here. My advice Hector, is not to look for Lucius. He is lost to us now," said Keevan with a little less animosity in his voice, and therefore realizing that nothing more could be learned, the older Vampire bowed his head to the Lycan Overlord, before motioning to Terry for the both of them to leave the pod.

"That wasn't good. Keevan would never cut a fellow Lycan adrift like that, especially the son of his dearest friend. It seems, he has much to lose, and Carswell has infected his mind. I fear something very dark indeed, my friend," said Hector, quickly descending the outside of the wheel, before heading across the river again in the direction of Fulham. The trip over the roof-tops of Chelsea took seconds, and after successfully navigating their way down Dawes Road and through the cemetery, they soon found themselves outside a modest Edwardian house by a large park.

"Hector, oh and Terence as well! What a surprise, how wonderful to see you both. Please come in," exclaimed Oscar opening the door with a look of surprise, before ushering his guests down towards the kitchen at the end of the hallway.

"Thank you Oscar," replied Hector, removing his scarf.

"My pleasure. You should have called ahead, I could have arranged entertainment. Some local girls I know, only too eager to please," said Oscar with a grin.

"No, thank you, we are only here for a short visit."

"Oh quel dommage. And how are you Terence? Well I hope. Trust there won't be a repeat of the previous unpleasantness, last time you were here?"

"Don't worry yourself Oscar. I'm here for Hector," said Terry with a grimace.

"Splendid. Oh, I'm not sure if you've met, but Hector, let me introduce, Errol McKenzie, my work colleague and house-mate."

"Yes, of course. My compliments, Senor McKenzie. Your name has been mentioned to me many times since my return; and congratulations on being elected to the Second Tier of the Vampire Council. And so young."

"Err, thank you," said Errol as he shook the Vampire legend's hand with more than a little embarrassment, before shooting an awkward glance towards Terry, who was standing behind him.

"Yes, Errol is one of our rising stars. He will make us strong in a new progressive future. So Hector, what brings you to our humble abode?" replied Oscar walking out of the kitchen and towards a drink's trolley in the next room.

"We are looking for Lucius Noble," said Hector, as his eyes followed his Spirit Son out of the kitchen.

"Lucius Noble? Now where do I know that name?"

"He's a footballer," scowled Terry, knowing full well that Oscar, being a regular season ticket holder at Chelsea Football Club for many years, knew exactly who Lucius was, and was playing silly mind games as usual.

"Of course. More of rugby man myself, but yes, been missing hasn't he? So what do we think? Someone bitten him? Well nothing to do with me. Steer clear of celebrities as a rule, much too messy. What about you, any dealings?" said Oscar throwing a casual glance towards Errol, as he returned with the drinks.

"Err no, just what I've read online, you know that he's missing," confirmed his housemate.

"Didn't think so. You might try Piers Trevelyan, lives over in Chelsea, loves a celebrity, feasted on Jimi Hendrix and Mama Cass by all accounts."

"Lucius is a Lycan," said Hector, taking his drink.

"Oh really? I didn't know that. Explains why he is so good at the old football, then. Well I could ask around, inform the Vampire Guards, so they can add him to their data base. Don't want a repeat of 1989, do we? Rogue Lycans wiping out Covens and all that nastiness."

"So no sign?"

"Sadly not, Hector. But, why the sudden interest? Just another Lycan who's jumped ship for a few days, isn't he? Probably find him in a forest somewhere, covered in stag's blood or something similar. He hasn't broken the treaty has he? I can get a message to Keevan if you like? I know someone on the inside of the Elite Pack. He's a savage of course, but can be quite reasonable if you catch him in the middle of the month."

"We have just been to see him," said Hector taking a sip from his drink.

"Is that so? I see. Err, did you clear that with Carswell? All contacts between Lycans and Vampires are strictly monitored these days. However, not to worry. You've been away haven't you? Probably didn't realize, but you see, we try not to…"

"Where is Lucius!" bellowed Hector, suddenly throwing his drink against the kitchen wall before reaching forward to grab Oscars face in his huge hands and stare deep into his terrified eyes. For nearly a minute, the two Vampires were locked in this mind meld until screaming at the ceiling, as if in excruciating agony, Hector released his Spirit Son from his grip.

"You dog! You hell hound! What have you done! What have you done?!"

"Look, you are not allowed to search the mind of a First Tier Vampire without getting written permission first. It's a flagrant abuse of power. Mark, you saw this Errol you saw what he…"

"Shut your mouth Oscar, shut your dirty, decadent, devil mouth. You killed him. You killed him. Four nights ago. He fought hard, nearly bested you. A mature Vampire like you is usually more than a match for a Lycan, but you needed help, didn't you? Four of you, he killed two. The last of the Benin pack. What misery, what horror. You have destroyed his line forever. What was his crime Oscar?! What was his crime?!"

"He needed to be silenced," confirmed Oscar, in a more assured voice, as he stepped away from Hector, while straightening his hair with his hand.

"Why?" demanded Hector, now with tears in his eyes.

"Because he wasn't playing the game. We have rules Hector. Those in charge, must stay in charge and…" but before he could complete his sentence, the older Vampire had raised himself up and proceeded to punch Oscar repeatedly in the face. It was a merciless attack, as pitiless blows, soon rained down on the Vampire's body, who, in a desperate bid to defend himself, countered with punches and kicks to the chest and knee, but it was to no avail. Hector was far too strong and Terry, in particular, had never seen his mentor like this. Furious, almost out of control, and at one point he almost considered intervening to stop the increasing bloodshed, before quickly realizing, it would have had absolutely no effect, whatsoever. Hector was the apex predator of apex predators, as even Carswell was wary of him, and so he watched in menacing silence, as bone after bone was snapped, until nearly fifteen minutes of painstaking carnage later, Oscar lay motionless on the floor of the kitchen, and whimpering like a whipped dog.

"I have watched you from afar. You take good words like Equality, Anti Racist, and Social Justice, and pervert them, so they mean nothing in the end. Dogs like you killed my dream in Spain. In Guernica and Malaga, soft boned ideologues caused my people to fight each other so Franco could just walk in and destroy everything. 300,000 Socialists dead and then when you have caused your devastation you move on to incubate yourself in another innocent host. I should kill you Oscar, I should rip your heart out now and drink every last drop of your disgusting blood," cried Hector pulling out a knife from inside his coat and placing the tip over the Vampire's barely beating heart.

"No Hector, don't," shouted Errol and Terry in unison, as for the first time since their own fight some months earlier, they now glanced at each other with something approaching goodwill in their eyes.

"I dare you to complain to Carswell you English scum. I dare you. I curse the day I made you mine," whispered Hector into Oscar's ear, pricking the Vampire's chest with the point of his knife, before quickly returning it to it's sheath.

"Senor McKenzie, you must report this to the Vampire Council, immediately. Attacking a fellow Brother in Blood is a very serious offense and must receive the appropriate sanction," said Hector, now returning to his former calmness, as the faces of the two younger Vampires stared back in complete amazement.

"Don't worry Pal, there's nothing to report here, is there?" said Terry, looking at Errol for a second, and then spending a few seconds to savor the moment, he grinned down into the barely conscious eyes of his old housemate, before grabbing Hector by the arm and marching him out of the kitchen.

CHAPTER SIXTEEN

Outside, the light of the moon, cast long shadows on the pavement, and as Terry drove his bike cautiously along the street, with a delivery for four Enchiladas and a bottle of Sprite, he made very sure to check all the rooftops as he passed by. He'd already had a few fake orders made to his firm, and only two days earlier, he had found a tracking device lodged in the engine of his moped. These were indeed paranoid times, and after the news of Oscar's beating had spread like wildfire through Vampire Society, Bloodsucker now eyed Bloodsucker with extreme suspicion. Unsurprisingly nothing was said. Vampires, especially the older ones, stuck to a very ancient code, so even Oscar, who had every right to place Hector, in some real jeopardy, imprisonment, loss of a finger, or even banishment, had no choice but to let it go. As usual, the familiars who had nursed him, couldn't keep their mouths shut, and by all accounts, Oscar's injuries were so extensive, that it had taken over three days for his wounds to heal, instead of the usual few hours, Vampire's unique DNA would have normally allowed. Of course, to save his fractured pride, Oscar was now telling anyone who would listen, that Hector was obviously suffering from an early onset of "some Vamp Alzheimer's" and therefore like a crazy grandparent you indulged at Christmas, he had let him "beat the shit out of him". It was an admirable spin on events, but fooled no-one, as everyone knew that Hector was in full possession of all his faculties, and therefore the whispered account of his violent encounter with Oscar doing the rounds in the bars and restaurants of polite Vampire Society only increased his legend.

Not that you would know this by looking at him, as for the next few days, in his new residence in Islington, having recently moved out of his apartment in the Great Hall, Hector sat in a large leather armchair and stared impassively into an ancient version of the Talmud for hours on end, looking desperately for some consolation. The death of Lucius had hard hit him hard, and when a few days later the Lycan's body was found hanging from a tree near Manchester, with traces of Fentanyl in his blood, he had screamed obscenities at the fireplace in Hebrew for hours on end, before he withdrew into a brooding silence once more. Another working-class hero had been eliminated by the establishment, and as with Fred Hampton fifty years before, a foul narrative was quickly spun. Drugs, mental health, an unbalanced mind. Only a madman, would live on a basic wage, and not enjoy the fruits of his success, the newspapers continued to murmur, as almost immediately, Vigils were held all over the world in his honor, while his fellow professionals, most of whom had been on the receiving end of constant ridicule from the dead superstar, now raised £20 million in less than two days and donated the money to various well known mental health charities. It was sick to say the least, as even Lucius' fellow Lycans, paid lip service to all the lies, burying their brother, the last of his kind, in an unmarked grave, instead of returning the body to the Benin Pack's ancestral homeland of Nigeria, for a full burial, as suicide was considered the most heinous and unforgivable of crimes in their culture.

Therefore the rancid circle was now complete, and as the months slowly passed and everyone soon forgot about Lucius Noble and his crusade against an unfair society, to be engrossed in yet another Tory scandal or a TV celebrity who'd sent compromising pictures to a much younger assistant, the world, it seemed, was returning to some kind of normality again. Even the perennial paranoia of Vampire Society had dissipated, well for the moment at least, and while a subdued Hector immersed himself in his studies, Terry continued to deliver trendy hamburgers to the bored and hungry masses, until one evening on his way back from a job in Putney, he received an unexpected text on his phone.

"I need to see you now, I miss you."

Lauryn.

It had been over a year since her last text and although, he had managed to stop stalking his former love and finally banished most thoughts of her to the darkest caverns of his mind, the anxious thrum he now felt inside his chest, told him something different. He was still in love with her and so quickly turning the key in his ignition he roared away from the kerb of the pavement to follow the beat of his heart, once more. Of course, it would be dangerous, but as the sharpness of the night-air, filtered underneath his helmet, he decided that he would have to take a chance for both of them, and anyway, as Hector had returned, he might just be able to persuade Carswell to lift his love ban. Anyway that was for another time. "She said she missed me," the Vampire mumbled excitedly to himself and after taking a quick turn off a main road, he soon brought his bike to a stop, outside a two storey house, he knew so well. Now, every cell in his body fizzed with anticipation and so quickly climbing up the side of the building, he successfully slipped the window lock, before finding his way into the bedroom and a soft kiss to end all of his hopeless misery. In the dark, his eyes recognized the familiar shape of her body under the sheets and he was just about to lean forward and whisper "I love you" in her ear, when his hand felt something odd and in a millisecond his entire world came crashing to the floor.

Blood, blood, blood.

It was everywhere, and the sight of such crimson carnage nearly made him topple over in shock, until his eyes were drawn to a huge hole in his lover's neck.

Vampire.

How?!

After his sentence, Lauryn's name had been put on a data base of protected mortals and even when he had been released from Bloodwells, he had made very sure to check and check again with the head of Vampire HR. "Yes, yes, she'll be safe, we've marked her house, in horses' blood, so there's no chance she'll be bitten" she'd said dismissively before returning to organizing some more DEI training for Beverley Di Franco.

No Vampire would dare break this order, as it would mean certain banishment or a long stretch in "The Pit", i.e. solitary confinement in "Bloodwells", thought Terry. In fact, it was the very first thing you did before you went out for a kill and in all his time as a Bloodsucker, he had never heard of anyone on that list being bled by mistake. Never, his thoughts repeated, as he fumbled for his phone and tapped her name into the Vamp App. Yes, there she was, still on the list. Who the hell could have done this? Terry's thoughts now demanded as he paced desperately around the blood splattered room looking for an answer, until his eyes fixed on a National Geographic magazine leaning against a vase, with a picture of a fit and healthy thirty – five-year-old entrepreneur on the front cover.

Oscar.

Lauryn had never bought a magazine in her life, never mind the National bloody Geographic, thought the Vampire and so grabbing the glossy picture of his nemesis and bringing it closer to his face, he instantly detected the unmistakable musk of his former house-mate. Now, his body started to shake in fury, and grabbing his face with both hands, Terry thought his head might explode from all the vengeance in his soul, until realizing Jordan could also be in danger, he quickly ran down towards a room at the end of the corridor, and thrust his head through a doorway. The bed was empty. Thank God, at least he was safe, thought Terry, before making his way back to the main bedroom to glance down at his former lover again. Her neck and stomach had been ripped to shreds and the damage was intense even for a Vampire. Oscar wanted to make a point here, alright. For every blow that he had endured from the fists of Hector, he had given one back, in kind, to Lauryn. However, despite the barbarity of the attack, her face was still at peace. Oscar had not managed to erase that, or maybe the bastard had left it unmarked, simply to increase his agony, thought the Vampire, as he ground his teeth together until his gums started to bleed. However, the sound of distant Police sirens, cut short his agony and thrust him back into reality again and after taking a final, despairing look at Lauryn on her bloodied bed, he slipped out of the bedroom window and away into the night.

For the next few days, Terry remained in a daze, while he listened to the Mainstream Media gleefully analyze the reasons for the brutal death. Male violence, a rise in domestic abuse during Lock down, even the Patriarchy, but despite all the outrage, there would be no "March in the Park" and clashes with the Police over a dead working-class black woman. Three months earlier a white woman from a nice London neighborhood, had been kidnapped and killed and there had been no end of Petitions, Fund-raisers, with thousands attending Vigils all over Capital, while Police cordons were breached and windows smashed in the local Town Hall. Not so for Lauryn and by the weekend, after her boyfriend had been taken in for questioning, the story had been quickly supplanted by a sex scandal in Hollywood.

Of course, after such a crime and his obvious connection to the victim, Terry had faced the inevitable questioning from the Vampire Guards in his flat in Warren Street, who, like the Police arriving so quickly at Lauryn's house, had turned up within an hour of the murder. Obviously Oscar was behind it all, but after a thorough check of his flat and testing his blood, it was confirmed that he was not responsible for the crime, and was removed from suspicion. In fact, at this point, he had it in his mind to make an "Official Accusation" to the Vampire Council against his former house-mate, but after a little re-think, he'd decided, there was little point. Against a First Tier Luminary like Oscar, progress would have been painfully slow, and as the blood of a victim only stays in a Vampire's body for 48 hours at the most, by the time any investigation could have taken place, all traces of Lauryn's DNA would have long departed his body. Of course, he still had the magazine but then it would be his word against Oscar's. How do we know you found it there? Where's the proof? You could have easily planted it with his scent? Maybe you hired assassins to kill your former girlfriend and now you're trying to frame a fellow Brother in Blood because he evicted you from his house? He'd probably end up getting charged himself, thought Terry, and in fact he wondered why Oscar hadn't planted his blood on Lauryn in the first place and just finished the job. It would have been simple enough to arrange, as the blood of a Vampire was always easy to find. Bleeding gums on a toothbrush, or a trace from the wound of a human or a fox. But of course, that wasn't the point, was it? Oscar wanted him to stay free, so he could endure the double blow to his heart and his ego.

Look what I've done.

I dare you to attack me.

Now who's smiling at my broken body?

Terry had never felt more impotent in his life, and although Lauryn's death surely demanded instant retribution, he knew, in his wildest dreams, he could never beat Oscar. Not only was he much older and therefore stronger, but he had fought with distinction in three Lycan Wars, actually winning the rarely awarded Marshall Medal (named after the famed 12th century warrior and Vampire, William Marshall) in his last campaign. He would snap him like a twig and even if Terry could somehow sneak up on him and deliver a fatal blow, he was so well connected at the Vampire court that Carswell and the rest would hunt him down and tear him to bits in revenge. It was hopeless, and so for the next few weeks, he remained locked in his flat, not answering any calls from Hector or Sophie, whilst drinking absinthe and snorting fentanyl to forget his cowardice and dull the pain of his loss. However, even Vampires have to pay the rent and so after another letter requesting immediate payment of arrears was slid under his door early one evening, Terry finally forced himself off his sofa of self pity, to return to work.

The chatter from his fellow delivery riders outside the burger restaurant, floated effortlessly over his head, as he sat back against the box of his bike and watched them show each other You Tube videos of cats trying to ride a bike or a fight between a pair of naked drunks, and he was just about to roll himself a cigarette, when out of the darkness an "Okay bruv," made him turn his head.

"Oh Jordan? Err, Hi."

"You still working here?"

"Yeah, usual. Look mate, I'm really sorry about your

mum. I read about it in the papers and I was gonna come over, but you know…"

"Thought you'd be at the funeral?"

"Well, err…"

"Mum loved you, you know. She was gutted when you left."

"Yeah sorry about that. It was complicated" said the Vampire quickly sliding off his bike and walking Jordan over to the side of the restaurant to avoid the attentions of his fellow drivers.

"It was cold Terry. You just left, not a word," said the young man, shaking his head.

"Trust me, it was for the best."

"I expected better."

"I know, I know. Look, I'm really sorry about everything," said Terry, with a pathetic smile, quickly followed by an awkward silence, until unsure of what to say next, he was just about to return to his bike, when Jordan leaned forward to whisper in his ear.

"I know what you are."

"Pardon?"

"In the bathroom with Blake. I still remember. You ain't human bruv."

"Bathroom, what bathroom?"

"Don't lie to me Terry, I saw you sucking on his neck and then fly out of the fucking window. That ain't normal and you don't come out in the day either, do you? I have never seen you in the day bruv. Probably why you didn't come to the funeral innit?"

"Look Jordan, I don't know what you're talking about…"

"The police told me there was a hole in her neck. A hole in her neck?! Who does that? It was you. You killed her right?" interrupted Jordan, pointing his finger in the Vampire's face.

"Jesus Christ, of course not."

"You're a fucking Vampire right?"

"What?! Are you joking. Look, you're obviously upset…"

"You're a fucking Vampire, Terry," shouted Jordan, prompting Terry's fellow delivery drivers to look over and grin at the bizarre accusation, before Terry grabbed the younger man by his jacket and pinned him against the wall of the restaurant.

"What? Are you crazy? There's no such things as Vampires Jordan."

"You're a Vampire and you fucking killed her, because she was seeing someone else."

"What? You think I could kill your mother? Seriously?" said Terry staring intently at the young man, and looking like he was on the verge of tears.

"Then why did you leave?" said Jordan, suddenly believing him.

"Like I said, it was complicated."

"Because you're a Vampire?" hissed Jordan.

"Don't be stupid?"

"I know what you are bruv, so you'd better tell me or I'll go to the Police."

"And tell them what? I'm a Vampire? You sure about that Jordan?"

"Well I'll think of some other way."

"I didn't kill your mother, Jordan."

"Then who did? She was my life bro'. Don't you understand. I don't want to live now and I'm gonna find out who killed her, and you're going to help me."

"I can't help you" replied Terry, but, now staring deep into the young man's eyes again, and surveying all the darkness in his mind, he also knew that, this time, he couldn't just walk away either.

Naturally, the choice to pass on the "Blood Curse" was always completely your own, as even Carswell couldn't instruct you to do it, and as a result, was seen by Vampires, as something separate and completely sacred. In saying that, most mortals were turned for relatively trivial reasons. Sexual desire, similar personalities, certain skill sets. He had even heard of one Vamp turning someone because they supported the same football team, but rarely was it ever done for revenge. This was definitely new territory, thought Terry as he continued to wander around young man's mind to see if he could be diverted from his chosen path, but all he witnessed was self- hate and incredible despair. He had even tried to kill himself and in all likelihood would probably try again. "I want to be like you!" Jordan's thoughts now screamed back repeatedly and so sensing his life would probably be forfeit anyway, Terry came to the conclusion that the best thing to do was grant his request. In any case, he felt that he owed it to his mother, at least, and so taking him on his bike to the banks of the Thames, and in front of the dome of St Paul's Cathedral, Terry revealed to Jordan that he was indeed a Demon of the Night, before explaining, in minute detail, the agonies of a Vampire life.

You live off human misery.

You lose everyone you have ever loved.

It's heartbreaking to sit and watch humanity make the same mistakes over and over again.

However, despite the warnings, Jordan had no hesitation.

"I want it," he replied defiantly, and so after some more reflection from Terry, the process of transformation began. No-one was quite sure how it really worked, even on a genetic level, but after three nights of deep meditation, some bloodletting and a great deal of vomiting, the process was complete.

"He is now your son," declared Hector handing Terry a glass of whiskey, while the two men looked down at the young man sleeping on a large double pallet.

"And, of course, the two of you will move in here now. I have more than enough room and the boy must leave his former life immediately and be with his own."

"Thank you Hector, that's really good of you. My flat is much too small for this kind of thing, but then again I may not be his Spirit Father for that long anyway."

"You're certain, it was Oscar?"

"You searched my mind. You saw the magazine. It was his scent."

"You know, he is far stronger than you Terry? You cannot ignore a 400 year advantage," said Hector, as both Vampires turned and walked back into the front room.

"But I want him dead Hector."

"I know. But my advice, if you choose to take it, is to bide you time. We have a long life for a reason, and someone as decadent and hubristic as Oscar, always makes a mistake. Keep it in your heart and then strike when you are stronger. Delayed pleasure is always the sweetest, my friend. Also you have greater responsibilities now," said the older Vampire, easing himself into his large leather armchair and motioning towards the bedroom, while Terry returned an uncertain smile and took a sip of his whiskey.

By the following afternoon, Jordan had started to come around from his deep sleep, while Terry and Hector now took it in shifts to nurse him into his new life with, at first, frozen human blood, then tomato and paprika soup, a kind of Vampire version of Jewish Penicillin (chicken soup).

Plus, there were a new list of instructions:

1. You only need blood once a month, if you choose human, once every 6 months.
2. Keep out of the sun or you will die.
3. Don't let the world know of our existence or we all die

And lastly and most importantly: "Do not take the life of another Vampire," said Hector, staring directly at Terry, as he made his final point. However, for the moment, revenge was the last thing on Terry's mind, as after three weeks recuperation, his young charge suddenly sprang out of his bed, like a new born colt, to embrace his new life. To say he was like a force of nature would be the under-statement of the century, as Jordan now constantly badgered Terry to go out into the night air and "exercise" his new found speed and strength. "Let's do the Shard bruv" declared the young Vampire bounding to the top of Tower Bridge and swinging by his arms from its iron beams, while he led his Spirit Father on a manic chase over roof tops and down the side of tall buildings, falling off here, losing his grip there, but pressing on regardless with youthful exuberance. It was insane, but for all the bother and disruption to his previously unattached life, Terry found that he could not contain his joy, as it seemed after all the misery and despair of what had gone before, life now possessed some greater purpose. However the Vampire, knew that his present happiness could be extinguished in a heart-beat, because every day, as the sun started to rise, and they retired to their pallets to sleep, Jordan would always bring the conversation back to the same topic.

Who had killed his mother?

*

The Beverley Di Franco's Tour for her latest book, "Acceptable Bigotry", continued for another three weeks, generating controversy and increasing hysteria on the way, before it finally returned to London for a special party thrown in her honor by a euphoric Lady Carswell, who now stepped forward to greet Errol, inside the Great Hall.

"Ah, wonderful to see you, my dear boy. Oscar and Jamaal have told me great things about you, and how you're such a natural organizer."

"Thank your Ladyship, I just did my job," said Errol, bowing his head.

"Nonsense, and so young. You know, we have incredible things planned for you my dear, and once we have changed the system, all will be possible. Oh and make sure you try some of the red, it's French. Four cyclists from the Dordogne, all nonsmokers, very rare," declared the Vampire Leader with a warm smile, before spotting Beverley Di Franco who had just walked into the Chamber to great applause, and so leaving the Vampire to his glass of wine. The red was indeed very good and as well as bringing life to a Vampire, healthy blood, such as this, also had the effect of relaxing inhibitions, like a form of liquid MDMA, and as a result, all around him, everyone started to giggle and feverishly speak their minds.

"I only bite Brexiteers now."

"I think all white people, well the poor ones anyway, should be taught separately from people of color to re-educate their minds."

"Nonsense, I think the only solution is to wipe out them out all together and just start again."

It reminded Errol of the famous Radical Chic article written by Tom Wolfe from the Seventies, he'd once read about, where the composer Leonard Bernstein, hosted a party for the Black Panthers and all the well heeled of New York society started to spout a form of far left-wing ideology, that they had absolutely no intention of living by themselves and therefore the Vampire wasn't at all surprised at the sudden intolerance of the "so called tolerant". It seemed to be nothing more than a performance, and one, they all knew was an enormous conceit, and so he smiled grimly for the next hour or two, pottering around the edges of the party while desperately trying not to punch anyone in the face. Soon speeches were made about the success of the book and the tour, which Errol found tedious and more than a little patronizing, especially when he was roped into the proceedings and told how "amazing" he had been for the hundredth time. Bet if he was Calvin Sewell or Glen Elder, the famous Black American Conservative, he wouldn't be considered so "amazing", thought the Vampire, grabbing another glass of red from a tray held by a Familiar, before seeking temporary sanctuary from all the claptrap, among some younger Vamps, on the other side of the room. However, this proved an even worse option, because not only were they wearing masks, for some reason, being Bloodsuckers, of course, with bullet proof immune systems, they hardly needed them, but then for the next half an hour, they just talked incessantly to him about "The Message" and the possibility of forming a Vampire Antifa. It was complete bullshit and the Vampire was just about to flee again until the sensitivity of his Bloodsucker ears suddenly picked up a conversation going on between Oscar and Jamaal, about ten yards to his right.

"That's a bit harsh even for you, geezer."

"Oh get fucked Jamaal. We are vicious, spiteful creatures, our blood is programmed for revenge. Of course I bit her. In fact, if I'm to be totally honest, I hypnotized her into having sex with me first, which I suppose is technically rape, but she definitely wanted it. It was the sweetest moment. That Northern bastard had been looking down on me for the last 40 years, and then when he smiled as I lay battered on the floor, that was the last straw, so to kill the love of his life was nothing short of exquisite. Hector might have humiliated me, but I got my revenge, alright. I even texted the pathetic fool from her phone and then left a magazine with my latest interview about Green Capitalism on the side-board, you couldn't have scripted it, fella."

"Way too cold bro."

"Well, aren't we all? Anyway enough of the faux jugment mon brave. Lets get properly wrecked" laughed Oscar handing Jamaal, a small wrap, before looking up quickly to make sure that nobody had overheard him. Errol could feel the glare of his house-mate on his back and therefore angled his head towards the nearest blue haired Vampire and started to giggle.

"This red is insane."

"Isn't it? I'm only biting cyclists from now on."

"Me too," gushed Errol, staying perfectly relaxed. The last thing he needed right now was the unwanted attentions of Oscar and so continued the pretense of talking to the younger Vampires for a few minutes longer, until, sensing the coast was clear, excused himself and fled to the toilets.

"Oscar had raped and killed Lauryn," Errol's thoughts now screamed, as he sat in a stall in the rest-room.

Terry.

Poor Terry.

Over the years, he had been witness to hundreds of mixed race relationships, and for the most part, had always felt that everyone was trying just a bit too hard. Trendy white guys trying to score points on their "Progressive Register" while ambitious Black guys flocked to the upwardly mobile world of "fucking a white chick" and although he would usually stop short, of the rationale of someone like Jamaal, who basically characterized all White /Black relationships to be a variation of some Slave owner/Slave girl, White Mistress/Mandingo fantasy, he also found, that he couldn't always discount it, either. Humans were addicted to fashion and approval, however, to his surprise, he found that Terry and Lauryn had never been like that. If anything, whenever he saw them together, they were more like the terrible twins, constantly laughing, constantly loving each other.

No actor, regardless of talent, could fabricate that.

So how did the hell, did he get here, then?

Even as a blood sucking murdering scumbag, he had always seen himself somewhere on the side of the angels, but this was beyond anything he could possibly endure, as inevitably the memory of the middle class swingers, Ben and Sarah, came back into his mind again.

They didn't deserve to die.

Blind hate and ideology had taken their lives

Damn Beverley Di Franco. Damn Carswell. Damn Oscar. Damn, even his Spirit Father, Jamaal.

This had nothing to do with Black Empowerment or Justice for "past and present wrongs" but rather a dirty power grab by the people who have always been in charge and so like every soldier in history, Errol suddenly realized, he'd probably been fighting for the wrong side all along.

Now, out of the maelstrom of his hellish thoughts, for some reason the words of Joe Biden, the Presidential candidate in the 2020 American election, appeared: "If you don't vote Democrat then you're not black".

"That so Joe" mumbled Errol to himself, and then pulling a phone out from his trouser pocket, he started to text.

CHAPTER SEVENTEEN

Terry couldn't really remember, the last time he'd felt this happy.

His heart was full, his step was light and even his permanent distaste for the British middle classes had, for the moment at least, begun to fade into the background.

Next, he'd be laughing at Four Weddings and a Funeral, thought the Vampire, smiling to himself, before leaning back on his chair and taking another sip of Hector's excellent wine.

Of course they was no mystery to his present state of euphoria.

Jordan.

He was totally brilliant.

Whether he was breaking Hector's private meditations in the Kabbalah with the sounds of Skepta or Kendrick Lamarr or rushing around the apartment with his phone held aloft showing everyone articles about Social Justice or Trans pets that made their own milk shakes, he was like a breath of the freshest clean air on a sticky summer's day.

Okay, it was like living with a Woke Vampire, but this was a version that dazzled rather than depressed, and as the months began to pass, Terry slowly felt himself falling into that dreadful cliché, where Jordan began to represent "The son he'd never had."

Of course, Lauryn still occupied his thoughts, how could she not, his love for her was deep, much deeper than even he had ever suspected, but somehow the presence of her son in his life right now, brought a welcome salve to his damaged heart. Maybe this could be a new beginning, mused Terry, as he watched Hector and Jordan engage in another one of their dinner time arguments, this time about what a better society might look like.

"Without Free Speech young man, we have nothing."

"Nah bruv, that just lets the Nazis in."

Terry couldn't resist a smile.

Bloodsuckers, arguing over what was best for humanity.

The irony, as always, was delicious, and so the Vampire continued to listen dreamily to the conversation at the other end of the table, until Hector rose to bring in the cheese board, so they could decamp to the comfort of the front room, with a nice bottle of Port. Obviously, this ritual provided little attraction to someone as young as Jordan, who promptly stretched out on the sofa with his phone, while Hector nibbled on a piece of Stilton before nodding off in his favorite leather chair. "Perfect" sighed Terry and he was considering following his old mentor and indulging in a post dinner snooze himself, when a ping from his phone, diverted his attention towards an unexpected text.

"Oscar killed Lauryn, we have to meet ASAP- Errol"

Now his heart quickened as he sat up in his chair, before glancing over towards Jordan on the sofa opposite.

"You okay?" asked the younger Vampire, pulling out an ear bud, as he noticed a frown on Terry's face.

"Err, United lost again."

"You should support Arsenal bruv, get a proper team," Jordan replied with a big smile, before returning to his You Tube video, while Terry frantically searched his mind about what to do next. It hadn't mattered so much when only Hector knew the truth, he was like a father, who cared little for ego, only the best outcome for the one he loved. But Errol was a different matter entirely. He was a contemporary and would demand blood. Of course, his lover's death should have been avenged. Everything in his soul had told him this, and even after all the platitudes and excuses had been trotted out by the more rational side of his mind, was he, in the end, nothing more than a miserable coward? Possibly. He still railed about the Iraq War, the first and greatest of the many lies that now defined the new century, and would have gladly bled out Campbell and Cheney, the real villains of the piece, in a heart-beat, had it not been expressly prohibited by Carswell and the Vampire Council. Yet he balked at Oscar, who had taken the "supposed love of his life". However, whichever way his thoughts now took him, honor, dishonor, brave man, pussy, everything still came back to one single consideration. Jordan. Any revenge, would only result in certain death for his Spirit Son and so, in reality, whatever his ego might protest, all bets were still, basically off. "Nice" Terry now mumbled to himself and happy that he could still look himself in the mirror in the evening, as contrary to myth, Vampires could see their own reflection, he quickly texted back his former housemate, to arrange a meeting for the following evening.

That night, he managed a relatively, undisturbed sleep, and after rising early, he made himself a healthy breakfast of muesli and natural yoghurt, before wandering over from North London to a boating pond in the middle of a park in Fulham, to explain himself to Errol.

"Hi," said Terry sliding out of the darkness and approaching a familiar shape sitting on a park bench.

"Mate," replied Errol standing up with a nervous smile.

"Thought we couldn't be friends," said Terry, with a grin and shaking his hand.

"Yeah fuck that."

"Crazy innit?"

"Crazy's the word. Been running around with Di Franco and all those fucking idiots and instead I should have reached out."

"Reached out? You're so Woke geezer!"

"Believe! Why can't they just say "contact", for fuck's sake? Oh, and you'll like this one. Been doing PR for a firm called Embrace Vegan, yeah?" said Errol, sitting back down and happy to see his friend again.

"Oh right? The ones who do the sausages?"

"That's them. Totally ethical apparently, you know bring in their ingredients by sailing ships to save the environment and all that kind of shit, But get this. First, they stopped their workers starting a Union with the help of that Lefty Democrat, AFM, you know Angelina Felicia

Mendes and then because of a backlash in the Press and their sales going down, to cut costs, they've secretly been getting their sausages and burgers made by a firm that processes meat. Actual fucking meat, bro'. Can you believe it? Saw the invoices the other day. It's hilarious."

"Don't surprise me."

"Yeah they're a joke" said Errol, shaking his head again before there was a brief silence between the old friends, until Terry started to speak again.

"So your text about Lauryn, then?"

"Yeah mate. Sorry about that, I was gonna text earlier when I saw it in the paper, but... Anyway, but I overheard Oscar and Jamaal talking at a party didn't I? They were out of it and Oscar was saying that he killed Lauryn, you know in revenge for what Hector did to him. Just thought you should know."

"I knew, already."

"What? You knew?!" said Errol suddenly rising from the park bench.

" He sent me a text from her phone and I went around and saw her on the bed."

"Fucking hell. You knew?" repeated Errol, while Terry slowly nodded his head.

"He can't get away with that mate."

"Look Errol, It's not that easy," said Terry firmly, looking up at his friend.

"You what?!"

"This is what he wants. Make me react so he can kill me in self defense."

"What? Fuck off Terry! Seriously? That bastard killed your bird."

"You know as well as me, he'd fuck me up in a second, plus I hear he's banging Carswell, so he's protected. It would be suicide, you know that."

"Ah, this ain't you. I've seen you stand up to older Vamps before. What about Parsons? You done 'im, remember?"

"Parsons is only 100 years older than me, plus he's a twat. Oscar is a different story."

"Don't seem right bro."

"Well, it's the way it is. I'll have to bide my time."

"Okay Tel. But you know killing her wasn't the only thing he did," said Errol, looking away a little embarrassed.

"Why, what do you mean?"

"Well, I didn't want to say anything, but he also said that… err…"

"What?" said Terry, now standing up from the bench.

"Well, he said that, erm. Well that he hypnotized her and, well you know. Said it was the sweetest thing."

"Fuck! You sure?"

"You know Oscar, that's his thing innit, power, revenge."

"Piece of fucking shit" replied Terry, now walking around in front of the bench, while he tried to process this new information, and was just about to turn around again to ask Errol something else, when out of the trees, a figure suddenly appeared.

"Jordan, what you doing here?" said Terry, moving towards the young Vampire.

"Who the hell is this?" said Errol turning towards Terry.

"He's Lauryn's son."

"What?! Well, hypnotize him quick, then" shouted Errol

"No he's one of us," replied Terry, and he was about to walk over and urge his young charge not to over-react to what he'd probably just heard, when Jordan sprang forward to grab the lapels of his black leather jacket and scream vengeance for his dead mother.

Now any chance of a better outcome would be lost forever, as Jordan's incurable curiosity had led him to follow Terry on a whim and had now overheard what should have always remained a secret. However, despite this, Terry sat the young Vampire down on the park bench and tried to reason hard with him, even enlisting help from Errol, who, gradually realizing the perilous nature of their situation, especially now as it included Lauryn's son, began to side with his old friend. But it was to no avail and so after an hour or so of back and forth in the middle of the park, where with tears in his eyes, Jordan begged for Justice for the death of his mother, Terry and Errol were finally forced to admit defeat and pledge all of their efforts to the destruction of Oscar.

Therefore, in light of this, the next few nights, were frantic to say the least, as the three Vampires met to try and formulate some kind of a plan. However, whichever way they worked it out every scenario seemed to end up, either in their own destruction by way of Oscar or later at the hands of Carswell and the Council, who wouldn't think twice about snuffing out the lives of Bloodsuckers so young. All the same, despite the ridiculous odds, by the third night, a plan did finally emerge and predictably, it was pretty basic. They would stay the night in Errol's cell in Fulham, and then before the setting of the sun, the three of them would walk along the corridor to Oscar's door and just as he came out for a shower, would take him by surprise and rip out his heart, which other than decapitation, was the only sure way to kill a Vampire. "Piece of piss" noted Terry dryly, and so for the rest of the week, they went over every detail of their plan, whilst drinking copious amounts of human blood, from Errol's private reserve to increase their strength. Terry, in particular, schooled Jordan relentlessly on how to anticipate the reactions of a Vampire and more importantly how to avoid being destroyed himself.

"The older ones are, on average, about five times faster than Vampires like me and Errol, so that means they are ten times faster than you. So don't mess about. We just need you to hold onto Oscar's legs for only a few seconds, before I drag his arms back and hopefully Errol can plunge the knife straight into his heart," explained Terry, as he repeatedly threw Jordan around his cell to concentrate his mind on anticipating the moves of someone as terrifying as Oscar. Every now and again Hector would stroll by, and take a peek in at all the rough and tumble, while Terry would smile and explain that he was just showing his protege how to fight off any rogue Lycan he might encounter. Obviously, all their problems would be over, if Hector was on their side, but he also knew that his Spirit Father would only try to dissuade them from their suicide mission, and as Jordan had made them all make a "Blood Pledge" which could not reversed, it was probably best to keep things as they were. Very soon Saturday evening arrived, and after being ushered into the house by Errol, they all stayed deathly silent in his cell until the next day, and then as the sun started to set, the three Vampires crept silently along the hallway to wait for Oscar to emerge from his usual weekend orgy of sex and Class A drugs. They had reasoned that this was probably when he would be at his weakest, and so remaining outside his cell door, the minutes seemed to tick by like hours, until finally they heard a click and then a familiar swish. In less than a second, Errol had leapt forward and delivered a huge kick to the older Vampire's chest, while Terry sprang to his right and grabbed one of the Oscar's arms.

"What the ..." cried Oscar, as Jordan quickly joined the fray and even succeeded in securing one of the Vampire's legs, while Terry moved around the side and managed to pull back the other of Oscar's arms, so at one point it seemed as if the day was won and Errol could plunge his dagger straight into their enemy's chest. However, at the last minute he hesitated, maybe killing a fellow Brother in Blood, proved too much for him, but whatever the reason, it allowed Oscar, time enough to wrestle free from Terry's grip, while a quick kick to Jordan's head, left the young Vampire unconscious, in the corner of his cell.

"Good Lord. Assassins. What larks. Well your chance has gone chaps and now you must pay the price. Like poor Lauryn. So very sweet" grinned Oscar as he grabbed both Errol and Terry by their throats and forced them up against the wall of the cell.

"Vampires should never kill one other, but as this is in self-defense I think the High Council will understand," declared Oscar with a savage grin, as he squeezed harder, causing both, Errol and Terry to flail around for breath, until their assailant was suddenly grabbed from behind and thrown to the ground.

"Hector! Thank god you're here. These three villains have just tried to kill me as I came out of my cell," spluttered Oscar, as he looked up at the older Vampire, who had now appeared in the room.

"I know. I read young Jordan's mind three days ago. Stupid plan. We should never kill one of our own."

"It is the law," confirmed Oscar, now getting to his feet, before raising his hand to straighten his hair.

"Yes, Oscar, it is the law," replied Hector and then taking the knife from the hand of his Spirit Son, in one swift movement, he plunged the dagger deep into his heart.

There was now a slow gurgling sound, which lasted maybe less than a minute, before the Vampire, slumped to the ground and immediately start to decay. The stench was nearly over-powering as Terry and Errol looked on in utter amazement, until Hector declared "You must go now," before walking over to a corner of the cell and starting to weep.

*

The guards hustled Hector into the middle of the meeting chamber, and glancing sheepishly under their brows, they loitered for a moment, until the figure standing on a purple dais, quickly raised her hand, and they turned to march away.

"You look tired Hector. A drink?" said the Vampire Leader, her voice echoing around the heavy wooden beams as she glided down the steps of the raised platform to approach her old comrade.

"I'm fine."

"Are you sure, it's very good" said Carswell walking over to a decanter sitting on a side table and then pouring herself a whiskey.

"The mortals are lucky don't you think. Live seven or eight decades, learn a few things, make a mark and then that's it. If you make a big enough mark, your ideas live on, and if you don't some woodland creature relieves himself on your headstone, but at least it's done. A beautiful release. Thinking about it now, that's how I should have left you, when I found you in the library of Cordoba serving under Abd al Rahman III. You were brilliant, are brilliant. Your name would be up there now with Omar Khayyam, Newton, Goethe, revered like a Titan for the rest of eternity, but your body, sadly long crumbled to dust. You could never adapt, could you? The challenge of a longer life? Always fighting a cause, not realizing, that it's all artifice. Fate makes the decision. She loves chaos. It's the best disinfectant, don't you think?"

"We have to try, Dierdra."

"Utopians always say that don't they? We have to try. We have to make a difference. Spare me, please. Such rot. Take Mother Nature for example. Forget the Patriarchy, she's the biggest misogynist of them all. Menstruation, Menopause, Men! A real bitch, if ever there was one and yet we learn to accept, don't we? Because in the end, loyalty is all we really have and it's Lady Carswell to you,

you pitiless dog" shouted the Chief Imperator, throwing her glass on the floor before flying across the room and striking Hector, hard across the face.

"Oscar was diseased," said Hector, defiantly.

"Then why turn him?"

"It was my one mistake."

"In hell's name! You are such a fraud, Hector! Plaguing history for centuries with your ridiculous compassion. Attracting acolytes and then drawing them to their death. You know Rousseau's children all ended up in an orphanage and Marx left his family in penury. Hypocrisy doesn't even cover it. Why can't you leave well alone."

"This is an old charge of yours."

"And still true. You are a snake Hector, worse than me, worse than the old one, who made us what we are today. You have all this power, and yet you try to share with those less fortunate. Prometheus in sack cloth and ashes, perhaps? What is it you used to say in the Vampire elections? Oh yes, I remember. If you are destitute vote for your own interests and if you are rich vote for the interests of the destitute? Weasel words. It changes nothing. In fact it only makes things worse, because all you really do is stop the underlings from hating you more and rising up to take your power."

"My power?"

"Yes, your power Hector. The power of the Missionary, the benevolent Billionaire, the random caring Celebrity. So bloody transparent and like you, they achieve very little, except, of course, to increase their own social capital, which is all hypocrites like you, crave anyway. Is that not right my dearest? You know, I knew Mother Theresa rather well, and every time, I searched her mind, all I saw was vanity, and pure self-interest, as I glimpse in yours, when your guard is down. The Legend! The Great Thinker! The Righter of Wrongs! Unmasked at last. That's why you believe so much in charity, isn't it? For that line in the newspapers or that little whisper at a party, "Oh he does such good work" Christ in heaven! At least I'm honest. I believe in charity, for one reason and one reason alone. Because it sedates. Starve a man and he may kill you in your sleep, but keep him just about alive and he may even thank you. I do the same as you, but with less mess."

"I am nothing like you."

"You are exactly like me. Exactly! You don't even like the poor, you pity them. What is that? Enlightened? And anyway why should we pity them? Who built this world? The 80%?, as that Lycan dog used to call them. No fear. They just sit there, like they have always done, waiting to be fed. They build nothing! NOTHING! We built it. We, the Elite, the gifted, the so-called chattering classes, you spend so much of your wasted life spitting venom at. Imhotep, Plato, Buddha, Al Khwarizmi, Francis Bacon, Alan Turing. Where the hell do you think these people came from? The Swamp? The Ghetto? The Housing Estate? Of course not. You know maybe I should kill you Hector. I was responsible for you, you were my making. Maybe should I take your life, as you did Oscar. He was dear to me, because he was your blood son."

"He was a monster."

"We are all monsters! " screamed Carswell grabbing Hector by the throat and lifting him from the ground with one hand.

"I am ready," said Hector, closing his eyes.

"I don't doubt you are. A martyrs death, you long for it, so? A worthwhile end to a lonely life, but I find, that despite the ways you have always found to hurt me, I still love you," said Lady Carswell, throwing Hector to the ground and then turning to walk back to the purple dais.

"Within a few hours, the Vampire Council shall convene an emergency meeting, in this very Hall, in fact. It is over 600 years since a First Tier Vampire was killed by one of his own, and so they will, most assuredly, insist on your demise. A slow end, stretched out under the Arctic sun for a crime, which is doubly egregious. A fellow Brother in Blood, and your Spirit Son. What should I say Hector," said the Vampire Leader, glaring back at the Spaniard.

"You should say yes."

"I should, but I won't. You are not supposed to die yet, your time is not done, I sense it. So I will recommend that you be interred for 500 years, a quarter of your life."

"I would prefer death."

"No you wouldn't and anyway I will be long gone by the time you awake and maybe the world will be more to your liking then. Goodbye Hector," said Lady Carswell, sharply, now turning her back.

"May I see Terry before I go," asked Hector, softly, with his head bowed.

"Your beloved? I shouldn't, but if it is your wish," said Carswell, remaining with her back to him, before dismissing him from the room with a wave of her hand.

As she predicted, the Vampire Leader used her considerable influence, to persuade the Council to defer the prescribed sentence of death for such a heinous crime to one of 500 years locked in a lead coffin in depths of the Blood Temple. Furthermore, the verdict of the Council was to be carried out within 24 hours of the decree, and so after getting his affairs in order and writing some letters to his Rabbi and a few close friends, Hector was then taken from his cell, to an inner courtyard.

"We could get you out, know," whispered Terry, as the two men walked a few paces away from the four guards in attendance.

"No my friend, they would simply catch me again. Besides my sentence is just."

"How is it just? You rid the earth of scum," replied Terry, shaking his head.

"That's as maybe, but I must pay for my crime. My only consolation is that you were not involved. They asked you questions, yes?"

"For hours. Even Jamaal turned up and nosed about the flat but got nothing."

"Excellent. Say nothing and tell Errol and Jordan to do the same, because, have no doubt my dear friend, if Carswell ever finds out the truth, she will not hesitate to kill you all. I have glimpsed inside her thoughts, when she probed my mind for the truth, and rest assured she hates you and blames you for my fate. Believe me Terry, she will destroy you if she gets the chance."

"Fuck her Hector. Anyway, who cares, this world is finished."

"How can you say that? Always the pessimist," said Hector, stopping to smile at his friend.

"What do you expect? I'm a Northerner."

"Well, you must keep your head, my friend. Of course,

everyone is crazy at the moment, but this is just because we are asking questions we have never asked before."

"I dunno Hector, this is bad, worse than I have ever seen. All we do is look back to the past, to smash each other over the head. Today it's Slavery, tomorrow it will be something else, we're fucking doomed mate."

"Not so fast my friend. Do you know where the word Slave comes from? The Slavs. When I was a boy, they were the dogs, and the only Slaves I saw in Spain were white. Then Black people were destroyed for 400 years, but very soon they will rise and probably become the masters themselves. In fact, I'd wager you a Caliph's Treasure House, that in a less than five hundred years, a Black historian will write, that the British Empire for all its faults was ultimately a great thing, in the same way Gibbons said that the Romans civilized Ancient Britain. Do you think the Romans were loved 2,000 years ago? Of course not. But from a safe distance, devoid of any real memory, we come to admire them. It is one of the only joys of living so long, my friend, is that you see how things really are. I have seen Empires come and go. Everyone gets their chance to be the oppressed and the oppressor, no? and then they disappear like the morning mist. Where is the Kingdom of Kush now? Where is Macedon? The Mongols, The Aztecs, or even the Spanish? I have seen it with my own eyes. For some reason, humans, need to dominate each other. It seems to be their path to progress. But little by little, inch by inch, it gets better. Look at today? What a world we live in? Do you know the average life expectancy 150 years ago was 40. Now it is double that, we have so much to be thankful for. Fear not my friend, despite Carswell and those who think like her, the battle will be won. So, don't give up, look after Jordan, soothe your angry soul and when I awake, we will rejoice again."

"But 500 years Hector?"

"Yes, think of that. 500 years ago it was 1522, and there I was in Venice, conversing with Michelangelo, reading Martin Luther with all of the Renaissance crashing into my mind. Think of what it will be like when I awake? Listen to me, Terry and learn. I have been a Vampire, a scourge of humankind, a Psychopath for over a thousand years now, but despite my sorry condition, I still see only the good in us all."

"I don't. This Woke bullshit is fatal, Hector."

"It's fashion, nothing but fashion. Sixteen hundred years ago the Huns ruled in most of Europe and they had a custom, of wrapping the heads of their babies when they were born, so they developed coned -shaped heads. Crazy no? But because they were in charge, the people who they conquered, started to do the same thing to their own babies, and not because they were forced to, but because they wanted to copy the new elites. Think of it Terry, they deformed their babies just to fit in!"

"Probably explains the Mullet as well."

"The what?"

"Nothing, a joke."

"A joke? Yes, yes, very good. A joke is exactly what we need right now. Like poor Kierkegaard, we must laugh at the absurdity of life. Even the Puritans among us will not be able to resist the power of that, in the end. Be strong my dearest friend and I will see you again. You know, you always had the most beautiful smile," said Hector, his eyes suddenly filling with tears, and then leaning forward to kiss Terry on the cheek he stared up at the night sky for the last time, before walking back towards the Vampire guards to meet his fate.

CHAPTER EIGHTEEN

The next few weeks were pitiful, as even Jordan's youthful exuberance seemed to have been completely flattened while the silence of the flat screamed out its grief for their lost friend. Despite this, Terry continued to deliver fast food, to keep his mind off all the misery, while Jordan watched Netflix, and munched constantly on Sour Cream and Onion Pringles. It was grim to say the least, and made even more depressing when Terry picked up a copy of the Metro one evening to read of the recent death of Joshua Norton, 25, from causes unknown. He had begged him to keep it to himself, not only because it was the right thing to do, but also as he feared that the Vampire Authorities, would pick up on the story and in their usual paranoid manner, do something drastic. Ten to one, they had a hand in his demise, and although Terry was genuinely sorry for the fate of the young man, who's life he had initially saved, he found that, in the circumstances, his sympathies were limited. As the man said, bullshit will get you every time, and the image of Joshua's face beaming out from News Websites all over the country for the last few weeks, while he pressed on with his high profile search for his "Delivery Bike Samaritan" smacked more of a desire for approval and acceptance rather than anything more genuine. Of course Joshua's conceitedness was hardly justification for his death, far from it, but to Terry, it presented further proof of a modern malaise, where a strain of Post Modernist thought developed in a French laboratory by those mad scientists, Derrida and Foucault, and then exacerbated by Social Media, was now out in the general population and causing devastation to everything it touched. My truth is the only truth. Words are more powerful than action. Morality should be based on consensus rather than objective judgment. Eventually, humans would develop an immunity to it's ravages and, in time, return to a more authentic place, but until then, the bodies of young men like Joshua would continue to pile up. However, Terry, still considered it to be, an awful waste and just added to the general dolor in the flat, and therefore it came as somewhat of a relief, when one Friday night, Errol suddenly turned up to punch a hole in the ongoing despair. "This is no good. Hector wouldn't want this. The place is like a bloody morgue, why don't you move in with me? I got to keep Oscar's house and its way too big, just for me. Be like the old times, geezer," declared his old friend clapping his hands together at the joyless Vampires slumped in front of him before busily going from room to room to pack their bags. Terry could think of a thousand reasons not to take this advice, but none for the moment came immediately to mind and so looking at Jordan, he shrugged his shoulders and mumbled, "Why the hell not," before they locked everything up, and followed Errol to Fulham.

With five spacious cells, a Swimming Pool, plus it's own Private Cinema in the basement, the house was still nothing short of amazing, and in an irony that even Oscar might have appreciated, Terry moved into his nemesis' old room, to marvel at the interior of a Private Gym, Jacuzzi and a fridge full of the best Vintage Blood, that even a Vampire Veggy like himself, could hardly turn down in good faith. So, the three Vampires settled in quickly, and as the months rolled by, Terry continued to deliver at Fast Food 4 U and help out at the local Food Bank, which was now doing nights runs because of demand, while Errol gave up his job with EVC, now taken over by Jamaal, and returned to being an electrician on the London Underground, at same time mentoring ex prisoners at the weekend, leaving Jordan to devote all his time to his new Podcast, called Bloodsucker J, and producing "Ethical Drill" videos, which prohibited any messages of hate between rival gangs. It was all going swimmingly, and except for the odd visit from a representative of the Vampire Council, to check that everything was operating within accepted guidelines, for the most part the three housemates were left in peace, and so by the end of any normal night, they would usually find themselves on a sofa, watching random daytime TV.

"You ever noticed with all the ads these days, that they just show black guys, and middle class white women, but no-one from the white working class" declared Terry staring at the TV screen with folded arms

"Oh no, not this again," said Errol, leaning forward to take a mini samosa from a plate.

"I'm only saying," said Terry with a grin.

"Anyway, that's rubbish bruv. white people are everywhere?" countered Jordan, putting another pringle in his mouth.

"Really? Okay, let's watch, then, shall we," said Terry, leaning back into the sofa as they all sat in silence, watching the television for the next half an hour or so, paying particular attention to the adverts.

"Right, I counted two, and both of them were as fat as fuck, and in one ad about the People's Lottery," said Terry, finally turning around towards his two housemates.

"So?" snapped Jordan

"So, is that the white working class then? Overweight and addicted to gambling."

"I don't get your point."

"Jordan, all my life I listened to black people say to me, that they needed to be seen and heard, yeah? Like if you can't see it, you can't be it. Which I totally agree with by the way. So don't the white working class have the same right, then?"

"They are seen," said the Young Vampire.

"Where? I don't see 'em."

"Nah, they're everywhere bruv?" said Jordan laughing

"Exactly, but not on the box, apparently. Okay, here's a question. What percentage of the UK population is black?"

"What's that gotta do with anything. That's racist."

"Is it fuck. What percentage, Jordan?" repeated Terry.

"I dunno 20 percent."

"You see? Everyone thinks that. I did as well. Actually,

the number is closer to 5%? So that means, there are over 80% of white people in the UK, most of whom are skint, by the way, but we don't see 'em, do we? Unless, of course, they're doing something racist or suffering from mental health."

"Yeah, but what about all the white people at the top, in Politics, the Media and the Boardroom," replied the younger Vamp after a moment of contemplation.

"That ain't most white people Jordan, use your loaf son. Most of the guys you're talking about, had really posh backgrounds."

"What about Midsomer Murders then?" interrupted Errol, leaning forward to grab another mini samosa and joining the conversation once again. "Don't see no black geezers in corduroy pants knocking off the local Vicar, in that one, do ya? In fact, I remember, back in the day, the only black face you would ever see on an advert was on a jam jar, or fucking Uncle Ben's Rice, so suck it up white boy. Anyway what does it matter who's face is selling car insurance or soap."

"Oh right McKenzie, but when it was all white faces, you never shut the fuck up about it, did ya? "Oh, look Terry, another advert wiv no black bloke in it! I remember pal," said Terry smiling at his old friend, before grabbing the remote control and increasing the volume as another advert came on the television.

"Oh right, here we go, here's another one. Let's watch, shall we? Black guy, check, nice white middle class girl check, horrible spoilt privileged kid telling everyone what to do, double check, but err white working class bloke, err… No. Oh and I bet, if you ever do see one, he'll be doing something fucking ridiculous. But you know, only saying", said Terry, while for the next five minutes of adverts, the three Vampires stared blankly at the huge plasma screen, until Errol broke the silence again.

"Yeah, yeah okay, you've a point," he said, scratching his nose.

"Nah he don't. That's just bullshit."

"No it's not, Jordan, and so the question you gotta ask yourself is, who decides who gets seen?" replied Terry, now turning off the TV, and turning to face the younger Vampire.

"I don't get you?"

"Why are there so many people of color on the box today?" repeated Terry.

"Because it's right."

"It is. But it wouldn't be happening if Carswell, or the Elites, didn't decide it, would it?"

"Well maybe they're right then."

"Or maybe they're just fucking with us. You hate cultural appropriation right?"

"Yeah bruv."

"Cool, so you remember that film we saw recently about those English gangsters from the 1960's?"

"Yeah, it was sick," said Jordan, with a big grin.

"Now those gangsters came from the East End, which was dirt poor at the time, not like today when it's all gentrified and shit, but the guy who played the main character in the film went to Public School and is really posh, so my question is. Why is it okay for someone to say you can't steal from black culture, but it's okay to take from white working class culture? And while we're on the subject of the cultural appropriation. Have a guess where black American street talk comes from?" interrupted Terry, folding his arms again.

"Oh fuck, not this again?" said Errol shaking his head.

"Yes this again. It actually comes from white blokes from England, who went to settle in the Deep South of America in the 17th century and were skint and looked down on by everyone else and they used to say things like "You be" and "Axe" instead of ask. So who's culturally appropriating who now, then?"

"No way, is that true?" said Jordan looking at Errol.

"Actually, it is. Thomas Sowell wrote a book on it."

"Well I don't care. They're white and it don't matter how broke they are, they still got privilege."

"I can't buy that mate. Okay suppose you got 50 black guys and 50 white guys in a room and you walk in and you don't know any of them. Which side you gonna walk over to first? You know instinctively?" said Terry, folding his arms.

"Err, well, probably the black side," said the younger Vampire, after thinking for a second.

"Exactly, so would most people. But suppose those 50 black blokes had gone to a Private School and lived a privileged life, while those 50 white guys went to a rubbish comprehensive and lived on an Estate. Cos of your upbringing, you'd probably have more in common with the white guys, but 9 times out of ten, you'd still go towards your own color, yeah?"

"Yeah, but, Terry, that's where your argument breaks down, innit?, because you wouldn't be able to find 50 black blokes who went to Public School, cos we're all broke, bruv," said Jordan, laughing out loud and clapping his hands, while Errol started giggling too, and even Terry had to crack a smile.

"Well there's a lot richer than you think, especially these days. Look, you know me, Jordan, I ain't some white guy who wants things just to stay the same as they used to be, am I? But all I'm saying is, once upon a time, there used to be loads of the white working class on the box and now there's none and that can't be healthy, especially if half the people in the country are still white and skint. I mean that's how you get Trump and idiots like him."

"Nah Terry, that's because they are racist, bruv."

"What all of them? You know he got 80 million votes in the last election. That's a lot of racists Jordan, and also over ten percent of people who voted for Trump in 2016, voted for Obama in 2012, and the time before that as well, so maybe it's not racism and it's about something else."

"Like what?" asked Jordan, still unconvinced.

"Like Class. Like a great big giant scream from poor people saying what about our jobs? What about our pay? Why has our lives been so shit for the last 40 years. I mean they talk all the time about Diversity, Equity and Inclusion, right? Well aren't poor white people included too? Isn't diversity about including their voices too? Or is it, sorry, poor white boy, you've had your bit, now it's time for the poor black guys to take over, so fuck off and keep watching the Oasis docs?" said Terry, sitting back in the sofa, in a justified huff, until Errol broke the ensuing silence again.

"Too right, as well. What did working class white boys,

ever do for us anyway? Except chase us down the street, calling us names or nicking all of our reggae rhythms to make million selling albums, and not giving us any credit for it. Lee Scratch Perry was twice as good as Phil Spector, and he didn't shoot no bird in his house either. But no-one knows about him, do they? And did we get paid? Did we fuck. Just a pat on the head now and again, like Peter Tosh with the Rolling Stones that time. Nah Terry, let the poor little white boy feel some pain for a change, might do him some good. But you know, only saying" said Errol, leaning forward for another snack, before the two older Vampires looked sideways at each other and began to laugh.

"Yeah, well, fuck it, anyway. I've got a lot of Brit Pop videos to get through haven't I?, so maybe we can take a little time off," said Terry, as he happily turned the television back on again, and for the next hour or so, the three Vampires watched and munched in relative peace, until Jordan suddenly reached forward and pressed the remote control.

"Oi, I was watching that," said Terry and Errol in unison.

"No look. I've been thinking about what you been saying. Maybe you got a point and we are fighting each other for no reason, yeah? So why don't we do something about it then?" offered Jordan looking optimistically towards his house-mates.

"Like what Jordan? We tried everything. Doesn't work. You can't beat Carswell and the System, they'll do anything to divide ordinary people. Look at what happened to Lucius Noble," said Errol nodding over to Terry with sad resignation, before he took the remote control off the younger Vampire to turn the TV back on again. However, Jordan was not deterred by their fatalist response and quickly exiting the front room, he grabbed his lap-top from the kitchen and began to type.

Within a week a new website had been set up by the young Vampire to encourage working class people of all colors to start interacting with each to change the national conversation, while he also persuaded Errol and Terry to start a new podcast, called *Friends not Allies,* to promote the new initiative. The channel proved to be an immediate success, as the personalities of the two Vampires blended perfectly, merging the old school bluntness of Terry's Northern delivery with Errol's slightly more Southern optimistic take on events. Suddenly *class not color* became the new zeitgeist, as young men and women, from similar economic backgrounds, started to swap ideas and compare the stories of their lives. Now white, brown and black faces beamed back over Tik Tok, You Tube and Instagram, about how much they had in common, rather than what set them apart. Even Onlyfans joined in with the new movement, with models from working class communities, offering discounts to those who had been on free school meals in their youth, whilst wearing various types of lingerie with the new tag-line *Friends Not Allies* emblazoned on the front.

They were fast becoming a brand, and so it made sense for the three Vampires, to set up an official organization to support their ideas. They called it the Hampton Institute, obviously after Fred Hampton, the Black Panther activist, who had spent most of his young life, trying to bring poor people of all colors together, and after garnering some early success, inevitably, they soon attracted the attention of Beverley Di Franco and others of her ilk. "White Ruse", "False Consciousness" and "Misguided Class Reductionism" were all leveled at the Institute and although, initially, the Mainstream Media, were generally positive, as soon as it became increasingly obvious that the new voices had very little in common with their own social class and values, predictably they started to push back, as well. Now Errol and Terry were accused of stoking a class war and promoting pointless division, while Jamaal, publicly denounced his Spirit Son, as being nothing more than a "House Slave", happy to undermine the real mission of destroying racism, with a color blind rhetoric, that only plays straight into the hands of the white supremacists. "Why can't you be proud you're a black man, brother?" his tweet screamed across internet as the inevitable online pile on quickly followed. Surprisingly, the normally pugnacious Errol, didn't seem particularly affected by these attacks, and instead laughed them off as old hat, while he tweeted back "Of course I see color, Jamaal, but the difference with me is, I do my best not to let it affect how I treat other people", before proceeding to co- host an event on the South Bank with the conservative, Calvin Sewell, called *Black People are Not a Monolith,* drawing huge crowds, and proving to be a big success. However, despite this support, rather predictably, Jordan, took this new line of criticism very badly and although he had been the real catalyst to the new way of the thinking, initially setting up all the Podcasts and Websites, in common with most of his generation, he did not want to be seen as anti-progressive or worse still, a racial gatekeeper.

It was to be expected.

Social Media had bent the minds of Gen Z, addicting them to approval and group think and so as a result, Errol and Terry advised Jordan to take more of a back seat, as abuse from the Social Justice Warriors and the Left-wing press, continued without mercy for the next few months. However, despite this pressure, the Hampton Institute, and especially Friends not Allies only increased in size, registering over 30 million subscribers by the year's end. There was even an appearance on the Billy Morgan Experience, the world's biggest Podcaster, who flew the two Vampires over to America for an interview, which drew the biggest audience in online history, and even had the effect of making a convert of the host, who, on air, committed himself to the ideals of the Institute.

Furthermore this new movement, also presented Terry with an ideal opportunity to promote something that he had been thinking about for most of his extended life; that being the idea of *Muscular Socialism*. For decades now, the Vampire had watched with increasing despair, as the conservative side of the argument in politics, almost always captured the idea of self- discipline and greater personal responsibility. Get your life in order, stop blaming others for your circumstances, the buck stops with you, were all well known tropes of of the Right, with the result, that the Left had nothing left to offer except "Extreme Empathy" or even worse an endless ridicule of vital qualities, such as self sufficiency, resilience and societal accountability. He had even read recently in a Socialist publication which he regularly subscribed to, that "going to the gym" was part of the Patriarchy and possibly even racist. However, as far as Terry was concerned, this attitude was a million miles away from the truth. Why should we expect less of the 80%? Why shouldn't we expect people, even in the most challenging economic circumstances, to seek out a system which makes their lives better? In short, why shouldn't the Left start to tell people to sort themselves out? In fact, all of his experience of working class culture, both lived and observed, had told him this was true, and that those, usually at the bottom of the social hierarchy, valued structure and self reliance, way more than the critics on the Left did, who regularly shouted down such instincts, as "Unnecessarily Cruel" or "Bootstrap Politics".

For as long as he could remember, Terry had always been confused by this opposition from his side of the debate and in his darkest moments, suspected, that these well fed activists only did this, because they knew a disabled Proletariat would be much easier to control. This was no way for a dynamic ideology to proceed, thought the Vampire and so over the course of a few weeks, he sketched out his own blue-print for change. *A Code for yourself and a Code for your community* was Terry's new mantra and using, in particular, The Ragged Trousered Philanthropists by Robert Tressell and Meditations by Marcus Aurelius, as his main guides, while, at the same time ignoring the stark intellectualism of Marx and writers from the Frankfurt School, Terry, drew on the rich history of the English Working Class, from the Peasant Revolt through to the present day Labour Party, to compile twelve aims or guidelines, for a better way ahead.

The Aims of Muscular Socialism were:

1. **Join a Trade Union.** *If you're not at the table, you're on the menu.*
2. **Defend Free Speech with your life.** *It is as important as the air you breathe. If it is attacked, drop everything and walk to the front line in your flip flops.*
3. **Employers should only ever be paid ten times the rate of their average Employee.** *This will be the ultimate incentive to pay their workers more, so bosses end up with a better return.*
4. **Have a Code for yourself and a Code for your community.** *Read The Ragged Trousered Philanthropists by Robert Tressell and Meditations by Marcus Aurelius. Let them be your guides.*
5. **Bring back the 1970's.** *Obviously, without all the racism, sexism and homophobia. Aim for a Star Trek socialism, where all the basic needs of the 80% are met.*
6. **Embrace Wisdom, Temperance, Justice and Courage in your life** – *the four tenets of a Stoic Life.*
7. **Wages up, Assets down** – *Nuff said.*
8. **Reject victimhood at all costs.** *It should have no social currency at all. The World is indifferent to your fate.*
9. **Get better heroes.** *Boycott all modern celebrities. They are the storm-troopers of Neo-Liberalism, who help the establishment control the majority.*
10. **Reject compelled speech.** *Ignore pronouns when demanded. Remember it's your choice to use them or not use them. You do not have to sing the National Anthem, so why do this?*
11. **Remember the obstacle is the way.** *Without hardship we are nothing and live very diminished lives.*

And the Twelfth and most important commandment.

12. ***Friends not Allies.*** *Melanin is just skin deep, Race is basically a social construct, and an oppressor/oppressed narrative will damage us all in the end.*

Terry, also intended to include some other rules, in particular, never referring to George Orwell's 1984 or the Emperor's New Clothes by Hans Christian Anderson, in any critique of Woke behavior, which every Political Commentator seemed to be doing these days, under pain of a heavy fine; but, in the end, the Vampire decided to just stick with the original twelve. Soon, the phrase, *I'm a Muscular Socialist,* was appearing everywhere, on Shoulder Bags, Coffee Mugs, and Mouse-mats, and even infiltrated the inner sanctum of the Vampire Council, when a Palace Guard was caught on Social Media in his local gym wearing a T Shirt emblazoned with the new catch-phrase, and, as a result, was confined to barracks on horse's blood for a week. Inevitably the establishment pushed back, especially regarding the point in the new Manifesto that encouraged "Bringing back the 1970's" which Carswell declared in a very rare interview with Vanity Fair, "would only make the poor, poorer" while Bane Vulpine, who had previously given qualified support to the new movement, now viciously attacked them on his podcast, The Bane Event, as "Nothing more than Communists" and "Much worse than the Woke". This anger only intensified, a few months later, when thousands of members of the Hampton Institute, joined the Labour Party specifically to propose a motion at the Autumn

Conference banning anyone who had attended Public School or Grammar School or indeed sent their children to said schools from being members of the party. The vote, despite being very close, was eventually rejected by Conference, but sent shock waves through an increasingly detached Commentariat, who now recognized that the battle was finally coming to their front door. Not even the continual vitriol from comedians like Tudor Dee, who had tried to ridicule Errol and Terry at every turn, could land a decent punch and therefore it was, of no surprise, that late one evening, the two Vampires received a visit from Bane and Jamaal at their home in Fulham.

"You have to stop Terry. Remember who the enemy is" and "Errol, you can't keep helping White Supremacy" quickly fell on deaf ears, until a phone was placed on a kitchen table and a video of their attempted assassination of Oscar began to play.

"A Familiar had been in the room all the time, satisfying Oscar's various urges, but after you made your attack, he was able to hide in the wardrobe and film the whole thing. Everyone thinks it was Hector alone who did for Oscar, but the reality was, it was you. Trying to kill a First Tier Vampire, tut tut. Probably death for Vamps so young. Now, it's simple. Stop this nonsense and go back to where we were, or Carswell gets it in the post" declared Bane, holding up the phone, as the video ended with a knife being thrust into Oscar's chest, and a clear shot of Errol and Terry standing smiling in the background.

*

" Hi Tudor."

"Oh, err, hi. Look you can't be in here, I'm on soon and …" replied the Comedian, spinning around from admiring himself in the make up mirror before staring anxiously at the Vampire who had just appeared in his dressing room.

"You sure? It's only just after 6pm. You have at least a couple of hours before you go on, don't you?" interrupted Terry, quickly grabbing the nearest chair and sitting down.

"Look I know who you are Terry, but like I said, I'm preparing for a show. Can't we talk afterwards? It's not the right time."

"Not even for a Brother in Blood? I only wanted an autograph, I'm a big fan."

"Yeah, yeah, very funny. Anyway, Carswell is coming tonight? I'm protected you know."

"Oh, I know you are, but I think I could still get away with breaking the odd nose or maybe crushing a few ribs. Could blame the ADHD. It's all the rage at the moment. HR would understand" said Terry with a pleasant smile.

"Err, okay then. What do you want?" said Tudor, now looking unnerved and losing most of his initial cockiness.

"Just wanna talk."

"Well, it's still not very convenient, and like I said, I need to prepare, you know get in the right place."

"Oh right? So it won't it be the same old crap then? Slagging off some low hanging fruit like Boris Johnson and Donald Trump, then throw in a bit of existential thought quoting Heidegger or Sartre just to show everyone how clever you are, before laying into a fellow comedian who happens to be doing better than you. Surely, that doesn't require much preparation anymore, does it?"

"Look if you just want to insult me, I…"

"My apologies, only teasing. Look, I just wanted a chat, you know, man to man, or Vampire to Familiar, if you will."

"Well…"

"I mean, I could make you. You are aware of my powers?"

"Well, okay then. What is it you wanna to talk about, then?" said the Comedian, irritably, and very unused to being boxed in a corner.

"Cancel Culture," said Terry.

"Oh for fucks sake, not that again! Look, how many times! There is no Cancel Culture…" replied Tudor dismissively, as he reached across to pick up a piece of paper with some jokes written on it, before Terry moved forward in his seat and slapped the Comedian hard across the face.

"Arghh! Christ! What was that for?"

"Gaslighting."

"Err?"

"Like a cheating husband, who tells his suspicious wife, you're just imagining things, its all in your mind. I'm not banging my secretary baby, just like when you say, there is no Cancel Culture."

"I thought you said you weren't going to hurt me."

"Only if you lie, Tudor. Helen Joyce, Kellie Jay Keen, Gillian Phillips, Leo Kearse, Tabia Lee, James Dreyfus, Alison Bailey, Maya Forstater, Suzanne Moore, the list is flipping endless. Oh and before you say it's just accountability and no-one is being arrested by the Government for anything they say, you and I know perfectly well, that's not the point and every day, ordinary people are losing their jobs or having their lives completely ruined for saying very little. So lets start again, shall we? Cancel Culture? It exists, yes?

"Erm, okay," replied the Comedian sulkily rubbing the side of his face.

"Lovely, now we have common ground"

"So, I suppose you'll slap me again, if I say something else you disagree with? Yeah, very free speech," protested Tudor, shaking his head at the sudden unfairness.

"No, that's the Woke way, pal. Heckler's veto, bang some pots and pans together, shut down debate, scream racist! Free speech is a right wing trope! Is the juice worth the squeeze? I've heard it all, but fear not brother familiar, I'm a much more open minded than the pricks on your side of the argument, and so now we've established the parameters, that will be your last slap. Say what you want."

"Look I can't see the point of all this? We don't agree do we? Your podcast and your Hampton Institute, whatever it's called, says it all doesn't it?"

"Well there's a start. Why don't you like the Hampton Institute? We bring working class black, brown and white people together. Challenge the system of crony capitalism, try to create real change, gotta be a good thing, yeah?"

"Well not if you're working for the Establishment and doing their bidding, it isn't?"

"Oh right. We're the establishment? Funny thing is, I thought, you were."

"Oh right, 'course we are," said Tudor, shaking his head again.

"Now is that misinformation or disinformation, I can never tell? Of course you're the Establishment and do you know how I know? The way you always know. It's always the ones, the best jokes are about, and today, that's your side. Jesus, I remember when your side, used to be my side. That's ironic innit? Spitting Image, Ben Elton, Mark Thomas, but now the Left just aren't funny."

"Yes they are, you just have to look"

"Oh I have and as far as I can see, it's laughing at people who "just don't get it". It's boring dude."

"You say."

"Okay, So you can say what you want then?"

"Of course. As long as you don't punch down."

"Oh right, so not like when you used to take the piss out of disabled children, then?" said Terry, folding his arms.

"Well that was another time."

"Oh just admit it Tudor. You can't say what you want. I mean I don't have to look in your eyes and read your mind to see that, do I? Do you know how many emails me and Errol get from Actors, Singers, Creatives, all saying that they secretly agree with us but can't say it in public? In fact, the next one who does it, I might bloody bite them for having no balls. Bet you're the same? Absolutely shitting yourself in case you place one toe over the line, and then when some poor bastard does, you all pile in to ruin his career. Another competitor out of the way. Another space on Taskmaster or Dave freed up. And don't make me laugh about "Punch down". What does that even mean? Humor punches anywhere it want's Tudor. I shouldn't have to tell you that. Up, down, around. That's what it does. A joke is always targeting someone isn't it? Someone is always getting done and that's fine, because at the end of the day the audience decides, don't they?"

"Well, times have changed."

"That's a crap excuse. What about Graham Sadowitz then?"

"Well..."

"Well what? He's just got banned from the Edinburgh Fringe, and then they canceled his tour for doing the same act he's been doing for the last twenty years. Thought he was supposed to be greatest inspiration to British Comedy since Monty Python or Billy Connelly? Thought he was a genius you couldn't categorize? In fact, didn't he give you your first break on Channel Four?"

"Well that was a long time ago and anyway he goes too far, doesn't he?"

"That's his job! He's a comedian for God's sake. He's supposed to find the edge. Christ, no wonder Dave Chappelle and Babylon Bee take the piss out of you lot."

"Babylon Bee? Really? They're a bunch of religious freaks for a start and Dave Chappelle isn't funny, he just says fuck a lot. You know, I hear this crap all the time, that the Left are the establishment. Really? Well, correct me if I'm wrong but haven't we had the Tories in for the last decade or more? And like aren't ninety percent of the media, far right? Err, the Daily Mail? Doh! Need I go on?" said Tudor, sitting up in his seat and desperately trying to re-claim the high ground again.

"There you go again, Tudor. Pointless hyperbole. You forget, I was born in 1918, so I know what the Far Right actually looks like and so do you for that matter. I mean the Daily Mail might be annoying but it's hardly Far Right is it?"

"Yes they are. They're really far right."

"Really? How? They believe in the NHS, no guns for the Police, Abortion Rights, Women's Rights, Gay Marriage. You think, Heinrich Himmler or the Grand Wizard of the Klu Klux Klan were up for all that? Behave yourself, son. You'll be telling me words are violence next."

"Well that's your opinion."

"Just my opinion? So, what about the BBC? Right wing? The Universities? The Arts? All right wing, yeah?"

"Well some of them are, more than you think."

"Who? Where? Survey after survey shows the complete opposite. 1 in 12 lecturers are Conservatives, 90% of all Humanity departments are Left leaning, and now the little brats, who have been brainwashed by these Apparatchiks are all over the Civil Service and big Corporations, eagerly spreading their bullshit creed about and canceling anyone who gets in their way. Hardly viewpoint diversity, Tudor? I mean I'm a Lefty, but it hardly seems fair, know what I mean?

"Well, what about the Royal Family then? We still have them, don't we? If that's not proof of the right wing running everything I don't know what is."

"What century are you living in son? It's not 1630. The Royal Family have no power, they are puppets of the past, and in fifty years they'll be gone, any dick knows that. But I tell who does have the power. Corporations and people like you."

"Oh of course, I'm in control, I'm the problem. I

mean, what was it you said in your little Jordan Petersen, Muscular Socialist, 12 rules for making the bed or whatever it was. Get rid of Celebrities. Of course Ant and Dec rule the world, don't they? I mean, once they're overthrown, it will all be dreamy. Give me a break" said Tudor, shaking his head, and pretending to look at his page of jokes again.

"Then why do you defend the status quo then?"

"I don't."

"Of course you do! praising big Corporations, Quangos who spread Identity Politics and getting people thrown off Twitter for saying nothing."

"Well it's a Private Company, they can do what they want."

"Yeah, until they do it to your side of the argument and then it's "stifling free speech". You see Tudor, this is why most people hate celebrities like you, because you have no utility anymore. You used to cheer us up but now you just depress us with all your hypocrisy. It's making us feel unwell and that's why there's a change coming, but not the one that you were hoping for. Gay men, like Andrew Doyle and Glen Greenwald, Trans men and women like Blair White and Buck Angel, Black men like John McWhorter and Coleman Hughes, Women like Inaya Folarin Iman and Batya Ungar Sargon, Matt Taibbi, Douglas Murray. Lefties, Tories, Independents, Free thinkers. This is the real progressive Nirvana, you idiot. You wanted to divide us, with all your bullshit, but the fact is you've achieved the complete opposite. The push back against the Wokeocracy will prove to be the greatest Anti Racist, Pro- LGBT, pro Women, pro Class project in History. You know, it's funny, but I used to think that the only way humans could ever truly band together was if the Aliens invaded, but now the Woke has turned up, there's no need. You're the fucking Martians"

"Oh, so you're othering us, then," said Tudor, now completely outraged.

"Without a shadow of a doubt."

"So you want to kill us."

"Not any more Tudor. I used to bite cunts like you all the time, thinking I was making a difference, but that's before I realized, that I was just turning myself into the very person I was claiming to hate. What was it Nietzsche said? Beware hunting monsters lest you become one yourself. Jesus, I was so bitter, an absolute joke. But then I woke up. It was my great awokening, if you will; and now I don't want to bite the white progressive bell-ends anymore. In fact I want them to live forever. Longer than Vampires in fact, so we can see what bullshit really looks like. So keep calling everyone you don't agree with, Far Right, or Racist or Transfuckingphobic. I don't care. Keep doing it, son, it only make us stronger. That's why I don't agree with toppling statues. The dickheads of the past need to be in plain sight so we can see them for what they really were" said Terry, suddenly reaching forward to clasp Tudor's face into his hands and then stare deeply into the Comedian's eyes.

"Be at peace my brother, I can see your pain. So, you're not as successful as you think you should be. It's a damn shame. Why can't the stupid masses not understand the genius of your innovative deconstructionism? Why did both of your BBC series fail, while Ross Label, with his working

class bombast and ever so predictable drug habit, conquer America? But you know this is wrong my friend. There's a reason no-one wants to interview you, and all you have to show for 30 years in comedy is a room filled with 500 social justice warriors, who think you're the Comedian's Comedian. If the audience think you hate them, they're not going to laugh are they? It's as simple as that. So stop being such a snob, stop pissing on the poor and try and be honest with yourself for a change. Forget all the hate Tudor, and be at peace, and I assure you, all that anger in your soul, will disappear. That's right, breathe deeply my friend, let the tension go, and so tonight, when you perform, shelve the Woke shit, and just go for the comedy, yeah? Say anything, it's only jokes, after all, and be a Comedian again. Be brave, you used to be good at it, and I guarantee it will make you happy."

"Oh, err, hi. It's Terry from the Hampton Institute isn't it?" said Tudor now blinking his eyes and slowly coming out of the Vampire's mind weave, before producing an uncharacteristically warm smile, which slightly disturbed his guest.

"Yes, that's right," replied Terry, now standing up.

"Oh wow, I love your Podcast, *Friends not Allies*, listen to it all the time. Errol is fucking hilarious, isn't he? Always going on about footballers diving and paying too much for Jamaican food. Totally brilliant. In fact, entre nous, I agree with more or less everything you say, but I have to keep it to myself, you know the fucking woke mob and all that? Drive's you nuts sometimes, doesn't it, but you gotta make a living, haven't you? So, anyway Terry, what are you doing here, did someone let you in?"

"Yeah. I hope you don't mind?"

"Not at all, it's fantastic, glad to see you."

"Oh good. Just wanted to wish you luck before the show."

"Oh that's really nice, thank you. Well grab a seat then and lets have a chat, I'm not due on for another few hours."

"Would love to, but I've gotta go I'm afraid. But, like I said, good luck for tonight. I'm sure you'll be brilliant."

"Shame. Err, maybe, we could do a Podcast together, you know in the future?"

"Oh definitely," replied Terry with a smile, before turning around and exiting the dressing room.

CHAPTER NINETEEN

"So what we doing here? I hate this fucking area," said Errol, as he sat hunched by the bar and stared blankly into his pint of craft lager.

"Crouch End is okay, mate. I remember Oscar used to bring me down here all the time in the Nineties. It was a lot of fun back then," replied Terry smiling at the sorry condition of his friends face after three days of non stop drinking.

"Well it ain't now," slurred Errol before nodding his head in the direction of a sign behind the bar that read *"This establishment does not tolerate Racism, Sexism, Sexual Harassment, Homophobia, Transphobia or any form of aggression. If anyone makes you feel uncomfortable at any point, please speak to the bar staff."*

"Yeah, it's a bit wrong, innit?"

"This is what we're giving up, Tel. In five years, every Boozer, Cinema, and bloody BBQ, will be like this. We were really getting somewhere, you know. Bringing everyone together against all this bullshit, it was fucking amazing, and now we're supposed to just walk away. Nah, geezer, that ain't right."

"Well we have to. Bane and Jamaal will tell Carswell and then Jordan will be dead, and that will be that. She's still grieving over Oscar, even now. Heard, she'd recently massacred 20 mortals and bathed in their blood, just for the hell of it. We've no choice, mate," replied Terry remorsefully, looking back towards his friend, who didn't seem to be listening, but was rather continuing to stare at the sign behind the bar.

"Oi mate," said Errol, looking down the counter.

"Err yes, can I help," replied a young barman, brightly, making his way towards the Vampire.

"I'd like to report, someone is making me feel uncomfortable," said Errol.

"Oh, really? Okay, who is it," replied the barman, as he shot Terry an accusing glance.

"Nah not him. It's you, innit."

"Me?" said the slightly shocked barman.

"Yeah you. I imagine you agree with what that sign says."

"Err, of course," said the barman turning to glance at the notice behind him.

"Well that makes me feel uncomfortable."

"Okay, but, err…"

"I mean this is a pub innit? A place for open discussion, a forum for the exercise of that most sacred right, freedom of speech. But now that sign tells me I can't do that."

"Well, of course, there is freedom of speech."

"So can I say a Transwoman is a Transwoman then?"

"Well, no that's hate speech."

"To you maybe, but to ninety-nine percent of the world, it's just basic common sense, innit? Okay, if I can't say that then, can I say that Critical Race Theory is a fucking scam and will drive working class white people and black people apart and at each other's throats?"

"Well that's racist, isn't it?" confirmed the barman.

"You think? Okay then, so can I say that you are a total piece of shit, whose neck I'm gonna rip open right now, cos people like you destroy the very reason to be alive?" scowled Errol rising from his stool, and grabbing the barman by the shirt, before proceeding to slap his face repeatedly for a few seconds, until Terry quickly stepped in to prevent a rather public homicide.

"He ain't worth Carswell sticking us in Bloodwall's and chucking away the key, is he?" said Terry now wrenching Errol's drunken fangs away from the young's man neck, and then after quickly hypnotizing the poor unfortunate barman and the four other regulars who were in the bar, he dragged his friend out of the pub and back home to Fulham. Predictably, Errol threw up when they got back and after cleaning him up, Terry laid him out on his pallet to sleep it off, while he poured himself a drink and wandered restlessly around the house for the next few hours. Errol was right, they had come a long way, a hell of a long way. The establishment was rattled, while the rank and file of everyday life, after years of impoverished impotence, were now walking around with something approaching a spring in their step. However, despite this progress, Terry couldn't let Jordan die. It was his last covenant with Lauryn and so after finishing off a bottle of good malt and visiting the local garage for some more cigarettes, he finally pulled out his phone and texted Bane. He would agree to their demands, but that it would take a month at least to provide the right excuses and wind everything down. Naturally, Bane argued for a week, but after a few more texts, Terry managed to persuade him that this would look a bit contrived and as a result got some extra time. However, when Errol awoke, he was predictably less than impressed.

"Two weeks! Two fucking weeks?!" spat out Errol, the next evening, in the kitchen, sipping on a hangover cure of frozen blood and valium, while Terry leant against the door of the fridge to try and explain the reasons for what he had done.

"Mate, they will show Carswell the video, and I don't really mind about me, but she will definitely kill Jordan. I mean, you know what a vengeful bitch she is. Look at what she did to Marilyn Monroe. Wouldn't share her lipstick in the bathroom at some film doo and the next day, she'd knocked her off. Imagine what she'll do to Jordan over Oscar."

"Ah, c'mon Tel, that's just a story."

"Yeah, well may be it is, but you could see her doing it, yeah? And what's more Hector told me before he got interred, that she hates me, blames me for Oscar and everything. Nah, I can't take the chance. It ain't happening pal. He's my Spirit Son for fuck's sake."

"Alright, I get it, but after all the work we've done, geezer. There has to be another way?" said Errol, rubbing his face in exasperation.

"Well, I can't see it."

"What about Maxwell then? She's nearly as old as Bane

and from what I heard, she fought in the first two Lycan wars and apparently fucked loads of 'em up before she decided to wear a dress."

"She's got Body Dysphoria, dude. It's not a lifestyle choice, is it?"

"Well, you know what I mean, Tel. She's powerful. Me, you and Maxwell, could easily jump Bane and Jamaal and then stick them in a coffin till they tell us where the phone is."

"You can't disappear Bane and Jamaal you nob. They're famous for God's sake."

"Nah, we don't kill them, do we? Just keep them there until they give us the film."

"You sure? Even if we do get them to tell us, that still leaves the Familiar," said Terry shaking his head.

"That's no problem I know the prick. Troy David, innit."

"The Premiership Footballer?"

"Oscar was banging him for ages. Look c'mon Terry, you've said it a million times yourself. What's the one thing they don't want? Ordinary Blacks and Whites working with each other, and now all over the world they are. There's even black Ramblers in the New Forest. I'm serious. Camping out with a load of yokels from Dorset and singing Bob Marley and oldie English folk songs together, it's beautiful. Do it bruv! Ring Maxwell. What have we got to lose? It will work, I swear," urged Errol as Terry sat and nibbled his bottom lip for a few minutes, while he considered the pro's and cons of the proposal including the risk to Jordan before another eager glance from his friend, finally persuaded him to pull the phone out from his pocket.

"Oh my god Terry? Long time, no hear. How are you petal? Where have you been? Thought you were avoiding me, so I didn't call. You were so naughty, walking out when you did. Was it something I said? Couldn't be, I'm fabulous, aren't I?Anyhoo, been listening to your podcasts and all your shenanigans. Muscular Socialist? Hilarious. I hear it's annoyed the fuck out of the High Council. Jamaal's gone nuts apparently, calling everyone white adjacents. It's glorious. Crazy about Oscar and Hector as well, wasn't it? Oh and sorry about your girlfriend by the way" said Maxwell, and as usual packing in every bit of recent news in his first sentence, until Terry cut her short to explain the reason for his call, before she launched off on yet another tangent.

"So it was you and Errol, then? Naughty Boys," giggled Maxwell.

"So, you in?" asked Terry.

"Why of course darling, wouldn't miss it for the world, But I get the Publishing Rights for any future books or films."

"Forget it, Maxwell. It's supposed to be a secret. They'll be no films, alright" snapped Terry, pulling the phone from his ear and shaking his head at Errol in amazement.

"Oh, there's always a film Terry, but don't worry, I'm thinking 100 years time," replied Maxwell laughing again, before agreeing on a plan to invite Bane and Jamaal over to her flat, and then springing a trap.

Over the next few days, more texts were exchanged between the conspirators until with everything in place, Errol and Terry, this time, without Jordan, just in case anything went wrong, traveled up to Manchester, to lay in wait in Maxwell's apartment for their blackmailers to arrive. As agreed, Maxwell had persuaded both Jamaal and Bane to come over for a dinner, whilst also inviting Kevin as well, to make sure everyone was relaxed, especially, as Bane had sounded a bit paranoid on the phone.

By 2am, the guests had arrived, and after a half an hour of drinking and taking drugs, Kevin came into where Errol and Terry were hiding, to signal all was well and that Maxwell had slipped a sedative into their cocaine. Another twenty minutes then passed, for Bane and Jamaal to pass out into their chairs, before they were ferried from the living area to two lead coffins that Maxwell had waiting in a room at the end of her apartment.

It was nearly 4am, when the first noises from inside the coffin began to surface on the intercom, prompting Maxwell, Errol, Terry and Kevin to make their way to the back room again to welcome their new arrivals.

"What? What's going on? Let me out. Let me out of here!" cried Jamaal waking up first.

"Give us the video."

"Terry Anderson, is that you? You're in a lot of trouble son. Now let me out! I'm a First Tier Vampire, you can't do this. Let me out," bellowed Jamaal menacingly, while in the coffin beside him, Bane had started to stir too.

"Oh my God, where am I? Get me out, get me out. I'm claustrophobic in these damn things. I need my pills," shouted the Right wing Pod-caster, banging the side of the coffin.

"This is treason, let me out," joined in Jamaal again.

"Give us the video."

"Errol? Is that you? What the fuck are you doing?

"We want the phone."

"Fuck you, McKenzie, and after all I did for you."

"You made plenty out of me, Jamaal."

"Piece of Grenadian shit. I should have left you, in that West London hovel, I found you in. Fucking traitor," spat back his Spirit Father.

"Anyway, it's no use. Do you think we haven't made plans? If we don't contact our Familiars in 24 hours, they give the video to Carswell."

"Nice try Bane, but that's only in the movies. No-one trusts a Familiar, they are mortal remember," countered Maxwell.

"Maxwell. Is that you? God. You're dead, you Tranny fuck."

"Tutt tutt. That's Transphobic Bane, and this is being recorded by the way, so if you continue, I may have to expose you on my website and let the Trolls have you," laughed Maxwell.

"Fucking lets us out," screamed Jamaal again in frustration.

"Give us the phone then," repeated Terry, as the two Vampires inside the coffins continued to bellow for their freedom, while amidst all the shouts and threats, Errol now turned to smile at Maxwell.

"I meant to ask. Why did you help us? Bane's your friend, isn't he?"

"He is and I love him, I really do but he is for the status quo now, which is soooo fucking boring, don't you think? It's like with Gary Lineker and Gareth Southgate. I remember, when they were just nice guys but incredibly tedious, but now everyone hangs on their every word, as if they have something terribly important to say. It's the age of bullshit and performance darling. If Diogenes or Lord Rochester were born today they'd be prescribed Adderall or locked up in an Institution. For some unknown reason, eccentricity has suddenly become a crime and so this awful little phase in our existence must come to an end, I'm afraid. I'm faithful to one thing and one thing alone. Art. In fact, I am bound by a sacred oath and anyway Walter Gropius would never forgive me."

"Who?"

"Founder of Bauhaus silly."

"Thought they were a band" replied Errol smiling again, and was just about to lean down and speak into the micro-phone to taunt their captives once more, when the door of the back room suddenly sprang open, and there in front of them, stood Lady Carswell, holding Jordan by his neck.

"Thank you Kevin, you can go now."

"Your ladyship."

"God, Kevin, you little bastard," declared Maxwell, quickly punching the younger Vampire on the side of the head.

"Now, now Maxwell, a little more decorum. You're a lady remember. So here we are, and guess what I have," said the Chief Inspector waving a mobile phone in front of the three Vampires."

"The film?" said Errol, a little shocked.

"I read Jamaal's mind and found his little hiding place. Of course, it only confirmed what I knew already. Hector would never have done this on his own account. Why kill his Spirit Son, over a dead Lycan? Not possible."

"I didn't tell him to help."

"Of course you didn't Terry, but Hector is a man of honor. Fatal for our kind. That is the true horror of living so long, nothing really changes, because nothing is supposed to change. By the way, do know how old I am?" asked the Chief Imperator, as she dragged a terrified Jordan into the middle of the room.

"I heard 5,000 years. Sumerian," replied Maxwell, before taking another opportunity to punch Kevin in the side of the head again.

"Ancient Sumer, of course, or what about Hattusa, where it was said, the first Vampire wiped out all the Hittites or maybe the Sea peoples, who were in fact, a race of Vampires from Sardinia, and caused the Bronze Age collapse. I have heard them all. In fact, it's way too early, Maxwell, my sweet little hypocrite. The first Vampire was actually a Druid called Barach, from the tribe of the Iceni, who in the first century, found a way to change his blood and achieve extended life. He served at my mother's court. I was the youngest daughter of Boudicca. I saw her flogged by the Romans and my sisters raped. I saw the fury in her eyes and the cities burn. Roman babies roasted over fires and men butchered like pigs. I saw Barach tell my mother not to fight the Legions on open ground, because he knew the power of the invader and then from a war chariot, my ten year old eyes watched as 10,000 trained Romans decimated 200,000 Britons without even blinking an eye. It was then, I understood how things really worked. The many are weak, and it is only the Elites who can make the world turn. Never again would I cheer when I saw the faces of the down-trodden or the weary, and when Barach chose me as his successor and gave me life, I knew where my mission lay. To let those with the power and intelligence take their rightful place. I was in Constantinople with Justinian, in Aachen with Charlemagne, besties with Eleanor of Aquitaine in the court of Henry II, it was divine. Spreading my influence, keeping the flame of progress alive, making sure the people who should be in charge, stayed in charge."

"Why don't you let the people decide?"

"Because they are scum, my dear Errol. They believe anything, eat anything, do anything. We are Vampires, we are the Elite. Mortals need our guidance. Once it was Catholicism, then the Enlightenment and now it's Woke. I don't have to believe in any of it. Personally I think Beverley Di Franco is a fraud. I have looked into her mind and it is so devoid of any integrity that she would have happily been a guard at Auschwitz, if it had served her purpose, but for the moment it works. The world is smaller and we are getting better, so we argue over nothing, because we're bored. Progress has always been about boredom."

"So what do we do now," asked Terry, staring in horror at Jordan's pleading face.

"Creatures like us, only live for 2,000 years, and that includes me, whatever the conspiracy theorists like to say. My position gives me no more right to a longer life than any Vampire, so I must pass on my legacy. You have ruined so much Terry, more than you can ever know. Oscar was my perfect replacement. Two hundred years of nurturing, prompting, even love, for what it's worth. But now I must start again and quickly, so I must be paid for my labour. You are in my debt, Brother in Blood."

"Look, I had no idea that…"

"People like you seldom do," interrupted Carswell, before pulling out a large knife and instantly severing Jordan's head from his shoulders.

"No, no, you can't…" screamed Terry launching himself at Carswell, before she easily deflected him with a flick of her hand, leaving him unconscious in the corner of the room.

"Here is the evidence you are looking for. I found the Familiar who filmed it and he was more than happy to hand it over," said Carswell placing the mobile phone on one of the coffins

"So now we die," said Errol, looking around at the devastation in the room.

"Die? Why, of course not. We need your opposition. Don't you understand, my sweet boy? That's how it works. It makes our job so much easier," replied Carswell, moving forward to open the second casket and guide Jamaal onto the polished floor.

"I have decided that he will be my successor now, oh, and, you can leave Bane in the coffin, his voice is no longer needed. My people will come by tomorrow to collect him" she added busily, before turning around and walking the dazed Vampire towards the exit of the flat.

*

Probably the best dive of his career, mused Errol, taking a sip of his coffee, as he glanced down at the headline on his phone again before reading how Premiership footballer, Troy David, had fallen to his death from his luxury East

End apartment block in the early hours of the morning, apparently after an argument with his girlfriend. Carswell tying up loose ends in her usually efficient manner, and now the phone evidence had been destroyed too, Errol allowed himself a brief moment of relief, before his thoughts returned inevitably to his friend again.

After the horror in Manchester, they had returned to London with Jordan's corpse, whereupon Terry insisted on taking it to the spot, Lauryn had been laid to rest, before falling to his knees and starting to dig. It was pitiful to watch, as the Vampire tore into the damp earth with his bare hands, while muttering foul accusations to himself in the stillness of the night.

"They would both be alive now, if they hadn't met you."

"Your existence is death."

"You must take your own life now, before you do any more harm."

Eventually Terry reached the polished wood of the coffin and after ripping open the lid and re-uniting his Spirit Son with his former love, he lay on top of the corpses, as if wishing to join them in death, before Errol managed to pull him out of the grave and drag him back to Fulham before sun came up. This desire for self destruction only increased in intensity over the following weeks, as Terry's mind, now appeared to be totally broken from all the guilt and the grief and as a consequence, Errol rarely left his side, as multiple times, he'd had to drag Terry back from the rear door of his cell, while he sought natural justice from the rays of the morning sun. It seemed he couldn't be reasoned with and Errol was genuinely at a loss as to what to do next, until a Vampire specialist, he had met during his time with

EVC, came over to prescribe "a secret tonic" containing of all things, Ketamin and Lithium, to finally bring his friend, some measure of relief.

Meanwhile, Errol, when he wasn't preventing his friend from turning into a shovelful of ashes, was still, continuing the work of the Hampton Institute, even setting up a hot-line, for those affected by the emerging Woke ideology. Authors not being published for unfashionable views, Speakers being no platformed for standing up for free speech, workers being sacked for sharing a tweet, bank accounts being canceled for political views, the Institute soon became the go-to place for those, Left and Right of the political sphere, seeking refuge and redress from an increasingly dogmatic world. Predictably Jamaal, who had recently taken over most of the day to day duties of the Vampire Council from Carswell, herself now retired to her estates in Cornwall to write her memoirs, pushed back with the usual tactic of denying that there was a problem in the first place. "Nothing to see here" and "So-called Wokeness is just an invention of a hard right press" together with the increasingly meaningless labels "Nazis" "Racists" and "White Supremacists" were all thrown in the direction of the Hampton Institute, which was doubly ironic, considering, not only, who the Institute was named after, but also that over 50% of the organization were now working class people of color. However, these attacks from the usual suspects, proved fruitless and despite his own Wikipedia page being changed so many times to "Far right commentator" by woke activists, that it became something of a standing joke, Errol's reputation as a "courageous spokesmen for the truth" was still assured. As a result, he became a popular guest on various podcasts, always engaging in lively discussions about controversial subjects, even getting himself into a much publicized spat with black American libertarian, Don Walsh, over of all things the philosopher Ayn Rand. Walsh, a big supporter of Rand and her philosophy of Objectivism and hyper Individualism, declared that not only, was she one of the most important figures of recent times, but also that the UK would be a much better place, if they adopted some of her principles, whereupon, Errol called the dead Philosopher, a self-obsessed fraud, and probably half the reason America "was completely fucked up in the first place". Admittedly, Errol, hadn't read too much of Ayn Rand's work, and based his opinion solely on the fact that even Oscar thought she was a bit nuts and had turned down her request to be a Familiar, but his comments were enough for his American host, to immediately terminate the interview before declaring, "All black British men to be scared of success," and vowing never to speak to any of them ever again. This suited Errol just fine. For years Black British men, like himself, had looked across the Atlantic for counsel and inspiration. It was natural. They were the richest, most successful, and most influential black men on the planet, but, in the end, did it really help? Were the Italians like the Italian Americans or the Chinese like Chinese Americans? Were they hell thought Errol, and so finally, after nearly seventy years in the land of his birth, Errol started to feel something he had hitherto, stubbornly refused to even contemplate. National pride. Forget Afro-Pessimism. Lovers Rock, Soul 2 Soul, Jungle, Grime, Drill, Stuart Hall, Idris Elba, the odd entrepreneuer on Dragon's

Den. All black, all British and all achieved in less than 75 years since stepping off the SS Windrush in 1948. It was new ground, and although he couldn't really see himself at the Last Night of the Proms, any time soon, cutting the umbilical cord to the United States was definitely the next important step for those from his background in the UK.

Elsewhere, in another dramatic twist, Maxwell, still smarting from her recent encounter with Carswell, boldly arranged a sting operation, where she forced Kevin, by threatening to incarcerate him in a lead coffin for 100 years for his former treachery, to seduce Beverley Di Franco and record all of their post coital ramblings. Within weeks these intimate discussions were released online, where the world could finally hear the best selling author admit that "The Wokies are nothing more than pampered rich kids, "Trans activists are complete fantasists" and "Critical Race Theory is so full of shit, that she only keeps pushing it because she is making so much money". Naturally this revelation caused an immediate sensation, and despite huge denials from Jamaal and Di Franco, saying that her voice had been digitally doctored and that she had been manipulated by a "spiteful Patriarchy," Corporations soon began to engage in damage control by distancing themselves from the social justice activist and her confederates.

Meanwhile, amidst all the uproar, Terry remained living with Errol in Fulham, and continued to maintain a low profile, whilst gradually reducing his reliance on his medication. Within, months, he was drug free, and determined to make the most of this new start, he quickly immersed himself in the teachings of the famed Psychologist Carl Jung with particular reference to issues regarding integrating his Shadow, ie. the darker side of one's personality which lies dormant in the sub-conscious. Of course, this type of "Shadow work" was generally ridiculed and seen as pointless by most Vampires, who were usually committed to more selfish and homicidal ends, but Terry found great solace in the practice, especially with regard to projection and transference and together with his on-going belief in Stoicism, began to seriously rationalize his guilt surrounding, not only deaths of Lauryn and Jordan, but also those of the many middle class people who's lives he taken because of his permanent feelings of class anger. Only in Britain were these feelings so pronounced, as if passed on from generation to generation, like a vengeful gene, demanding on-going retribution for some unspecified crime from a distant past. For the last eighty years now, this was all he knew and therefore determined to finally break free of these toxic chains he decided to start his own podcast, named "The Bridge" in an attempt to broker a true rapprochement between the established factions in British society. Progress was slow at first, as neither side wished to participate in any kind of a meaningful way, but gradually, through the Vampire's newly acquired relaxed manner and openness to all perspectives, the channel started to take off. Soon, Supermarket Staff sat down with University Academics, Heads of HR with Self Employed Plumbers, as even an unexpected invitation to talk to a group of students from a notable public school, presented itself to the reformed Vampire. In times past, Terry might have preferred to pull his fangs out with a pair of rusty pliers or go for a noon day stroll in the middle of Death Valley, than stand in front of five or six hundred of some of the most privileged teenagers in the country, but now he found that he almost relished the challenge. Fair enough, half of them could probably code and speak Chinese mandarin by the time they had left Prep School and had the kind of social safety nets that most people could only dream of, but, in saying that, they were probably just like the billions of young men, who had walked the earth before them, awkward, a little lost, and with a terrible urge to fit in.

"Who should be in charge?" said the Vampire, looking out towards his night time audience in a large School Assembly Hall, while he placed both of his hands on the lectern.

"Truth is no one knows. Marx thought he did, and dreamt of a blissful Utopia, but without consent from everyone, that was always going to be the path to hell, because like it or not, human nature will never, ever, EVER, be held back. Forget all that Rousseauian cobblers you might have read, that deep inside, we are all just dying to get back to a Garden of Eden somewhere to frolic about naked and write poetry in an Egalitarian paradise. It's complete bullshit. In fact, the real truth is Mother Nature loves nothing more than a hierarchy, and so whatever system we choose, be it, Capitalism, Communism, Fascism or Democratic Socialism, the likelihood, is the majority will probably always end up being ruled over by a bunch of smart – arses, who think they know better than anyone else. It's called the 80/20 rule. I'm sure you all know it. 80% of the consequences, comes from 20% of the causes. You can even see it in dating. 80% of the girls go for 20% of the guys. That's why there's so many punch ups in Kebab Houses after the Clubs kick out. And for my money, this concept, above all others, is probably the defining principle of our existence and should be the very first thing any child is taught when they first go to school or even before. In fact, I think it's so important, that Vilfedo Pareto, the guy who who came up with this theory in the last century, should be up there with Socrates, Shakespeare and Einstein, in our estimation. So, knowing this, what do we do about it? Let the cards fall where they may? Well that's been tried, but then no-one is happy, are they? The 20% feel guilty and start decolonizing the museums, while everybody else just feels excluded and starts eating Pizza and watching porn for the rest of their lives before finally dropping down dead from diabetes. Any other options? Co-operation perhaps? We've done it before, even without resorting to a big dirty war or a Global Pandemic. Just take the band, Iron maiden. The lead singer was posh, while the rest were skint. That worked, if you like heavy metal of course. Then the film Withnail and I, Withnail was upper class, Mick and Keef in the Stones, or Larwood and Jardine in the cricket" said Terry as some of the boys laughed at the comparisons, while someone at the back shouted out.

"So how do we do it on a larger scale then?"

"Well, that's the question, isn't it? First thing I would say is, let's start from the bottom up, this time. Let working class people, of all colours and creeds take control of their own destiny for a change, and don't think you have to get involved, just because you feel some natural sense of injustice at how the world works. You could be doing more harm than good. Remember Kropotkin and Lenin, the architects of the Russian Revolution of 1917, came from very affluent backgrounds, as did the 1970's Marxist's terrorists, the Bader Meinhoff gang in Germany and the Red Brigade in Italy, and even today, most of the Left- wing activists from Antifa to Extinction Rebellion are, in general, the sons and daughters of the wealthy and well connected. *Political ideology should never be based on middle class guilt,* as, ultimately, it only turns into a tragic kind of theatre sprinkled with a lot of misery. I mean, if these people, had ever stopped to ask those they were trying to help, what they really wanted, they would have got some very different answers from what they eventually chose to do. No bugger wants to end up in a Gulag eating fish heads do they? And although, I've been a Socialist all my life, I've never believed that the ends ever justifies the means, however good the cause. And so while we're on the subject of guilt, the second thing you guys should do, is not feel shame about your privilege or being posh or middle class or that your dad is well off or his dad was or his dad. It's all nonsense in the end, because what we should be really focusing on, is what actually matters and if the paradigm of the 80/20 rule is always going to be with us, which all the stats, up to this point, tell us is probably correct, then wouldn't it be better for us to recognise this fact, and act accordingly. We all know the 20%, are gonna do okay, whatever happens, so we don't really have to worry about them, do we? Maybe dish out the odd plaudit now and again, perhaps a knighthood here and there but nothing more, because the real job of a society should always and ever be, to sort out the 80%. Sort out the 80%, then the 20% don't have to feel so guilty, in turn the 80% don't have to feel so resentful. Job done my son, and after thousands of years of Tribes, Empires and Governments, we can finally learn the most important lesson from history. That being the proper negotiation between the Classes. Those with the power, and those without, finding an effective equilibrium, so we can all have a shot at hopefully living the good life" declared Terry with a warm smile, before, to his absolute amazement, he received a standing ovation from those in the Assembly Hall, plus an invitation to stay for a drink afterwards in the teacher's common room.

However, he politely declined, because even as a reformed class warrior, a dry sherry or tea and crumpets may have been a bit of a reach for the moment, and so after shaking a few hands and posing for some selfies, he strolled happily, out of the Public School towards his bike in the car park, where, unexpectedly, he was stopped in his tracks by a familiar voice.

"Hey Terry, what you doing here?"

"Sammy Stagg! Bloody hell! What am I doing here? What are you doing here? You on a demo against Private Schools or something."

"Err, well, no. Actually my son goes here."

"Your son goes here?! You're pulling my wire?" laughed Terry, shaking his head.

"Yeah, I know. Wife's idea really. Didn't like the Local Comp, thought he'd get bullied. Not that I should be worried about that. He's just shoved some Trans kids' jacket down the toilet, so I've had to come up and try and sort it out."

"Boys innit?"

"No excuse, really. Just lucky the Headmaster's a big fan, so I talked him out of expelling him. Gave him a few free tickets for my next tour."

"Ah well, all sorted now."

"Yeah, suppose so. Anyway Terry, great to see you again, but better go, wife's waiting in the car, she who must be obeyed and all that. But definitely we should catch up soon. Still can't believe, how young, you look."

"It's the smashed avocado, Sammy," replied Terry and for a moment, he stood and watched the old Eighties protest singer slink away into the darkness, before getting onto his bike and heading towards the high street.

CHAPTER TWENTY

Terry looked down at the latest tweet from Jamaal on his phone as he took another pull from his cigarette.

"What the hell has happened to Tudor Dee. It was like listening to Ricky Gervais! The Chief Imperator was there and not impressed. It was a complete disgrace. I've never heard such racist, transphobic, unprogressive garbage in all my life. We shall be reviewing his First Order Familiar status without delay. Tudor, you are on a warning!"

It was naughty, but the Vampire couldn't resist. His recent mind trick, shown to him by Hector, of being able to hypnotize a mortal's mind for up to 24 hours in advance, had been a roaring success, and more than enough time for the Comedian not only to deliver his "Unwoke" stand-up routine, but also send a long tweet in support of the banned comedian, Graham Sadowitz. It was delicious, and although Tudor was probably, being re-educated by Jamaal's goons as he was looking at his phone and would therefore be back to his annoyingly "on message" self in no time, it still provided the Vampire with something to giggle about.

However, despite this punch upwards towards the nether regions of the Limousine Left Establishment, and unusually hitting it's mark for a change, Terry's joy was soon replaced by the reality of what his life had actually become.

Jordan and Lauryn were still dead, and as much as he tried to wiggle around his conscience searching for some kind of redemption, it was becoming increasingly clear to the Vampire that "a price had to be paid", and, as a result, early one Sunday evening, he walked into the kitchen to make an announcement.

"I have to die."

Immediately, Errol raised his hands in protest, as a thousand objections crowded onto his tongue, before realizing that, after all the horror of the last few years, there was probably little point in arguing with his old friend, and so grabbing a bottle of rum from the cupboard, Errol followed him down to the banks of the Thames to wait for the sun to rise.

Now, in the stillness of the night, Dr Alimantado sang "Poison Flour" from a mobile phone, while Terry passed Errol a big fat joint, and the two Vampires sat in a happy silence.

"God save the Queen," shouted Terry raising a bottle to the night sky.

"Bollocks to the British Empire," cried Errol.

"Ban the Commonwealth Games!" shouted Terry.

"Nah, keep them."

"Oh yeah? Why's that?"

"Why my mum came here in the first place, innit. Nah keep the Commonwealth spar?"

"Thought the British Empire was evil. I mean, you don't see Germany having the Third Reich games do ya? Like every four years Israel, Poland, and the Ukraine all get together to chuck a few javelins and remember the good old days."

"Not the same thing Tel."

"Well okay, if it your mum wants it, we'll keep it. What about reparations?"

"I dunno. Used to think, we were owed, but after all the BS of the last few years, I think who would pay and who would get paid? Anyway would feel a bit insulting, like we're children or something. Fuck it, give us the Isle of Man and Shepherds Bush and we'll call it quits" said Errol, passing the joint to Terry.

"Done. You know I heard, Maxwell is now developing an App, where you can change the cast of any Film or TV show into your preferred racial or sexual taste."

"What! So you can get an all Trans, Die Hard" said Errol

"Yep. Or an all Black, Dad's Army," said Terry.

"Could be the answer. Keep everyone happy. Then again I dunno. Only one race, innit?" replied Errol rubbing his nose.

"What the human race?"

"Yep" said Errol, taking back the joint again.

"Yeah, but you're a Vampire."

"Decent point. But you know, despite all the shit of the last two years. Fucking George Floyd, CRT, pulling down statues, it's been worth it for one damn thing."

"Oh yeah? What's that then?"

"The English can no longer go around feeling all smug about how great and compassionate they were, during the British Empire. That train has definitely left the station" said Errol, blowing the reefer smoke out of his mouth.

"Yep. You really fucked that one up for us, alright. Had a good run though," said Terry with a grin.

"About 60 years, until you all got sussed. The shit we were taught at school. You know, I only found out a few weeks ago from this Pod-cast that before the Empire, India had a better GDP than Britain. All that crap about bringing trains and modernising everything. If the British hadn't gone anywhere near the fucking place, they would have still industrialised and got the trains anyway."

"And we pauperized the gaff. Fucked up their textile industry, with our our big Northern mills and then made them buy our products back, so they got shafted twice. By the time we left in 1947, they were skint and that's without the East India Company being pricks, the Amritsar Massacre, and of course, all the Famines. Gave them Cricket though."

"Well, yeah, of course that makes up for everything, doesn't it?"

"Look, I ain't gonna stick up for the Empire am I? Did fuck all for anyone where I came from, except maybe give us the odd day off for a Jubilee, and then we were still left potless and living on dripping. But I do have to disagree with you on one thing, me old fruit," said Terry, nudging the shoulder of his friend.

"What's that then?"

"Slavery."

"Not having that," said Errol, shaking his head.

"Dude, it cannot be denied. Since the dawn of recorded civilisation, there's been Slaves, and no-one ever had the idea of freeing them, until we did. You gotta give us that mate."

"Bullshit. Would have happened anyway. There were Slave Revolts, all over the place at the time. Toussaint L'ouverture in Haiti, revolts in Jamaica, plus I read it wasn't profitable any more," said Errol shaking his head in disagreement.

"So why they still doing it now, then? There's more slaves today than back then. Nah mate, what we did was pretty cool, and also those revolts you're talking about were at the start of the 19th Century. Granville Sharpe and William Wilberforce were trying to abolish slavery back in the 1770's way before all that and they did it because they saw it was wrong. Plus when they eventually did abolish it in 1833, the British spent years blockading Africa and South America to stop any one else from doing it. 4,000 blokes in the Navy lost their lives through disease because of that."

"But what about the millions, we paid to the Slave Owners, then? We've only just finished paying them off a few years ago."

"Shows you how much it cost us to do it then, don't it?"

"Nah, can't agree with that, Tel. Money should have gone to the Slaves instead."

"Of course, but they thought different back then, didn't they? Anyway, everyone's been a prick to everyone, haven't they. I mean, how do you keep a score on human misery? You know, Hector reckons in 500 years time, they'll be a Black historian who'll say the British Empire was the best thing ever to happen to Africa."

"Probably be called Cecil Rhodes as well," said Errol passing the bottle of rum to Terry.

"Ha! That's funny. Wanna know a secret?" said Terry, now looking sideways with a grin.

"You're into Pegging."

"Nope. I voted Tory in 2019."

"Fuck off!" said Errol, now sitting back in amazement

"It's the truth. Reckoned you'd get more sticking a gun to Johnson's head than trusting a party of middle class tossers."

"You fucking sell out. Wanna know an even bigger secret?" said Errol.

"You're a Virgo."

"Nope. I voted for Brexit."

"No way!"

"Yeah way. Thought it was better we make our own laws."

"Cool."

"And my favourite film is *Zulu*," continued Errol.

"Really? That's genius. I'd say mine was the *Sound of Music* but I hated those little Von Trapp bastards."

"Me too. Only time I ever cheered for the Nazis" replied Errol, laughing before throwing the end of his joint towards the river. Now in the silence of the night, the two Vampires sat in a moment of blissful tranquility, before turning to stare into each other's eyes, suddenly all the memories of their shared lives flooded through. Nights out, tear ups, lost dreams. In the end, they were brothers and leaning forward, they held on to each other tightly in the dark, letting their hearts beat as one until a glimpse of the early morning light started to appear from behind a dark cloud.

"Now we're proper allies" said Terry, letting a large tear from his eye drop onto his cheek.

"Nah, bruv, we're friends."

"We are that. Sun's up," said Terry, fatefully, looking towards the sky.

"Don't do this Terry, there is so much to live for, don't do this, spar."

"I have to go, Errol. I can't bear it any more."

"We have to bear it, that's what life is, yeah? I mean you're right. Fuck the past, fuck the horror, fuck feelings, live for today, because that's the point innit? You have to endure. Stay, Terry, I love you man."

"And I love you but I'm doing this, pal."

"But what about all that Muscular Stoicism, then? What about persist and resist?"

"Epictetus. Wise man. But it's been a bit too much resist. I'm tired now, mate."

"Well, okay, fuck it, I'm staying too then."

"No Errol, you can't save me any more."

"I'm staying."

"Look, my brother, I don't want to live. I can't explain it, but I just don't. I love you, very much. You are my friend, my best friend, but I just don't want to stay. My heart is broken."

"It will heal. Fuck, I've had loads of birds who broke my heart. You get over it, it gets better."

"This won't," replied Terry plainly before Errol looked straight into the eyes of his friend one more time and realising there was nothing more he could say, he glanced up at the sky for a brief moment, before quickly disappearing into the half-light towards the street above.

Now, a solitary Nightingale chirped from behind the river bank, and as Terry pulled his knees into his chest, and stared out across at the dawning of a new day, a man with a metal detector and a torch suddenly came into view on the wet mud in front of him.

"Oi mate, you missed one. There's a Roman Denari, just to your left."

"Very funny" replied the man, sourly as he carried on walking along the river, while Terry laughed out loud, before placing a final cigarette in his mouth.

"I've seen things you people wouldn't believe. Hen nights, with sparkly dresses off the shoulder in Blackpool, I've watched C-beams glitter in the dark near Wigan. All those moments will be lost in time, like tears in rain. Time to die" shouted Terry with his arms outstretched, and satirising a line from the end of *Blade Runner* his favourite film of all time, causing the man to look up again and shake his head. Seconds later, the sun started to rise in the East, and while the Vampire's flesh began to singe and slowly burn, he retreated into his mind to feel the soft lips of Lauryn again.

"I love you Terry."

"I love you so much Lauryn and I'll be with you very soon."

"No my darling, I don't want you to."

"But I can't stay here."

"You must. I want you to live my love," urged Lauryn, and then touching his face with her hands, she kissed him again, before whispering in his ear a phrase, that Hector used to quote, from time to time.

The wisdom is about transforming our darkness into light.

Now Terry lowered his head and paused for a moment.

Yes it's all bullshit.

There is socialism for the rich, and rugged individualism for the poor. Left and Right are the same, both ending up like the ends of a horse-shoe in the same authoritarian hell, but despite all this, it's still life in all it's nonsense and contradiction. It's still life and it's beautiful thought Terry and suddenly feeling a greater desire to live than die, he gazed into Lauryn's eyes one last time, before turning his scorched face towards an opening in the river bank.

"Flipping hell. Hope Errol hasn't rented my room out yet, the bastard," Terry now mumbled to himself, as he scrambled into a small hole under a metal girder and in the damp stillness of his new sanctuary, he placed a cigarette on his lips and started to smile.

EPILOGUE

Vladimir: So this is the end of the world then?

Estragon: I fear so. Just the two of us left and in a few minutes, the Sun will turn into a Red Dwarf

Vladimir: Thought they said, it was going to be a white one

Estragon: No, it's definitely red, my brother told me and he lectures at MIT

Vladimir: Suppose he'd know, then. Shame though innit?

Estragon: Well yes, but we must take into consideration, we've had a pretty good run. Addressed Racism, Sexism, Poverty, Hunger, Homelessness, Addiction

Vladimir: Homophobia, Depression, Greed, Cruelty, Climate Change

Estragon: And let's not forget War, Violence, and of course the Patriarchy

Vladimir:	Yeah, that was nice. Didn't quite manage to get to grips with Class, though did we?
Estragon:	Oh God you're still not going on about that are you?

Now, Estragon, in his protective suit, makes his way across the dusty plain, towards the ever brightening orb in the sky in front of him, while Vladimir lags behind, staring intently at the back of his companion's head. "Posh Twat" Vladimir mumbles into his helmet just as a blinding light flashes across the surface of the earth and incinerates everything in it's path.

Sean E Boye, at present, lives in North London, with no partner, no friends and a limited future. However, this is more than offset by his love of Newcastle United, Daim bars and the music of the Electric Light Orchestra. Fred Hampton's Blues is his first published novel with Troubador Publishing.